MEN

WALKING

ON

WATER

MEN
WALKING
ON
WATER

EMILY SCHULTZ

Alfred A. Knopf Canada

PUBLISHED BY ALFRED A. KNOPF CANADA

www.penguinrandomhouse.ca

Alfred A. Knopf Canada and colophon are registered trademarks.

Library and Archives Canada Cataloguing in Publication

Schultz, Emily, 1974–, author
Men walking on water / Emily Schultz.

Issued in print and electronic formats.

ISBN 978-0-345-81101-1
eBook ISBN 978-0-345-81098-4

I. Title.

PS8587.C5474M46 2017   C813'.54   C2016-905989-8

Text design by Jennifer Griffiths
Cover design by CS Richardson
Cover image: (skyline of Detroit postcard ca. 1905–1939)
© Universal Images Group / Getty Images

Printed and bound in the United States of America

2   4   6   8   9   7   5   3   1

Penguin
Random House
KNOPF CANADA

For Tom Schultz

of Detroit and elsewhere

The hard sand breaks,
and the grains of it
are clear as wine.
—H.D.

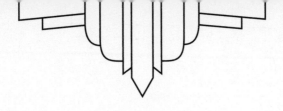

BOOK ONE

DECEMBER 1927

= { 1 }=

THE MAN WHO connected them wasn't a man anymore, but a body, hidden deep beneath the green ice of the Detroit River. The group of rumrunners huddled on the shore, consulting on what had just happened. All knew the doors of the old Ford had been removed for ease of exit in exactly this circumstance, yet apparently Alfred Moss still sat inside. The Doctor claimed to have seen the car go under and no one had seen the driver since.

Moss was dead: to begin with. "There is no doubt whatever about that," the Doctor said.

Perhaps Moss had heard the ice cracking, had managed to get one leg out the door, had been caught mid-jump as the vehicle plunged under, its grille like a falling arrow headed for the mud. If so, the fabric of his trousers now flapped grayly, silently. A lone black shoe balanced on the baseboard, poised to leap. This the men imagined. They also knew that Moss's hands might still grip the wheel— or perhaps the parking brake or the roof's frame, whatever he had grabbed—ridges of knuckles white with fear, mouth ajar and the water swirling strands of dark hair around deaf ears.

Willie Lynch could picture this more vividly than the others. As the kid in the group, he often rode with Alfred Moss. He knew that the Murray's Superior Pomade in Moss's hair would already be undone, though inside Moss's coat pocket the couple on the orange tin would still smile. His fedora would already have fallen away into the murk.

Or perhaps Moss had managed to get free and swim, had made it up to the crusted ceiling only to bump against the ice, unable to break through or find air before sinking back down, arms and legs limp as strands of seaweed.

Willie watched as the other men scuttled back and forth, searching, still hoping they were wrong. After a while, he climbed down from the bank and started to venture out on the frozen river but was called back. He could feel his face cracking beneath his cap, his eyes glassy. This was the worst thing he'd ever seen; it was intolerable to be forbidden from stretching out his body on top of the frail ice and freezing to death himself in search of the lost man. It had been Alfred Moss, not his own father, who'd finished teaching him to drive. Two brown moles beside Willie's eye consulted as he squinted. He spat. A small white gob landed on the white ice: proof he wasn't about to cry.

To the northeast was the anchorage site for the bridge. The men had read or heard that it would be nearly fifty feet wide and rise above their river by 135 feet, but in the dark it was just an island of dirt heaped up on either side of the waterway, a place where the sandhogs worked in hard, short shifts, going down into the concrete tubing below the surface of the water to excavate. The construction site was a rubble of wood and sacks of cement. In the distance, in the moonlight, the round concrete caisson seemed to mock Willie and the men with its shape: a giant life preserver.

The gang turned on the headlamps of their cars, positioned the beams so they could see across the ice. Although the light died at a hundred yards, they agreed the skid Alfred Moss had been pulling, heavy with Scotch, must be gone too. They snapped off their lights. Willie Lynch put his hands in his pockets and scrunched his shoulders. *Why do they fucking care about the poteen?*

"Where is the second car?" the large man in the homburg bellowed. This was Vern Bunterbart, the heavy, the one they answered to.

"I am the second car," the Doctor said grimly. He was supposed to be out on the river too, coming back from Canada, following behind the Ford, bringing half the shipment. Sometimes it was Willie and sometimes the Doctor, whose real name was Ernest Krim. The men glanced up the bank where his old truck sat parked. They were silent for a moment.

"You saw it or you heard it?" someone finally asked.

"Both," Krim replied. He was a thin man with a face like a hammer, and eerily calm about the whole matter, considering he'd known Moss the best of all of them. Willie stared at the Doctor's frosty green eyes.

"What did you see?" Willie asked.

"Just a spot of dark, then splintering, a sound like a tree struck down the middle. Then the dark dipped. The spot just disappeared."

"You are sure?" Bunterbart demanded. "How can you be?" He turned around, holding his homburg with one hand and the collar of his fine coat with the other. "A long way out."

At his words, the group turned again and stared. Along the opposite shore, a hem of lights blurred between Willie's eyelashes.

"I'm sure," Krim replied quietly.

The men cursed and clutched their coats closer. They pulled their hats lower. There was a strong wind coming across the vast ice, but Willie didn't flip up his collar.

"How many cases?" Bunterbart asked one of the others. His voice was like a razor flicking over a strop.

The man chose his words carefully, so carefully he said nothing.

"That many, ya?" Bunterbart huffed, and turned his large body away.

Willie shot a glance at Krim. He didn't care for the Doctor, but didn't know why. He liked him better than some, but that went without saying since no one liked Bunterbart. It was something about Krim's manner. He stood differently from the other men, his eyes often looking up. Willie's father had called him Krim the Prim. He was a *citizen*. But then Willie remembered what Alfred Moss always said: the Doctor was a *true pal, a blood brother, the one phone call you get*. The Kid turned and again searched the frozen river with his eyes.

"Enough that it would have gone down fast," Krim said. He wasn't a real doctor, only nicknamed that by the others. He was a pharmacist, which meant he had a legal right to deal liquor and got it officially. The unofficial work he did at night was for extra income— debts the other fellows could only guess at. Willie noticed Krim looked uncomfortable as he scratched at his ear with a gloved hand and cleared his throat. "He can't have felt anything but cold."

If this was said to comfort the others, it had the opposite effect.

Now, collectively, they felt the ice gapping, the temperature of the gloom that rushed the lost man's mouth, like swallowing snow. Willie pictured the bottles shifting in crates in the backseat of the vehicle as it nose-dived. Overloaded, soundlessly tipping, falling, the quarts of liquor gliding from their boxes and denting the roof like bullets, hitting the windshield, glass on glass, leaving large puncture marks as if the car had been bombed from inside. Alfred Moss wouldn't have had a chance to swim, the bottles would have knocked him cold, and now the bottles too were wasted. Whiskey mixing with water in the manner of a stingy bartender. The men peered across the ice, through the dark, at what was just a slick of silver, the hole where it had gone down.

Each thought, *Could have been me.*

One of the men, Gerald, dressed in an old coat, turned away and began counting the cases that Moss must have delivered before attempting his second trip.

He called to Bunterbart. "Vern . . . Going by his first run . . ."

Willie watched as they spoke together in low voices.

Then Bunterbart lifted a white spat and kicked softly at the corner of one of the cases and his voice lifted and Willie heard him declare gruffly: "But sold, more than three times that. Load it." He was calculating. *The fat bastard.* Gerald and Jake began plugging the cases into the pickup vehicles, which stuttered in the still night air.

Jake, unaffected or pretending to be, claimed, "There's always more booze to be had. That right over there is a country of snow and gin."

"Cash," Bunterbart demanded. "Was Moss dropping off cash?" He glanced around, eyes settling on Willie, clearly expecting the boy to know. Willie stared back. Bunterbart's love of drink blurred his facts for a day or two after a binge.

The Doctor cleared his throat. "Yes," Krim said. "I believe so."

"How much?"

The answer was a mute headshake.

Bunterbart returned to the huddle of tweed and houndstooth, where the rest of the men stood uselessly, hands in pockets. He spoke to Willie again, clapping his shoulder a little too warmly. "What do you weigh? A dollar and a quarter, ya?" The manner of the big German was amicable, but above his mustache his eyes were ice. "Is, after all, your chance to be a hero. Walk out. You can see if the skid is there or sunk. A bag perhaps. What is left. Far enough to see only," he cautioned, holding up a thick leather finger.

So he was to let Moss freeze but put his own life on the line for the hooch? Willie's voice constricted with shame. What was he to do if it was there? The answer came quickly: grab the bag and come back.

Willie spat again then off he went, his steps uncertain across the slick, semisolid river, feeling the spot between his shoulder blades stitch with worry.

Behind him, he heard Bunterbart grunt. "Pity. Who will go wake up Frau Moss?"

Willie knew the others were watching as he stooped in the dark and picked up two random bottles. In front of him, maybe fifteen feet away, the hole was black, the water seeping up over the rim of the freeze. He searched to see into it, but there was nothing. It didn't seem big enough, or ragged enough, to swallow his friend. It didn't seem possible—but he knew the world held many impossible things. He felt a hiccup and smashed his lips together before it could come out a sob. The surface where he stood felt too slippery and he edged back. It began to snow and the wind and flakes hit his lashes, making him tear up.

Soon it seemed as if the shapes of the men were coming closer to him, but it was he who trudged back toward them.

"The bag? The money, ya?" the big man called to him. The boy shook his head.

Willie heard the Doctor say, "I'll handle the woman."

Bunterbart turned away. "Get this load where it is going." He nodded at the two fellows by the cars. "Rest of you, scram now."

As Willie's feet hit the shore, one boot toe caught on the crusted snow and rock. He pitched forward slightly and dropped one of the two bottles. He had almost forgotten he was holding them. It shattered on the rim of the frozen river. The men swiveled at the sound, and the Kid felt the burning in his throat as if the wind from out on the ice had become trapped in there.

$$=\!\!\{\ 2\ \}\!\!=$$

THE CEMETERY WALL was low enough that locking the gate was unnecessary—any kid could vault over it. Nonetheless, Vern Bunterbart pulled out a key and the gate creaked open. He moved slowly, dragging the loaded dolly behind him. If he were the sort to worry about being caught, he would have used a wheelbarrow with a tarp—a more common sight for a groundsman in a graveyard— but Bunterbart worried about little. It was easier to bribe a police officer with a bottle or a few bills than to engage in subterfuge. He left that kind of acting to women, the ones who built bottle-carriers into their girdles and walked across the border, heavy hips swaying. Bunterbart was a walk-in-and-get-it-done man. Never mind that his head throbbed and his muscles felt watery from the workout he'd given his liver earlier that day. Because he viewed himself as a Christian, Bunterbart tried to abstain at least two days a week, but today hadn't been one of them.

He wheeled the two crates of whiskey past tombstones to the cellar entrance and peered down to where he knew there was another gate. Darkness. The Reverend Prangley wasn't there to meet him. He took the crates down the six steps and parked them against the gate, the bottles clanking. On the other side, he knew, were another seven steps and a landing that led into a long dirt tunnel that eventually wound into the church basement. Peering in, he saw only more blackness. The far end of the tunnel had a gate across it too, but Vern didn't possess keys for this one. Prangley housed a portion of their product there—"the reserve" he called it—but given his occupation, he didn't care to have Bunterbart too close and Bunterbart's coming and going was always prearranged. If they weren't completing a drop, Vern stayed away from the church. To discuss business, they met in roadhouses or they telephoned, with Bunterbart always announcing himself as "Mr. Muller." There had been a third partner, an Irish fellow named Seamus Lynch, who did go to meet Prangley in the church on occasion—for a men's group, he told people—but Lynch had died an awful death the year before and Bunterbart asked no questions. He'd liked working with the Irishman about as much as he liked working with the Jews on their ragtag team—not much. The boy Bunterbart had sent out on the ice to inspect the hole and look for the skid of booze was Lynch's son. When he'd asked Prangley a year ago if they should keep the Kid on, there'd been a slow nod, then: "Extra hands cannot hurt."

Bunterbart suspected Prangley had thousands stashed away, and more than once he'd wondered if he could enter the cellar, find the loot, dip a paw in. Unlike the rest of them, Prangley could not go around buying fanciful things.

Vern and the reverend seldom saw one another in the daylight, and in the years he had known Charles Prangley, Bunterbart had begun to think of him as "The Yellow Shadow," because he always seemed so backlit by lamppost or flashlight beam—and perhaps, too, because he planted in Vern a hard kernel of fear. There were things a priest knew about you—discerned in a glance—things about your sins or your usefulness. And it felt to Bunterbart as if Prangley had seen it all.

Bunterbart pushed back the homburg. He mopped his brow with a handkerchief. He thought he heard something behind him, and his hand went instantly to his lapel, which housed a tough old .38—but it was soon clear the sound was only the wind snapping through tree branches. He waited a few more minutes before mounting the stairs. He crossed the cemetery to the adjoining parsonage and banged a staccato rhythm on the door. But Prangley wasn't there either. Well, the liquor could stay where it was, for the night at least. The more pressing issue was the loss of the man. Alfred Moss had been fast, strong, and clever enough to have recently done some negotiating for better prices on his own.

Bunterbart exited the graveyard, relocking the ornate entrance. He stopped for a minute, contemplated going home to his wife and kids, crawling in and sleeping away the shivers that gripped him. But that was childish. Bunterbart considered himself a man of great fortitude, even when weakened by spirits. And he knew now where he would find Prangley; he just didn't relish making the cold trip across the waters to Canada—especially tonight.

={ 3 }=

MISS ROSINE PERRAULT's tavern, the Riviera House, was inside a large, dull redbrick building. A white railing encompassed the yard, winter outlining the details, softening them. A garden that, in summer, was set firmly within a circle of stones was now a bulge of snow. Below plain rectangular windows, a veranda hugged the building. The gutter running down the house corner was slick with ice; accidental daggers decorated the tops of the porch columns. The grandest part of the structure was a pentagon turret—and what went on within its suites. A sign sang in the wind, croaking with every other gust. Its painted red-brown letters read:

Open All Year
Specialty: Fish Chicken Wine Cigars

The word *Wine* had been painted over in white during the Ontario temperance years, leaving a gap in the advertisement. But everyone knew what the house contained and no one had bothered to readvertise it. Similarly, on the opposite side of the sign, the name of the previous owners was still vaguely visible, although ten years had passed since Miss Rosine Perrault had taken over management. The place had once been a hotel and restaurant catering largely to American tourists, perched on the edge of a park renowned for its

amazing mineral waters. There had been merry-go-rounds and cro-
quet tournaments. A band shell and fireworks. Healthy entertain-
ments for families. Then the sulfur dried up, and the crowds left. The
parkland remained, stretching vast and stoic with wind and tall grass.

Inside the inn, Rosine Perrault lifted her black-and-white spaniel
from behind the shiny bar and plopped him onto its surface, which
he shared with three or four empty lager pints. *"Assis,"* Perrault said
around a cigarillo, although whether she was addressing the dog or
her patron was hard to say. The dog knew more French than her customers did. She poured a shot of Hiram Walker's Canadian Club into
a glass and set it in front of one of her final patrons.

The man wrapped long yellow fingers around the glass and reeled
it in toward his vest. There were people upstairs, but he was the only
one who remained in the ballroom. Rosine knew he was grateful for
both the drink and the privacy. She observed how his tall frame tightened and hunched within his clothes, even now when the reverend
ought to have been at his loosest.

"Rosine, you treat him better than a man," Prangley said, fishing
below his vest and coming up with a nickel.

"Here, the men receive good treatment," Rosine said. She tipped
her head back, eyeing him. Her hard, thin face was framed to the
chin by dark curls, which ran straight and glossy along a high forehead. She always managed to look dubious and convincing at the
same time. She took the short, blunt cigar from her mouth and set
it in a tray. She stroked the dumb-eyed animal beneath its jaw, then
behind its ears where the black and white was fringed with amber.
Its feathery tail twitched in response, gently tapping the drink she
had poured. She put one finger down on the coin and slid it back to
Prangley. "Save your tips for the girls."

"They've already had them."

"D'accord." Into her apron pocket it went.

How old? he wanted to know. Four months, replied Rosine. What name? She shrugged. She hadn't settled on it. A new one every day, she told him with motherly excitement. *Napoléon. Chief. Charlie Chaplin. Hershey. Attaboy. Nifty. Doughboy. Garçon. Lindbergh. Petit Chou. Pickles. Pixie. Toots. Coco. L'Amour.* Her face was rigid, her tone matter-of-fact despite the childish names that poured out of her mouth. The syllables floated like small, unattached dreams, then disappeared.

"For—for what befalleth the sons of men . . . hmm . . . befalleth beasts." Prangley stumbled on his words, leaned his wiry frame farther across the counter, then nodded before continuing. "Even one thing befalleth them: as the one dieth . . . so dieth the other."

She opened her mouth, but he held up a finger. Although he hunched, he was six foot three and could, when he wanted, intimidate.

"The exciting conclusion: Yea they have all one breath; so that a man hath no pre-eminence above the beast: for all is vanity. Ecclesiastes 3:19," he finished. The reverend gestured to the dog without touching it. "What kind?"

"He's a Charles—like you, Charles. But he's King Charles. English. Not French. I wanted a French spaniel—the Brittany. But this one is more expensive. He must be better."

Charles the man took his drink slowly. Charles the dog attempted to step off the mahogany counter but, realizing he was trapped on the narrow strip, plunked back down. "So," Charles the man said, "have you been there?"

Rosine had begun wiping up. She stowed the bottles into a hideaway shelf behind the bar that she didn't need to use anymore but still did out of habit, turning the panel to face inward. Legal or not, she found that patrons wouldn't harass her for more if it was all tucked away. "Where?" She could hear the weariness in her own voice.

By the end of the night her skin always felt looser than her thirty-six years.

"France. The Riviera," he clarified.

Through the ceiling, a hurried bumping came, followed by three exaggerated female squeals, rhythmic as a cash register, then silence. Beneath thin, black drawn-on brows, Rosine smiled, her lips twitching into place as if amicability were a familiar shape, but one that was nevertheless a size too small. "When would I have the time?"

Prangley bobbed his head and a chuckle burbled out of him, the sound similar to that of a baby spitting. To Rosine's trained eye, the reverend was almost handsome. His dark pupils turned up slightly so that one could see a sliver of white beneath them; he had a forceful nose, a deep dimple in his upper lip, and longish black hair that was receding in such a way that it had—and needed—no part. His skin was olive, and his eyebrows were fine, like a woman's.

"I saw a picture of it once. Beautiful as a screw on a Sunday." Rosine smiled more widely now, exposing the gold filling in the back of her mouth, as she whisked Prangley's glass off the counter.

"Well ... It's got to be Monday by now." Prangley dug out his pocket watch.

"Then you are hours past last ferry. You don't drive across the ice, do you?"

The sound of someone rattling the outside door startled them. The spaniel jumped up barking, surprisingly loud for its size. It scooted off the counter and hit the floor at Rosine's feet, bleating at the distance of the leap.

Rosine Perrault put her hand on Prangley's jacket sleeve. "My watchman would have set off the buzzer. One must not worry. Always an owl or two late at night, *c'est tout*." She left her station and the still-yipping puppy. She pushed the fringed blind aside, then let the man in. She had seen him before.

"Bunterbart," Prangley croaked.

The big man entered, stamping the snow from shoes too fashionable for the weather. Prangley's face told Rosine that he would take a room after all—a place to conduct business.

She headed behind the bar and plucked out the room key, but before she could pass it over, Bunterbart said, both voice and chin quivering, "It is all balled up. With Moss. We have lost it."

Rosine stopped and watched. She never interrupted men in business.

"How much?" Prangley demanded, his voice hardening.

"The man, a half load, gone. And money."

Prangley's face turned red as if his tie had choked off his circulation. "Fucking cunt—"

The large man pretended to brush the snow from his lapels. He never seemed comfortable in the Riviera; Rosine had noticed how he often pulled out a white square and blew his nose into it repeatedly—as though the smells of perfume and sweat wafted in and released something from his nostrils.

"I apologize for my language, Miss Perrault," Prangley said.

"Cards, canned heat, and cunts. That is my business, and I am offended by nothing except debt." Rosine set the room key firmly on the counter.

When the men had gone upstairs, she scooped up the puppy in one arm and opened the panel in the wall with the other. She poured herself a drink while the dog squirmed. *"Monsieur Malfaisant,"* she whispered into his curly ear.

⊨{ 4 }⊨

CHARLES PRANGLEY DRAPED his jacket over a wire hanger and placed it in the closet with precision as he fought to control his temper. Vern Bunterbart had dropped onto the edge of the bed, spats facing in separate directions, hands hanging between his knees. He breathed out heavily. It was clear to Charles that Vern was in no hurry to admit his own sins. Bunterbart was a fantastic grotesque, but he didn't possess a strategic mind—that component had been missing from their business for some time.

Prangley went to the clamshell-shaped sink in the corner and rinsed his hands, lathering them with a bar of soap as swollen as a potato. Bunterbart was the one who should know if the river was solid enough to drive on. Prangley rinsed his face, peered at himself in the ornate mirror, patted himself dry with the towel, arranged it back on its bar, and brought a gold velvet chair that had been nestled against one wall into the middle of the room before placing himself upon it.

"Do explain what happened," Prangley asked, his voice more even than it had been downstairs. Either Rosine had numbed him with Canadian Club or it was the delayed effect of the girl who had entertained him earlier that evening.

Bunterbart took off his hat and swatted it softly against his knee. Then he pitched it onto the table. It landed beneath the lamp, a miniature cast-bronze girl, naked, holding up a globe of white light. "Moss went under the ice. Most of the shipment, too. I sent the Lynch boy out to get his shoes wet, but he saw nothing, recovered nothing."

"Downstairs you said only half."

Bunterbart nodded.

"Fuck the man and the liquor. Those are replaceable. Tell me about the money we were driving over." Prangley's brows twitched and he drew a finger along the seam of his lips. Bunterbart coughed into his palm. "I will not hit you, Vern. Look at your size. I would be a fool to become angered." It was a lie. He often became angered and Bunterbart, although he was a giant, had good reason to fear him.

After a long silence, Bunterbart said, "You should check the ledger. I would say ten thousand, ya?"

Prangley turned pale. He felt as if he might plummet from the chair. Then he stood and dashed the table lamp onto the carpet. The bulb burst, and the nude statue lay facedown on the rug. The room was dim now, lit only by the bulb above the clam sink in the corner.

Bunterbart shifted uncomfortably but didn't move from his spot on the bed. "But you know how I hate to guess."

Prangley held up a hand while he collected himself. Then he said, "Tell me, when was it we agreed to trust this much to Moss? And who was riding with him?"

Mr. Krim had been the second man on the job, Bunterbart said, but he'd been late.

Prangley pulled his tie loose and glared at Bunterbart, wondering if he should yank it clear around the fool's throat.

"You know you are a smart man," Bunterbart appealed to him. "We will recover this loss. You know how to use information to make money. *Erpressung*."

Blackmail, extortion, he meant. Prangley had heard him use this phrase before. Prangley folded the tie and set it aside.

Bunterbart went on: "The women of the church love to talk to you. About husbands. We have made it work before—and very well." His voice remained casual and bright, but his eyes said he was feeling otherwise. When Prangley merely swallowed in response, Bunterbart said, "Or we take up a collection, a campaign. We must do something."

"Certainly. The Purples care nothing for *your* losses." Prangley watched as Bunterbart shifted again, uncomfortable at the words "your losses."

"What you do not pay for protection, they will find a way to take from each of us. They are rotten. Those people all are."

"Don't make it personal with them," Prangley barked. "Lynch knew that. He handled the Purples, he handled the money, and he handled our men on the water. All you handle are your balls." Prangley sat on the chair and pulled his watch from his vest, examining it as if it held answers.

Bunterbart rose to his feet, a long crease running across his forehead. "Ya, and Lynch is dead a year, and now so is Moss. So what?"

"Sit," Prangley growled. Bunterbart did. Prangley swiveled on his chair to face the wall above the bed where there was a portrait of an anonymous young woman in a cloche hat, smiling coyly. It looked as though it had been torn from an issue of *Redbook*, framed, and placed on the wall. His lips parted in a smile—the first moment of levity he'd felt in an hour. Not everything about Rosine's stage settings was perfect, and knowing that pleased him even in the middle of his woes.

"Mrs. Moss—Elsie—was a member of my church once." Prangley squinted at one corner of the room. His eyes fixed on one of the shapes on the wallpaper. It looked uneven there, as if the paper had been smoothed up to cover peeling plaster. "It has been a couple years now since we saw her." Over his shoulder he said, "Send something for her in the morning."

"Alfred was a man who talked sometimes too much."

"Was he now? You are taking care of her, right?"

"I sent Krim."

"Speak to her yourself."

The German got up and crossed the burgundy rug. He moved heavily to the other side of the room, where he undid his trousers, fumbled to maneuver, then released a protracted stream into the clamshell sink. "My teeth," he grunted. "Every time I think it, to die that way, like Moss did, I feel a shot of cold right down in my gums."

"What, are you pissing? You kraut dog." Prangley shot out of his chair to remind Bunterbart how he could tower over him. "You dumb tit. Get out of here before I beat you like a mutt!"

Without another word, Bunterbart hiked up his pants and left.

Charles Prangley ran water into the sink then removed his shoes and his socks, which he paired and tucked inside the mouth of one of the Florsheims. He stood and turned the light off before continuing to get undressed and fold away his things in darkness.

Bunterbart had sobered him up, though, and he wished he were drunk again. He lay down on the bed and closed his eyes. *This cold . . . down to my gums.* He heard Bunterbart's heavy voice wheeze and so he turned his mind instead to the girl he'd been with earlier. She couldn't have been more than sixteen, and although he suspected he was not the first to trespass, he sensed that nothing had prepared her for the profession in which she found herself. She was as small, stiff, and silent as a porcelain doll brought down from a shelf. She had smelled of rosewater and had nipples that were hard and brown as acorns. He hadn't taken off his clothes, had only yanked out his cock, pushed aside her gratuitous layers, and stuffed himself into her—deep inside where it was warm. On top of the bedding, Prangley felt his breath pull from him, his body fall, as if through water, into sleep.

AFTER BUNTERBART LEFT, the men on the riverbed lingered. If any of them had been religious, they might have been moved to say a prayer. But with one Baptist, two Presbyterians, two Lutherans, two Jews, three Catholics, and more than one thoroughly fed up with God anyway, no one said anything for a long few moments. Then Jake, whose hair was as black as his face was white, yanked the remaining bottle of Scotch from Willie's hand and unscrewed its cap. The others took off their hats, raised the bottle each in turn, and said, "To Alfred!" "To Alfie!" and "To Moss!" tipping the bottle back and taking a quick belt before passing it on to the man on their right. Inside their mouths, the liquid tasted smoky and bright like a flickering candle flame, but when they swallowed, a velvet shadow followed.

Around the circle the bottle went, to all but the Doctor. He removed his hat like the others but then excused himself, climbed into his vehicle, and sped off to inform the new widow. His abstinence was expected; the men knew Krim did not drink, and although they ribbed him often for it, none had ever thought to ask why. Gerald said Krim thought himself above them, but Jake said maybe he'd gone wino after the war. After each had taken a glug from the bottle, the men divided up their routes—several heading out of the city to deliver to farmland and small-town contacts, and the others off to make their city deliveries. That night, it was an unspoken pact between them that each stop should include another drink. Separately together, the men became dull with grief.

Jake and Gerald pulled Willie along with them on their run. Jake Samuel was the younger of the two men by a handful of years. Where Jake was pale and thin as an icicle, Gerald had the shape and complexion of a turnip—five-eight, slightly rotund. Gerald had a past as a boxer, Willie knew, and though one might not see it at first glance, he was still solid and carried himself in such a way that most others would avoid crossing paths with him. Some of the men called him Sleepy Z. Willie rode behind the two in the dark backseat and said nothing, his chin resting on his adolescent chest as if it had been glued there. The week before, he had bought himself a pocket watch. It was slim and gold and accented with onyx and enamel, and he couldn't stop fingering the latch, flicking it open and closed in the dark. It clicked like a rosary.

The first delivery was to a rooming house. They supplied the landlord, and the landlord supplied the tenants. They distributed to a few little grogshops, but most were off-limits, unless they wanted to find themselves running up against the Purple Gang—who took a chunk of their cheese and looked the other way. This had been told to Willie many times, by his father and by Moss, and by Gerald and Jake and others too. Follow the rules, they said; the dollar you make on the side is the nail in your coffin.

In the basement laundry room, the men stacked the bottles gently in the bottom of a bin, and piled clouds of barely white bed linens back on top. Less gently, Gerald belched. "We need a warm-up. Give us a quilt," Jake said, friendly but commanding, and the buyer opened one of the bottles he'd just purchased.

Upstairs, the fellow said, for tumblers. They trudged up to the main-floor apartment and he took out four glasses and poured it for them, the liquid gleaming in the dim sitting room. He didn't hesitate to take one with them.

"How'd that taste to you?" Jake asked the super after his first gulp.

"Fine," the man responded warily.

They sat down for a grim party. "It should," Gerald asserted, unbuttoning his coat. "It's an expensive blend."

"Comes at the price of a man," Jake said, his voice at once sarcastic and sorrowful.

Willie pulled his newsboy cap low and clicked open his watch.

"That so? Sorry, then."

"Alfred Moss, you remember?"

"One with the vest?" the buyer asked.

"The very same."

"One that had the baby boy? What happened to your man?" the buyer asked.

"Drowned. Under the ice."

The circle drank again somberly.

"Poor fellow. He always did wear that vest, didn't he? Bit of a peacock."

"Indeed. A nine-inch peacock," Gerald said, smirking.

"We should only say good things of the dead."

"It is a good thing."

"You sure you got your measurements right? He told me there were some marital troubles."

"Well, ain't you heard? Everyone's got some marital trouble."

"Spoken like an expert." And the three men snickered sadly while Willie stared into his glass.

"Going to be hell without him," Jake said. "Bunterbart can be—"

"A hot piston," Gerald finished.

"A Jew hater, I was going to say. I'm sick of it. Practically walks around with the *Dearborn Independent* under his arm."

"I'll give Krim and Moss that, they keep Bunterbart focused on business."

"They *did*, you mean."

Another round. As Willie drifted on the flow of the drink, the yellow roses on the wallpaper seemed to nod.

"Hey, Willie? You gotten any nookie yet?"

Willie squinted. He bit at a hangnail and said nothing.

"Leave the Kid alone."

Willie pulled out his pocket watch and consulted it, then sucked back the rest of his Scotch.

"I heard Moss had his own girl on the side."

"You never," said Gerald. "His problem was dope—straight up. How'd you think he met that wife of his, anyway? They sure wasn't playing pinochle."

"You two were close. What'd you think, Kid?"

Willie got to his feet suddenly, wobbling with rage. "Weren't you the one sayin' earlier to only speak well of the dead?" Willie glared at Gerald, then seized the bottle from the buyer's tea table and poured the rest of it into his own glass, leaving the three grown men staring into their empty tumblers.

"Weeeell," Jake said, tipping his hat to the boy and glancing sideways at Gerald, "look who just started shaving."

Within three deliveries, Willie could barely stand and slurred all his words like a toddler trying to expel a meaningful syllable. He spat his *b*'s and swallowed his *s*'s. He knew he was doing it, but couldn't stop. He'd lost his cap somewhere along the way and his ears turned red as wine. Meanwhile, his face yellowed with nausea. The watch chain had snapped when he'd yanked it too hard while stumbling, and now the chain was balled up in one pocket and the watch in the other. The bottles vanished slowly, dwelling by dwelling, but to Willie each load became heavier, and finally Jake and Gerald lugged it up porch steps and walk-ups without him, handling more than their usual share while Willie staggered behind or took up sentry.

At their last stop, Gerald straightened himself on the bend of a staircase and grunted, putting a gloved hand to his lower back. "I could go for one of them forty-hour workweeks right now."

"Nah, Moss had one of those. Think you got it made. Lay you off three-quarters of the year and then where are you? Back on the river with us or else riding on the ferry with bottles rigged in your sock garters. 'Sides, Ford's a fanatic. Catch you at the gates with the tiniest bottle, they confiscate it and can your ass that very day."

Jake peered out the landing window, though in his half-drunk state it was more a place to lean than to enjoy the view. "You're not gonna lose your cookies again, are ya, Kid?"

"Fuck off and let me carry," Willie retorted, though he was clinging to the rail.

"No wonder he's blotto," Jake said sideways to Gerald. "Moss took him under his wing when his father died last year."

"I can hear you." Willie felt hot and rubbed at his forehead.

"Moss was a good guy for a jackal. Give me another minute to catch my breath," Gerald said, lighting a cigarette. He breathed in. "Just wait till you're thirty-five."

"Clam it, Zuckerwitz," Jake dismissed him. On his own he moved a couple of the cases a few stairs up. Willie grabbed for one and hefted it a few steps, then lost his balance and fell three stairs back, catching the case on his chest with an *oof* at Gerald's feet.

"Productive, Kid." Jake paused. "How old was our pal, anyway?"

"Alfie?" Gerald's gaze consulted the landing's window frame as if it held an answer.

Dawn light fell grayly across dusty floorboards where Willie struggled to right himself, pushing the case away in defeat.

"Went to school with Krim." Gerald butted out the Lucky.

Groaning, he and Jake hefted the cases all the way to the top of the next landing while Willie promised to sit on the step and not hurl. He was sure he could keep half the promise. The men rounded the corner and faced the final set of stairs.

Willie listened as they struggled up, thumping, the din only slightly louder than the blood in his ears.

"Watch that corner—four more steps."

Gerald huffed from beneath his hat. "Tell me why our guys always live on the fourth floor."

Jake picked up their running joke: "So they can see the coppers coming."

They hefted the last three cases up, letting them drop onto the floor instead of setting them down as they'd meant to, the glass inside ringing. There was a rap on the familiar door. When no one answered, Jake became impatient, from either the exertion or the alcohol. "Hey!" he hollered, banging. "Time to let the dog in!"

Willie turned and looked up, wishing for the work to be done so he could go home or just lie down somewhere.

At the top of the stairs, Gerald swooned, putting a hand to his jacket collar. As the door opened, he spun around, grabbed the newel post, and yelled, "Fire in the hole!"

They all watched as Gerald retched down the stairs. The sick settled just shy of where Willie sat.

≡{ 6 }≡

ERNEST KRIM PULLED his truck around the circle of Roosevelt Park, which was near empty at that time of night in spite of the number of passengers the train station served. He parked and got out, slamming the door. A Sweets' Pharmacy logo was painted on its side: blue over gray. In front of Krim, the three arches of Michigan Central Station gaped; beyond the station depot was the taller office tower, its windows dark. In daylight this was Detroit's cathedral of mobility, and Krim remembered the awe he'd felt when it had first been built, before the war. Even after being in Europe, Krim still thought it grand in its own way. Although the tower was visible from across half the city, he'd never had occasion to frequent it—until tonight.

From beneath a tarp in the back of his pickup, Krim yanked out a suitcase. He fumbled in the dark for the luggage tag, and began to write: *Al—*

He paused. The suitcase had Alfred Moss's name neatly stenciled on it. Moss had instructed him to put it on the train with a tag addressed to Alphonse Novarro, but Krim wondered now if the different name on the luggage would muck things up. He decided to do as he'd been told; any mix-up was Moss's problem. How was the name spelled, anyway? *Novarro* was like the actor, but *Alphonse* was anyone's guess. The pencil in Ernest's hand stopped. *Alfonz Novaro*, he printed as cleanly as he could. Would Moss be on the train, Krim had asked; but Alfred had been cagey on that point. Stashing the pencil in his pocket, Krim tied the card around the Bakelite handle. Suitcase in hand, he walked toward the station.

In the lobby, a redcap took over the bag. Krim waited, studying the vaulted ceiling, which even in the middle of the night was brightly lit. Looking up, he recalled that he'd been inside the station once before, had come to see his mother off on a train to some event in Chicago. It must have been just before his parents divorced—when they were still moneyed and his mother was campaigning for temperance with her lady friends. The station couldn't have been open long then. The porter checked the tag and glanced up expectantly, and after a minute Krim realized the man expected something from him. He said, "New York, please."

He quickly fumbled for two bits and left the bag in the porter's care. Krim explored the passenger atrium. There were more people here than he would have expected at three in the morning, but Moss was not among them. A finely attired dark-haired man in a black coat and houndstooth trousers was sleeping with his briefcase as a pillow, but when Ernest drew nearer, he saw the man had too fat a face to be Moss.

Reluctantly, Krim exited the station. He climbed back into the Sweets' delivery truck and headed for the center of the city, where the Moss house was located.

THERE WAS A LIGHT on in the back, and although the drive was empty, a blue Packard parked on the street two doors over let Ernest Krim know what he would find: Elsie Moss was awake, but not alone. Moss had intimated as much—several times, in colorful language— but Krim hated to believe the worst of anyone, especially a woman.

It was nearly three thirty. He approached the house slowly. The first lie had been harder than Krim had imagined. All eyes had been on him—Bunterbart's and Zuckerwitz's and Samuel's and Bob Murphy's, as well as the others'. They all took it more personally than he'd anticipated, but especially the boy, Willie Lynch, who'd looked as though someone had put a shot right through his gut. Krim couldn't recall the last time he'd lied—maybe during the war to his officer, or to his mother—but he hadn't remembered it being so damn hard. The words had felt like little stones on his tongue. *Three thousand*, Moss had promised him, and he'd wire it. The idea of money moving like electricity made it seem hot and unreal, something only a fool would touch. Krim realized he should have asked for cash, that a part of him had hoped to find Moss at the train station for that reason. He ought to have haggled for five, or even the full ten Moss said he was taking. But he was a friend.

Elsie had been left out of Moss's orchestrations. He'd given Krim no instructions about how to tell her the news. Several times in his mind on the way to the Moss house Krim had gone over what he might say, but his knock wasn't nearly loud enough. He raised his fist and banged again, then a third and fourth time. His hand was on the knob to open the door when a light came on and the wood gave way on its own from within.

Mrs. Moss clutched one hand to her throat, holding together her pink robe. She had not bothered with slippers. A wave of gold hair curled and puffed up over her forehead as if she had had it styled until recently. Her face pulled together at the center of her forehead and the corners of her lips, tightly. "What is it?"

Krim reached up and touched his clean-shaven chin, certain his face had turned red with embarrassment at the sight of her. It hadn't. If anything, he was white as marble.

"Mrs. Moss," Krim began, stepping inside the foyer before she could ask him in. He removed his hat.

He knew that, when he took off the fedora, he became a respectable man—slick dark hair parted down the middle, a strong, straight nose, pink lips, and brows like parallel lines—not the type Elsie Moss would expect to come knocking on her door in the night. Her facial expression rearranged itself as she recognized him as a friend of her husband's.

"I didn't know you without your glasses. You're the one from Sweets'?"

He nodded. "Ernest Krim."

"'Ernie,' Alfred calls you. 'The Doctor.' But he's not here. I'll tell him you called."

Krim gave her a hard stare.

"What is it?" There was a note of fear in her young voice.

Without prompting, she retreated into the living room and he followed.

"Elsie, it's Alfred . . ." he said to her back. She hadn't told him her Christian name, but he knew it. He had prescribed her a few weeks back. She came in often with prescriptions for minor ailments, accompanied by a fussy newborn in a buggy. He'd skipped the shotgun wedding, and when she came to his shop, they usually skipped the small talk, but certainly he'd heard enough about her from Moss.

She fumbled with a lamp, illuminating the tidy room. The house was new and in a fine neighborhood, and it had trim around the floorboards and ceilings, yet it struck Krim as drab and empty—Moss could afford enough to buy it but hadn't had the money to properly outfit it. It smelled of pipe tobacco and pine, although presents had not yet been set beneath the Christmas tree. The only other decoration in the house, aside from a small cabinet full of saucers, was a framed piece of fabric that said in blue stitching, *God Bless Our Home*. A Victrola on low in the other room floated plaintive piano notes through the still house. Gene Austin was singing in that polite manner that made Krim certain the crooner didn't believe his own words: *Bluebird, Bluebird, this is my lucky day. Now all my dreams will come true* . . .

"Did the Bureau pick him up?" Elsie said. Through her thin dressing gown, her shoulders hunched. "You work with him, importing?"

Krim said nothing, and she sighed.

"Well, you don't have to admit to a thing. I suppose I knew it would happen eventually. I don't know why he couldn't just be content with his line work."

Beyond the dark expanse of the dining room, down the hall, he could see a ribbon of light beneath the bedroom door. She glanced anxiously over her shoulder at the door, as if Krim's gaze had called hers to it, then, seeing it was still closed, she snatched up a cigarette case and extracted one, turning it over in her fingers. Her robe fell open slightly, a ginger chemise showing. She sat down on the sofa, leaving the worn wing-back, which was Alfred's, to Krim.

"I suppose we'll have to come up with bail." The record that had been playing faintly came to the end of its song. It was a forlorn little tune—people found it sweet—but why anyone would want to ball to it, Krim couldn't fathom. He heard someone flip the switch that would lift the heavy needle and move it away from the record. If she'd been alone, the arm of the machine would have continued circling the spindle, playing static. It was hard to feel sorry for her then. And perhaps in time she would be better off, as Moss had said. At any rate, it wasn't Krim's concern. His concern was to say the lines, get in and out.

From beneath his coat, which she'd not offered to take and he hadn't bothered to remove, Krim pulled out and extended a bottle.

He waited until she poured it without question into two small glasses she retrieved from the side table.

Then he said, "It's actually much worse than getting ten stripes."

"What could be worse than being nabbed?" Mrs. Moss asked without emotion. Then a look crossed her face and she sat down again abruptly.

"Yes, what?" His face and voice were colder than he meant them to be.

All of a sudden she made a sound, something between a laugh and a howl. Her unlit cigarette fell from her fingers onto the carpet.

"I suppose you'd better drink that," Krim said, without lifting his own glass.

Elsie Moss tossed back the drink in one gulp, and shakily placed the glass on the table. She removed a new cigarette from the case, leaving the first where it had rolled beneath her chair. This time, Krim crossed the room and lit it for her.

"Was it—? Oh God," she breathed.

For a minute he felt genuinely sorry, but the feeling dispersed when he glanced again at the glowing line of the bedroom door. Mrs. Moss pulled the smoke in and out. Then she said, her voice flat, nasal, but not teary as he might have expected, "How did it happen? Did they shoot him?"

"That might be better."

"Don't say that." Now her voice sounded hollow. She looked straight into Krim's face.

He worked his tongue around his mouth, as if there was something there, a grain of dirt or sand that he was trying to dislodge. What he saw in her face was pure numb shock. Worry lines had gathered in small clouds around her mouth and eyes.

He told himself that if he said it plainly enough, she would believe him.

"He went through the ice. There's no finding him, Elsie."

She believed him. He could see it immediately in her eyes.

Elsie lurched from the chair and flailed out, ramming her hand through the stained-glass section of the cabinet where the glasses had been kept. As she saw the red gash on her wrist, her eyes widened and she let out a low, shaky howl, as if she couldn't believe what she'd done.

Krim grabbed her from behind, seizing her bloodied fist in his own. It was his professional instinct to try to help her—but this wasn't vapors or indigestion. She hammered an elbow against his ribs. He hadn't expected that, and the blow was sharp, but he didn't let go. Glancing about for something to wrap the wound with, he noticed she had dropped her lit cigarette on the carpet. He stamped on it before it could burn and pulled her farther into the dining room, where he shuttled open a bureau drawer. A wail arose in the next room—the baby. Krim grabbed a white linen napkin. Elsie stopped struggling and the two of them watched as the blood seeped through the fabric.

"Goddammit," Elsie muttered, her hair fallen over her eye.

"Stay calm." Krim hustled her directly past the nursery and the closed bedroom door and into the bath, where he tugged on the light and blasted the water, and she didn't protest as he held her hand securely in the cold stream. Her body relaxed against him. He could smell the vanilla of her hair wax, and the tinny scent of sweat, and other bodily fluids. With his free hand he ran his thumb and forefinger over his eyelids as if trying to erase something.

When the water had changed from pink to clear and it was obvious there would be no permanent damage, Krim released her and said, "You've had a shock. I'll see myself out."

"No, no, I'll—" Elsie protested, but her arm was still lying limp in the sink, her head braced against the wallpaper. She was wet all down her front, her nipples shaped like Chiclets, and it occurred to him that she had probably been drinking before he arrived. Her robe had fallen from one shoulder. If she hadn't cried before, she was crying now.

Krim managed to choke out a feeble condolence, then left. It was only as he edged past the bedroom door that he remembered the other person inside; the door hadn't opened, even at the height of the drama. Moss had said he didn't know who it was his wife ran around with—he suspected there was more than one, and the baby could be anybody's. But the Packard at the curb told Krim it was someone affluent; the fact that the man had not made an appearance during the crying said everything else. The woman might be weeping now, but like Alfred, she'd make a new life. In the nursery off the dining room, the infant was still blubbering, unseen in the dark. The door to the nursery was ajar and Krim poked his arm through and found the crib. He fished around and found the soother for the child, silencing it, before closing the door gently.

On his way out, Krim stooped to pick up his hat in the parlor. Beside it he found the first cigarette Elsie had fumbled, the one she hadn't bothered to light. He pocketed it. Outside, the air was cold and refreshing. He breathed it in, then fished out and lit the cigarette. It tasted woody and sweet, and he felt relief gather in plumes against the dark sky.

He clambered into the truck and whipped through the neighborhood, enjoying the emptiness, accelerating, appreciating the sound of the old engine thrumming. The pickup was nearly through a stop sign when Krim hit the brakes. The truck skidded in the snow and stopped a couple of feet past the brand-new red octagon. With no one nearby, another man would have run it. But the thought made Krim shudder. He had learned long ago that he couldn't be that man.

={ 7 }=

"YOU CAN COME OUT," Elsie called, but only after the front door had firmly closed and the truck outside had coughed twice and motored off into the night.

His suit already on, the few silver hairs on his head re-combed, and his tie straightened, Frank Brennan emerged from the bedroom. He touched Elsie briefly on the elbow, as if they had only just met.

Elsie pulled her chemise closed and tied it. "I feel so cold."

Brennan fetched a blanket for her and sat her down in the living room. "I'm sorry," he said. Again he touched her arm gently.

"I acted like a fool," Elsie told him. "Is there any Scotch left?"

"Some aspirin might do you better." Frank got up to fetch it. While he was up, the baby chirped and cried again, and Elsie said to bring him. Frank went into the nursery then called, "How should I pick him up?"

"Pretend he's a puppy." Elsie closed her eyes against the ache in her wrist. Why had Mr. Krim delivered the news? She had known he and Alfred were old friends, but if they were business associates, she'd blocked it out. Then again, maybe Alfred had mentioned being out with him now and again.

Frank came back, holding the baby securely if awkwardly under the arms, legs dangling. He handed her the boy, then, when the two of them were settled, the aspirin.

"It's not like I haven't thought of what might happen if my husband were hauled in. It's just that I thought the biggest danger might be from other men. The police." She pulled her dressing gown down and covered her breast and the boy with the blanket as he nursed. "You lie awake at night and imagine beatings, or maybe coppers and fines. I figured there could be other women. No, I knew it. Dancers. Certainly I think about that with him going in and out of social clubs and apartment buildings for deliveries. There's so much to think about when you marry someone who does whatever he wants. But—"

She began to cry again, and Frank stood to go to her then sat back down again. She could see he was uncertain how to comfort her while the baby was in her arms.

"I never considered death." Elsie grimaced at the child's weight on her injured hand. "Of course, now I don't know why it never occurred to me."

Elsie was only dimly aware that she was crying again. She was more aware of a throbbing—in her arm, all the way up it, to her throat, then farther up, behind her eyes. That was all. A throbbing. She couldn't say when she laid the baby down, or when Frank let himself out.

⬊ ⬋

FRANK BRENNAN OFTEN drove along the river at night, so that he could see the place where the bridge would be. He could visualize it in his mind—there, hanging in the air. Steel cables, girders, tension, symmetry. Even now, he still had to do this to convince himself it would be real, that it would all be worth it. And so this is what he did when he left Elsie Moss's house and made his way home.

"Home" was a relative term. Brennan had as many homes as there were bridges in America—or at least that was how he felt, driving beside the long, lonely river. There were large bridges and small bridges—and large, elaborate apartments, or just rooms with a bed and a sink and a telephone in the hall and a landlady in rag curlers. Still, no matter the size and place, he had done this in every city he'd worked, with every bridge that would be—walked or driven the path that offered the best view of the future structure.

It was a pity about Elsie's husband, Brennan thought as he drove, keeping the car centered and straight. But then again, it wasn't, because he could only recall one favorable thing she'd said of the man in the brief time he'd known her: *he has a smile that could make anyone feel happy just seeing it.*

Brennan had come to Detroit three years before, directly after working on the Bear Mountain Bridge in Peekskill, New York. That bridge had surpassed in suspension length the one before it, and this new one would soon surpass it. So it went: each monument replacing the last, if not in grandeur, then in size. It had been that way since he began working. The minute the Williamsburg Bridge had opened in 1903, Frank Brennan had sat on his suitcase to press it closed, then boarded a train heading to Pittsburgh. From there he was off to Colorado, where he met a girl, married her, then packed her up and whisked her back to New York to work on the Manhattan Bridge. And soon he was off again, leaving his towheaded mountain girl alone in an apartment in an unfamiliar metropolis, until one day he came home and realized he was married to a New Yorker. As the years went on, he worried much less about leaving her than he did about the bridges he'd miss out on—like the Silver, over the Ohio River, set to open around the same time as this one. He'd never work on that. And he felt as if he was still waiting to work on this one.

For three years now, the project had been in stasis, and all he'd been able to do was buy himself the Packard and drive the river. He'd learned to drive ten years before—as fascinated by engines as he was by engineering—and it came in handy in his line of work. Still, at his advanced age, he was proud of the skill. The Packard was a gift to himself, one he deserved after all the years when he was at home, between projects, listening to the *snip snip snip* of his wife with scissors in hand, coupon clipping. Her thrift had paid them back, and she could afford the best fashions now. Meanwhile, the Packard had cost him nearly three thousand, but it was a majestic vehicle. *Just ask the man who owns one*—so went the slogan, and Frank found it to be true. Looking at its round headlights, the alluring smile of the grille across the front, he'd fallen in love with it. It was roomy and reliable, sleek and blue as the night, and it purred like a woman.

The first thing he'd noticed about Detroit was how dark it was, at least to a New Yorker. As a boy, he'd known that darkness, but now the splendid electric lights of his home city never seemed to fizzle. Here, though the river town was industrialized and working constantly, alight, stars could still be glimpsed like small gasps. The buildings yawned low and black against the horizon—excepting the train station and the stone corridors downtown, where the department stores and apartments offered a peak or two.

Brennan thumbed the wheel, steering his long car over to the shoulder. He climbed out and, leaving the door open, walked a few paces toward the water. The air was damp in his mouth as the whiskey he'd had with Elsie. It was a terrible business with her. A young woman was bad enough. A married one, worse. And now a widowed one, *worser*. He laughed at the word in his mind—wordplay, he knew, was an incurably Irish trait—but his body trembled. It had become harder over the years to extract himself from such entanglements. At sixty-two, he was too old for such things—and probably too old to go tramping around in the night, looking at empty sky and water.

There was a highway tunnel project headed by a Norwegian engineer competing with Brennan and his team for who would open first in Detroit. The tunnel was located right downtown, and if that company pulled it off, they would open the third underground vehicular crossing in the United States. The idea of an immersed tube positioned deep against the riverbed fascinated Brennan, but it also made him short of breath.

He'd grown up with the Brooklyn Bridge finding its shape beside him—though they had called it the East River Bridge then. As Frankie Brennan grew, it also rose. To look at it was like looking at a cathedral: Gothic arches that wanted to reach for God, wire rope triangles that cut the light into pieces as if to throw it down, something brilliant portioned out to each onlooker. The third of six brothers in an Irish family in Greenpoint, Brennan was five when construction began, and he was a man, just turned eighteen, when it opened. Fireworks were lobbed overhead and cannons boomed. Later in the opening week, there were rumors the bridge would collapse, and twelve people died in the crush as the crowd ran trammeling. But Brennan knew it would never collapse. Mr. P.T. Barnum and his circus elephants were brought in for an elaborate publicity stunt. With Jumbo in the front, twenty-one elephants had marched across the bridge. Brennan had been too young to work on that grand structure, but he'd been old enough to study it. Once, he had even shaken Mr. Roebling's hand. Brennan had been a bridge man ever since.

Now Brennan stared at the iced-over water and the concrete foundations on the Detroit side. He fancied Elsie, he thought, and his heart went out to her; but there had been as many Elsies as there had been bridges. With a start, he realized there was something out there: a small dark hand lay on the white moonlike beginnings of his bridge. He removed his glasses, rubbed at them with his scarf, set them back on his nose. A lost black glove, its empty fingers turned upward and flapping slightly in the wind, waved to him. One of the workers had left it behind, no doubt. But then an awful thought came to him: an image of Elsie Moss's husband's face, though he'd only ever seen it in the one wedding portrait that hung in her house. Brennan coughed twice, and quickly turned back and clambered into the car, which he drove faster now than he meant to, away from the river and between the gaping factory lots, toward Dearborn—the fingers of the glove still waving behind him.

8

ELSIE MOSS WAS SLEEPING in her husband's chair when the knock came.

"Just a minute," she rasped, although there was no one to hear her. She pushed herself up from the armchair and peered through the pane in the door before she opened it. At first, it looked to Elsie as if her visitor was a salesman—big, broad, and loud-suited beneath his winter coat. Then she saw he was too expensive a man for that line of work. She unlatched the door. He had his hand out before she could ask what he wanted.

"It's early but yet I want to come 'round, ya?" he said. His arm was locked around a tall blue box, which he hugged to one side of his barrel chest. He gave his name, which sounded like flatulence.

"Excuse me?" Elsie said, and before he could say "Bunterbart" again, he had hefted himself through the door frame.

"This is not a good time," Elsie said.

"You do not know me, but I know you, Mrs. Moss," he said. "I am sent to tell you how to do things. Very sorry, but we will need you to make the police report."

Elsie stared at him from inside her aching skull. Her brain felt like a wadded ball of Kleenex and in her chest her heart felt even smaller and flimsier than that. "Coffee?" she suggested. She didn't take his coat and left before he could answer, heading into the kitchen at the back of the house.

She took longer making the coffee than she should have. This man would bribe her not to tell what she knew from Alfred about their operations, she realized. Whatever was in the blue box was for her, but it likely wasn't money because that would have come in an envelope inside his coat or a bankroll in his trousers pocket. Of course, it was possible there was *also* an envelope, she told herself as she poured the milk into a blue and white china pitcher. When she picked up the tray, she felt her wrists shake; she set it down again on the counter. She pulled her robe tighter and felt in the pocket for a handkerchief, which she pressed to her nose. How could she stand there thinking about the possibility of an envelope or the contents of a box, she wondered, when no one had told her anything about the body yet, or how death had come, or how they knew it had? Had it been terrible? There was that question too, but she knew she didn't want the answer. When she lifted the tray again, it shook once more, and the two cups rocked black liquid into their saucers. She took a breath and carried it out anyway, her robe knotted tightly and her head held high.

"You had a visitor last night?" Bunterbart asked, his hand out for the saucer before she had even set down the tray.

"Where'd you hear that?" Elsie said, taking her seat. She watched him pour the milk and stir it. His spats pointed outward, his feet and knees encircling the small table and the tray. His hand was so large on the spoon; he was like a bear invited to a child's tea party. Elsie hiccuped a laugh and reached forward for her own cup. She took it black to avoid having to negotiate space with Bunterbart around the tray.

"Mr. Krim, the Doctor. He was here, ya?" Bunterbart pointed to the floor between his shoes as if asking whether Krim had sat in that very spot, which in fact he had. "He told you the news. Did he tell you what happens next?"

Elsie didn't say anything. She stared sullenly at the fat man's feet.

Bunterbart took a sip of coffee and the two sat in silence, the morning sun growing stronger through the gauzy curtains. Mrs. Moss continued to stare at the man's shoes and he stared at the hem of her nightdress, then at her bare feet and her toenails, which were varnished like an automobile, and then, absently, at the blood on the carpet next to the china cabinet. There were still shards of glass across its surface and, following Bunterbart's gaze, Elsie realized she should have asked Frank to clean it up the night before.

Finally, Bunterbart drew a napkin across his mustache and said, "That was very good. Thank you." He set the cup and saucer back on the tray. He rose to his feet and Elsie looked up at him.

"Here is what you do, Mrs. Moss, exactly what you do: you tell the police Mr. Moss, he needed some air, went down to look at the new bridge construction."

"But there's nothing there to see, is there?"

"Then tell them he ice-fishes. He never comes home. That is all. They ask more, say: I don't know. Say it."

"I don't know." Her voice trembled.

"Good. Convincing! You may be the wife, but they do not expect you to know what your husband does at night. Nothing, you say nothing about me, Mr. Krim, business. We are your friends, your husband's friends, so you say nothing. What do you say?"

Elsie didn't understand. She faltered. "I don't know?"

"That is good, ya."

He picked up his coat, which lay on the back of the chair. "I am very sorry that your husband will not come home again. With

Mr. Moss—well, we just do not know what happened. Ice crack and *er stürzte herab.*" He made a gesture with his hand like an elevator dropping—but Elsie's own parents had been German and she knew the words from her childhood. Bunterbart shook his head. "Should not have happened."

He retrieved the blue box from beside the chair where it had been leaning, and extended it to her above the tray. She watched her hands, against her will, reach out for it and seize its corners.

"Please . . ." Bunterbart said, and helped her with the ribbon because her fingers were trembling. With thumbs as large as revolvers, he quickly split the lid open.

The rich brown fur inside the box spilled out and Elsie barely caught the sleeve of the garment before it could fall into the creamer. "Oh," she said, and took it back into the chair with her, clutching it as if she had caught a human falling. She wrapped her arms around it and hugged it. She pressed her face into its soft layers and wept.

"I see you like it," Bunterbart said. He smiled tentatively. His mouth beneath his mustache looked suddenly small on his oversized skull. "It is a task to come by a fur like this. Worth a couple hundred, easy, ya."

Elsie began to sob.

"Is very warm. Most flattering fur for the female figure," Bunterbart tried again. When she didn't stop, he lifted his own coat back up onto his shoulders and buttoned it. "I must go, Mrs. Moss. I am sorry for this business."

Elsie stopped crying. She didn't know if he meant the business of being dead or the business he and Krim were in, in general—and perhaps, given Mr. Bunterbart's expression, he didn't know either. She sniffed, stood up, and pushed her arms through the sleeves of the mink. It was tight over her dressing gown and her wrists were exposed by a good three inches. She dug underneath the mink coat into her bathrobe pocket and brought out a handkerchief, dabbing at her eyes.

Bunterbart felt in his pocket, took out his wallet, and peered into it. He fished inside and brought out a few bills, which he pressed into her small, cold palm. Elsie gazed down at the fist that held on to four thin and wrinkled twenty-dollar bills.

"No," she whispered. "I don't want it."

But Bunterbart had already turned away and was plucking his homburg from the peg where he had hung it up himself in the hall.

Elsie pushed the bills back at him, and he stopped for a second before snatching them almost angrily.

"But still you will say 'I don't know,' ya? Do not say I don't help you."

Elsie nodded, and watched him go.

The thump of the door closing woke the baby, who shrieked to be fed, while Elsie stood in the middle of her living room in a fur coat two sizes too small.

9

MEN HAD BEEN ARGUING about the damn thing for nearly fifteen years: a bridge that didn't yet exist. That was how Faye McCloud
saw the situation, anyway. Her fingertips grew linty with newsprint
as she perched behind Reverend Prangley's desk, having a peek at his
newspaper. She would refold it and put it back where she'd found it
before he arrived. It wasn't even an argument about where or how,
but about from whom the money should come. All arguments were
about money. Just get the thing built and done—that was Faye's feeling. But now there was a competition: the bridge over the water by
one man and his company, and downtown the tunnel under the water
by another.

Faye's father had argued about it, and he had died while the war
was still on, although he hadn't gone to Europe, had simply expired
at home of influenza like so many. It was even before that—overtop
of her unruly adolescent head capped with a large yellow bow—Faye
could remember talk of the need for the bridge to Canada. For decades
railcars had been rolled onto ferries, loaded with travelers or heavy with
import goods. Either way, the process of transport was slow at best.

What Faye hadn't known—but the article took the opportunity
to tell her—was that shipping interests and railroad interests had been
at war much longer than she had realized. The evidence was right
there before her in fuzzy type. The nation was webbed with rail lines,

and Detroit was the big black spider in the center of the lacing: the
Michigan Central Railroad ran to Kalamazoo to Jackson then Detroit;
Des Moines ran toward Chicago then on to Detroit; St. Louis to
Detroit; Cincinnati up through Sandusky and on to Detroit; Baltimore
to Pittsburgh to Cleveland to Detroit; Philadelphia to Pittsburgh to
Cleveland again and once again to Detroit; New York to Buffalo on
through Ontario over to Port Huron down to Detroit; Boston to
Albany to Rochester to Niagara Falls to St. Catharines to Detroit;
Portland in the northeast to Ogdensburg to Kingston to Toronto to
Port Huron again and finally to Detroit; from the Atlantic to Montreal
down that same Grand Trunk Railway to Detroit; and from the west,
Duluth to Marquette to Mackinac to Saginaw, Lansing, Detroit. Even
over water, the routes bled into one another, the Great Lakes trickling
down—to Detroit.

The fact was so startling that Faye almost knocked her coffee over,
as if she had discerned the face of Jesus in rail maps. It had never
occurred to her that she lived in a place where all things must pass.
But there she sat, with her glossed hair dark and circular on her head
like the black dot of Detroit on the map before her. She steadied the
cup in the now-wet saucer and carefully set it to one side, on top of
Reverend Prangley's hymnbook, which she knew even as she used it
as a table she should not be doing, but did nonetheless, and turned
the broadsheet page.

The problem had always been that vessel boards opposed the
building of piers, claiming they would interfere with the shipping
industry. In competition with the railroads, shipping organizations
as far away as Buffalo, Cleveland, Toledo, and Milwaukee had rallied
against the very notion of *bridge*. In 1871, James F. Joy, the president
of the Michigan Central Railroad, had privately hired an engineer to
begin the first tunnel on both sides of the river. The Thames had been

tunneled in 1843; why not the Detroit River? But labor disputes, hard-pan, boulders, and finally sulfurous gases leading to two deaths shut the project down before it could gain more than twelve hundred feet from the American side, less than four hundred from the Canadian.

There was a knock, and Faye jumped up from Prangley's chair, a hand at her chest. Then her shoulders relaxed: it must be Kitty, because the reverend wouldn't knock. Faye left the office and unlocked the side door of the church.

Beneath her fedora, Kitty looked slightly dazed, as if she had been up half the night, or more likely all of it. She let out a plume of breath and hopped up on the stoop. In spite of the perky show of impatience, her eyes were dull smudges in her face. She clapped her hands slowly together. "He here?"

"Not for another hour, I expect. Come in, take off your hat. What are you wearing?" Faye didn't know why she bothered asking—she could see Kitty's trousers beneath the coat hem.

"Tea?" Kitty inquired instead of answering, and she threw her fedora on a hook in the cloakroom before following Faye up six stairs. She left her coat and scarf on.

"No, coffee. I'll get you some."

"I went to some show last night, let me tell you—" Kitty called to her sister's back.

"Please don't," Faye said. She brought the cup back, steaming. "In here." She carried it through to the office and took up her spot again at Prangley's desk, his paper in front of her.

Kitty glanced about the room. "Doesn't worry you take tea in here? You said he likes things just so."

Everything in the office was dusted and oiled until it shone. There were ashtrays, but all had been wiped clean. The diploma on the wall was straight and its glass bright.

*Master of Divinity
awarded to
Charles Prangley
from the Lutheran Theological Seminary, Philadelphia
on this day of May 10, 1912.*

"I'm always careful," Faye said, though, reminded, she dabbed at the desk with a napkin where the creamer had left a drop behind. "I don't know what could possibly go missing—Reverend Prangley keeps half those drawers locked. I just make sure the blotter is centered before I leave."

She remembered how Kitty had told her once that she thought all men of the cloth were bent, or broken, and that, no, those weren't the same things. Now, as she saw Kitty incline her sharp face in such a way as to imply this, Faye said, "What?"

No sound came from Kitty except a loud slurp. Faye said, "He likes women. Or at least, women like him. These old ladies in the congregation, they find him very charming. Besides, Lutherans aren't Catholics. Reverend Prangley can marry."

Kitty nodded. "The old ladies, yes. What about the young ones?"

Faye said nothing. The reverend did engage with the young girls a lot, perhaps too much, but she would concede nothing to her sister. Instead, she held up the newspaper and said, "Listen, did you know this—"

"How can I know if you didn't say it yet?"

"Listen . . . Years ago, in 1873, the Detroit River froze solid and for two months straight there were no ferries. Twelve hundred freight cars had nowhere to go—travelers were stranded for two months!"

Kitty unwound her scarf from her thin neck, which was knotted into a man's shirt and a dark blue tie. "Why do you care about that stuff all of a sudden? That's not like *you* to care about that."

Faye ignored her, glancing instead at the clock on the wall, and at the door. She continued reading silently. Three bridge proposals had been drawn up, but no one could agree on which to pursue. Congress would authorize the secretary of war to examine the issue. Then again, here were more private companies, more railroad barons, more private bridge plans than Faye could keep track of—she downed her own coffee and listened to the cup ring when she dropped it in the saucer. Where was Prangley? Well, thank goodness he was late . . . She read about more starts, more fails, operations north of the city, operations on Grosse Ile. A proposal in 1912 for a peace bridge, commemorating a century of peace between Canada and the United States, abandoned as the war in Europe demanded attention, then retaken up as a symbol of unity within the war. But no . . . And finally . . . The first spike had been driven on May 7, 1927, but even this was a kind of lie, a trick. Joseph A. Bower, by way of the American Transit Company, had been authorized by the United States Congress provided the construction of the bridge commenced on or before May 13, 1927. One spike was all that was needed to meet the deadline, and so it had been driven in by Bower's daughter Helen in a ceremony for ceremony's sake. Yet this did appear to be the firmest plan so far for an actual *happening* bridge. Full construction had begun in the summer and now, just five days ago, the cement caissons and their excavation had been termed "complete."

"I've never been to Canada," Faye said suddenly, looking up into her sister's eyes, which were as green as her own, but softer in some way, dreamier she always thought, although maybe that was just older-sibling jealousy. Kitty's eyes were constantly tired, but at twenty-one there wasn't a wrinkle around them, nor did her hair, short though she kept it, contain a single gray twig. "I can't think of when or why I might have the occasion to go, but . . ." Faye let the words trail away.

Kitty swiped her hand across her forehead to remove the one loop of hair that was long enough to fall forward and place it again behind her ear with the other waxed locks. "Just bust out a quarter and ride the ferry. I mean, there it is." Kitty gestured broadly, holding out a hand to the office as if offering Faye the world.

"No, of course," Faye stuttered. "But you . . . you've been. Do you still see her? Your friend?"

Kitty moved the spoon around in her cup. Though she'd already drunk the liquid, there were sugar granules pooled in the bottom. She'd forgotten to stir them in. "You don't have to say it like that, Faye. You're such a virgie. *Her. Her.* Do you still see *her?* She's not some stripteaser."

Faye stood up, lifted her own cup, and gestured for Kitty's, which was passed to her. Their gazes met. "Well, I don't know what she does . . ." Faye blurted.

"Yes, you do," Kitty breathed, looking down at the floorboards.

Faye turned away with the dishes. Kitty sighed, leaned forward, and neatly folded up Prangley's paper, replacing it where she was certain her sister must have meant to. Then both left the office and walked through the silent church, discomfort between them.

Faye had met Kitty's friend once, by accident, one afternoon the previous summer. The two of them had been bumping down the street arm in arm. Kitty had introduced her: *This is Rosine.* Faye had assessed the woman, from her thick dark hair down to her pearl-blue heeled slippers. Rosine's mouth had been rouged, but most of it had come off on her cigarillo. The pair were a bit tipsy in the middle of the afternoon, enough to be chummy. Faye had made the briefest of pleasantries, as if she and Kitty were not sisters at all but acquaintances, and sped off in the other direction. She had felt a little ashamed of herself, but also ashamed for her sister.

"She's a businesswoman," Kitty said as they reached the church kitchen. "Like you. Like anyone."

Faye didn't answer, hiding behind the sound of water running in the sink.

"Besides, serving up giggle water is legal there. Don't ask me how a bunch of frogs and hayseeds figured that out before we did."

With that, Kitty left her sister to the washing up.

When Faye came back into the cathedral, Kitty was sitting at the Steinway to one side of the stage. She had exposed the keys. Her fingers rested on them as though they were old friends or lovers before she began to move them. She fumbled the notes purposefully, fast and hard—and to Faye they sounded like someone walking down the street, tripping over his own shoes.

The song ended and Faye's voice was thin across the distance between them. "You've got no respect for the church."

When Kitty opened her eyes and turned, she saw her sister holding her hat. "I got respect for the music," she grumbled. "Time for one more?"

Faye came over with the fedora. "What was that?"

"You don't know it? That's last year's song. Jelly Roll Morton, 'Dead Man Blues.' Except it's supposed to be horn—I'm better at it on trumpet. Hey, let me know when you get an organ in here." It was a running joke between them, as whatever money came into the church seemed to vanish before improvements could be made. It was Faye's job to balance a budget that never lined up. The secretary before her had been an older woman, and when Faye was hired, the church trustees told her that they suspected Mrs. Hoffmann's mind was going even before her sudden illness. Anything Faye could do to sort things out properly would be appreciated, one of the trustees put in. "But we don't expect you to work miracles,"

Prangley had said gently, leaning forward. "We'll leave that for God."

Kitty put out her palm, lifted her brow, and wagged her fingertips.

Faye dropped the hat into it.

Kitty tossed the hat onto her head and tried again with the hand motion.

"You need to get yourself a job."

Kitty cocked her hat to one side. "I have jobs. I stroked the keys a bit at the club last night."

"A real job."

Kitty stood up. She put her arms around Faye and pulled her close. "Don't worry," she said into her hair. "I won't ask again, and I'm coming for that Christmas concert."

Faye shrunk away from her. "Not dressed like that, I hope."

Kitty smirked. "I'll see what I can do."

Faye nodded to the side door. "My purse is in the cloakroom, but for God's sake leave me enough for supper."

Kitty rolled her eyes heavenward as she backed out of the seating area. "For *God's* sake. You have no respect for the church either."

"But I have respect for my job."

The door at the front of the church scraped open and, hearing it, Faye headed toward Prangley's thin, dark shape. She waved her sister silently out of the cloakroom at the side entrance as she passed, and by the time she greeted Reverend Prangley, she had heard the other door softly close with a *fum-fum*.

"There's a lot to cover before the service next week," Faye said in a bright, crisp tone. "I was just making some notes in your office for us to go over."

Reverend Prangley gave Faye a pained look. When it was just the two of them, he was sometimes distant and taciturn, moving with unease, his dark eyes darting to the side like a rat that had accidentally come inside the house. This was in contrast to how he was in front of the congregation; when he was performing—which he would not have called it, though Faye thought of it that way—he was benevolent. Then his movements held grace.

Prangley was finely attired this morning, his suit a series of lines and firm creases, as if he'd had other business already, yet his eyes were sunken with sleeplessness. Faye offered to get him some coffee and toast, but he curtly refused her kindness. As they walked together down the side aisle, Faye noticed that her sister had left the cover off the keys on the piano, and although she didn't dare correct the mistake just then, she resolved to replace it later.

"I have some things on my mind this morning," the reverend said abruptly when they reached the door to his office. "If you don't mind, take your notes with you for now and come back later."

Faye retrieved her notes and had barely exited the office when she found herself examining the wood of the door, already shut tight behind her.

10

INSIDE HIS OFFICE, Prangley moved across the room. He stood behind his desk and, before he'd even taken off his coat, unlocked the desk drawer and fumbled for the leather ledger. His finger scanned the columns and rows and stopped at a number in his own writing—a number that he nonetheless wanted to argue with: $20,000.

He slid down onto his hard office chair and sat unmoving for a quarter of an hour. Staring through hungover eyes made the numbers much worse, because what he saw instead of lost income was the price that would be delivered personally upon the round, dumb head of Vern Bunterbart if their operation failed to pay. That price was made not of stick figures but of lead pipes. He knew he should pull the telephone across the desk and dial Bunterbart. Instead, he tapped the number with his finger several times as if it might magically change beneath this touch. Then he keeled forward, his hands rubbing backwards through his turbulent hair, his forehead pressed against the desk. He contemplated his options.

Yes, there were women who came to see Prangley to talk of their marital troubles. Bunterbart had suggested making up the shortfall by using this information—but Prangley knew they could never make thousands at it. Just last week, a Mrs. Hess had come to see him, handkerchief in hand. But Mr. Hess was not influential in any way. He ran a shop on Michigan Avenue. Prangley drew a finger across his lips.

Perhaps it was important to Mr. Hess to maintain a reputation, but Prangley did not think any scheme could tease out more than a couple hundred from the man, and if he were honest with himself, he liked Mrs. Hess too much to hurt her household. She was virtuous, he could tell—younger than her husband was, scarcely twenty-one, petite and blond, and she sat there wringing her delicate hands and shaking like a bird ruffling its feathers to shake the rain off them. There were women he liked much less—why couldn't one of them have come to him with information? Prangley bit his thumbnail. He was getting soft. He blamed it on the hangover.

Moss should never have had the money, Prangley thought, tapping the number again. He picked up a pencil and put it to his lips, tasting the eraser. Even through the ache of his hangover, he was reasonably sure he had asked Bunterbart to make the trip himself—so why had Krim been in the second car? Flipping back through the schedules, he saw Krim and Moss often did the night runs together, the same way Zuckerwitz and Samuel were partners. When it wasn't Krim, it was the Lynch boy. The boy's father, Seamus, had had no fear of the water, and if he'd been alive he would have made the run himself, especially when there was cash to exchange. It was Bunterbart's job to keep the men in line. The big German didn't like to get his shoes wet, though.

Hearing the clatter of Faye's typewriter, he went out into the hall and decided it was safe enough to head to the basement. There, he walked the long corridor, unlocking the door and the gate at the far end, and headed to the second gate, outside of which he could see his two crates of whiskey. He hefted them inside and carried them to a room off to one side that he kept locked tight. He did so with some annoyance: Bunterbart ought to have sent these bottles off into the night to be delivered, especially since they were light on the shipment. It was simply another in the long list of mistakes.

Prangley heard a noise above him—something rolling on the floorboards. Given his own location, whatever or whoever it was must be in the antechamber. He hastened to lock up and sprinted the stairs. He was seated in his office, sweating, when he heard female voices.

=〔 11 〕=

NO ONE HAD TOLD Elsie Moss how much a baby cries. At the hospital, for seven days, the nurses had tutored Elsie on how to change it and bathe it, how to put it to her breast, how to tilt its strange, misshapen skull toward her and squeeze her nipple upward until it pointed at the ceiling then slip it quickly inside the infant's feeble, untrained mouth, but they had not told her what to do when it stared up at her, unwilling, and howled for hours. They assumed because she had been capable of removing her dress and mucking about and showing a man her jelly roll that she also knew what a baby was. They assumed she'd had sisters or friends with babies, relatives and neighbors whom she had helped when she was a girl, that she had learned these skills over the years. But Elsie didn't, and hadn't, and even after a week's worth of instruction the baby was startling. Everything about the baby was startling.

Before it was born, Elsie had felt it moving—a quiver, a thick gasp in her abdomen—and a love unlike what she knew with anyone, even Alfred, shook her. She'd thought, *I'm ready*. But she wasn't ready.

She and Alfred named the baby Johnny after someone she didn't know—a friend of Alfred's who he said had died during the war. They named him Johnny, but mostly they called it The Baby. They'd swaddled it in a brilliant pink blanket and took the boy proudly home, but by evening of that day Elsie realized she was alone with it in their house and there was no one there to tell her what the baby needed. She put it to her breast and the baby closed its eyes and screamed until its small head quivered and reddened. She laid it down and the baby still screamed. She took off its clothes, and unfolded its diaper, and the baby wailed as if she had stuck it with pins. Was it cold? She wrapped it again, heavily, and picked it up, sang to it, and bounced it. The baby yowled. She paced with the baby and it began to nod off, then spread its arms suddenly and whimpered. She collapsed in the chair and rocked while the baby blubbered. Did it have gas? She patted its small belly through the white cotton of its gown. The baby grunted and grimaced. She put it to her breast again, and again it cried until tears formed and ran from the corners of its angry eyes. It was hungry, and then it was colicky, and then it was wet, and then it was hungry, and then it was colicky and wet again, and when it was those things, it stubbornly refused to feed until it was again crying due to the hunger.

The baby persisted in this manner for weeks.

Alfred would come into the room and say, "What's this rumpus?" Then, "Stop it, shut it up. I don't give a flying fuck how, but if you don't silence that runt, I'll go nuts." And finally, "What's wrong with you that you don't know how to comfort your child?"

Once, he had sent her flying with a backhand across the mouth. And the baby had cried, and then Elsie had cried, and then Alfred had left. He stayed away longer hours, working, he said, importing, making money for the li'l one, he said, though he gave her very little, and when he returned, it was only to leave again, sooner, more and more frequently. She only knew the thing ate enough because it grew. Its feet extended out of its gowns, and during the thin hours it slept, she sewed new clothes for it. And the baby cried again. And the supper was burned again. And Alfred left, and Elsie ate the meal one-handed though it tasted like tar. The fork was gripped in one hand and, using her other, she bounced the baby on her hip and thought, *Please, God, don't let me kill it.*

At night, she dreamed the infant underwater, its body wrinkling, its whole head turned blue. She always woke from these dreams shaking, grasping at the bedclothes for the baby as if to pull it out, save it. She knew there was something wrong with her, but she'd no time to even think about it. She was so tired she felt as though her bones were made of straw and her lungs full of sand.

It was only a little more than a year before when she'd been a waitress at a speakeasy in Rivertown with her girlfriend Judy. She'd met Alfred there—his white vest, black coat, hat pulled low as if he walked out of a picture show and not the assembly line he really was from. Many of the drinkers became sweet on her, especially when the hour grew late—had pawed her ass or slurred promises of lifelong devotion. Alfred did not. He ordered his drinks and smiled.

Elsie and Alfred had never really spoken until one morning after close, when Alfred stayed for business with the owner. Elsie had wiped the tables down as the morning light cut into the smoke. Alfred left the office and, on his way out, stopped and asked her, "Would you like to take in the movie *Wings* with me?"

"It's not playing yet. Not until next month."

"It's playing in Chicago. If we leave now, we'll make the matinee."

Elsie grabbed her coat and the two drove to Chicago that morning. Along the way she talked about the poetry of Dorothy Parker, how much she loved *Enough Rope.*

"You know about Dorothy Parker? Jeez. I knew you weren't like the other girls."

Elsie missed three consecutive Sundays of church because she was studying the whiskey sour with Alfred. By the seventh Sunday she was most certainly pregnant, and by the twelfth she'd got herself hitched. When they married and moved in together, she took her copy of Parker's *Enough Rope* out of a fruit crate and showed it to Alfred. "Remember this?"

"What's that?" he replied, blank-faced. His lies never seemed to stick. The child was the only permanent thing about Alfred Moss.

THE FIRST THING to rattle her from the terrible blue-baby dreams was the same thing that had started it all—the horizontals, though not with Alfred. He had been attentive throughout the pregnancy, but not in that way, and he hadn't shown any interest since. It began like this: Elsie went out with the baby in its carriage, in another attempt to stop the shrieking. Earlier, she'd walked away and let the baby cry for an hour in its crib because she felt it was safer there than in her grip—although the closest she'd ever come to hurting it was opening her arms and letting it fall, twelve inches down onto the soft bedding. At the grocery, a canned good in one hand, she had been debating the price of dinner while pushing the carriage slowly back and forth, not enough to go anywhere, just enough to keep the thing quiet. At the end of the aisle, a man she'd seen before in her church had been descending a stepladder. Apparently he ran the shop. Elsie had watched his shape move, the brisk musculature of him even though he was older than Alfred and at least two decades her senior. When he caught her eye, he smiled. He was tall, unlike her husband. He smiled into the carriage and then again at her. "I haven't seen you in a long time," he said.

It was an ordinary fact. Elsie had disappeared.

Two days later, this same man simply raised his hand and removed her cloche. His palm reached out and touched her hair, her ear, her cheek. How had he convinced her there was something in the stock-room he would retrieve for her? She asked herself this question, yet she already knew the answer. His gesture marked the first time she'd felt like a person since the baby had come. He had not needed to convince her of anything. She had left the baby with her neighbor *just for a few minutes while I run to the market*—why hadn't she thought of it before?—and she'd flitted along the street in the deep blue of late November, the wind catching in her chest, free for the first time in months. Under the grocer's hands, her body tensed. She forgot what she had come there for. The room smelled like sawdust and cauli-flower. He opened her blouse two buttons. He pitter-pattered fingers over her stockings, beneath her skirt, found the soft flesh between garter belt and drawers.

During his ministrations, Elsie didn't think about what they were doing, what she was doing. That he was married, that she was married, that they'd once been members of a congregation together. Instead, she stared at the stockroom wall where a row of hand-painted signs for the next day's specials stared back at her in blue ink. *Chicken breasts, Porterhouse and T-bone steaks, long-grain rice, Real Canadian maple syrup, fresh squash, canned peas, canned corn, Kellogg's corn flakes, Quaker oats, Strawberry Faygo, Windsor salt.* His cock sprang up and surprised her. She wrapped her hand around it. *Woodbury Soap: You too can have a skin you love to touch,* a large printed poster on the wall declared. He backed her up against a stack of kraft paper packages. Beneath her rear, King Coffee. It was a strange sensation, feeling good. Her head felt fuzzy, as if she'd swallowed a glass of whis-key in one go.

He wasn't the only man. There were men, men everywhere. That she had a husband and a child seemed of little consequence to them.

Her body without the baby was different from her body with it, or her body before. It felt like a new body, in some ways not as beautiful as when she'd been a virgin, but in some ways more so. The nursing had drawn her waist in quickly, and her breasts had swelled to unexpected proportions; it was as if this body wanted to be seen, to be felt, as if it were designed specifically to attract men at this particular time, in spite of the lines that still ran faintly across her belly.

She wasn't always a pushover with the men who paid her attention; usually it was just conversation, an exchange of glances. It brought her back to herself, out of her blues and into the world. She felt like she hadn't talked to anyone but the baby for weeks. That was how it started with Mr. Brennan. He was kind—kinder, maybe, than even Alfred had been in their early acquaintance. If there had been anyone to confess to, she still might not have said she was goofy on the old fellow. He was twenty years older than her father. She had her shame. But for the first time since the baby had arrived, she felt as though she might like to keep living.

And then, a man showed up in the dark one night and told her that Alfred was gone.

She had only guessed before that he worked with her husband. Ernie Krim was a respectable man—as respectable as men could be, anyway, which lately she'd doubted more and more. She had seen him just a few weeks before, when she and the baby were standing in line at Sweets'.

Now Elsie sat in the wing-back chair in her parlor—it was *her* armchair and her parlor now, she realized, along with any debt that came with it—and examined the cut on her hand from the previous night while the baby nursed at her breast, cradled on her forearm like a football. The cut was a perfect line, red. When she'd stuck the fist through the glass, for a second she'd experienced the same thing she felt when she was screwing: an angry exhilaration. It served her right and it was good, she decided, clean.

"Your daddy's dead, and your mama's a whore," she told the baby.

It stopped suckling and gazed up at her with large eyes that she noticed now had lost their cloudy blue-gray color and become brown, like its father's. When it drew its head back, Elsie Moss waited for the baby to cry, but instead it sneezed. Then, amazed by its own explosive, watery sound, it looked up at her, parted its lips until she could see its pink gums, and smiled.

Elsie took this as a sign. She went to the closet and took down her dress coat—not the new fur, but her faded black wool. She should put on a black dress, too, she realized.

={ 12 }=

THE RAP AT THE DOOR came within a minute of Prangley scrambling back up the stairs and into his desk chair. Faye McCloud was apologetic as always, saying there was a woman there to see him, and in some distress. "I can't be sure, but I think it may be Elsie Braun."

Prangley shut the ledger and quickly hid it in a drawer. "If it is her, it's Mrs. Elsie Moss now." The words came out hoarse; he could stand a drink of water.

Elsie was quite a bit smaller than he remembered, though perhaps it was the way she hunched into her coat. He paused, observing her, how her hair shone in the half darkness. At seventeen, she had been a beautiful girl: thin-limbed and plump-lipped, her breasts like small stones behind her dresses, a great devilish flicker in her eyes. Now, a few years later and less than half his age, she was already stooped, though in all likelihood the night's events had helped in bending her. A terrible cry rang through the cathedral, startling him. It was only then he realized that Elsie was hunched into her coat to talk gently to the baby she cradled inside it. The noise he'd heard while downstairs must have been the wheels of the baby buggy. Turning, he saw it through the double doors, parked in the front foyer.

"Is this your son? We included him in our prayers when we heard he'd been born," Prangley said, softly approaching and peering down into the face of the child. The infant fixated on him and stopped its bleating. He focused on the child to avoid too much eye contact with Elsie, though he stood close enough to inhale her vanilla scent, and the layers of wet wool.

"He must like you, reverend," Elsie said, her tone more defeated than pleased, though she straightened up inside her coat and held the baby out to show a certain amount of pride.

It had been a long time since they'd seen each other. Prangley noticed Elsie's face growing pink. Her hand inched up to check her hair and push the gold curls around. The reverend smiled, the divot in his upper lip pressing in, deepening into a flat, gray dime shape. He could see she was recalling how she'd thrown herself at him, years ago. A floozy who'd turned afraid at the last minute—he couldn't think of a worse type. She would do fine without her husband; he'd wager hard cash on the fact that she would find another within the year. Prangley reached out and poked at the baby's blankets, feigning interest. The tiny boy caught his finger in its fist.

"What's his name? Are you here to arrange the christening?" Prangley knew better than to glance at Elsie. Lies were easy to discern in a gaze but difficult to catch from the tone of voice. "Yeeesss, yeeesss," he cooed at the homely thing. Its face was wrinkled and red as coral. "You're a strong boy, aren't you? Nice and strong."

"Oh, oh, I suppose we will want that sometime," Elsie stammered. Then she sank onto the last pew and the baby went with her, though it still had Prangley's finger in its grasp.

"My, you *are* a strong little fellow. Look!" he exclaimed with artificial gusto. "See how he's caught and kept my hand."

But the woman's shoulders were truly hunched now; if Prangley had extracted his hand a moment later, her tears might have touched his skin. "I see I am mistaken, forgive me," Prangley said soothingly. "It is a bad time?"

BENEATH HIS DESK, Prangley rubbed the seam in his pants between forefinger and thumb, as if to pleat it more firmly. He hadn't slept in the pants, but felt as though he had. He also felt unusually warm, though the day was cold.

"My husband, he's a good man, you know," Elsie began, almost blurting this, as though in response to an accusation.

Prangley said nothing. He left the seam alone and picked up his cup from the tray Faye McCloud had arranged for them. Elsie acted quite nervous now that they were alone in the confines of his office, and he wondered if she expected him to launch over the desk at her. What a preposterous woman, coming to him for help, blushing and yammering, then jumping at his slightest movements.

"He works for Ford, you know. Or he did until the autumn layoffs—"

She spoke in a roundabout way, and it reassured Prangley: she knew nothing of the commercial relationship he had with her husband. He reached forward and lifted a cup toward Elsie. Above his stiff shirt collar, his smile was guiltless as a dog's.

She accepted the cup reluctantly.

"I see. The layoffs. You are facing some financial woes, then?" Prangley inquired, keeping his tone calm and his gaze fixed on the sugar bowl he offered.

"Yes, but no, it's the other business he's in—"

"The other business?"

Her gaze fell to her saucer, and her cheeks pinkened again. "Last night, two men come to the door. The middle of the night, early morning." She set the cup down, sloshing the untouched coffee. "They tell me my husband is gone. Alfie is gone—*dead*—that there is no body and they don't know what happened. They give me no explanation. They—"

She plucked through her purse for a handkerchief as she fought a sob.

"Oh dear. These men . . ." Prangley looked carefully at her face between words rather than during them. "They are known to you?" Prangley probed, his hand suddenly coming up from beneath the desk to pull at his bottom lip.

After reflecting, she shook her head no in reply, then dabbed at each nostril individually with the embroidered cloth. "Rumrunners, I expect. I hate to come to you with this tawdriness." She held on to the top button of her dress, the handkerchief still clutched in her fist, a dash of white against the black.

"Temptation calls to each man now and then," Prangley said, stretching his arms out across the desk to her. She set down the handkerchief but didn't immediately accept his hands. Her mouth downturned, then she let herself reach forward. "The question," Prangley told her, "is how we answer."

As he gripped her lightly by the fingertips, she drew a shaky breath.

Prangley inclined his head and whispered a passage from Isaiah, all the while trying to keep down the gastrointestinal reflux that threatened his throat, a side effect, he told himself, of the previous night's libations. "Fear thou not, for I am with thee. Be not dismayed, for I am thy God. I will strengthen thee."

He swallowed the offending bile.

Elsie made the mistake of thinking the reverend had finished. He felt her pulling back, and clutched her gloved fingers tighter between his.

". . . Yea, I will help thee. Yea, I will uphold thee with the right hand—" He swallowed again, then finished strongly: "—with the right hand of my righteousness."

Elsie began to cry. She said she had been an awful wife, a real *wurp*. She'd been so blue and distracted she hadn't attended to any of the household needs, and hadn't been there for her husband in months the way a little wife should. She knew the baby was a gift from God, and she should be happy and grateful, but it yowled constantly. Had the two of them driven Alfred out? And had he met a terrible end because of it? Was his death her fault?

Prangley observed this spectacle with detachment and a suppressed chuckle. Did all women hate themselves so much?

He watched as her gaze wandered around the office, settling on his topcoat where it hung beside the door. It was a lovely mohair. He hoped she wouldn't ponder it too much, and vowed to wear a shabbier coat to the church from now on. He'd worn it only because he had come directly from Rosine's and the ferry that morning.

Elsie's voice trailed away as she glanced at the half-open door, down the hall, as though wondering if the child was being well tended. Prangley could hear Faye babbling to the baby in low tones.

"Do you remember the church picnic?" Prangley said suddenly. "Remember how I found you there by the lake? You were still in high school then, I believe?"

Elsie was clearly caught off guard. She retrieved the handkerchief, hid her lovely mouth behind it. Her triangular chin tilted. She looked sad suddenly, which surprised him. "I remember. I was only seventeen."

"Seventeen," Prangley echoed, but his voice struck the word more softly than Elsie's had. There was a coldness to her he didn't recall noticing before. Perhaps she was in shock.

She looked out the small, high window to the right of them, though it showed only a blue wisp of sky. Prangley watched as she dug in her purse for her cigarette case. She didn't ask permission before lighting one. The stimulant rearranged her face as she drew upon it. When she spoke again, her voice was steadier. "As I said, I hate to bother you, reverend. We wed at my husband's church, but I admit, I don't know that congregation well."

He leaned back, amused. "Yes, why didn't you marry here, I always wondered?"

"Please." She drew a breath on the cigarette and rushed on as if she hadn't heard him. "Will you tell me if you hear of work for me? I know you are acquainted with so many good people."

"Mrs. Moss, you are not yourself. Give yourself time," he said, forming a steeple with his fingers in front of his mouth. "You should not have to think about such things now. Especially when you have the most important task at home." He glanced down the hall now too, indicating the child. "We will take up a collection for you. It is Christmas. It is the time for giving."

He instructed her to come to the service the following weekend and bring a photograph of her husband. "In the meantime," he said, turning around in his chair so that its wooden back was to her, "perhaps— But no, what would you think of me?" He glanced over his shoulder at her.

Elsie Moss stubbed out the cigarette in his spotless ashtray. Prangley turned back to his task and unlocked a drawer in a bureau behind the desk. He labored over it for a few minutes, weighing his options.

The collection would benefit the business. He could pay the Canadians for the whiskey, in part at least. That would leave less of a hole in his own profits. With some persuading he could take in a thousand from the congregation, of this he was sure. A small portion could go to the widow, a hundred or two. A gesture made now, larger than that which had come to her from her husband's unknown but supposed business partners, would secure her faith and keep her unquestioning when he delivered less than expected from the donation tray. He could see she was easily manipulated. Really, she always had been.

Inside the drawer was a small valet, which he opened. In it, five pocket watches and two wristwatches gleamed. Prangley took care to shield them from Elsie's eyes by stooping over them. As he whisked one finger along the row of them, he realized that a grieving widow and a missing man could be more than just one collection. It could yield a full season of sympathy. There were any number of searches and missions that could be staged, if he preached properly and drew effectively upon the empathies of others. With each idea, the sound of dollars whispered in his ears—or was it just the tinnitus of the hangover?

He chose a pocket watch in sterling and gold with a full hunter closure. It was neither as handsome nor as valuable as the ones beside it, but that wasn't what stopped Prangley's hand as he passed over it. It was the feminine pull of that particular piece. He touched it gently at first, then more confidently extracted it from the velvet case. The front was engraved with blossoms on a vine, and the watch face inside was filigreed.

His hands shook as he locked the valet. He began to talk, winding the watch.

"Really, I should not have kept this, and I am ashamed that I did. You see, we are all human and we all have our affections." He paused on the word, mulling it over. "This was given to me as a gift . . . by a woman . . . whose husband had also died, I might add. She came every day and we prayed together. I told her she must trust in God and His plan even when she was most distraught and uncertain. At the end of . . . that spring, she made her way to family on the east coast. Her sister had had a baby and she was going to help there. Her life had a new purpose. She left this because it was her husband's." Prangley found the words tumbled out, as if they were given to him. Stories took shape inside his head as simply as rainbows after rain. He already felt as if he could visualize the fictional woman he spoke of. "A sad reminder. But she wanted to make a donation to the church and had little to give, so she parted with the watch."

He looked up finally at Elsie. Her face had twisted through the hour from grief and shame to curiosity and hope, which, in his estimation, was exactly how one ought to enter and then exit a church; it told him he'd done his job well. He held the watch out to her, cradled in his palm.

"Like I say, perhaps I shouldn't have kept it. Maybe it ought to have been sold and the monies put into the ledger." Prangley sat down again. He watched as Elsie bent forward, admiring the timepiece but afraid to reach out and touch it. "I guess I waited for her to write to ask for it back. But it has been six years now since we heard from her."

Elsie sat silently as a cat sits in a window at night, watching. Prangley knew then that she wanted the piece. He didn't dislike her, he decided, in spite of her defects. He could have given her something with greater value. It was just that there was no point to it, business-wise. She posed no threat. His tactic had always been to surrender as little as possible while still reaping the greatest profit. Except words— those he had, and gave, in abundance.

"Every object has a purpose. And now I see this object's purpose." Prangley tapped a long, straight finger alongside his nose. "It was given in kindness, in gratitude and praise. And now in kindness, it must be given again. One kindness must beget another," he finished, releasing the watch.

Elsie reached forward slowly. She opened the jewelry, and stared at its gleaming insides until her eyes also gleamed. "I won't be able to pass it on to anyone in kindness," she protested.

"You will, though!" Prangley exclaimed. "You will use the money from its sale to feed and clothe your child—and you'll teach him and raise him in kindness, and so the cycle continues."

Suddenly he felt his voice hitch, and he began to cough violently, until Elsie leaned forward and poured more liquid into his cup and he used it to wash away his words. He fished out his silk pocket square and ran it over his eyes. When he looked at Elsie again, she was placing the watch in her purse and snapping the lips of the bag shut.

"Thank you," she said.

Something about the way she looked at him made him feel sick, as though he were yellowing before her eyes, and he felt terrible, but only for a moment. He coughed again and drank.

"What do you think I should do—about the men who came to my door? Should I tell the police the truth?" she asked.

Prangley froze, his cup still resting against his lips. He set it down slowly, exactly in the circle of the saucer. "I suppose you could turn them in, these associates of Mr. Moss's. But then again, perhaps they are not the sort of men one wishes to anger. Perhaps . . ." He glanced up and met her eyes for the first time in an hour. ". . . you should do whatever they said to do?"

Her lips became slack and the color left her. She nodded, then promised she would come back the following week. As she was gathering her coat and standing to go, she asked suddenly: "Do you think there's any hope for him, though, reverend?"

"Hope?"

"Yes, for my Alfred."

Prangley let his gaze fall, trying to interpret the question. He began rearranging things on the desk. He picked up a book and contemplated its weight.

"It is possible, of course."

"Do you think so?"

Prangley swallowed. "I do. We should not assume a man is dead just because others say that he is. You must have hope." He set down the book and clasped her arm firmly, feeling the thin flesh through her dress, patting it twice before he released her. The silence in the office told him he'd trespassed, that her grief was not big enough to permit him this. She shrank from him and yanked the door open before he could say or do anything more.

As he watched her fumbling her coat on and crossing the door frame, he realized too late she'd meant was there hope with God. He shouted after her, "God always forgives!"

={ 13 }=

OUTSIDE THE BAR, the snow shone white as fondant as it fell on Manhattan. Inside, Alphonse Novarro fiddled with his ring, scrutinizing the crowd, his crisp black hair slicked back. The owner of the El Fey Club, Larry, wasn't there; Novarro had entertainment leanings and he'd hoped to persuade Larry to invest in a film, grab a nice credit as producer. Now his business for the night was the kind that didn't end in money. He let his drink sail by his teeth, and signaled for another.

Jessie, the girl he'd brought with him, was dancing as if she knew he was watching: shimmying until her pearls flew out and knocked the other girl, her friend, in the teeth. No tits, all ass, both of them. Heads like snow globes and hair as glassy. Alphonse Novarro had no doubt that Jessie even tasted like snow. Like Christmas morning, which it was—almost. Wet and anticipatory. Her white stockings exposed half up the thighs as she turned her feet in and out. The El Fey Follies had nothing on her. When the number finished, he'd be there with the girls' favorite cocktails, Mary Pickfords. What was the other girl's name—Doris? Dorothy or Dottie? Yes, that sounded right: Jessie and Dot. He had a corner table that would fit all three of them. He looked magnificent in his new pinstripe suit, a new white vest, and the emerald on his pinkie.

The emerald had cost as much as he'd promised old Krim. But Krim could wait; he was the patient type—forgiving.

"Come on," Novarro said to Jessie, slipping his arm around her, under the strap that held all those glittering sequins up.

"Let me catch my breath, Al," she pouted.

He saw that her friend had already noticed the size of his ring. Unlike Jessie, she had no shame over being a B-girl. He watched as she smoothed one hand along her hair. She smiled coyly as she twirled it into a tighter pin curl. "What did you say your name was? Mr. Nova?"

The three of them walked by a caged tiger on display in the middle of the club. It paced furiously, amber eyes glancing angrily at its surrounds. Its large ears twitched and rolled as the horn player launched into a solo. Alphonse looked directly into its face as they passed, and the animal parted its black lips at him, showing yellowed teeth.

"Novarro," he corrected, and steered the ladies down on either side of him, his hand already on the friend's garter, if over her dress.

"You don't look Mexican." Dot laughed and covered her mouth.

"Spanish—but name only, really. My grandfather came here when he was a boy. Said California was as beautiful as Madrid."

"Dot, I told you. He's a movie producer. Talkies! He took me to a film last week an' told me the secrets!"

"Here to meet with writers. Got Dorothy Parker hooked on to write the scenario. *The Sun Also Rises.*"

"Oh, what's that?"

"Why, it's simply F. Scott Fitzgerald's greatest book—and it's going to be *the* sound sensation of the decade. DeMille's directing."

"Listen. You know what I asked Alphonse? I asked, 'What do writers do at Christmas?' And you know what Al said?" Jessie was animated as she laid it all out for her friend.

Alphonse Novarro's hand crept back onto Dot's garter, this time beneath her hem. He noticed the date she'd come with was across the room, arguing loudly with someone, about to come to blows. So far as Alphonse was concerned, the fellow was as good as streeted.

Jessie's voice rose above the din, exaggerated for the performance. "He said, 'All's you can hear is the clatter of typewriters. Four in the morning, bang bang bang, like tap dancing.'"

Alphonse laughed as a hand from Jessie's side landed on his knee. "Well, either that or they're on the roof."

"The . . . roof?"

The friend wasn't quick, but he had no beef with that. "Yeah," he clarified. "I mean, out cold drunk."

"That true? Where you staying, Mr. Novarro?" Dot bumped her glass against her mouth as though she'd prefer to bite into it. She was high, with starry eyes—and he reckoned not just from the effect of his story. She had a deep, earthy scent; he'd noticed it when she bent her head near. Like reefer. She was a pretty little viper.

"The Algonquin."

"I heard they spent a million dollars on that place," Dot put in, just as Alphonse turned and sank his teeth into Jessie's shoulder. These girls were cheaper than whores, and a lot more fun. For one thing, they believed that everything was an experience.

"Oh, Al! Stop," Jessie squealed, and pushed him off, but only a little.

"A million's nothing," he said, reaching up Dot's leg to bare skin. He winked. "A million's a steal."

"Big talk." Jessie gulped her martini.

"Isn't at all," Novarro said, raising his arm for the waiter, signaling another round. But none of the wait staff spotted him in the crowd, so he took out a twenty and held it aloft, snapped his fingers, and yelled, "Over here!"

The band slid from a raucous number into a fast-paced version of "God Rest Ye Merry, Gentlemen." A man lifted his glass in a toast and shouted, "Comfort and joy!" along to the song, and soon everyone joined in.

"Coulda stayed at the Plaza, but who cares. I been there a hundred times. Thought I'd try something else."

The girls exchanged looks.

As new drinks were fashioned and circulated, Novarro slipped a thin box from his inside jacket pocket. "Think I'm tall tales, do you?" he said, but Jessie already had her hands on the box, opening it, the bracelet falling into them with a flutter. "Some *ice* to go with your drink," he chuckled as the diamonds were revealed.

"Oh!" exclaimed Dot—but not in response to Jessie's new jewelry. Novarro's middle finger had made its way past her silk tap pants. He stroked the velvet veil of hair he had found, then stopped, leaving her to think about it. Jessie was too distracted to notice.

"Ain't it swell?" Jessie exclaimed, fastening the bracelet around her wrist, holding it out to show off. She had her mouth on his now, tenderly, while below the table's edge he could feel someone massaging him into full erection.

"Ab-so-lutely," Dot sighed.

"Gold," Novarro whispered, keeping his eyes on Jessie and putting his hand back on Dot. "Like your hair."

Across his lap, Dot said to Jessie, "Mr. Novarro comes all this way from Hollywood, winds up meeting us. It's so romantic."

"I'm sure I can find a little gift for you too—back in my room," he assured Dot, and she reached out and drank down her new martini, then the rest of his. The three of them teetered out of the bar and wove through the streets of New York, their coats pulled on haphazardly, the girls' purse straps tangled, threaded half under and half over their clothes.

"You've only been here a week. I barely know you," Jessie protested suddenly, pausing on the corner to look at the white-gold filigree. He could see she was uncertain whether the stones were real. The cold had awakened her.

Novarro raised his hand for a taxi. Two that were already occupied surged past.

"Jessie, who cares? I bet it's worth a ton of kale," Dot hissed behind her hand, as if he wouldn't hear her.

With one palm Novarro gestured again for a cab, and with the other he gave the doubting girl's buttocks a violent squeeze. "Careful," he warned her, pulling her close and looking down into her frightened, drunk eyes, "my mother and father met and married in far less time than that." He bit her lip then pushed her into the waiting vessel, practically on top of her friend, the flopsy and more willing Dot. He clambered in himself, threw instructions at the driver, then buried his mouth into the low neckline and triangular breasts of one of the girls, without looking to see which it was.

An hour later, Dot lay passed out, drawers still hooked over one leg but not the other. Jessie had covered herself and sat twirling the bracelet around and around her wrist as she smoked. Music bopped from the seams of the city into the room. Jessie exhaled, "I always thought about being an actress. People say I have the looks. I once won an award when I recited some poetry in front of my class. Only thing I ever did win."

Novarro didn't respond. Beside her, he sprawled naked, his glossy black hair spilling across the pillow, the pomade undone. His cock lay flaccid against one thigh.

"How do I love thee? Let me count the ways," Jessie began, drawing herself up where she sat in the bed. Her voice was tinny and her boroughs accent showed. *"I love thee to the depth an' breadth an' height / My soul can reach, when feeling outta sight / For those ends of Being and ideal Grace."*

"Oh, those *ends* of Being. Yours are particularly tasty." He reached over and gave her thigh a pinch.

"Why do I think you're a bad man?" she said, tipping her head back against the headboard, part indignant and part playing at it. "I know, it's that ink there." She pointed at the Kewpie doll on his shoulder.

"Not everyone in the movies is a soft boy. I did my service." He sat up and tossed his hair back from his angular face. "Have you thought about having a head-and-shoulders shot done? It's industry standard."

He told her he'd give her his card and get it set up for her. All he needed was ten dollars to cover the photographer's costs—and that was a special rate. "I know the guy who discovered Joan Crawford."

Jessie searched for her purse, reaching across her friend for it. Then she yanked the sheet back up to cover Dot. "She's so loose. Honestly, I don't know why I pal around with her. I can't believe I have to be at my mother's for Christmas in a few hours." She dug around in the beaded bag.

"Well, she hit on all sixes tonight. Hand me that, will you?" He gestured to her friend's half-smoked reefer on the bedside table. "You go around with her 'cause she makes you do the things you want to do but wouldn't otherwise," he said, lighting it up. "And contrary"—he hissed the thick, sweet smell inward—"to what you may think, I *am* a good man. Just one who's been good far too long."

Jessie squinted across the room to where his luggage sat. He followed her gaze. It was stamped clearly with the word *Detroit* and had another man's name stenciled on it. She put two fives on the bedside table, saying she'd pay for the head-and-shoulders shot but that he'd *better call her.* She snapped her wallet shut.

Novarro leaned back and closed his eyes. He felt his mind turning sideways with the marijuana, and saw behind his lids the black bars and black stripes of the tiger in the cage at the El Fey bar. Magnificent and fierce. Quietly, he laughed.

={ 14 }=

IT WAS NEARLY eight on Christmas Eve, but Ernest Krim was still outfitted in his white coat, the neon pharmacy light a yellow beacon to many—those who were ill and those who were also looking to get ill on 100 proof. The line continued, though he'd already told his assistant to lock the doors. The faces and bodies before him were varied: the impatient, the nearly nodding off, the nervous, clutching their prescriptions, dressed to the nines rather than for sickbeds. A pair of pretty girls leaned together, giggling behind their hands. Krim could hear singing in the street, the stuttering of car horns, both angry and joyous, the clatter of high-heeled boots, and the deep clong of church bells, but he didn't look up again from his desk until he had completed the capsules, sealed and labeled them, and stapled the paper bag closed. His assistant pulled another crate of whiskey from beneath the counter, each bottle marked *For Medicinal Purposes Only*.

"Does that one need delivery?" his assistant inquired, nodding at the pills while bagging bottles as quickly as possible. His name was Irving. He was a shy and serious young man, with a curious nature, and a long lock of hair that had a habit of falling over his eye.

"I'll take this one. It's for my mother," Krim said.

One of the waiting customers, a Mrs. Volks, overheard them. "What a good boy, visiting your mother on Christmas Eve."

Krim and the assistant looked at each other. At thirty, Krim had not been a boy in a very long time. Then again, Mrs. Volks was close to fifty and half-baked. She had half a dozen children between the ages of ten and thirty, and came in twice weekly for her prescribed bottle of whiskey.

She leaned on the corner, one arm flopping out dramatically. "How is your mother, poor dear?"

Krim grimaced, but stepped forward to ring the woman up. "She's in a delicate state."

"Oh, bless her," Mrs. Volks sniffed, counting out dimes.

After she'd gone and as Krim filled the next prescription, Irving whispered, "Is it still bad?"

Krim sorted the carbon receipts. Without looking up, he said, "I thought you knew: my mother thinks her head is made of glass."

"Pardon me?"

"No, you heard correctly. It's a ridiculous notion, but recently she's absolutely convinced of it. It affects the way she sits and stands and carries herself at all times. I think the only time she's perfectly happy is when she's lying down on a soft pillow."

Irving left to clear another few customers. Krim had told the boy when he was hired that he was sometimes called away to deal with his mother's medical issues. He hadn't been forthcoming, he realized now, and felt guilty for being ashamed.

"I'm sorry. But why glass?" the assistant asked, coming back to the prescription table a few minutes later. It was a question Krim had heard before and he supplied his standard answer.

"If I knew that, I'd be a doctor, not a pharmacist." Krim handed Irving a bottle of Arzen Nasal Oil and another of Nembutal elixir. "This one is for Mr. Johnson, but put this one in the delivery.

"Merry Christmas, Mr. Johnson," Krim managed cheerily for the next patient, and he stepped to the till and took Irving's place. Counting, he could see there were only seven more to go—two with real medical needs and five with deep thirsts. He gestured two elderly patients forward in the line, not just because of their weakened states—everyone in line was weakened in some way—but because the drunks were more difficult and took longer to serve: each wanted to share a story.

Soon Krim was back at his desk filling capsules while Irving dispensed the liquor bags. The assistant called over, "I forgot to tell you—I got to Crowley's in time. I picked it up like you asked. In the back." Irving nodded toward the locked storage room, the blond lock bouncing to conceal his right eye as he did so.

"I gave you enough to cover it?"

Irving nodded again. Nickels rang in the till as he finished with the last of the boozehounds.

Krim passed him the final prescriptions and made his way into the back, where he found the gift box, small as an orange and wrapped in bright paper. Carefully, his thumbs eased the lid off and he stared down at the tiny powder pot inside. It was an opaque jade glass. He hadn't bought her the powder, only the jar. It served a small purpose, but more than that, it was beautiful—and beauty was as much as one could hope for, Krim supposed, when the hours passed with so much discomfort.

"Help me retie this." Krim carried the small bowl back to his desk. In his free hand he held a silk ribbon. He and the assistant crouched over the delicate object, each making attempts at a bow. Then they stood back and appraised their work and decided it would do. "Hopefully she won't pitch it at my head," Krim concluded.

"You never know. May be the best idea you've had." Irving nodded, then knelt to heft his box of deliveries for the evening.

"We'll see. It's a way to communicate—I'm just not sure what I'm saying." Krim came up beside him and examined the orders. "You must have plans. I can take some of these."

But Irving assured him that what plans he had he'd rather put off. "Besides, your mother needs those pills."

In the fall, Krim had taken a day away from the pharmacy to view the Sanford Hospital for the Psychopathic, a private facility that specialized in nervous and mental diseases. It had the presence of a grand hotel—brick with white pillars beside the door, a small cupola on the roof. Driving up the lane, he was struck by its elegance; inside, he'd felt a sense of peace. The attendants were skilled in the application of electricity and massage, and the director combined the studies of psychiatry and neurology in order to diagnose and treat—or so Krim had been told by a woman as pretty as she was efficient. He made the mistake of calling her "nurse," and she had smiled as she corrected him. She was a medical student, after which she would start full-time as a doctor at the facility. After that information had been given, he did not know how to address her, settling eventually on "ma'am" since she was not yet a doctor.

"The hospital seeks to maintain patient dignity," this student had informed him. "Your mother will be encouraged to tell the doctor, in her own words, about the development of her disorder."

"My mother has a lot of words, ma'am," Krim said, "many requiring a strong constitution."

The student doctor smiled and told him that during her internship she had already heard a hundred words not in any dictionary, but—she consulted the form he'd filled out—whatever Gertrude's *peculiarities*, she was sure his mother would find *serenity* at the Sanford. Superb care and rehabilitation were the goals of the hospital. And his mother could stay as long as he, and she, found it a benefit.

"Serenity," Krim echoed, his eyes wandering down the gleaming white halls.

There were outpatients and inpatients, forty beds, and his hope had been that Gertrude would soon enjoy the sunporches and the view of elms outside, where she could watch the leaves change—one of the few things she still seemed to take pleasure in. But the leaves had now fallen and Krim still hadn't put together the money he needed. It was one of several reasons he'd said "no problem" to Moss's impulsive demands.

"Tranquil. Very professional setting," Krim said now to Irving as he described the facility, although he wasn't sure why he felt the need to reassure anyone, much less his assistant, of the hospital's quality. "I almost have the down payment. I'm just waiting on some funds to come in." Krim gathered up his things then walked around the shop making adjustments here and there, his face showing dissatisfaction even though the assistant had swept and tidied up earlier. "It will come soon, though," Krim said, in answer to himself. "Well, good night, then, Irving."

"Good night, Mr. Krim. Merry Christmas."

"Have a good one." Krim pulled on his hat and coat and let himself out.

HIS MOTHER WAS perched very still in the window when he pulled up. The house was small and most of it dark. It was not the one he'd grown up in, since they'd had to sell that after his father took up with another woman and his parents had divorced. His mother had lived in a decrepit apartment while he and his brother Morty were away in the war. Krim didn't think of this newer house as his, though he'd made most of the payments. Through the ruffled sheers, he could see his mother holding her shoulders straight, as if a plank had been inserted down her back. He sat for just a minute in the darkness before getting out of the truck.

The hired nurse met him on the walk. "I'm sorry, Mr. Krim, but I just can't do it anymore. I'm serious, no more." When he apologized for being late on Christmas Eve, she said, "No, sir, it isn't that at all. She threw a hairbrush at me."

Krim coughed and swallowed, unsure how to aid the situation. The nurse knew his mother abhorred having her hair combed. Her head—or illusions of her head's material—was much too sensitive for such common rituals. Krim held out the envelope with the small bonus in it, hoping to change the woman's mind.

"I know she can be difficult."

"It isn't that," the nurse repeated, "it's that I threw it back at her! Then, Lord, she burst into a terrible round of tears and wailing. For two hours, and I'm sure they could hear her all the way to Central Station, and I had to say to myself: 'What is wrong with *me* that I would throw an object at a woman who believes she is made of glass?' I cannot do it anymore, Mr. Krim. I am simply not good enough, and I can't. I can *not*."

"I understand," he said, and bid her good night and Merry Christmas. He almost called after her that if she were to change her mind . . . but he didn't, because he was quite certain she wouldn't.

Inside, Krim sat in front of the phone and jiggled the receiver. "New York City, please. Plaza Hotel."

"Hold for toll transfer."

As the operator connected his call with radio-like chirps, Krim took out a small notebook from his back pocket, worn and shaped to the contours of his ass. He had noted in handwriting unnaturally small all the debts owed to him that he could not list in his real ledgers down at the shop. Written beside an amount of $3,000 were the initials A.M.

"Plaza Hotel. How may I direct your call?" The voice had that five-dollar toll call timbre, flat and mechanical.

"I'd like to speak to a guest. Last name Novarro. First name Alfred. I mean Alphonse."

Krim circled the sum of money in his notebook with a short pencil, drawing several stars around it.

"There's no guest by that name here, sir."

"He checked out?"

"No record of that guest at all, sir. Least not this week."

"Thank you."

Krim hung up and looked down at the figure of $3,000, now illuminated by scribbles. He crossed it out until his pencil broke.

$$=\!\!\!=\!\!\mid 15 \mid\!\!=\!\!\!=$$

THE CHRISTMAS CONCERT at the First Lutheran affected Elsie Moss more than she'd thought it would. In the two weeks since Alfred had gone missing, Elsie had dealt only with the police, the banks, and the baby's cries, and now to find herself surrounded by strangers and half acquaintances brought her back into her body. Voices rose in song, the tenors, the altos, the sopranos: together, they were both deep and quavering. The reverend had promised that part of the collection would come to her, but at that moment, Elsie didn't care. She *did* care, of course—because the banks had been impossible, and because the insurance company insisted that without a body there was no policy fulfillment to discuss—but Elsie only had the energy to be inside the humming song. She closed her eyes and listened to the way the voices could stand out or mingle. She stared at the empty cross above Reverend Prangley's head.

When she left the church, Baby John wrapped and sleeping in spite of the din, she walked straight to a pay phone and dialed Frank Brennan.

"I'm sorry, I know you wanted to see me tonight, but I can't," Elsie blurted. "Yes, I know you had a gift for me, but I can't take it. I can't see you anymore, and I—"

"Don't be foolish, Elsie," he said on the other end. "If anything, you need me now more than before."

Outside in the snow, happy passersby from the church continued to flow around Elsie and the baby carriage while she stood holding the pay phone and trying not to weep in the street. All the warmth she'd felt half an hour before seemed to have left her. When she was singing, she had felt God close to her, just as she had when she was young. But now, she felt the ice beneath her shoes. "It's not right," she breathed.

FRANK BRENNAN WAS already dressed in his blue suit, his few remaining leaden-brown hairs combed across his head. He stood in the hall in half darkness, the phone in one hand, the Packard keys on the table ready for him to pick up. His forehead wrinkled every time he thought about Elsie. Why was he getting new wrinkles over some woman, he wondered. Wrinkles should be created only by his own children.

"Look," Brennan said, trying to reassure her with his tone. "Whatever happened to your husband, it's not your fault. It's not because of us."

The girl took her time replying. He could hear her shaky breath.

Brennan didn't want to make his argument too strongly; he didn't want to fall in love with her more than he had, especially now that half the obstacles had been removed. Ten days before, she'd had a husband, however truant, and he a wife, however far away. Frank reached into his pocket and fingered the striped paper of the gift he'd been planning to bring her. He couldn't bring her jewelry because that would have alerted her husband. He had thought for a long time about it, and settled on poetry. The volume he'd wrapped up for her was by someone called simply H.D. He normally didn't read such things, but he'd bought the book while traveling and read it on a train between New York and Detroit. The verses were stark, sexual, with nature intruding, but every piece deliberately constructed, baffling and intriguing him in a way that little—except perhaps Elsie herself—did.

"There have been others, you know," Elsie said, her voice suddenly angry.

Frank Brennan pulled his finger back from the gift in his pocket quickly, as though he'd been burned.

"All right," he said. "We won't see each other right now." He hung up the phone and then picked it up again. She was gone, and he realized he couldn't phone her back because she wasn't even at home. He snatched up and felt the jagged car keys in his palm, contemplated driving across the city against her wishes to be there when she arrived back at the house. But then he set the keys down on the table. He took out the wrapped book and dropped it there too. He prided himself on being a man of his word, and he'd just told her they wouldn't see each other. He unknotted his tie as he walked through the dark hallway back to his bedroom.

={ 16 }=

JUST BEFORE THE Christmas concert at his church, Prangley had spotted Vern Bunterbart lurking in the cemetery—the big man's homburg a brown halo above cherubic cheeks that had turned pink with the cold. Prangley strode quickly across the grounds and made a show of shaking Bunterbart's hand, even while glaring at him.

"We will be seen here. People are arriving." Prangley nodded to the fence and the street beyond. He turned to lead Bunterbart back to the parsonage but at the last minute became uncomfortable with the idea of inviting him inside. It seemed too personal. Prangley indicated his car, and the two men got into the green Buick coupe. It was a small vehicle, and Bunterbart had to squeeze himself into the seat just to close the door.

"You need a bigger car," Bunterbart declared, taking off his gloves and exposing his red hands. Clearly, the man had been waiting awhile but hadn't had the guts to knock on the parsonage door. Prangley relaxed slightly; he had taught his accomplice well.

"I have cars," Prangley remarked. "But I do not drive them."

"I have a car—new, nice," Bunterbart continued. "I would sell you, then maybe you sell it back to me when the business with the Purples is passed?"

"Did you miss our payment with them?" Prangley stared out the windshield as if they were driving, though he hadn't taken the keys from his pocket.

Bunterbart peered ahead too.

"Ya, you have to give me something."

"I did."

"Not enough."

"You make plenty in this job, Vern. You should have something of your own to put in."

"Ya, well, my wife and the children are good at swallowing money. They eat it up like mashed potatoes." The man tried to smile but settled for a small parting of lips.

Prangley considered for a few minutes. The Purple Gang had begun with four brothers—the Bernsteins—who were so rotten that supposedly even their parents had given up on them before they graduated high school. Soon they were being mentored by older local gangsters: Russian and Polish Jews in Paradise Valley. Groomed into bank robbers and extortionists, they imported muscle from New York, and had been taking over the booze business—so successfully that even Capone had been coerced into working with them. It was that or a street fight. A shopkeeper in the neighborhood where they'd grown up called them the Purples, a term journalists had embraced; the brothers were like bad meat, turning a rancid color. Or perhaps they were Purple because one gang member who had been a boxer had worn shorts of that color. Prangley tried not to learn the truth behind such folklore—you did not make chitchat with such men. You paid them and kept away from them as much as possible.

Prangley tipped his head back and stared at the roof of the car. "Do you remember last February, the Purples killed a cop? Their gang is not to be put off. And in March, they chewed up the hallway of their own apartment like a shooting gallery. Put three men down. Did you see the pictures?"

"First time I heard of them: tommy guns." Bunterbart blew on his hands, glancing at Prangley in the hope he'd start the car or offer a blanket.

The Milaflores Massacre had made all the local papers, and Prangley knew that even though Bunterbart could hardly read English, he understood the meaning of the black spots like ash marks that had marred the walls in the photographs. It had taken but a day for two men in the Purple Gang, Abe Axler and Fred Burke, to be arrested—but they couldn't be charged and had been released.

Prangley let the conversation sink in. With women he used banter, but he preferred to use silence with Bunterbart. His patience was rewarded: after a moment the big German confessed he'd gone door to door to every business they worked with, politely demanding a protection tax. He'd managed to drum up an extra two grand. Couldn't Prangley help a little?

"Of course." Prangley smiled. "I can match that."

"But we owe them . . . thirty percent of twenty thousand." Bunterbart closed his eyes and Prangley wondered if he was doing the calculations very slowly in his head.

"It is getting late and I must get to the church. Tell me what you want."

"They will shoot me, Charles, over what? Two, maybe three thousand. They shoot me and my family. You want that?"

"Of course not." Prangley patted the large man's shoulder. "You should do something."

"What?!" The big man shifted uncomfortably in the small space. His homburg fell off.

"Pray." Prangley smiled and got out of the car.

Bunterbart climbed out too, and slammed the door. "You want to work with me, ya? I am good for the business, not . . . replaceable!" He moved quickly around to Prangley's side of the vehicle, grabbing at the reverend's sleeve. "So you help! You have seen these machine guns? Sleek round barrel. Zip, zip. Like doing up a coat."

"Pictures, that is all I see," Prangley confirmed. He moved ahead of Bunterbart. The man's desperation was agitating. "They will not kill you, Vern. They will take your car and house before that. Have faith: they are businessmen and they care more about money than death."

"But you give me more money. Better yet, get me one of these Thompsons." Bunterbart panted in his effort to keep up.

Prangley turned abruptly, almost bumping into the man's chest. "I will get you more. Now I have a concert in an hour. Get away from my church or I'll stamp some lead in you myself."

AFTER THE CONCERT, Prangley entered the church basement, ducking his head. He could see the dust on the low beams; his secretary was not big on upkeep, and that was a good thing. He'd hired the woman for her ability to show up on time, and that's all he wanted. The fact that she hadn't seemed particularly interested in religion at her job interview last year had been a selling point for Prangley. Believers felt a sense of ownership. The previous secretary had come down the basement stairs far too often. What a relief when she died suddenly one day after eating her bread and tomato soup in the small kitchen. She ate the same thing every lunchtime, at twelve sharp. That day, she'd lain down on a bench in the ladies' room afterwards, complaining of shivers and stomach pain—"women's pain," Prangley had told the ambulance driver, though Mrs. Hoffmann was past fifty. He missed Mrs. Hoffmann's abilities with a rag and a bottle of Murphy's soap upstairs, but he did not miss her intrusions, and as time went by, he found he could not for the life of him remember what her face looked like, though he'd spent every day with her for nine years. He wondered why that was.

No, Faye McCloud was much better as a secretary. She stuck to typing, scheduling, answering, and greeting.

He progressed down the corridor and stopped to find the key on its large ring. Just before the basement narrowed and the flooring turned to dirt, he turned and unlocked a door. It stuck at first, then let him in. The Scotch was cloaked with a heavy tarp; he peeled it back, revealing the cases. He plucked a bottle, opened it, and sniffed. He took an empty brown bottle of aftershave from his pocket. On a ledge at the side of the room, he found a funnel and began to fill one bottle from the other. He replaced the lids and put the Scotch back in its place and the "aftershave" in the interior pocket of his suit. He replaced the tarp and darkened the room before locking it tight.

He stooped where the basement was lower and entered the long dirt corridor at the end, carving footprints in the dust. Charles had told Faye when she started that there were some old tombs here, going back to the 1880s, and she'd pursed her lips and lifted an eyebrow. If the girl was frightened, she didn't show it—but she never asked for a tour, either.

The far end of the corridor opened up like a cellar into the tiny graveyard behind the church. Large metal gates were locked across both entrances. As he came to the one on the church side, he unlocked it and hunched along until he arrived at the third catacomb.

He entered the room without hesitation and fumbled for the lantern he kept inside. The place smelled of mold and damp cedar. He worked in the near darkness to light it, then faced the simple wood casket.

"Vern Bunterbart, you swilling, self-drowning crumb," he said on an exhale, gazing at the coffin, which sat on the cobwebbed brick shelf. "How much do I give you?"

The casket was over six feet long, darkened with grime. Though old, the lock was not yet rotten. Prangley opened it carefully and stuck his hand inside without looking. Beneath his fingers, stacks of money. The feathery feel of the bills always thrilled him, but tonight it was a duller sensation than usual. He rubbed his thumb along the bundles and drew one out. He looked at it, put it in his pocket. "One for me"—his hand went under the lid again—"and one for you." He put a second stack of cash in a different pocket.

He had been in touch with the Canadians himself and, after a few conversations with raised voices, had convinced them the money for their shipment had indeed been left for them, hidden in the reeds along the river where the men had picked up the booze. If they had not received it, he said, they had their own countrymen to blame—someone else had absconded with it. They had argued back that they needed some payment if his men wanted to continue to do business on their side of the river. A middle amount was agreed upon.

Prangley stepped back from the casket and examined a calendar pinned to the wall inside the small room. In contrast to its surroundings, it was crisp and white, with a picture of a car on it, and the name of Seamus Lynch's dealership. As Prangley touched the page, it occurred to him that he would have to find a replacement calendar in a few days. Every third Monday of the month was circled—their payout day to the Purples for the privilege of operating. Prangley's men sold to those who didn't want to deal directly with the Purple Gang: Irish saloons, German beer halls, tiny corner grogshops, landlords, and farmers. The Purples would collect their money from Bunterbart on those third Mondays. Prangley expected they wouldn't relent on snatching their cut, no matter the circumstances, and the payment date for that month had already come and gone.

Still deliberating, Prangley cocked his head. He turned and opened the casket lid fully, gazed on the immaculate, clean bills that filled the entire coffin, each bundle circled with a paper band. He ran one finger across the topmost bills, delicately, the way other men might stroke the back of a cat or dog. He started to withdraw another couple of bundles, but paused. He didn't like the space left behind.

"No, you lug-headed boozer. You fucked it up, so now you work."

Prangley shook his head and let the lid drop a little too forcefully; a puff of dust shot out from the boards. He locked the casket.

When he left the room, he stood in the passageway, smiling crookedly. Then he ascended the stairs and walked back through the empty church. He'd told Miss McCloud that they needn't tidy up right after the Christmas concert, and as a result, small, bright flyers littered the pews. The floor by the entrance was still wet from the many boots that had trudged through. He grabbed a mop and gave the floorboards a perfunctory swish, pushing the dirt to one side, then he darkened the great room and locked up. He abhorred mess, but he had more important matters to tend to.

Back in the parsonage, he struck a match and illuminated a thick red candle. It cast a dancing light across the bare front parlor. The room contained only a table and a pair of tired-looking armchairs. He walked through to the bedroom and snapped the light on. He slid off his pants and stood there in his silk boxer shorts. He placed his old black derbys under the bed. He opened the closet and took his time selecting from its array of designer suits and separates. It was only a medium-sized closet, but he had managed to fill it tightly. He reached past a raccoon coat and gently pulled down a pair of deeply creased baggy trousers.

An ornate Louis Vuitton shoe trunk sat open, and inside its compartments rested thirty pairs of Florsheims, Selzs, Stetsons, Manfield Waukenphasts, Goodyear welts, Hamilton-Browns with imported genuine kangaroo leather, custom oxfords from England, and wingtips from Italy. There were black and whites, blunt-toed brogues, stylish semi-brogues, and crocodile-skin cap-toes. Prangley sat on the bed and changed his footwear, stepping into a pair of two-tone tan and whites. He went to the dresser and from a collection of bottles selected the night's cologne, which he dashed onto his palms and chin.

When he had chosen a handmade shirt and silk tie, he returned to sit, impeccably attired, alone, in the dark front room on the worn chair. He was due to meet a man about a plane, but not until midnight. Bunterbart had disagreed about taking the operation to air, so Prangley hadn't confided his plan. Of course Bunterbart disagreed— there was nothing in it for him. Without the river, who did Prangley need? The men he'd gathered were useless. For Prangley, the question was one of cost. Stocks were easy, play numbers you moved from one column to another. But he hated to part with cash. The same was true of planes—machines and flyboys cost a few beans. But paying off the Purples cost more, he reckoned.

A sudden snow blew against the window glass, whispering.

Something about the sound agitated Prangley, and he got up and paced around the empty part of the parsonage. It was decorated with books and framed Biblical quotes and held very little else. He turned on the radio and spun the dial until he found a show he knew. It played new classical compositions, and he listened as the host announced that the next piece was Anton Webern, String Trio no. 2. Webern composed in Vienna, though tonight an orchestra in New York performed his piece. Prangley listened to the scratchy, plaintive strands. It made him think of lines running at opposing angles. It was a nervous-sounding piece, but he liked that nothing seemed to come easy. He went into the back again and took out a box of imported cigars from his humidor. Returning with a fragrant brown stick in his mouth, he leaned down to the candle flame and puffed until the cigar glowed. Then he opened a drawer, empty except for a deck of cards. He sat down at the bare table in all his finery and laid out six piles, turning over kings and queens, sixes and sevens.

At exactly quarter to midnight, Prangley restacked the cards and tucked them in the side bureau drawer. He put on his mohair coat and locked up the parsonage. The air outside was still and damp. Prangley got into his Buick coupe and drove to a speakeasy downtown.

The fellow he was on his way to do business with called himself King Canada, but his real name was Blaise Diesbourg. At the speak-easy, he found Diesbourg's guys—two baggy wool–slacked slicks, one with a smile like a dagger, the other with no smile at all.

"Airplane," the first man said, grinning. He made a buzzing noise with his mouth, his hands held up like wings, as if he thought Prangley didn't speak the same language.

Prangley nodded; he could see the second man assessing him.

"Why you interested in them?" the unsmiling man asked.

"It takes too many to move product across the ice. It is too easy to lose both men and product," Prangley said, looking him in the eye. He held up his index finger. "So far as I understand it, only one man flies the plane."

At the next table, a fat man who looked too much like Vern Bunterbart for Prangley's liking was leaning into a blond-haired woman, who in turn was leaning into her beer. Prangley watched as the stranger planted a fat, wet kiss on the girl's earlobe.

The second man put a hand below their own table and, without looking, Prangley filled it with a thick stack of bills.

"Being careful takes time," the man said.

Next to them, the mismatched couple grew handsy, and Prangley eyed the two Canadians. It was a good time for them to finish their drinks.

"I understand," he said. "The other way takes even more time in the end: five to eight federal. Gentlemen, I assure you, I know the value of waiting."

⟹ 17 ⟸

THE TABBY CAT shot out the door the second it opened, even though it cracked only a tiny bit. "Watch it!" Bunterbart yelled. "Lose that cat again, I dare you." He stared as his son bent to grab the creature by its tail, but the boy still clutched one of his toys and the cat was too fast. Out it went across the snow, all stripes and flattened ears, its paws barely leaving behind a trace.

"Hansel!" the boy yelped as the door bounced wide open, jingle bells on the wreath tinkling. The partner cat, Gretel, the shy all-black one, remained inside under Bunterbart's chair. From where he was sitting, Bunterbart could see only his eight-year-old son, Peter. He figured the person who had knocked would be one of his wife's friends, someone dropping by with a fruitcake. He certainly didn't expect a man at the door with sleepy eyes that looked as if he'd taken a few too many blows to the head.

To Peter, this stranger was just a man at the door—and that was how the boy put it to Bunterbart: "Papa, there's a man here." The eldest of five, the boy clutched a new clockwork train engine against his pajama shirt.

Bunterbart lumbered over. "Your sisters cried for hours last time you lost that goddamn—"

Then he saw who it was. He turned and mouthed silently to Frieda, who recognized the wild look in his eyes, even if she could not interpret the shape his mouth made. She gathered the children quickly and pushed them into a back bedroom, in spite of their protests—each attempting to run back to the tree for their new treasures. Slaps were delivered, followed by crying and hushing.

The man at the door was one of the Abes. Half the Purple Gang was named Abe, and the other half Irving. Or so it seemed to Bunterbart, who was obsessed with the markers and signs of Jewishness. He had learned English by reading the political essays of Henry Ford, as published in the carmaker's personal newspaper, the *Dearborn Independent*. The paper had fortified Vern and Frieda with pictures of important people buying American-made cars, alongside warnings from Ford about threats to this good life by Communists and Jews. Bunterbart had a copy of *Mein Kampf* on his shelves, mailed to him by a cousin, and had jumped right out of his chair when he saw the name Henry Ford—the only American mentioned within its pages.

"I said I would bring it," he protested now.

"Then you oughta. It's a week past. These ain't library dues."

Bunterbart drew a breath. He reached inside his trouser pocket, yanked out the bankroll, handed it across the door frame.

"You have such a bright young son. Such nice manners," the man in the doorway said as he flicked through the bills. How could his black eyes droop so and still hold so much menace? All the Bernsteins had messed-up eyes. He was half Vern's size, yet Bunterbart didn't think of him as small. When the man made a clucking sound in the back of his throat, to Bunterbart it sounded like a trigger being cocked.

"It's light."

"We lost a shipment, ya. Like I told your brother," Bunterbart said, gesturing to the car that sat idling at the curb.

"Not my problem."

"It is in the bottom of the river."

"Is it now?"

"Ya!" Bunterbart scratched at his neck. He knew his face was reddening.

"What else do you have for me?" Abe's hard face was unreadable.

"I will have more soon." Bunterbart attempted to take up as much of the door frame as possible so the black-eyed young man wouldn't see any more of his home, children, or personal effects.

When Abe didn't leave, Bunterbart's fear turned to agitation. "Please, it is Christmas." He jerked his thumb over his shoulder.

"It's your fault, Bunterbart," came the reply. The man leaned casually in the door. "The river's been frozen solid for over a month. It's thicker right now than your dumb Kraut skull."

"What is it you are saying?"

"I'm saying I don't give a fuck where your shipment is, but if you think it's in the river, you're dumber than you look."

Bunterbart's hand balled into a fist. "Get out of here."

"Listen." A nod at the driveway. "You rather lose your car or kneecaps? I'm helping you out here. Don't be an idiot."

Bunterbart could feel his neck burning. He was reluctant to fetch the keys but was prompted by the sound of one of the children behind him crying. He reached into the closet and fished beneath his coat, thumb brushing his .38. He paused and peered out at the other man in the sedan at the curb. Probably Little Joe Bernstein, said to be the toughest of the crew in spite of his size.

Bunterbart sighed heavily. The keys slipped from pocket and hand to hand. He knew the gang would not count it for what it was worth. Against the debts, it was a puff of gasoline.

The man in the door took the keys and turned away.

Vern puffed himself up and shouted after him, "You people come here, to my home, on our day. Rats! All of you. *Ratten!*"

The man stopped. He stood very still for a few seconds, then he came back swiftly, delivering a punch to the groin with his right. Bunterbart attempted to block it, but the man had surprise and momentum on his side. Vern doubled over, sucking in air at a high pitch. Inside the man's fist was a small sap, and it came down across the back of Bunterbart's head like a stone dropping. Bunterbart tasted cement and snow, the grit of his front porch. Pain spider-climbed across his skull.

Through eyes scrunched in agony, he saw his son Peter run out of the room where his mother had cloistered them. The boy hung in the doorway again, his bare feet dancing on the threshold, uncertain whether to step down to aid his father. The hem of his flannel pajama trousers fluttered white above the snow.

"Stop acting like a woman and maybe one day you'll make money," Abe said. His shiny shoes padded through the snow. He got into Bunterbart's brand-new Model A and backed it out of the driveway. The Bunterbarts had owned it for only two weeks. The second fellow drove away in the car the Purples had come in.

Peter helped his father up. "Why did he say that to you, Papa?" the boy asked, his face soft, warped with worry. "You are not a woman."

As soon as Bunterbart stood up, he slapped the boy hard in the face. But his anger subsided as he took a step forward through the house and realized he needed his son's help. Together they hobbled in, the small one sniffing back tears, the large one wheezing with pain.

ALL DAY VERN moved the ice pack from his neck down to his trousers then back up again. Over the course of the afternoon he drank eighteen beers, until he shivered and hiccuped with sickness. After dinner, without explanation, he entered the kitchen and slapped his wife repeatedly, hands instantly turning one of her cheeks blue.

"You spend all my money! All my money on that automobile, and now—gone!" he yelled, disregarding how he'd loved the vehicle too.

Bunterbart pushed Frieda hard against the icebox. His son Peter dropped his new green engine and hollered, and Frieda yelled in German that the only danger they faced was from Vern: get out or go sleep it off. He did, by and by, although not before scaring her again by pulling a large army trunk out from beneath the bed and fumbling with its lock. It contained his guns from the war. Eventually he managed to pry it open.

Bunterbart lifted his Savage automatic from the chest. Kneeling beside the bed, he loaded it. It was a 1907, a .45, a small gun, really, for his purposes, but it fired ten shots. He studied it. It was the first gun he'd ever owned, but in spite of its age it remained a nice weapon. He only wished he had two. From the small arsenal he selected a Colt 1911, an uglier gun in Vern's opinion. As he handled them, he snorted. "Ya, if you were a woman at a dance, you would be the ugliest." He set it down and picked up a New Model Iver Johnson.

"It is late, and you are drunk," Frieda said quietly behind him.

He flicked a set of stockings off the bed, using the gun. Then he turned and aimed the gun at his wife. He laughed when he saw the solemn expression this evoked, a gray fear stretching across her black-and-blue eyes. "I wouldn't, but I could, ya."

He cursed, lowering the Iver. He silently stashed all the guns back in the trunk and pushed it under the bed. Then the weight of his frame fell forward onto the blankets, with a grunt followed by snoring.

═{ 18 }═

THE WIND WAS harsh and Faye McCloud pulled her scarf over her nose. Bessie Smith's "Backwater Blues" hummed through her head, sliding the way her boots did through the snow. Her sister had bought the recording for her as a Christmas gift, though whether it was really a gift for her or Kitty's way of owning it, Faye wasn't sure. It was the gesture that mattered, even if the money that had paid for the album had, in a roundabout way, been Faye's own. At first she'd been skeptical that she would enjoy it, but she could admit that was natural, as she was skeptical about most things. As the days passed, she had put it on more than once—including that morning—and listened closely as the piano rolled in like clouds, the song bumping up against itself. It was mournful but not despairing, and Faye supposed she could appreciate that. The morning was dark, although it was already eight o'clock. Up ahead a boy bent, shoveling the sidewalk—no, she saw he was a young man, old enough that perhaps he wasn't in school.

There was no official name for this area north of midtown and just below Voigt Park. Henry Ford Hospital had been built there first, and then the homes had come, like small echoes of its large voice. When she'd worked at the hospital, she'd bused promptly to and from her door, had never had time to wander around the area. Now she found it was lovely, really, in the snow, if not for the cold—the white folds of the lawns and the homes' serene brick faces with their large windows. Walking through the impressive neighborhood, Faye had to remind herself that although Mrs. Moss lived in a stately new home, she would soon not be able to pay for it. The money in the envelope in her purse felt heavy suddenly, too much of it in coins. Faye felt a pang at delivering so little, and the song in her head started up again. There was one hundred and two dollars, sixty-seven cents inside the envelope, and Faye had counted it twice. The previous Sunday she had felt with her own hands how loaded the plate was when it passed her—a layer of paper bills on top, crisp as snow. There must have been at least five hundred. She didn't like the math on the back end. Prangley had delivered the Christmas collection in the New Year, and Faye wondered now if it was paltry too.

Faye pulled out the card she carried with the address, and checked it.

The young man stopped shoveling as she passed him and she saw he was doing the walk of the house she needed. She nodded and said good morning. Beneath a woolen cap, he gazed with ice eyes. He had two moles by his eye and the weedy grass of a juvenile mustache. He mumbled, "Ma'am," and watched her cross the tiny path he'd just scraped clean up to the front door.

"It's good you have help." Faye gestured back at him after Elsie Moss had shown her in.

Elsie parted the curtains in the living room and leaned between them. "He's out there again?"

She looked thinner than Faye remembered, as if she hadn't eaten since the New Year. Faye unwound her scarf, though it was cold enough inside the house that she almost wanted to keep it. She frowned and stamped her boots on the woven mat underfoot. Prangley, she imagined, might have begun the visit with a light touch or squeeze, might have asked in a low, calm tone how Elsie was doing, whether Christmas had been hard. Elsie was wearing a dark wool suit; she had dressed for the reverend but also for the coldness of the morning. Faye wondered how soon she should bring out the money. Administering was easy; house calls were outside her experience. Prangley had said to make his apologies for not coming himself, but Faye didn't like the idea of issuing apologies on behalf of others. Glancing around the interior, she saw that the table had been set with a cloth and a tray of cheese, jam, and seedy-looking bread. Prangley had said he had business that morning, but when Faye checked the schedule there had been nothing penciled in.

Elsie reached for Faye's coat. Her long painted nails were chipped around the edges. The place smelled damp, almost like rain, and earthy. Faye glanced about and her gaze settled on the sagging Christmas tree, now browning, in the far corner of the living room.

"I'm sorry it's freezing," Elsie apologized. "I couldn't get coal until next week. If you want, we can go into the kitchen next to the stove. That's where I have the baby. Moved his crib in there. Just for now."

Elsie offered something warm to drink, but Faye replied, "Really, nothing. I'm fine." She preferred to keep the visit short.

"That boy's been coming ever since Alfie disappeared," Elsie said, walking back toward the living room window. "It's so strange. Like he wants to look out for me."

Faye opened her purse and took out the envelope. She laid it on the sideboard in the dining room while Elsie had her back turned, still looking out the window.

"Had you seen him before?"

"Never," came Elsie's quick answer. Faye heard the whisper of a match lighting a cigarette. She moved to stand beside Elsie in the sulfur and the smoke. There was something about the smell that drew her. It reminded her of her father—so she told herself. They both stood back about a foot from the sheer curtains so the boy wouldn't see their outlines if he glanced up.

Faye appraised him. "I don't suppose he's any threat?"

"What? To me? He's half my age."

"Not at all," Faye remarked. "Just a handful of years, really."

Elsie turned suddenly, accidentally bumping Faye. She drew hard on the cigarette and looked more closely at her.

What did Faye do at the church, she asked, and Faye answered, clerical.

"My father used to say that those who did the bookkeeping were the most valuable—the ones who know the secrets."

"He sounds like a wise man."

Elsie waved the cigarette dismissively. "Oh, the only thing he's wise about is how to brew beer." Then she amended, "Maybe that's a fib. He was respectable once."

"Well, I don't know any secrets," Faye said.

"Sure," Elsie said. "But I suppose the reverend told you about my husband's disappearance—about his business. I really didn't know much. He could have been involved with anyone." She waved the cigarette again, as though it didn't matter to her, but Faye could see that it very much did matter.

The two women glanced back out through the snow at the taut shoulders of the boy as he pushed the black shovel down the drive, making a sound like sleigh runners.

"A boy?" mused Faye. "Would a boy be in your husband's business?"

"There are lots of boys who smuggle," Elsie confirmed, and Faye felt a slight flush of excitement at the word, the trust Elsie showed in her by naming it. "My husband told me there was one he was teaching to drive. Lost his father a year before, I think Alfie said. It's funny now how I remember it. There are so many things I remember now. And I only recall the good things about Alfie. Isn't that funny? I think I love him more every day. It's terrible, really." She sucked back on the cigarette. "Are you sure I can't get you something warm to drink? I'm not much of a cook, but please, there's breakfast if you're hungry."

Faye advanced toward the spread. She knew she was expected to stay, make pleasantries, give comfort—things that were not in her job description but nonetheless came along with working in a church. At the hospital, when she'd been employed there, people had died, but she was only expected to type and bookkeep. In contrast to Elsie's three layers, Faye wore only one—and she hunched her shoulders so the sleeves of her dress would cover more of her. The feeling in the house was too much like that in her own after her father had died.

"I went to the bank, but they wouldn't let me touch our accounts," Elsie said, inhaling. "All that they told me was that he took out a big sum of money two days before. For Christmas, I reckon. I can't help myself from wondering what it was he was planning to buy us."

Faye looked around the sparsely furnished room. Was she supposed to guess? "A radio?"

Elsie crossed to the china cabinet. She opened the cupboard and took out a cup and saucer even though, Faye noted, the glass pane had been taken out completely, leaving the cups in the open air. As Elsie did this, her gaze fell on the envelope. "Oh, you brought this?" Before Faye could apologize for the amount, Elsie's shoulders fell and she said abruptly, "I told Reverend Prangley I would need work. He said to allow him to work some magic. Not that I'm not grateful—I am. For every bit." Her fingers worked the envelope.

Faye sighed; she supposed the amount might get Elsie and her child through a few more weeks. "I shouldn't speak against the reverend, but . . ." Faye took a plate and piled it with bread and cheese slices as she tried to avoid saying anything more. She bit into the bread and chewed and swallowed, then stared at the crusts on the plate. Shaking her head, she said, "Men will never encourage you to labor. It's not in their nature. It doesn't mean it isn't a necessity."

Elsie took the envelope and pushed the money into a drawer without counting it. She sat down across from Faye. "How long have you worked?"

Faye said she'd always worked. Her father had been a shopkeeper. When he died, they lost the shop, but she had found work in an office at the university—and was able to sit in on classes there sometimes, too. She reckoned she'd been employed now for almost a decade at this job or that.

"It's tragic, of course, that you've had to come to it this way. You mentioned your parents. Can they help?"

Elsie shook her head. She described how, when she'd phoned and told her family the news, her mother had said Elsie must have driven Alfie to it. Her parents had suggested she come over and tie one on with them. "I almost agreed to it," Elsie confessed.

"Friends?"

Some girls had come by to offer condolences and help with the baby. "One was here last week. She's dating a race man. I didn't know what that meant. He took her to a revue at the Palms. She talked for two hours before I realized she meant he was colored. Based on her description, I had told her that he sounded like a great fellow, a businessman, and a real up-and-comer!"

"Well"—Faye fiddled around in her handbag—"perhaps he is."

From her bag, Faye unfolded an announcement with a photo of Alfred on it, a photo that Elsie had supplied. She held it out. "I thought you might like to have this. It went to all the parishioners twice for the collections. And Reverend Prangley asked me to tell you he's so s—"

The baby woke and began to cry from the kitchen, the warmest room. Faye breathed in relief as Elsie hurried away—although, alas, she closed the kitchen door behind her, taking the last waft of heat in the house.

"Shall I see myself out?" Faye called hopefully a few minutes later, but Elsie called back, "Please stay!"

Half an hour later, Faye could hear the baby continuing to fuss through the feeding. She stared at the photo of Alfred Moss on the donation announcement. Something about him was familiar, but perhaps he was just that sort. In the picture, his lips were gray and his eyes were gray but his hair shone so black it was almost blue. His nose was sizable, but he was undeniably handsome, with thin, slanting cheeks. Had Elsie married him because she was young and impressionable and he so handsome? Or, thinking of the drunken parents she'd mentioned, Faye wondered if it had been a simple way to leave home. Alfred Moss squinted somewhat, giving the impression he was laughing even though his mouth was a closed straight line. She could tell that his teeth were a bit large behind his lips—something about the fullness of the mouth, its curvature.

Suddenly Faye put down the announcement and began to pace around the living room. She walked over and placed her hands on the radiator, but it was cold. She went into the closet to gather her things. There, she brushed past a mink. Without thinking about it, her thumb briefly caressed the hem. She closed the closet door and pulled her own coat loosely around her shoulders. This shouldn't have been her visit to make.

Prangley had been a bear since Christmas. Was it the number of times he'd shut the door to his office practically on her foot, or the way he came in later than usual and said less? Just to give herself a break from him, she'd started leaving early in the afternoons to see a film, with the claim she'd finished most of her work in the morning hours before he arrived. Perhaps he had troubles with some woman. Or perhaps, like everyone, he was secretly inclined to drink. Faye didn't like to speculate. She'd found it easier to stay at jobs longer if she didn't tell herself stories about those she worked with.

From the other room, she could hear the baby and the mother shushing it. It was a most intimate battle, and Faye felt her face turn red, then a rush of anger as she thought again of the paltry envelope contents. She blew on her hands to warm them.

A phonograph stood in the living room and she went to it. It was a portable with small doors that opened up to the speakers, not much larger than a breadbox. The Victrola sat atop a separate table, where the collection was stored.

The records were motley—a few hymns, a few popular songs, names she'd heard from Kitty, like Count Basie, Duke Ellington, McKinney's Cotton Pickers, Miner's Melodians, and others too that were foreign to her, names and sounds far outside her world. There was an old one, a version of "If You Were the Only Girl in the World." Faye pulled it out, held it in her hands, something well-played and showing its scratches, then she slipped it back inside, letting it rock back into its slot in the table a little too hard. She had danced to that tune once. The record must have been Mr. Moss's—Elsie was much too young to remember the song, and she knew from the announcement that he had been thirty.

As she moved around the missing man's home, an ache coursed through her—part cold, and part stinging anger that Prangley had made promises to the widow he hadn't kept. She pocketed her hands and unpocketed them again. She sat down and drew her coat around her knees.

She heard the boy dragging garbage cans up the drive and leaving them alongside the house. When he rapped on the door, she got up and opened it tentatively.

"I'm sorry. Mrs. Moss is preoccupied with the baby," she said into his youthful, piercing gaze.

In his hand was a folded newspaper. He brushed the snow from it and extended it to Faye. "Tell her I can come back again if there's more snowfall." The voice that came out was a man's voice though he was still half the size of one.

"Thank you. What's your name?"

He hesitated before extending his hand. "Willie Lynch, ma'am."

Faye looked over her shoulder at the kitchen door, where it still sounded as though a wrestling match was occurring. Her gaze fell on the dry pine tree in the far corner. She stood aside and gestured him in, then pointed to the tree. "There's something you can help me with, Willie."

Willie said of course, and got right to loosening the base while Faye took the dozen or so ornaments from the boughs and laid them carefully on a side table around the lamp and its doily.

"Is it true that Mr. Moss taught you to drive?"

The boy hesitated, his face unyielding for one so young. Instead of answering her, he lifted the tree and tested its weight on his shoulder. He hoisted it and headed for the door.

"I'm sorry to pry," Faye said, and started to close the door behind the bush and the boy.

At the bottom of the porch, the boy set the tree down. "Tell Mrs. Moss not to worry. I can come again."

"Coal," Faye called after him. "If you want to do more."

Willie nodded. He dragged the tree to the curb, then returned and picked up his shovel. He nodded again and Faye closed the door. She heard the shovel trail down the path he'd carved, and farther, all the way down the street. It occurred to Faye that the boy was the same age or possibly older than she'd been when she'd danced to that old waltz, the record from the Victrola—that would have been 1916, twelve years ago now. Kitty was right. Faye did need more music in her life.

Finally, Elsie reappeared, now with the baby on her hip. He had grown since Faye had cared for him at the church. Baby John's face had filled out and he was almost able to hold up his head. In contrast, Elsie looked much worse than she had an hour before—a fog had settled over her eyes, and Faye wondered if she'd joined the child in some crying.

"You know, I worked clerical at the hospital before the church. The nurses there, they will happily help you if you need more instruction. Nursing children is hard work," Faye said, trying to keep her tone bright. "I've never done it personally, of course, but I hear it can be as difficult as learning to drive."

"Thank you," Elsie said quietly. Then, "I heard you talking with the boy."

"Willie."

"Willie," Elsie echoed. "So my Alfred was the one who taught him?"

"He wouldn't admit to so much, but I believe so. I had him lug the tree. I'm sorry, I didn't see a broom." Faye gestured to the tide of needles the boy had left behind.

"Thank you," Elsie said again, the words catching in her throat.

While knotting her scarf tight, Faye said suddenly, "I lost someone once too. It changes you immediately."

Elsie looked up from where the baby was chewing on its bib. She didn't say anything. Faye came back into the room and sat down.

"In the war? You must have been young. He didn't come back?" Elsie leaned forward.

Faye nodded but didn't elaborate.

"You know, there *is* something else you can help me with," Elsie said with quiet resolution. "Something I need, well, taken from here. I found it. It was in Alfred's drawer, and I don't—" Elsie stopped to jostle the baby and burp him. "The state I've been in. Honestly, I'm not cuckoo, but I don't entirely trust myself with it."

She stood then and left the room with the baby, and when she came back, Faye was startled to see that she held the baby on one side and a pistol on the other.

FAYE WALKED DOWN the sidewalk the way she had come, a greater weight in her purse than the dollars, quarters, and dimes she had brought to Mrs. Moss. She waited until she had left Atkinson Street. She turned onto wider Second Avenue, and at Second and Clairmount, where there ought to have been less privacy, she found shelter against an apartment building. She gazed around her carefully, though there was no one out in the cold, then opened her purse to peer in and look at the object again. The small, snub-nosed revolver stared back at her. It had an almost pretty carved pearl handle.

A popping sound in the distance carried over the rooftops. She looked up suddenly. It came again: a quick cracking. Faye jumped back against the building, as if the weapon in her bag were the one that had discharged. One hand clutched at her chest nervously. The flap of the purse flopped closed.

$$\equiv\{\ 19\ \}\equiv$$

VERN BUNTERBART STOOD waiting. He was not a man of regrets—though he did regret not taking himself out for a better meal at the Hofbrau Haus, Gies's, or Edelweiss Café. But other than that, he could see no use in contemplating the small details. In an hour, they would be meaningless. The day seemed unusually gray, and his coat heavier than it ought to have been even with the weapons inside it. On the opposite corner, a dentist's sign smiled at him, grinning widely two stories above his head. *Dr. McArthur's Dentistry.* Inside a large lit-up circle: nose, mustache, and full set of pearlies.

Finally, the streetcar came, and he boarded. He dropped his coin in the box and lumbered three or four steps before finding a pole to grip among the working stiffs and the women who were off to run errands. Bunterbart turned over logistics in his mind. One of the other importers, Gerald Zuckerwitz, owned extra cars for running the river, he remembered as the bus lurched and he shuffled on the spot to keep his footing. Bunterbart pictured them: broken-down 1917 and 1918 jalopies in a field behind Gerald's small house. An old King, he remembered, some kind of touring car, and a green delivery van with a Prezel logo painted on the side. Perhaps the whole operation would go smoother if he borrowed one? But Gerald lived almost as far as the River Rouge, and Bunterbart did not have time for that. He was a decisive man, and going in the wrong direction struck him as indecisive. Gerald was also Jewish, and Vern wished to owe him no favors. So he remained on the street-car, his great heft bouncing up and down as it rattled its way north on Woodward.

Soon, despite having stood outside in the snow for so long waiting, a cold sweat began to leak out from beneath his homburg. Bunterbart removed the hat briefly. He dug into his coat and lifted his handkerchief to mop his brow. As he did, he caught sight of a fellow eyeing the Savage beneath the coat. He glared at the man, allowing his anger to narrow to a point and directing it into a single glance. He pinched the coat shut again and buttoned it. The man, spectacled and frightened-looking, clamped his lips together and stared straight ahead.

The pool hall the Purples frequented was on Blaine. It was in the Jewish quarter, where Bunterbart had never been. He was used to driving and did not know much about the streetcar routes, so although there might have been a more direct option, he decided to stick to the streets he knew: Woodward up, Clairmount across, and a short walk down Twelfth. He'd traded in his Model T for a Model A, and now both cars were gone—thanks to the Purples. Was it anger or nerves that made him sweat so? Bunterbart shifted his weight. He peered out the window, the perspiration trickling into his eyes. He didn't dare open his coat again.

At the corner of Grand Boulevard and Woodward, perched up in the old crow's nest signal box, was a uniformed officer. All the traffic signals were going automatic, but there the officer was, as if he had been stationed there to make Bunterbart nervous. The man hovered slightly above the streetcar windows as it passed, and Bunterbart watched him intently. His gaze flicked down to his spectacled new friend, who looked up momentarily at the giant German and looked quickly away as if he very much wanted to disembark.

It was almost 9 a.m. by the time Vern switched trolleys. Between rides, he stopped at a pay phone and dialed home. Perhaps Frieda had changed her mind and returned to him with the children? Ringing filled his ears; no one answered. He wouldn't have fought with her, and she wouldn't have left, if it hadn't been for that stupid fur coat he'd given away. This whole state of affairs came down to Alfred Moss. Moss was the one to blame—but he was gone and the Purples remained.

He hung up and dialed Prangley at the church and spoke to him briefly. "I will show them *der donnergott*. God of thunder! When I finish, they will remember my name," he shouted into the receiver. "They will speak my name same as Henry Ford."

"Vern, are you drunk?"

Why was everyone always asking him if he was drunk, Bunterbart wondered. It was as if they did not hear him. It fueled his anger and he hung up on Prangley mid-sentence.

LARGE HOUSES AND APARTMENTS lined either side of the street. Bunterbart passed chic dress shops, candy shops, grocery stores, and restaurants. He passed by Boesky's Deli, which advertised *Vienna Products*. There was also Hebrew lettering on the awning. Vern scratched his mustache and squinted at the place, his broad face reddening. He trudged on, keeping his eyes open for any of the Purples. For there to be this much city so far from downtown was startling— and he realized he seldom left Germantown except after dark, when the jewelers were removing their wares from windows and even the corner stores were shuttered. The places he usually frequented involved back rooms and basements. Or was it only that the streetcar ride had been long, and now the walk too was long, and too crowded with nobodies? With each step, Bunterbart tried to visualize his

martyrdom, but what he saw instead were doors opening and closing, people coming and going quite normally under the long gray sky.

The pool hall looked like any other, and Bunterbart didn't hesitate. He pushed open the door, which was unlocked. He drew the
Savage first, and put two shots into the first person he saw—a kid in
an apron, polishing the brass bar. The boy was clearly neither a gangster nor Jewish. The shots rang hollow in Bunterbart's ears, and the
boy slouched to the floor, his shirt covered in blood so dark it was
like spilled ink.

Bunterbart advanced and shot again—he could see that the men
in the back were already on their feet. One shot glanced off someone's
shoulder. The man twitched and cried out, a rose bloom of a wound.
Bunterbart looked for Abe, the dark-eyed one, but spotted only one
of the slim blue-eyed brothers, Ray. Bunterbart pressed the trigger,
but his shots ate into wood. They hit the bar and split the pool cues
as the Purples were already drilling back at him, eight hands and
eight guns. He didn't see the one he wanted before his chest opened
up raw and wide, even beneath his fine coat. It felt like flames tearing
from his gut to his throat, and his imagined glory was over as quickly.
Bunterbart jerked with the bullets and fell over on his hat, and then
two were above him, looking down, although Vern couldn't tell their
faces from their guns. He opened his mouth, but all he could hear was
the slick of blood rolling on his tongue.

"Who the fuck is that?" one said to the other.

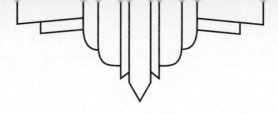

BOOK TWO

JANUARY
1928

DETROIT NOT ANOTHER CHICAGO? TOO LATE

Editorial, *Detroit Free Press*,
January 16, 1928

More than any of the other 47 states, Michigan knows that the ideology of prohibition is a compound failure. We were the first to be operated upon by federal surgeons and since then we have been resoundingly, wringingly, wet. Now, with last week's butchery at the Cue Club on Blaine Street, Detroit has inherited the violence that comes with such readily available vice.

The police deny knowing why Vern Bunterbart, an unemployed father of five, entered the club with a Savage Automatic rifle and opened fire. This paper, and any local citizen with eyes sharper than the police (that is to say, any and all), knows that the Cue Club is one of the many establishments controlled by the Purple Gang.

It was not the crack of pool cues to be heard that morning, but gunfire. The shots that cut down 16-year-old bar porter James "Jimmy" Hinckley, and then Bunterbart himself, could be heard blocks away by residents like Faye McCloud, a 28-year-old secretary who was running errands for her church. Good people like Miss McCloud are getting accustomed to such crimes. The Purple Gang were featured players in last year's "Milaflores Massacre" and no doubt the stars of future, similarly extravagantly named, acts of brutality.

Prohibition has empowered these gangs in our city, much as it has crowned king the beer barons of Chicago and larded the corrupt pockets of Tammany Hall in New York. In the wake of this most recent shootout our mayor has assured us that "Detroit is not another Chicago" but we counter that it is too late. Our able new mayor had campaigned on repeal of 18th amendment and that was wise. No one likes it. No one wants it. No one heeds it. It is time, however, to turn campaign promises into fact and work towards the abolishment of the law. Michigan was the first state on the sinking ship of prohibition and let us be the first off. We are, after all, already quite wet.

={ 20 }=

ERNEST KRIM WAS WELL AWARE that there were lots of reasons to drink, but none had prompted him to do so before.

The holidays had been rough—long days and more prescriptions than ever to fill. He'd hired a series of temporary nurses for his mother, yet she'd still managed to set the Christmas tree on fire on New Year's. What was she doing with the candles, he'd demanded, and Gertrude's voice had been thin and high when she said she wanted the tree to be as bright as the ones of her youth. No one puts candles on the tree anymore, he'd scolded his mother, dragging the charred branches through the house and then knocking the broom against the furniture while she sat in the corner, very still, letting tears slide silently down her cheeks. Krim couldn't tell if it was anxiety or dementia that she suffered from, but her condition seemed worse than ever.

Then, on the second Wednesday of January, he walked into the pharmacy and Irving the assistant, usually flat-faced and somber, had waved a newspaper in his face as if it were a movie ticket for *Spoilers of the West*. The headline announced that a man had died in a shootout over in the Jewish quarter.

Krim hadn't liked Vern Bunterbart at all, if he was completely honest. So what if the fellow had been chewed up by the Purples like an old boot? What nibbled at Krim was the question of what would happen to the operation if Bunterbart wasn't there to oversee the shipments. Could the hulking profile Bunterbart cut on the waterfront be replaced by Gerald or Jake, Herman or Otto, Tom or Bob? The answer was clear.

Krim snuck another glance at his assistant's newspaper. Now, at almost ten in the morning, it lay on the counter at the back of the pharmacy, its sections folded together imprecisely, next to a prescription for Mercurochrome. Irving hadn't the slightest idea that Krim knew Bunterbart, so when the young man shook his head and said, "More holes than a cheese grater," this exclamation came from an honest sense of awe. Krim knew Irving didn't mean to be cruel.

"He deserved it," Krim said as he picked up the slip for the Mercurochrome, and his assistant looked startled, the excited smile falling from his youthful face. "One doesn't get that way by accident," Krim expanded. "At least, not in the middle of the day."

Krim took up the paper in his other hand. He stared at the big photograph: there was the pool hall with the county coroner's truck outside and a police inspector standing at the door. Krim felt a coil of fear in his guts as he peered at the washed-out face of the inspector. The crime scene was big enough to draw attention, and if it involved the Purples, it could pull in agents from the Bureau of Investigation. Bunterbart had never struck Krim as the kind of man to keep records, but someone in the business must be. What if all their connections to each other became known? *Disbandment*, Krim thought, and immediately touched his wallet in his back pocket, knowing it contained a single bill.

Krim set down the Mercurochrome prescription and turned the page. There was a portrait of Vern Bunterbart and the story continued. Bunterbart's steel eyes scrunched above his mustache, collar and tie choking his throat. Krim ran a hand over his own face. When he looked up and saw the assistant staring, he fought to open a dry mouth and said, "Looks like an ordinary fellow, I guess."

He couldn't carry on the ruse beyond that. He tossed the paper down and went into the back room hastily.

He went to a cabinet where they kept the liquor locked up at night. He saw the key turn, his own hand unscrew the bottle, raise it, then the twisting amber ribbon between green lip of bottle and the clear column of glass he couldn't recall having picked up. It was poured tall, and there were at least four shots in the glass. Before he tipped it back, he said to himself, under his breath, *Do everything*—a joke and a tribute to the temperance reformer Frances Willard.

Moss hadn't wired Krim the money he'd promised to send. Bunterbart was dead—probably because Moss had taken a good chunk of green when he left. Krim raised the glass again. He drank it fast so he couldn't change his mind. It tickled, then landed with a punch. He breathed out hard, feeling the drink's fire.

Krim glanced into the front of the store, then poured again. The alcohol left his lips tingling, his throat numb. He put the glass to his mouth once more, then stopped. He abruptly turned around and dumped the liquid down the small sink. It wasn't the supposed immorality of alcohol that perturbed him—it was the inefficiency of it. Drinking wasn't going to put the three grand Moss had promised into his hand any faster, and it wasn't going to keep shipments coming across the ice at night, either.

Krim had never been pious, but his mother was. He remembered standing beside her when she went to see Billy Sunday preach. What had he said? *Come on you slanderers; come on you assassins of character.* As if he was baiting his audience for a fight even though most in the crowd were on his side. There he was, crouching and slugging an invisible enemy across the stage while wearing spotless white shoes and a white silk tie. Krim had been a pimply-faced kid then, and only a month later he was off to Europe, where the real fight was. But looking back, those weren't such innocent days for him. There had been that awful night with Moss at graduation. Krim could push it out of mind within moments of thinking about it, yet Moss had saved his hide that night and would never let him forget it.

Krim had a sudden memory of how, in those youthful days, the sweat used to gather all along his hairline, as if he were being pulled upward and out from himself—how shamefaced and desperate he had felt all the time. He touched his brow.

Then he shook off the memory, rinsed the glass, and filled it with water.

The prescription slip from earlier still sat on the desk, and he picked it up. He was beginning to feel less disturbed—that was the booze, he thought. The tension slipped away from him like heat rising above asphalt in summer. He squinted at the scrip then fumbled for his glasses.

MERCUROCHROME.

Irving appeared. "You busy, Mr. Krim?"

"I'm mixing the Mercurochrome for Mr. Richard Slater," Krim said, reading the name off the prescription. He couldn't remember any such man coming into the pharmacy before.

If Irving smelled the drink on Krim, he didn't show it. The young man swiped his hair off his forehead with two fingers. "There's a customer. A question about bunions."

"You can handle bunions. Read the box," Krim told him.

As he put together the prescription, he examined the slip again. People sometimes gave false names alongside true addresses. Once, Charles Prangley himself had stood at the counter asking for a fill on a scrip with exactly that discrepancy. That had been a couple of years back, when Krim had only just begun to run rum with Moss at night, but he remembered it well.

Prangley had walked up to Krim's counter and quietly asked for Mercurochrome.

"What dilution, sir?"

"Please understand," the tall reverend had said, leaning on the counter in a confidential manner—or was it because standing was uncomfortable? Whatever the case, the reverend had spoken in a low, calm tone. "It is a sensitive matter. He could never come in for it himself, you understand."

"Is it . . . for the treatment of venereal disease, sir?"

Krim had recently read in pharmaceutical journals about early tests for an amazing bacterial medication, but until it was approved, the treatment for gonorrhea was more punishment than palliative: a one percent solution of Mercurochrome flushed into the urethra with a metal-tipped syringe.

Three times daily.

The reverend shifted again from foot to foot and glanced over his shoulder to check how close the nearest customer was to him. "That would be the sum of the matter. Yes."

"Has he been to the doctor? Is there a referral—"

"I assure you, he's an expert in these matters. Very experienced." The reverend shifted again, a strained look on his wolfish face.

"How tall is he?"

"My height."

"That tall? And his weight, the same as yours?"

Prangley winced his way through an unseen pain. "Same."

"Are his discharges frequent?"

"The tears of the Devil himself."

"He'll have to come back in an hour. I mean, you can come back in an hour and collect it for him."

KRIM PACKAGED THE PRESCRIPTION for the unknown Mr. Slater and put it in the morning delivery pile. He plucked his hat and coat from the stand.

"Try this one," Krim said as he passed by his assistant and the woman with bunions. He tipped a box off the shelf with one finger.

"Thank you, Mr. Krim. What time will you be back, Mr. Krim?" Irving called nervously.

"I have some business to attend to," Krim said vaguely. Instead of taking his vehicle, he strode to the curb and hailed a cab.

"First Lutheran," he instructed the driver, his face a mask of alcohol-numbed confidence.

={ 21 }=

FAYE CLOSED THE PAPER on Prangley's desk and went to the side door, where there had been knocking. She expected to open it to Kitty's hungover face, but a man she'd never seen before stood there, his head down as if he hadn't expected anyone to answer.

"I suppose churches don't exactly 'open' for business, but . . . are you open?"

The man was dressed for business, and had kind gray-green eyes. Faye stepped back by way of answer even though she knew the heat in the church would go out the door. Most people came to the front, not the side. The man came inside, removing his hat. His hair had come slightly unparted and curled a little at the edges. He looked around studiously.

"These places don't change, do they?" A touch of a smile bent his lips.

"Not really."

"I don't mean to offend you, of course."

"You haven't." Faye held her hand out for his coat.

But the man kept it on and sat down in one of the pews. He handled his hat for a bit before he tossed it down on the bench beside him. There were four long wrinkles in his forehead and, below them, a stern face with a large, straight nose like a structure around which the rest of his features had been built.

"Is he here?"

134

"Reverend Prangley usually gets in around now. I'm sure he won't be long."

The man set his gaze on the cross at the front of the cathedral. "What's your name?"

"Faye McCloud. I'm the secretary here."

"Miss McCloud, I've got to tell you, I'm in a terrible place." The man swept his hands across his face and breathed out.

The comment hung there, making Faye more aware than usual of the dust and the mildew smells that had crept in around the edges of their conversation. Tentatively, she sat down in the pew beside him.

"It's not that bad in here, is it?" she said lightly, and glanced around. She didn't know where her sense of humor had suddenly come from, but it seemed to work. She watched the man shake his head. Her comment brought the smile back, the corners of his eyes crinkling.

"You're a smart lady," he said appreciatively. He unfolded a pair of glasses from his pocket and put them on, picked up a Bible from the pew in front of him, began thumbing through it. "Don't listen to me. I took my first drink this morning. First one I had since I was seventeen years old. God, but my mother would disapprove—she campaigned, you know. Hit me—bam!—right there." With two fingers he gently tapped his forehead above his glasses. He scrunched his eyes shut and opened them again. The Bible slipped down into his lap. "Expected back at work. Walked out and left a soda jerk tending the place. What kind of man does that?"

Faye bit her lip. "Do you . . . want to pray?"

He took off the glasses and folded them, holding them in his hand. "Absolutely not."

She smiled. "That's good. I wouldn't really know where to start."

They sat in silence for a few minutes. Faye had never been alone in the church with a man besides Prangley, and she wondered why she wasn't more nervous about it. But in spite of his admission of drinking, the fellow beside her seemed calm—particularly for someone who claimed to be in a bad state of mind.

"What happened?" she blurted. "To make you drink?"

The man put the Bible back and stood up as if she'd made him uneasy. He tucked his glasses away.

"I shouldn't trouble you," he said. "I'm sure you've already had an earful."

Faye didn't move. "It's no trouble."

He leaned against the pew, his coat opening. Beneath it, an ironed shirt and vest covered his slim torso. "I've got to stop hanging around peanut-brains. Over here, the no-goods and over there, the hoodlums," he elaborated, gesturing with separate hands as if the no-goods and hoodlums were opposites when they were really one and the same. "No thoughts these ones, no scruples. Selfish. It's the selfishness more than the lack of education." He turned away from Faye and wrapped his hands around the wood lip of the pew—talking as much to himself, or to the space around them, as to her. Faye wondered if it was shyness or preoccupation that made him not look at her when he talked. "I've got a friend who cut out. Gone. He owes me a swell sum." The man drummed his fingers lightly against the pew. "Another friend, this smart fellow, goes and blows up my business in a show-off move. He thinks he's the Big Cheese, doesn't consider much. Like a stick of dynamite in a pond. A lot of us will get hit, float to the surface. Sure we will. Did you ever get yourself into a spot where you were earning less than you needed? I mean, well, you're a woman, maybe it's different?" He turned back to her, and she realized he'd been talking to her after all.

"Money doesn't see male or female, does it?" she put in.

"Good point. Money doesn't have eyes."

"No, just the faces of the presidents."

"Huh. True." He tapped the pew again with his hand as if contemplation had a slow musical beat. He touched his brow now and said simply, "I've hogged your time."

Faye admitted she wasn't much of a talker either—better with numbers than people, she said.

A bemused expression filled the man's serious face. "If I *had* asked to pray, what would you have done?"

It had happened before, she told him, but only once or twice. Now she reached out and plucked the book from the shelf along the pew. Opening it, she said, "I might have suggested that these psalms often give people comfort." She could see that he was watching her mouth as she spoke.

Her finger scanned down the page, stopping at the one Prangley used most, twenty-three. Then she skipped ahead: seventy-three, for lack of faith.

Taking the book from her but not fishing again for his glasses, he asked, "Do they give you comfort?"

"I prefer Song of Songs."

"For comfort?"

"For the beauty of its language." Faye could feel herself blushing as if she'd been caught at something. The act of not believing, or something else?

"Ah, language," the man said.

Faye heard a shuffling and she and the man turned as one to look at Prangley. He was standing, watching them, from the doorway—who knew how long.

={ 2 2 }=

CHARLES PRANGLEY SCRUTINIZED his secretary and her visitor. They sat, their backs to him, engaging, their voices intimate, their limbs practically touching. From where he stood, he did not recognize the man the others called the Doctor. It was only when the man turned away from the secretary and Prangley saw his profile that he recognized Ernest Krim. Before that, he'd mistaken the fellow for some suitor or friend of Miss McCloud's, so easy did the two seem with one another. Now his body shot rigid with distrust and he faded back slightly into the foyer.

He could hear the pair, but not their exact words, just the odd phrase that lifted. Her voice carried more than his. *Money, church, faith, comfort.* Prangley watched her flip through the Bible.

Prangley had learned of the pool hall shooting from the radio, but he was not entirely surprised. When Bunterbart had phoned him from a booth en route to the Purples' neighborhood, Prangley had known no good was coming. Bunterbart had never hung up on him before, and even though he'd been angry when he heard the connection sever, he had thought: *Well, that is that.* To hear Bunterbart's end announced had been no more or less real than the phone call. But one of the distributors arriving here, in his church—*that* was real.

Prangley fought to stay still and silent, though his impatience with the near stranger pulsed through him. The voices of Miss McCloud and Mr. Krim lowered and he could hear nothing now. Wary of let-ting the two converse too long, Prangley drew his shoe across the floorboard, scraping the hard-worn sole. The pair turned and looked at him. He fixed what he hoped was a neutral expression on his face and stepped forward.

Krim nodded at him across an expanse of pews. Prangley unwound his scarf and removed his coat. He watched Faye put her hand on the Doctor's upper arm, as if they were old friends, and lead him forward.

"Reverend, this is—?" Her hand fell as she faltered.

The man extended his arm in an open handshake. "Ernest Krim. But we have met before. I believe I've served you at the pharmacy I run—Sweets'."

Prangley glared and moistened his lips. After a long moment he said, "Ah. I see. Nice to meet you. Come with me, Mr. Krim. We shall see what I can help you with this morning."

⬉ ⬊

KRIM WATCHED PRANGLEY'S back as he followed the reverend down the narrow hall. He noted the tension in the reverend's shoul-ders. A fidgety feeling Krim didn't remember from his drinking years had crept up on him.

"I thought we should talk about Vern Bunterbart," Krim said as they passed the threshold to Prangley's office. He pushed the old wood tightly shut. His hand left the door handle and he turned, but the reverend was already right in front of him, grabbing him and throwing him back against the closed door. Prangley's face had a fierce snarl, his thin lips pulled back like a dog's. Krim shoved at Prangley's shoulders, but the reverend was stronger than he looked.

Both he and Prangley were tall and slim, and Prangley had ten years on him, yet Krim could tell immediately they were evenly matched.

The reverend grabbed in his fist the long crucifix on a chain that dangled round his own neck and thrust it into the skin under Krim's eye. "I could pop this like a bubble."

Krim glanced down the bladelike silver stick. It jabbed against his lower lid. Looking at it made him dizzy. He'd got drunk and made a terrible mistake by coming here. Slowly, gently, he raised his hand and laid it on the arm that held the cross like a weapon. He willed himself to look into Prangley's eyes. "We are on the same side . . . We want the same thing. Money."

Prangley lowered the cross. He stepped away slightly, appraising Krim. "This is a house of God, and it allows me to operate. You—you primitive haulers of booze, you money handlers, you mules—you are not to come in here. I will talk to you and do business with you, but you do not come here again."

Prangley backed off, then crossed the room to his desk.

Krim coughed and kept his distance.

"What did you say to the old girl?"

It took a second for Krim to realize that Prangley meant the secretary. To Krim's eye, her skirts and her coiffure both fell a bit longer than the current fashion, but her hair contained only one gray curl at the temple, and her frame was still erect, her manner restless with the self-consciousness of youth. He answered decisively, "Nothing."

"How dare you bring up that unfortunate incident in front of her!" Prangley barked, referring to the Mercurochrome prescription from several years back.

"Perhaps those words were ill considered," Krim conceded.

Behind the desk, Prangley pulled out a leather-covered ledger. "Even

Bunterbart never set foot here. Just came round the back, scratching around in the cemetery like a stray dog." Prangley sneered, then his tone changed significantly. "Good thing, too, with his picture in all the papers now. If you expect me to continue to do business with you, you must be more forthcoming. Did you tell Miss McCloud you knew me?"

Krim realized from Prangley's tone that he was expected to sit and endure a grilling. Reluctantly, he lowered himself into the chair opposite the desk. Looking down, he saw one of his legs shaking— adrenaline from the fisticuffs; the euphoria of the whiskey was gone. He felt around in his coat pocket for a handkerchief, and used it to wipe his brow. "I told her I had my first drink in fourteen years today."

Prangley nodded. "Charming. What else?"

"Nothing. That I needed help." Even as he uttered these words, Krim realized the truth was that he had said rather more. The whiskey had been poured tall, even if it was only one glass.

Prangley pursed his lips. "You're the one they call the Doctor. You saw Moss disappear?"

Krim's hand went to his neck, feeling the tender area where Prangley had squeezed. He nodded slightly.

"Bunterbart spoke of you. Trusted you." The reverend opened the ledger. "But I cannot trust you if you come here again."

Krim nodded again. "That *has* been made clear." He watched the reverend's face rearrange itself, as if weighing something.

When he spoke again, Prangley's voice was amicable. "Well, you are the only one of the men to come forward. How did you get into this work, if you do not mind my asking? I mean, you have your official channels for bringing in alcohol. Why risk the unofficial ones?"

Krim paused, reluctant, unsure.

"Debts?"

"My father was prone to drink," Krim admitted, his gaze falling on the desk. "Left my mother for another woman. Mountains of bills. Then my brother . . ."

"Following the family tradition?"

"Shows up when some bookie wants to break his knees. Once, they took me for ten large. Moss was the one said come fix it by working with him, talked me into it. He always was a good talker." Krim pressed his lips together. In his lap, he held one hand in the other. They were cold, dead cold. How had this gone from an assassination to a job interview? The quickness with which Prangley could change frightened him. "Mother has some . . . medical issues to address."

"So you need more."

"We all need more."

"What were you thinking, coming here?" Prangley's stare was cold, and having already been attacked by him once, Krim's confidence was weak.

"I wanted to know how closely are we tied to Bunterbart? How deeply will they investigate his crime? That's the first thing I thought when I saw the papers."

"Bunterbart leaves behind nothing." Prangley tapped his ledger. "Even his wife does not know about me. So don't you worry about your little business, your little life, your debts and your little house. I am the only one who keeps track." The reverend's dark eyes shone. "You are honest enough. I will give you that. You show some stones waltzing in here. And you are educated, which never hurts. We have debts to pay and we still have shipments coming in. Can you manage the men?"

Krim cleared his throat: Was it wise to continue importing at this time? Can we afford not to? came the quick reply. Krim shook his head. "I suppose I could manage the men. The Purples will be on us for more money, though. And the Purples are worse in some ways than the Bureau. Bunterbart didn't think about what he was leaving behind."

Prangley ran a hand over his dark, receding hair, pausing at his forehead as if he expected to find more there than there was. He smiled, and for one who had just lost an entrusted colleague, that smile struck Krim as far too broad. It made his face seem narrower. "That is it exactly. No one ever thinks about what they are leaving behind." Krim watched Prangley transform into a reverend again as he brought his arm down and steepled his fingertips lightly. "It is easy to think yourself a hero rushing toward glory; it is harder to be a man. Fellow had a family, too—poor fools."

Then they got down to business: numbers, the little island hiding spots along the Canadian side of the river where cases were to be gathered, addresses for distribution. Krim wasn't sure if he would remember everything. He could feel a headache on either side of his eyes, settling in like a fog. It seemed clear that Prangley had masterminded most of the deals; he named the men who were brewers as if he knew them better than he knew the men who brought the shipments over for him.

Before Krim left, Prangley cautioned him: "You are German. I sincerely hope you don't share Bunterbart's hatreds. Look where it led him."

"I believe in nothing," Krim muttered as Prangley looked at him with those unblinking eyes. "If Bunterbart is here . . . then I am here." Krim planted a finger on the rightmost and leftmost corners of the desk.

Prangley stood and opened the door to signal they were done. "Men come to me every day with their lack of faith, despair, vengeful thoughts . . ." His face yielded as he parted his reedy lips and softened his sunken eyes. "I should have seen this coming from a long way back, the way one sees a boat on the horizon over water."

As Krim let himself out the same side door he'd come in, he spotted Faye McCloud at the back of the cathedral, engaged in polishing the pews with wood soap as if she'd realized the space had indeed become suffocating with dust. She swiped and scrubbed with a dove-gray cloth that might or might not have been white before she began.

THE NEXT NIGHT, the men gathered at the dark water's edge. Ernest Krim clapped his gloves, but they made less sound than he intended, and anyway, he'd worked with most of the men going on three years already; they would either pay attention to what he said or they wouldn't. Nonetheless, Krim scanned their faces seriously, and said, "Bunterbart is gone. Sorry to tell you, but we have hard work to do. We're in hock and the sum is whopping." He cleared his throat. "Have to pull ourselves out, no other choice, it's that or disband. So—" He appraised them, then turned and gestured to the crates. "Let's get to it."

The men moved together, stepping carefully along the edge of the ice, swinging cases into cars. The scuffing of boots in snow, the squeak of dolly wheels, and the rattle of bottles in wooden boxes filled the night. In puffs and plumes their breath kaleidoscoped upward as the labor drew them in. Their losses were stacking up and the weight of whiskey didn't soothe any of them. No one raised a hand and said, "To Bunterbart!" because none had liked the man. But beneath their coats, each sweat more than usual with an unnamed fear, a shivery, wordless feeling, that soon, maybe this time or maybe next, they wouldn't be able to continue to get away with what they were doing.

={ 23 }=

ALFRED MAXWELL, AS ALPHONSE NOVARRO had recently renamed himself, leaned against the wall of the club. The *H*'s of chair legs upturned on the tables seemed to spell out *Go home*, but no one was moving fast. Behind the stage hung a banner: *Prince Dixon and His Kansas City Knights*. A boy swept dust out the open back door into the dingy light of dawn. The musicians had grabbed their own chairs to sit in, their arms looped over the backs of them and legs stretched out. Tuxes had been opened, white collars showing black skin. Drinks still swirled in palms. A couple of them passed a reefer back and forth. Two white women in gowns lounged around one of the musicians on a bench seat, their limbs languorous, eyes drooping. The bar staff threw tired glances in the direction of this last knot of stragglers, but with resignation: lingering was a regular part of the night in the hour after instruments had been packed up.

"Listen, fellas, here's what I'm saying—" Alfred tried again. It was hard to talk business in any earnestness with the Kansas City Knights, because they had developed a good sense of timing from playing together, and part of their rhythm involved interrupting and soloing, even in conversation.

The saxophonist, Stanley, held up his hand. "Everybody's got it, Mr. Maxwell. We're excited you're taking an interest in us, but—"

The trombonist joined in. "Speak for yourself, I want to sign."

The bassist slapped one hand against the other. "This is it, man. If he says he's from Maxwell House, that's the real deal."

Stanley finished his drink, set it down, and pushed his hands deep in his pockets. "I'm not saying I don't want to do it. But we're a band. We aren't individuals when it comes to the songs. We can't do anything except have our drinks unless Prince says he likes it."

"You got these contracts with you? Let's have a look," said the trombonist.

One of the guys knocked back his drink and said, "Maurice, why do you always rush? We gotta talk about the songs. I mean, the best ones. That's the thing to be decided."

Alfred Maxwell stooped, picked up his briefcase, and opened it. He squinted as if carefully studying the papers there, then shuffled inside it while the Knights launched into a terrific row about which songs would be their top hits.

Most of the musicians were in their twenties and their faces were smooth as water, even at the hour when faces usually turn ashy and begin to droop. Maurice was the youngest by far—by Alfred's estimation he was barely eighteen, his limbs still like sticks and his chin too supple to shave. Their youth and their enthusiasm: that was what Alfred had seen right away from across the room. They had bopped half the night, sweating barely more than a few droplets on their upper lips, and the dance hall had been packed. They played with their eyes mostly closed, as if they didn't see the ladies lifting their skirts, the men's feet tapping and thumping, or how the audience swooned during solos—played as if they only had each other, gazes clicking across the stage as each man took his turn then handed the melody over.

The saxophonist, Stanley, and the bandleader, Prince, were the oldest. Prince had to be closing in on fifty. Onstage, his walrus proportions were shoved into a tuxedo, his double chins quavering, his caterpillar eyebrows arching . . . and then the notes of his trumpet took off like a flight of birds. When he sang, his voice folded up and expanded like an accordion. Now he was nowhere to be seen and Alfred had seized the moment. Stanley, still slim at thirty and less intoxicated than the others, was the only holdout—but as they argued music, even he started twitching with eagerness. He had a ditty he wanted to put forth as one of their best—"Lord, Lord, Louise!"—and no doubt he'd penned it himself for some set of gams with the very same name.

"Gentlemen!" Alfred called. "There's no need to argue. You've convinced me. I'll take 'em all!"

The bassist climbed onto the stage and brought down the sheet music from one of the stands.

"Genius!" Alfred exclaimed, looking the notation over, stroking it lovingly with his fingertips then sweeping it into his case.

The papers came out, and Alfred produced a pen from inside his white vest. He got a signature from Stanley first, while he was caught up in the moment, thinking only about his own greatness, not bothering with the fine print.

Several of the musicians, even the one who'd been too occupied with the ladies to contribute much, gathered around. Maurice was chatting as he reached for the pen: "So when will our songs air?"

"I know my family will want to put this forward immediately. As you know, the Maxwell House coffee brand is big in radio, we buy the most ads, and because of that, we have a lot of pull. A lot of pull, you know what I'm saying? We keep the lights on at NBC. Now, I can't promise for sure—" Alfred put a hand alongside his mouth, and said on the other side of it, "Really, though, I guess I can, and I am"—and then, without the hand—"but I should think if we can get a recording done quickly so they can hear what I'm talking about, you gentlemen may be looking at a booking within the month."

"But we haven't recorded yet at all," one of the musicians clarified.

"Oh, it would help so much. I wonder . . ." Alfred's fingers formed an *L* over his chin and nose as if something were just occurring to him. "If there's a studio in town, if we could sneak you in bright and shiny tomorrow—"

"Today-tomorrow, or tomorrow-tomorrow?"

"Today!" Alfred exclaimed. "After a few hours' sleep, of course. Only thing is, studio time is expensive and I'm on vacation. I can put in some of my own kick, but I wasn't supposed to be signing up bands, you see. Just checking on our Kansas City business. That means I don't have access to the company account, at least not until Monday. And I got to be getting back to Nashville by then. Now, how can we do this?" Alfred stared in the direction of the door of the bar as if there were some answer out there in the dust.

"How much is it?" asked the drummer, digging for his wallet.

"I couldn't let you fellas do that," Mr. Maxwell said, seizing the contracts as the last signatures blossomed upon them. "But I suppose I *could* wire the money back to you. Thirty dollars from each of you would cover the studio time, and then I could take this big sound to Nashville, and when my people hear it, it would be *irrefutable*. Prince Dixon and His Kansas City Knights goin' to be the words on everyone's lips."

"Those are the words on everyone's lips round here already, so just where are you talking about taking us?" Prince Dixon himself wobbled into the bar from a back hallway. His voice had humor and so did his eyes, and Alfred Maxwell noticed a thin young woman scurry out the side door, one hand pushing at her hair and the other rearranging her skirt as she walked.

Alfred let the musicians answer for him, until Prince tipped his head back and said, "Oh, you're a radio man? Well, let's get you a drink, then."

Drinks were poured for both Alfred and Prince, and the trumpeter sucked his back quickly. Grinning, Prince extended his fist for the contract. He took out a pair of small wire spectacles and examined the document. "One thing I love about America. It's money. Ain't no black and white. Just money. That's all that matters. That's why I love this country." He bent over the papers, moving them back and forth to try to find more light.

"Oh, I see. Here's where it gets good." He held the papers back and squinted at them. "How many rights of ownership you aim to take from us? All of 'em?"

Alfred Maxwell held up one hand. "A standard contract. Always glad to strike a clause, if need be."

"He's from the Maxwell House family," Stanley broke in, a sudden and unexpected defender.

"What do you mean, *family*?" Prince set the contract on the bar, swirled his drink, though by now it was only ice.

"His parents own Maxwell House Coffee. He's tight with all the radio producers."

"Didn't you see the Duesenberg out in the lot?" another of the musicians offered.

Prince Dixon craned his neck. "The one with the *New York* plates on it?"

Alfred could feel the sweat in the creases of his shirt, but he smiled, showing all his teeth. "Acquired that on my travels. You heard of Duke Ellington? Saw him at the Cotton Club there."

This wasn't far from the truth. Alfred had been close enough to the Cotton Club. He'd promised a little gal he'd take her there—was it Jessie or Dot? He never could remember. The two of them blurred in his mind, just like candle flames on a birthday cake. New York had looked the other way while Alfred tried to shake the whole city's hand, so he'd set out for Philly, and after Philly he'd driven straight here. He downed his drink and reached to take the contract back.

That was when Prince Dixon began to laugh: a boom through the air that hit all the musicians and changed the expressions on their enthusiastic, drunken faces. Prince scooted the contract off the bar and into his lap. "I think I'll hang on to this for you, Mr. Maxwell." He turned to his bandmates. "See, this peckerwood has been selling us a load of shit thicker than the farmers spread on the fields."

Alfred quickly cut him off. "Now, I understand if you're nerv—"

But Prince had more to say. "As the fellas here know, I myself am originally from Nashville and I can tell you, ain't no Maxwell family to speak of at all. Just the name of some old café." Prince swept his spectacles away, hefted his butt off the stool, reached over the bar and grabbed a bottle, refilled his own glass. "Aren't you lucky I got the prettiest little lady here tonight—I'm so damn worn out I can't think of slapping the white off you. Oh, but you boys go right ahead. I know, if I were you, I'd be plenty pissed."

Prince Dixon knocked back his final drink of the night, still guffawing. He crumpled the contract in one hand and used it to pound out a beat on the bar.

Alfred barely made it to his car in the parking lot—his case was grabbed along the way, scattering sheet music. Considering how

inebriated they were, the musicians were surprisingly spry—a defi-
nite problem with youth, Alfred realized too late. He managed to
swing the Duesenberg out of the lot, and watched in the rearview as
Stanley chased him for nearly a quarter mile. He snorted and laughed
even as he examined in the mirror the quickly blueing side of his eye
where the saxophonist had managed to get a good swipe in. "Fuck,"
Alfred swore softly to himself.

The cream-colored Duesenberg swerved, throwing up bursts
of dust that settled across its shiny curves. Alfred tossed the battered business case over his shoulder into the backseat. "Lord, Lord,
Louise!" he sang with vigor, rolling down the window, but as he drove
on, his face began to rearrange itself, until fatigue and disappointment showed. Under the blue-black wave of his hair, forehead lines
appeared. He'd spent through half his Detroit take in the two months
since he'd started his new life. In New York he'd taken another ten—
not from the club owner but from an interested listener with a love of
the cinema—but then he'd lost fifteen at cards, and there were also
girls and hotel rooms, luxurious dinners and fine shirts, not to mention the car that had called to him, the one he drove now. As the day
brightened, he scrunched his eyes together. He knew he'd have to
pull over soon, but the highway yawned ahead, a long purplish tongue
through muddy fields.

={ 24 }=

IT WAS THE FIRST Elsie had seen of Frank Brennan since December—six weeks ago—and he said he hadn't expected to see her, either. He had simply found himself turning the Packard in the direction of the Moss house. That's what he told her when she opened the door. She'd heard the big blue vehicle ease into the driveway. He'd cut the engine and climbed the walk. After he rang the bell, Elsie stood blinking at him in an ordinary housedress, her hair not styled. But she didn't protest; and then she was in his arms. Now they were playing records and dancing. Ruth Etting's "When You're with Somebody Else" trilled through the brass horn of the phonograph in the living room, and Frank held Elsie closer. They'd barely spoken, and they hadn't kissed because the baby was sitting up in its chair, a sleigh-like wooden rocker. Brennan said he couldn't believe how the boy had grown, or how he followed them with his gaze while they danced.

When the song finished, Elsie pulled back and studied Frank. "I can't help it. It's like *he knows*," she said, but she didn't mean the baby. "I feel so terrible about the lies I told him. That's why I promised myself I wouldn't see you again."

"You didn't lie, though. He was never around." Brennan was matter-of-fact as he stroked her hair with one hand. She tried not to give in too quickly.

Above her, Frank's forehead arched high, topped by a thin silver peak of hair, like snow on a mountain. His eyes, blue as dusk. He had a strong Celtic face, a snub nose, and lips that must have been cherubic in his youth. Now, his face was creased all along the edges, but to Elsie it was a lovely kind of wrinkling, like handwriting that has been practiced. She sighed and took in a noseful from his vest, a whiff of wool and snow and Aqua Velva. "Let me go put on a better dress at least," she said, trying to detach herself.

"No," he said, looking in her eyes. "There's no point. We both know I'm only going to take it off you."

"Not yet." She glanced at the baby.

"But eventually."

ELSIE STARED AT THE CEILING in the bedroom. A silvery pool was quickly soaking into one side of the bedding where Frank had pulled out before finishing, and they both edged over a little to avoid it.

"I never got angry before." His statement wasn't connected to anything they'd been discussing, so she let it linger—turning over, pulling the blanket up, her calf hooked over his. "When you said what you did on the phone at Christmas, about being with other men," he clarified. Frank put his arm around her and pressed her into him, his fist between her breasts. He kissed her neck. "I didn't expect it. Didn't expect to be mad, didn't expect to be afraid either."

"How many years have you lived away from your wife?" she asked, rubbing her leg between his. Frank Brennan's skin was surprisingly smooth. Even though the hair on his head hadn't given up, the hair on his body had. She didn't mind the softness of his skin, especially given how hard the rest of him could be. He was in good shape for his age. But, like an older man, he was patient, and took his time with things—the attention he'd given her breasts, for instance, was as though he were memorizing them in case he never saw them again. To be so adored exhilarated her. She remembered now that he'd been like that from the first. She tried not to compare him with Alfred—who was as electrifying as he was fast—but Alfred hadn't touched her since early in the marriage, which made it easy to forget.

Brennan made a *tsk*ing noise in his throat, said it would be easier to calculate how much time he'd spent *with* his wife than how much away. He saw his children every few months, or less. Each time he met them, they were new children, he admitted. And now they weren't children at all. Sarah was a wonderful woman, he said, remarkable really. He didn't know how she'd done it.

Elsie swallowed. *Sarah*. She hadn't known the name. She hadn't meant to ask so much.

"She would be largely unaffected if I were to leave," said Frank.

"Why do you say that?" Elsie sat up.

"Because I've been leaving her for the entirety of our marriage."

"You'll leave here too. When you finish the bridge."

"I've already had an offer to go back to New York and do some work on a bridge there. A large one—supposed to be six lanes, and double the span of this one." Frank rolled back on the pillows. "But so what? So I go and come back again. I have a brother here, you know—Gabriel, the youngest. He's done well, works for the Bureau." He let out an exasperated breath of air. "One day I should retire. This is what everyone tells me. So the only question is, where? Where does a man who lives nowhere go?"

What was he offering? She didn't answer him, in part because she was trying to picture herself as the wife of a dignified man. A wife. But she was already a wife—the wife of a lost rumrunner.

Brennan continued talking, not romantically so much as logically. "You know that you'll do better with me than without me." The tone threw her, and she didn't know how seriously to take him. "It's been a couple months now since he disappeared. No one would fault you—"

Elsie rolled on top of him, closed her eyes against the few silver hairs that coiled in the center of his chest, laid her head there, and listened to his heartbeat instead of his words. "I can't love right now," she said. "I just don't have it in me."

He slipped his hand along her buttocks and stroked between them slowly. They had already made love and she knew he didn't have the energy for more, but the sensation prickled. Elsie's skin ripened with goosebumps. "You do, though, Elsie. Your body tells me you do."

He kissed her deeply then. He brought one hand up and touched her lips, and she could smell herself on his fingers. "Tell me," he said, "tell me who first kissed these lips."

"It was at Palmer Park."

But Elsie didn't tell any more as his mouth covered hers again. She closed her eyes and saw sunshine.

THE SUNLIGHT WAS SHARP, glasslike, broken by the jagged shape of leaves. Elsie Braun lay almost in the water, her foot still entangled in the undergrowth that had tripped her. The pain was exquisite, the most precise thing she'd ever felt, so much so that she couldn't budge. So many of them had run to the bank of Lake Frances, laughing, all of them giddy with a momentary freedom, ranging in age from twelve to seventeen. The boys skipped stones and the girls pointed out a kissing couple floating out there in a boat. Entranced, Elsie watched the young man and woman necking, and suddenly she turned and found herself alone. The rest of the group had gone. As she raced to catch up to them, she caught her ankle on a branch.

She had been there almost half an hour now, and two attempts to stand and walk had quickly dropped her again to her knees. Hadn't they noticed she was gone? She was new to the church group, and had largely joined because of the promise of excursions such as this one, the lure of adventure and socials.

She called out, but she could no longer see the couple floating out there on the looking-glass water. They had been there when she first cried for help, but, lost in their own world, they didn't hear, and now they were certainly gone.

The voice came cutting through the trees. Her name, almost whistle-like: "Elsie! Elsie!"

The tall reverend came into view, ducking between branches when she answered. His hair wasn't thick, but there was still enough and it was longish then, and a leaf had gotten caught in it—no bigger than her thumb—the kind of thing she might have laughed at with the other girls on any other day, but in that moment she was in too much pain.

"Take my hand," Reverend Prangley instructed her, but it became clear before he'd stood her on her feet that she was unable to limp along beside him.

"I can't," she said, even as he pressed her alongside him, lifting her.

"Stop it!" An irritated expression came over his long, smooth face. Elsie immediately felt sorry for protesting, and put more effort into her own rescue.

"Thank you for coming, reverend," she panted, gathering herself and putting great weight on her ankle, taking two or three steps before collapsing in the path. It was like hobbling on top of a ball of barbed wire.

"You really can't, can you?" he said softly, gathering her in his arms and hoisting her up, wedding night–style. Her arm looped around his neck and his hand propped beneath her feet, he walked a few steps along the path. The irritated expression had gone, and he was stony now—with regret, she thought, that he'd spoken harshly. She'd always known him to be patient before.

What happened next had scandalized her. He'd stopped right there in the path and kissed her. He stuck his tongue forcefully inside her lips. When she gasped, he set her down lightly and propped her against a tree.

"Reverend Prangley—" Elsie blurted, though it was not quite a protest. She'd seen him look at her before but had thought it showed an affection of a familial nature, the kind she expected of anyone she might meet at the church. She stared at him now, but didn't pull away. Then again, even if she'd wanted to, where could she have gone?

The fact that she wasn't unwilling seemed to anger him. He said nothing, but grabbed both breasts forcefully over her blouse. Her breath raged through her rib cage, and before she could decide if they were having a romantic encounter, he pressed his full body against hers. His hand went up beneath her skirt and he punched at her undergarments, not as if he wanted inside them exactly, but as if he wished to wound her. She closed her eyes and thought of the couple in the boat, circling on the water. Was this what it was like? Was this what it felt like to have someone make love to you? In films it was always fast and impulsive, but it hadn't looked that way with the couple on the water. Elsie grabbed his hand to slow him, but he twisted her wrist. Then his fingers were inside, in a place no one had touched. Elsie winced, and began to cry as she shifted her weight thoughtlessly onto her bad ankle.

They breathed hard into each other's faces, his hand still inside her drawers but not inside her anymore.

"Please, not like this," she begged him finally.

"The others—they're waiting for you. By the log house." He exhaled and pushed a hand through his hair, freeing the leaf, which tumbled yellow onto the trail between them, small as a petal. He left her there, unable to walk, though she told herself it was because he hadn't been able to control himself—that every man was allowed one indiscretion in his lifetime. It was that which had made him stalk off, not cruelty.

={ 25 }=

THE WOODEN TOOTHBRUSHES leaned into one another, their bristles kissing. Frank Brennan stared at them before his hand ambled along the medicine cabinet shelf, hoping for something that would assist in erasing the stubble from his chin. There was nothing he hated more than to start the day without being clean-shaven. Not finding a razor, his gaze returned to the two toothbrushes. What did it mean that Elsie hadn't been able to bring herself to throw Alfred's away? He bent and washed his face in the sink, cupping the water in his hands and splashing.

Impulsively, he took Alfred's toothbrush, snapped it in half, and deposited the pieces in his trouser pockets. He thought back to the nuns of his childhood and wondered what kind of sin—venial or mortal?—would be the destruction of a dead man's toiletries.

He could hear that the baby was up and Elsie was puttering about in the kitchen finding it a spoon, a bowl of solids, applesauce, or some sweet mush. As he toweled off his face, he listened to them. Elsie was babbling something to the child and Johnny made eager squeals. Could Frank listen to the sounds of such a scene every morning? Elsie had changed in the time since he'd seen her last—that was obvious. She'd become less upside-down, more resilient. He hesitated to say she was growing up, even to himself—but perhaps his semi-proposal the night before was not the worst idea in the world.

When he said goodbye to her, he gently set one palm against her long neck. "Think about it," he said, knowing the words needed no elaboration. He could see in her fixed expression that something in her didn't trust him, or maybe didn't trust anyone after what she'd been through with Moss. He knew the odds were stacked against him. Still, he pressed her. Even if he'd made the argument somewhat impulsively, it was now one he was determined to win.

"You know"—Brennan gestured to the car in the driveway—"any other girl your age would see that machine and say, 'Now how can I hitch myself up to him?' Not you—you don't even think about money."

Elsie's face cracked in a stunned expression, then she burst out laughing. "I do, though! Money is all I think about!"

He put his trilby on. "Well, all right, then," he said, as if they'd come to an agreement, but as he climbed into the Packard and started it up, he knew: he'd found himself a girl who didn't believe she deserved happiness. What he wanted with such a gal, he couldn't say—except that she was resolute and beautiful, and that every day now he felt more and more as though his own life had somehow sped away from him. He waved out the window, the pieces of a dead man's toothbrush in his pocket, and smiled as he backed into the street, fully aware the neighbors could see him, and hoping it wouldn't be the last time.

={ 26 }=

"THERE ARE MISSING MEN," Reverend Prangley almost whispered, when the din in the church had died down. "Men destroyed by drink, taken from their families, disappeared in the night. Alcohol makes ghosts. Right here, in our community—a young man, a husband and father—gone, two long months now. I am speaking, of course, of Alfred Moss." Prangley gestured behind himself to a blow-up photograph printed from the one Elsie had lent the church. It was a bit blurry in reproduction. "Let me tell you about this man, though he could be any man. He was an athlete at school, a talented musician, good-looking clearly—"

The women tittered, then presented more sober expressions as they realized they were admiring the quite-possibly-dead.

"Although she was unable to be here today, his wife is a member of our congregation. I have known her since she was a young woman." He flicked his gaze to the rafters, as if remembering her as she was then, and cleared his throat. "Next week I will baptize their infant son. Fatherless now." Prangley smiled through the lie. Elsie had been too busy working as a dishwasher to schedule the baptism with him, but the words sounded genuine, and a child always brought out more coin. "What temptation did Mr. Moss fall into? Did he begin drinking, as many do on occasion—a secret glug of this or that because it seems . . . joyous, celebratory? Then, perhaps a bit more," he said, jiggling his hand as he mimicked a pour. "Perhaps to excess. Wandering home late at night in that state, he may have been beset upon by thugs, bad men made more ruthless by their own consumptive habits. Or he may have simply lost his balance and fallen into the river. We cannot know. He may have turned to loathsome activity to support his young family, and wound up out there on an icy river, alone. We men believe we can walk on water. We think we are capable of anything. We are not." Prangley set his large hand down hard on the pulpit. "We are mortal."

A young woman smiled at Prangley from the front row, her hair looped around a rhinestone comb.

"But I know that Alfred was a good man," Prangley boomed. "Just as we all have good hearts here in this room, warmly beating, so was his. Drink seems so harmless. How can the Devil fit in a glass in your hand? And yet, in these ten years since the Amendment, we grow lazy and negligent. We believe we know better. Still, this little glimmering substance"—he held up his hand as if his fingers wrapped a glass— "takes a good man away.

"And by God, with your help, I will find him, and if I cannot find him, I will at least—at the very least, I promise you—stop others from bringing this poison to our shores. We will send a message!"

The women clapped and cheered him before moving on to tea, coffee, and platters of fruit and pastry. They filed from their seats, stirred up, chattering.

"Did he say he was going to use the funds to secure a boat?" a woman in gold velvet asked as Prangley passed by her.

"You mean to tell me he'll be there himself, patrolling up and down the river?" he could hear a woman in a black teardrop hat ask.

"Yes, and if he has enough, he'll get planes!" exclaimed another attendee.

"No!"

"He's so magnanimous!"

"He's so good-looking! Oh, we must talk to him," the woman in gold clucked. And the trio pressed past the refreshments to where the reverend stood, in his fine attire, surrounded by other women.

Prangley eyed the woman in the gold dress and the woman in the black hat, and he saw beside them also a fawn of a girl. He broke through the crowd to say hello. "How do you do, Mrs. Abbot? So good of you to join us," he said. He reached for her hand and shook it warmly, and she gripped back even harder. His eyes settled again on the girl between the two women. "And who is this elegant young lady?"

Mrs. Abbot replied that it was her daughter, Hilda.

"It is wonderful to see a young person such as yourself so *engaged* with social causes. You must be as clever as you are charming. Really, isn't it thrilling!"

The older women blushed and beamed while the young woman stared at the floor.

As Prangley shuttled them around the room, introducing them to other donors to his cause, he was careful to engage Mrs. Abbot while guiding her daughter with a gentle nudge now and again, a finger on the shoulder, once the small of the back—never more. He promised himself he would think of those glancing touches later, while visiting more pliable women across the water at the Riviera House.

REPEAL GAINING MOMENTUM? NOT ACCORDING TO REV. PRANGLEY

The Detroit News,
February 10, 1928

Rev. Charles Prangley looks like a scholar with his fine frame and studious glare, but the heavy hands he pounds on the pulpit betray the brawler he really is. Angered by an editorial appearing in our newspaper this winter calling for the repeal of the 18th Amendment, the good Reverend has begun organizing local meetings of Americans Against the Repeal. At a coffee and cake fundraiser he held this week at his midtown church, the First Lutheran of Detroit, Prangley spoke about the need for our country to show resolve and to "not descend once more into the savagery of the drink."

For all his fire, Prangley is also possessed of charm. He welcomed the visiting ladies (and they are all ladies) from the national organization as well as his own parishioners, who seem to be the distaff half of Detroit's leadership. There was the wife of Police commissioner Mrs. Tom Morgan chatting over sponge cake with Mrs. Charles Abbot, the wife of the district attorney. This reporter also counted three Fordettes under the church's vaulted roof.

Given that august company, Rev. Prangley will have no trouble continuing to raise funds for his operation, but he still gave a show for those who gathered and donated over several thousand dollars. "The danger to America," he declared, "is not from within but outside. A virtuous man once walked on water, but today men walk on the water surrounding our city, pouring in the poison and disease that dissolves the bonds of home, faith, and country."

For those not versed in oracular subtlety, the Reverend was talking about booze from Canada. Not afraid of seeming the bad neighbor, Prangley promised those gathered to use the money raised to purchase motorized boats, capable of chasing even the fastest of bootleggers once the river melts. "I promise to do what our government has failed to do," Prangley said. "I will patrol that river and I will make it mine."

={ 27 }=

CHARLES PRANGLEY LEFT the Riviera House before dawn. Outside, Charles the Spaniel was pissing against the veranda, one leg held stiffly up. Prangley veered close to the dog and raised his own leg as if to kick it, but the dog scampered off before he made contact, jumping through the thin snow.

Growing up, his father, Mr. Ralph Lewis, had owned a Boston terrier. The children had wanted to call it Blackie, but Prangley's father had insisted on Duke. Duke spent most of the day licking itself and farting. In keeping with its name, the dog had a royal sense of entitlement. It received the only affection in the household, and ate better than the children. The terrier had been won with a pair of aces, and it wheezed every evening as his father walked it proudly around the block on a leather lead, thinking himself quite grand.

Prangley walked along Sandwich Street toward town, past other roadhouses that had long ago become respectable teahouses. In the windows of residences, lights were just twinkling on, pale as the ice-colored sun over the river.

Rosine Perrault had supplied him with a young Indian maiden—although Prangley had been too tired, it turned out, to test Rosine's ethnographical promises. He yanked, and the girl yanked. She might have been mixed-blood, or just dark-haired and angular like many of the French farm girls in the area. At any rate, she did not arouse him. His mind kept turning elsewhere—the fundraiser he'd held, the throngs of gushing women who'd given away their dollars as if they were old shoes, and then Bunterbart and his widow and all his hungry brood, not to mention the Purples, whom Krim had said were pulling half the earnings right from his pocket—until finally Prangley had laid a trembling hand on the girl's forehead and pushed her away, perhaps more forcibly than he meant to.

"Tell me when you get a Chinese," Prangley had said on his way out, and tipped Rosine anyway as he left the dining room where four raucous patrons were hollering at each other across a small table and shoveling in some 3 a.m. spaghetti. The proprietress had sagged on the bar, a curl falling over one eye, her cigarillo the only thing that never seemed to wear down.

It would take an hour to walk downtown, all the way to the ferry. He had only just reached the bridge construction when he passed a feminine-seeming young man—fragile and weaving along the sidewalk, clearly half-corked. The fellow tipped his fedora by poking one finger up and touching the rim, lifting it off a smooth forehead then letting it sink down again. He carried a trumpet in a case. There was something odd enough about the encounter that Prangley halted and watched as the figure tripped through Sandwich town, following the same path he had himself just taken. Looking at the musician from behind, Prangley noticed a womanly slope to his hips; he wondered if it had been a man at all.

Across the river, the bridge project had erected a small X on the horizon. Though the land had been cleared on the Canadian side, it held only a pier and a huddle of cranes poking up like party hats. He couldn't imagine how the structure might hang over the tiny university situated there. The snow lay undisturbed outside the Jesuit church, Assumption College, and Prangley gazed up at its spires and stained glass. He had never been inside, but felt a pang almost like envy at how lovely it must be. He couldn't say why he still craved beauty when so many other forces competed for his attention. The campus was quiet in the pinkish-blue of dawn, and he expected the students were all sleeping in their residences, or perhaps—the enterprising ones—just waking. So young and full of belief they must be, he thought, bodies and minds as clear and agile as they'd ever be. Or not. He reached into his coat and took a belt of whiskey from his aftershave bottle, grimacing. Then he glanced about hurriedly and saw a taxi waiting, and soon he was riding along the waterfront toward the docks.

At the foot of Ouellette Avenue, Prangley boarded the first ferry of the day. There was an interior area where passengers could sit or stand for the ride. Cold though it was, Prangley preferred to linger outside, away from others, clutching the rail and wincing into the spray, watching the boat dip and cut through the choppy gray water. The icebreakers had cleared its path, but Prangley could look down the length of the waterway—steely under the dark wool sky—and in doing so he felt a certain amount of satisfaction, like one who held dominion over the water.

On the other side, as he waited to be questioned by the border guards, a man in line ahead of him caught his eye. The fellow shifted and turned as he waited nervously. A mop of curly hair pushed his hat up. His mouth was slightly swollen on one side around an old scar, and his eyes were pale gray like pebbles. There was no mistaking him. Prangley pulled his own hat low and turned his collar up, hoping to go unnoticed. Soon the fellow was before the guards and Prangley relaxed. He noted which way the man headed when the officials were done with him, then stepped forward. His method was to answer only the question he had been asked, and to always look a person in the eye. But taking in his fine clothes, even though his breath nearly bled alcohol, the guard asked Prangley few questions.

At the base of Woodward Avenue, all the signs called for Prangley to drink Vernors, learn a trade, and ride the *Ste. Claire* to Boblo Island Amusement Park. He made sure to walk on the opposite side of the street from the pebble-eyed man. But it was no good. There the man was suddenly, at his elbow.

"Lester!" the man exhaled, not bothering to lift his hat from his curls. "Well, I'll be damned. Lester Lewis. It *is* you."

There was no point in pretending. The fellow was so close they could smell each other. A curt hello and get on with it was best. Prangley nodded. "Ezra Harris. Gee, I hardly recognized you." He kept walking, but the pebble-eyed man kept pace.

"Lester, I ain't see you since Cherry Hill! I almost can't believe my eyes. Boy, it's good to see a friend! Remember how hard they worked us." He jerked a thumb at his back. "I still got lash marks. You come here for work? I mean, what you doing way up here?"

"Keeping busy." Prangley strode on, glancing from side to side though the streets weren't busy.

"Know what they made me do after you left? Oh, round '22, I suppose, they got those of us in Block 12 who were good with carpentry building an electric chair. I said, What the hell, I'd rather build 'em than sit in 'em—but I always thought, *Too bad I can't tell ol' Lester Lewis. There's a man who'd laugh with me.* Fucking Philadelphia! Callaghan busted out in '23. Did you know him? He's still at large! I got out, and right away I won some money got me here. Say, you got time for some joe and a sinker? I got so much to tell ya." The fellow's face was gummy with optimism.

Prangley smiled politely and took Ezra Harris by the shoulders. Ezra had been a boy when Prangley knew him, in for assault and battery with intent to kill, just like Prangley, sentenced to ten years. Unlike him, Ezra must have done all ten. Dumb as a handsy monkey.

"Sure," Prangley said through thin, smiling lips. "Come with me. I know a place that'll do." He led the young man down an alley. He took the aftershave bottle from his jacket and offered it.

"Weren't you in divinity school before you were in the can? Well, guess you ain't a man of the cloth anymore, huh? Makes sense after what you done." Ezra grinned and unscrewed the lid. He took a long thirsty drink.

"On the contrary." Prangley took the bottle back. Holding it in his palm, he smashed it four times against Ezra's temple and cheek. Then he lost his grip and the bottle fell and shattered. As the young pebble-eyed man lost his footing and sank to the cobblestone, Prangley took out a silk handkerchief and wiped the smears of blood off his hands. "The thing about God is this: He forgets about you unless you have something to be forgiven for."

From the ground, the man stared up at Prangley through dazed eyes. He swore and put one hand up against his face to assess the damage. He found a face split down one cheek like a sideways jack-o'-lantern grin. Prangley knelt.

"Pray for me, Ezra."

Ezra looked at him, confused. Prangley snapped out his handkerchief and Ezra reached for it—but instead of passing it to him, Prangley wrapped it around the man's neck, pulled the ends across, and threw all his weight down.

THERE WAS A BLIND PIG Prangley visited sometimes, not far from Grand Circus Park, and it wasn't until Prangley was standing inside it, leaning against the bar and ordering, that he noticed his hands abraded and shaking. He folded them together, hoping the shake wasn't obvious to anyone else. But no one there would have noticed anyway. Next to him, a man was passed out across the bar.

"What a way to end the night—or start the day," the owner said with a sneer, as if he and Prangley were on one side together and this poor fellow on another. The proprietor twisted a white rag inside a glass before filling it and setting it in front of Prangley. "Don't you be like him, now."

"Hope not," Prangley said, watching the patron drool onto his shirt sleeve.

But within an hour, Prangley too was wiping his mouth with the back of his hand and nodding into his drink until he wore a beard of beer foam. Although he knew the sun must be up, there was no way of telling from inside the dark watering hole.

"Get outta here," the barman said, prodding Prangley's elbow.

"What?" Prangley said haughtily, one eyebrow raised.

"It's already 7 a.m., pal. I seen you before. You look a well-employed man. Why don't you take a walk?"

"Why don't *you* take a walk?"

The barman held up his hands and said, "Easy."

"My mother taught me nice manners," Prangley muttered, as if someone had said otherwise. Looking over the heads of the other boozehounds still filling up space, the barman agreed that, yes, she must have. "To my mother." Prangley held his glass aloft.

It was his mother who'd urged him toward a religious education. She'd said a person couldn't go wrong with that. He'd wanted to make her happy, and at the time he did believe. He had always been a good reader and a clear speaker. He read the only book she possessed aloud to her, and she would beam—it was always either the Bible or the Gimbels catalog. When Prangley closed his eyes, he could see her face: calm and dark-eyed, the same eyes and brows that looked back at him from the mirror, only lovelier. He saw her as she'd been when he was a boy, as a young woman, and she was more real to him as he washed down the rest of his drink than any image he could conjure of himself as a young man. A young man . . . had he really been one?

"Lester," his mother had said, "you help people. And you get *paid* to help. To lend a hand."

Prangley snickered to no one. How naive and beautiful! He'd never been paid much, and it seemed to him that no one had ever much accepted his help.

He held up his hand and examined it. The writing fingers were calloused and he had a wart on one fingertip. His palm was bisected by the light burn of his handkerchief; when he turned his hand over, the back was knotted with blue roadways of veins that pulsed beneath old skin—skin the color of white roses that had been cut and dried, wrinkling into husks of their former selves. Young men. Impetuous and passionate, full of themselves. Like he had been. Like Ezra Harris had been. The name Jimmy Hinckley came floating to him, though he knew it only from the newspaper article about Bunterbart's final act. He swallowed a burp.

"There is no help for people," he said aloud to the barman.

Prangley reflected that he seemed to do his best work when he was lying. He'd never expected that his lies could come back to haunt him from as far away as Philadelphia. To his mind, a lie was only a lie if it hurt someone, or held no grain of truth. Most aphorisms were lies, but they sounded like truths and brought comfort, so did it not stand to reason that lie-lies performed that way too?

He drew a finger through a puddle left behind by an ice cube and drew an eye shape in it. The eye of God: that was what the skylight in prison cells was designed to represent. The penitentiary where he'd spent his time was laid out in a radial, and long hallways arched up, cathedral-like—everything was stone and metal. The pen was a beautiful building only if you could call something beautiful that had trapped and caged the essence of sorrow. There had been the skylight above his head, a rectangular slit—but the inset reminded him of a lid, that was true, and through it a pale light had wept every day, as if to remind him of the outside world and all the things he couldn't have. The light had streamed down onto his bed, hitting him in the face, giving him no peace. The walls had been clean and white, but the doors of the cells were cut low so that the prisoners had to bow when passing through them, bow down in repentance. There were stories there of the old days, when prisoners were made to wear masks to keep them from speaking. Solitude and reflection: what the space was intended to inspire.

Unlike most of the others, he had prayed. But the only answer he got was the moan of men down the hall as they cried or scratched themselves, or else the sound of boots far off in the passageway. He served less than half his sentence. When they let him out, he discovered his mother had died and no one had written to tell him. More than likely his father was responsible—a hotheaded man skilled only at brutality. But if so, Lester's cowed siblings protected their father with silence and, during his first supper as a free man, barely spoke to their criminal older brother. Because Prohibition had not yet taken hold, they drank Schmidt's from the bottle—even his youngest brother, who was only thirteen. In lieu of conversation, they sat smoking cigars their father had brought home from his job as a tobacco roller. While his father was passed out drunk, Lester took everything of value in the house and put it in a suitcase, then boarded the most immediate train, which happened to run to Toledo.

Many nights he fantasized that he'd killed his father instead of leaving. He supposed he could have disembarked at Pittsburgh or Cleveland—but those cities seemed still too close. He could have gone on as far as Chicago, but he didn't have a large-enough bankroll.

In Toledo, he found a forger of documents who, after Lester pawned some of his personal effects and paid him in hard cash, was willing to give him a new identity, including a beautiful certificate replicating the degree he would have achieved from the Lutheran Theological Seminary if only he'd finished his studies before his incarceration.

Lester—now Charles Prangley—didn't see this new identity as a lie. Not a real lie. He had done the work and he would have had the genuine piece of paper if only he hadn't stolen three thousand dollars from the campus church and tried to strangle one of the other priests—a self-righteous prick if ever there was one. Lester had learned the Bible as well as anyone else in the seminary, and if anyone were to question him in theology, they would be convinced of the thoroughness of his study, whether his name was Lester or Charles or Joe. So the crime lay in the assault, not the forgery.

Deprived of female companionship for five years, Prangley was quick to diddle the daughter of an elite family with an estate upriver on the banks of the Maumee River. The family wintered in Palm Springs and summered in Europe, and that left them just a slice of a season in Toledo for Prangley to discover the comely girl, golden-haired and smelling of lilac rub, a little disheveled and lonely from traveling. Did he delude himself that he was in love with the girl? Perhaps. A crush. He remembered how, on many occasions when he was alone, he would conjure the image of her hair, the rose of her cheek. At the age of twenty-six, he had little understanding of sex. If he wanted her, he had thought, that desire must be a sign from the heavens, fate. At sixteen, she was old enough to consent—though it turned out her father did not agree.

The girl's father might have been a temporary resident, but he wielded a permanent amount of power in the town. The choice for Charles to migrate from Toledo to Detroit was made an easy one. He was personally chauffeured to Detroit, and as he found himself driven into the grand, bustling town, a part of him that had been sleeping since college was awakened. The state of Michigan had just gone dry, ahead of all the others. Here, here was an opportunity! A place to be and become. A place of prospects, where he could do truly fine work. The way Prangley saw it, he could labor away a whole life the way his father had and wind up with only a modest home and a few trinkets to show for it, alongside a wealth of rage and despair—or he could grab what was there right in front of him, waiting to be taken. That didn't make him a bad person. It made him smart.

"WAKEY WAKEY, BUTTERCUP!" The bartender was punching Prangley in the shoulder, none too lightly.

Prangley sat up and, missing the handkerchief he'd left around the neck of Ezra Harris, wiped his mouth on his shirt cuff, even though it was one of his more expensive ones. He squinted at the barman's ghostly face. "What was I saying?"

The barman sneered. "When?"

Prangley found his hat. He put it on, and held up a finger. "'Let no one despise you for your youth . . .'" He stopped, either because he couldn't remember the rest of the quotation or because he didn't want to be known as a man of the cloth in that venue—in his inebriated state, he didn't know which. He held his finger higher, as if there was more to come—then slowly put it down again.

AN HOUR LATER, inside the booth, Prangley gripped the telephone receiver. "Yes, Hinckley," he said to the operator. "H-I-N-C-K-L-E-Y."

The unseen woman on the other end checked the directory for him, and said in a nasal voice, "Clarence Hinckley on Euclid or I have another Hinckley here . . ."

"No, that sounds right. Where did you say?"

"Mr. Clarence Hinckley is on Euclid and Byron. Or there's an Edward Hinckley on the east side, and that number is—"

He thanked her and said he thought the first Hinckley was the one he was looking for. In fact, he was certain of it. As she rattled off the Hinckley particulars, Prangley took out a roll of bills and examined them. He hung up the phone but kept his back to the street, as though still in conversation, while he weighed his situation.

He bowed his head, his features hardening. To put a bullet in a kid was a stupid move on Bunterbart's part—and pitiful. Jimmy Hinckley had just been the porter, probably not a real associate of the Purples so much as a gopher, hauling ice and whiskey—no different from the boys Bunterbart had used in their own crew. He recalled there had been a farm kid named Bob Murphy, and there was the Lynch kid, Willie, though Prangley had never met him. He was still unsteady on his feet, and so he leaned on the pay phone as he cursed Bunterbart. He tapped the roll of bills against his teeth and then put them back in his pocket. When he stepped out of the booth, he passed a man waiting to get in. Prangley's face was now serene and he attempted to walk with poise; to his relief, the man didn't give him a second glance.

Outside the Hinckley residence, Charles stopped, the money in his fist. He stood, blinking at the fine house, finer than he'd expected. Even in the snow, it was well kept. The sidewalk was shoveled, and the driveway too. Did grieving parents have the inclination to shovel? On the way over, he'd imagined the boy Bunterbart had killed. So many different drawings of him—sketches almost—filled Prangley's mind: the shape of an any-boy smile, shoulders and arms, a generic child on a bicycle or at play. Perhaps his drunk imagination had placed Jimmy closer to twelve or thirteen than the sixteen he was. Prangley climbed the porch steps and banged on the door. What did this man do, this man with the son who caroused with known gangsters? It looked like a doctor's house. No one answered. A light upstairs told him the residents had risen even if they hadn't got themselves clothed and presentable yet. He was about to bang again when the car in the drive caught his eye a second time.

He pocketed the money.

He walked over to the automobile, bent, and examined it. He ran his finger along its side. He stooped and looked in, taking in its plush brand-new seating. There, tucked in the cushion, almost hidden, was a matchbook. Prangley turned his face sideways to read the matchbook script: *Edelweiss Café*. It must have slipped from Bunterbart's pocket and gone unnoticed.

The goddamn bereaved were driving a dead man's car! It was the Bunterbarts' brand-new Model A, swiped by the Purples on Christmas Day.

"Son of a bitch! Well, I suppose, why *not* give it to the Hinckleys?" Prangley mused aloud as he glanced back up at the stately house. Here was Prangley himself ready to give them something and he'd never even met their boy. Nonetheless, an unaccountable rage filled him—and in spite of the cold, beneath his coat a rush of heat spilled through him. He swung and thumped his fist against the side mirror, breaking it clean off. The metal flew and glass shattered against the garage door. His fist burned from the blow.

Now they were up. A man opened the front door and stepped onto the porch in his bathrobe.

"Hey Hinckley!" Prangley hollered. "You rotten rabble! That is right, you may not know *me*, but I know this car, and it is *bent*." Prangley made a furious *tsk*ing sound in the back of his throat.

Hinckley turned and called inside, "Edna, get the police on the phone!"

Prangley, undeterred, rummaged beneath his coat, unscrewed the gas cap on the Model A, and let loose a long stream of urine into the tank. Then, the fire inside him still not out, he pulled back and sprayed the tires and side of the car.

"Try driving it now. Fuck you, and fuck your dead boy too!"

As he ran through the neighborhood, Prangley felt embers inside his lungs. A terrible hammering crept to his temples. Pressure gripped his skull, making him feel deaf. After four blocks, he collapsed and vomited under a rosebush that someone had cocooned in burlap to protect it until spring. Then he wiped his mouth with his scarf, stood up, and walked away, like a gentleman out for a morning stroll.

=〔 28 〕=

KRIM SPOTTED MOSS'S widow in line in the pharmacy, and studied her for a few minutes before she made her way up to him. When she handed over her scrip, her expression was dazed and she seemed barely to recognize him. In truth, he barely recognized her. She wore a plain black dress and an apron under her coat, her blond hair flat against her head, no longer curled. When he inquired how she was faring, she blinked rapidly, as if this were a question she hadn't been asked in a while and had given no thought to.

She said she was working as a dishwasher at the Cream of Michigan. "I pay the neighbor to watch Johnny," she said. It took him a second to realize she was referring to the baby by name, and Krim winced slightly. "I tell ya: first time I really knew I loved that baby was when I walked away and left him for the whole day," she said, as much to a woman in line next to her as to Krim.

When she passed the prescription across the counter to him, Krim saw that her hands were bitten by the bleach, and her arms had thickened with muscle. In Elsie Moss's eyes he saw a flat darkness like the surface of an old mirror. Whatever Mrs. Moss's indiscretions, Krim couldn't help but pity the tired figure in front of him. Her face powder had streaked along her hairline where she had sweat, making her look sallow, ghostlike. She'd stopped wearing rouge and lipstick, and her penciled brows had been half wiped off—probably from the hot kitchen. Though her shoes were fashionable, she stood with her weight on one hip as if her feet had taken all they could. A brown hairnet peeked from her coat pocket as if trying to escape, a rising tuft of crisscrossed lace.

Krim reached out for the scrip, and his hand shook. "I'll get this ready for you right away," he said, looking at the paper instead of her.

She might have been guilty of everything Moss said. No one with a healthy marriage had a visitor into their home at three in the morning, as he knew she'd had the night he reported Moss's disappearance to her—and yet, Krim thought now, homes were seldom wrecked by one person alone. Looking down at Elsie's drawn face, Krim knew: Moss had rooked him. At the time, he was hardly in a position to say no to Moss's plan. But he was glad he'd done little more than provide a false report to the gang. Moss wanted him to dispose of the car, and he'd refused. Nonetheless, he saw now he'd helped Moss jilt her, a young mother. Moss said he would leave money for her—but then again, he'd promised Krim money too. None had been wired.

After he'd readied the prescription and Elsie Moss had left, Krim went into the back room and threw a glass canister against the wall, watched the fragments shatter and bounce. Alarmed at the noise, his assistant came running. Krim said he'd turned too quickly, knocked the jar off the shelf.

He sat down on the stepladder and stared at a box full of bottles. The week Bunterbart got himself shot up was the first time in years he'd even thought of being so irresponsible as to drink; normally he didn't really notice the bottles. He carried them, delivered them, boxed and bagged them, and soberly joined the men in watering holes, or more likely fished them out of them, all of the recklessness passing him by. But having slipped once, he now felt more vulnerable, a feeling he didn't care for.

He cringed as he remembered what he'd told Prangley's secretary, Faye McCloud. It had been a half-truth. Yes, he'd been sober since seventeen—but the choice had little to do with his mother's campaign for temperance. The feel of a steering wheel beneath his hands, a throbbing in his head, and the sight of red on the road: those memories were what kept him on the wagon. Their high school grad hats tossed in the back, Moss beside him in the passenger seat, punching him in the shoulder, bidding him to wake up and see what he'd done. Krim hadn't even remembered agreeing to be the driver. It was Moss who'd got out and checked the body, toeing it, saying, *Jesus, Krim. Help me move him.* Krim could still remember how shaky he'd felt as he climbed out of the car. Moss was somehow calm, said they should roll the poor fellow to the side and phone in the accident once they reached a diner. But when they reached a pay phone, Krim couldn't do it, couldn't turn himself in.

"Listen, Mr. Krim," Irving said quickly, grabbing a broom to sweep up the pieces of glass, "if you're tired, I can work more hours."

Krim knew Irving had met a girl at a dance the week before. Clearly, the boy was eager to bank a few more bucks with which to take her out.

Krim smoothed his hand over his mouth and examined the other hand, the one that had picked up and wielded the glass jar. He nodded. "A good idea."

"Why don't you go see a picture show?" Irving suggested. "There's a new Chaplin, I hear. Nothing needs mixing that I can't do."

KRIM HAD JUST STARTED down the street, turning up his overcoat collar, when he spotted his brother Morty around the side of the pharmacy. Feet planted wide in the narrow alley, Morty was spraying a dark stream on the wall.

"Here, Morty?! Really?"

"Ernest!" Morty called happily, and lifted one hand in a parade-worthy wave. The other busied itself with buttoning his fly.

"I have a toilet in the store. You know that, right? You're thirty feet from a bathroom that I'd let you use."

Morty looked more sunken than ever, thought Krim—a man who might have had the height and the looks in the family if he hadn't spent his days stooped, slurping down whatever anyone put in front of him—including moonshine that bordered on poison. He'd clearly stood so far away from the razor, he might as well not have shaved at all. Ernest almost hadn't recognized him.

"You got a soda counter yet? How can you call yourself Sweets' Pharmacy when you ain't got no sweets? Oh, those bring the girls. When you goin' to get yourself a girl, Ernie?"

"I didn't name the place. You know that." Krim glanced over his shoulder toward the pharmacy, wondering if his idiot brother was right—would a soda counter fit into the shop, and how much extra would it bring in per month?

"Sure thing." Morty clapped him on the back hard enough to make Krim grimace. Morty acted as though they were pals—he always did—but the truth was they hadn't seen each other in four months. When Morty did show up, he usually stank like a ditch. This time was no exception. Krim sighed. It was good luck to find his brother outside rather than have him intrude on the business. He took Morty by the elbow and guided him swiftly along.

"Hey, slow down. Where we goin' so fast?"

"The pictures."

181

"The pictures?"

"That's where I was headed. You're welcome to come."

Morty stopped to argue in the way that brothers, drunk or not, will. He demanded to know what they were seeing, but Krim didn't argue back. "Don't know don't care. You can pick."

Morty insisted there was something he wanted from the shop, which was partly why he'd been coming to see Ernest.

"I know what you want," Krim said. "I have some. In my truck. The only question is whether or not I'll give it to you."

"Why wouldn't you, though?" Morty spread his hands, palms up.

Now the argument was on, and Krim realized Morty wouldn't give up—he'd whine and wheedle and talk all the way through the picture. Blocking out the world was hard to do if the world kept jawing in your ear about something, as Morty was likely to do. So they doubled back to his truck, and Krim reached in and pulled out a bottle from under the seat. He tucked it discreetly inside his brother's coat and cautioned him not to open it until the film had begun. Then he hustled them off again. But now Morty had a new issue. He was mad because he'd discovered that their mother's nurse had been replaced months ago, and madder still that Ernest was in the process of putting their mother in a home.

"It's not happening quickly. And how did you know about that?" Krim asked, fishing out a cigarette. His brother's eyes said he could go for one of those too, but Krim didn't offer one immediately.

"She phoned me up and told me."

"She phoned you? Gertrude actually picked up a telephone and held it to her ear—her ear that is supposed to be made of glass—and told you all the latest? How'd she even get hold of you? I call you and there's no answer. I thought you moved out from that place months ago. Didn't even see you for Christmas."

"Well," Morty drawled, "I been busy." He flapped his arms on either side of him, against his dirty coat. A funk drifted in Krim's direction.

Even as kids, they'd been opposites. In those days, Morty's rebellion had awed Krim, and although his brother was pushy and demanding, Krim had never minded. But after the war, Morty had seemed to plummet. He had just two years on Krim, but these days he looked ten older.

They stopped in front of the movie house.

"Seriously, what'd she say?" Krim now held out a cigarette to his brother.

"Said she had a new sweater, one you bought her. So thick it protected her from cracks. But that she hadn't let anyone touch her at all since December, when you let what's-her-name go. She said you drove her to a swanky place with trees and showed her all round, but that she didn't trust any of 'em 'cause they asked her so many questions."

Krim stubbed out his cigarette. "They asked her to speak for herself. That's a good thing. Psychoanalysis, it's called."

"Sicko-analysis. She being bathed?" Morty's brow furrowed.

Krim had to refrain from rolling his eyes. "You're one to ask."

"Well, aren't you the good one?" Morty said, his eyes narrowing. "Kill her if she knew how you make your money."

"That's why you don't tell her," Krim shot back.

"She'd cry and never stop. Go to pieces. She really would shatter."

Krim tipped his head back and examined the marquee. Irving had been wrong about the Chaplin. That film was playing at one of the other cinemas. The curving sign above him advertised *7th Heaven, Janet Gaynor, Charles Farrell.*

"Oh, I been to this one before," Morty said, following his gaze. "They had it last year. 'S all right."

Krim paused, but Morty said no problem, he'd see it again. Krim stepped up to the ticket booth.

"Why don't you wait for me in the lobby?" he suggested when Morty lingered, clearly hoping to start a conversation with the ticket girl. "Go on."

"You ashamed to be seen with me or something?" Morty asked, smoking the cigarette down almost beyond the nub before flicking it away.

"Well, you could use some new duds," Krim admitted. He paid for both tickets and, while he had his wallet out, handed Morty twenty dollars. "Save you from asking," Krim said. This time he did roll his eyes.

"They kicked me out last time I came here," Morty said, almost gleefully. "I seen a Louise Brooks film. Caught me with my hand down my pants, popping one off to her."

"Jesus, keep it down." Krim ducked his head as he headed toward the dark theater.

"Well, I didn't think no one was lookin'!"

Once they got inside, the brothers hunched in their seats. Morty uncapped the bottle and took a surreptitious drink, and Ernest pulled his cap low. The organist passed by, took his place, and arranged the score. Ernest concentrated only on the screen as it flickered to life, and let the music swim past his ears. *For those who climb it, there is a ladder leading from the depths to the heights—from the sewer to the stars—the ladder of Courage.* Beside him, Morty belched quietly. Onscreen, a woman, out of drink, whipped her young sister with a riding crop and commanded her to bring her more absinthe. After fleeing, the girl lounged against the wall and regained her composure. Krim could see that the young beaten woman was meant to be beautiful, however anxious. She was no Myrna Loy, yet she had her own quiet magnetism. Something about her struck him as familiar. Her hair was a swept-back dark cloud around her shadowed face. She held her shawl around her shoulders for comfort and stared dreamily into the distance—clearly willing herself elsewhere.

The picture was only ten or fifteen minutes in when the older sister chased the girl into the street, thrashing and choking her, intending murder. A sewer cleaner popped almost comically from the grate and rescued the girl. Krim noticed Morty was already snoring.

The street washer who saved the girl wound up taking her home, and they played at husband and wife—a necessary ruse after a half lie told to the police. Partway through the film, Morty seemed to awaken momentarily. He clutched at Krim's coat and mumbled something. Krim swatted him away and Morty muttered again, this time more clearly: "I'll meet you in New York, Alfie."

Krim was instantly alert. "What did you say?" he asked, grabbing his brother's shoulder. "Morty! What'd you say just now?"

His face slack with confusion, Morty's lids fluttered several times, and then he smiled. "Hi there, Ernie. Whatcha doin' here, pal?"

"Don't pal me," Krim said, even though they were now being shushed by a lone watcher in the front row. There were a couple of other patrons in the back of the movie house, but they were kids, and too caught up with each other to care about whispers. Krim pressed on. "You mentioned an Alfie. You've seen Alfred Moss? You seen him anywhere since December?"

"Moss? Ain't you been friends since track in high school? Why would I—"

Krim shook Morty—just once—firmly by the lapels. "But did you, though?"

Morty's eyelids were dropping again. "What?"

"Did you see him? Did he pay you?"

"Shhhh!" came from the front.

But Morty was asleep. His head thumped back against the seat and his battered hat fell and rolled into the aisle. Krim could see it was useless; it was five o'clock and his brother had sunk into the denseness of his intoxication. Morty knew Moss, but not as well as Krim—a couple of years had separated them, even though they'd all grown up together. If there was one thing Alfred was good at, Krim knew, it was talking. He'd always had a way with the ladies—class-mates, teachers . . . hell, everyone. Had Moss solicited Mort's help and promised to pay him off too, Krim wondered. A few paltry bottles would buy Morty.

Krim sat through the rest of the film but couldn't concentrate on it. Unsurprisingly, the man on the screen decided he liked having a wife after all. Krim stared up blankly at the actress. She had gone from sulky to ecstatic, under now-tidied hair, her trembling, dimpled chin. He watched the characters move and the intertitle cards change. He read them without really seeing. It was a sweet tale, overly so. He couldn't concentrate on anything beyond their faces. The man went to war. The woman learned of his death just as armistice was declared and people celebrated. She denounced God. He burst in, blind but living. In the face of this miracle, she again accepted God. The film finished, but Morty still slept. His head tipped forward and drool pooled on his shirt, making a dark, wet spot. His face was long and jowly, like that of an old basset hound. Krim stood up, picked up his overcoat, folded it neatly, then left it over his brother's shoulder for him to keep.

Outside, Krim watched the woman who'd shushed him from the front row walk down the street, pulling on her gloves as she strode along. Her brown hair bounced thickly above her shoulders, not unlike the actress's hair in the film. It was Faye McCloud, Prangley's secretary. Krim looked at his shoes for a moment, ashamed. When he glanced up again, she was a good distance away. She had not seen him; he followed her with his eyes. Then, without fully realizing he was doing it, he regarded his watch and marked the time and the day—as if he wanted to come back and find her there again. Did she often sneak out to the theater?

Without his coat now, wearing only his sweater, cap, and scarf, Krim ran in the opposite direction, back toward Sweets' Pharmacy and his truck. His strides gained grace and length as he went, his body still remembering the way, in his high school track days, the gravel flew in gray constellations away from his shoes. He knew it wasn't the movie that had broken his funk—and his brother certainly hadn't—but still, a boylike elasticity came to his limbs. He opened his mouth and exhaled, timing his breaths to his footfalls. By the time Ernest Krim climbed into his vehicle, his heartbeat had found a happy rhythm inside his swelling chest.

THE WAVES SLAPPED the sides of the tugboat, hiccuping and hissing. Elsie Moss had a feeling of slight nausea and they hadn't even left the dock yet. She watched Reverend Prangley as he stood at the bow of the boat with a megaphone, a fine brown overcoat shielding him from the spray, his collar poking out just enough to show some authority.

The river was warmer where the tributaries emptied into it. Frank Brennan had told Elsie that—not that they'd ever had much time for talk. But like any woman, she'd been sure to ask him about his work. Her experience was limited, yet as early as fourteen she'd been taught that men liked to talk of their occupations; even during the briefest small talk, it made them feel important. Frank had mostly spoken of cables and trusses, but sometimes clay and rock bed and water flow. He always spoke in a low voice, and even when she repeated the same questions, he acted not as if he were explaining something to a child but as though he were offering a wonderful secret. Now, standing on the small tug the Reverend Prangley had hired, Elsie suddenly missed Frank terribly, though she knew it was her husband she was meant to be thinking of.

Sometimes she thought of Alfred like a smile in the dark—something one felt more than saw. Other times she looked for his face in her mind and it was like staring into an empty closet. The details were already packed up and stowed away.

Although Prangley had admitted to Elsie that he didn't expect to find much evidence of Alfred and his lost vehicle this far from Detroit proper, he'd assured her that the ice had broken up in this one stretch, so they would start their search here and expand their course later on, when the weather was warmer. That Prangley acted as if the ice broke due to God's will—and not the coastguard, working on behalf of Ford—was not lost on Elsie.

"Are you all right?" the secretary, Faye McCloud, said to Elsie. Faye stood on the dock, next to the rope that kept the tug tethered. There was a worried expression on her pert face as she focused on Elsie.

"Just wishing I had the baby with me. Funny, isn't it? A few months ago I felt nervous just tending him, and now every time I walk out the door, I'm uneasy about being away from him."

"I'm sure it's a big change—all of it," Faye McCloud said, overly brightly.

Elsie remembered the gun she had pressed upon Faye a couple of months earlier. She couldn't believe she'd forgotten about it until now. Heat coursed up into her face. She nodded stiffly. "Will you come?" she asked, reaching her hand over the rail to touch the secretary's glove.

"Oh, I'd be useless," Faye replied. "I have no legs for it." She shielded her face from the wind with her hand. "The weather is going to lion-and-lamb you today."

The boat blew its horn, and the red-faced captain whom Prangley had employed for the day shouted, "All aboard!"—as if the boat were grander than it was. The captain—a wary-eyed man whom Prangley had introduced to her as Clement Couture—stood above Elsie, watching the forty or so extra bodies now traipsing onto his deck. In spite of the wind, it was a bright day, the sky gleaming white and cold as an icebox.

Elsie scanned the dock, hoping to see her friend Judy and her new man. She didn't know if they went around together in the daylight or only at night. A black man would have stood out in the crowd, but there was no such couple among the faces clomping forward.

To Prangley, the secretary called out, "Coffee! I've got an urn all arranged at the restaurant. We'll bring it down after!"

The preacher waved to her and nodded.

"Never been on one of these before!" exclaimed a woman, grinning, as she boarded.

"Looks like an old soup can," said her dimpled friend. "Let's hope she floats."

"Oh damn! Don't say it!" The first woman squealed, grabbed the other's hand, and scrambled toward the center deck. The vessel was large but filling quickly. They stopped beside Elsie to assess the best place to stand, then spotted someone they knew on the upper deck and headed that way.

The Red River emptied out near Zug Island. It was more a marsh than an island, and Elsie remembered how, when she was growing up, she heard ghost stories about Indian graves out that way—somewhere close to Ecorse, wasn't it? Or was it here? The ice was yellowed along the edges, but there was a passage, however narrow. The reverend had said they would travel out onto the St. Clair River then back in again, all the way up it to the Ford River Rouge Complex. Members of the First Lutheran congregation, and wealthy women in finery too, clutched binoculars around their necks, smiling gamely, as if they were sightseeing. The boat was not far from shore when the wind picked up and cut into their eyes, and Elsie pulled her hat down low and watched as these luxurious women she did not know whooped and tried not to cry. She heard one tittering, "We are all on Prangley's 'Mad Mission'!"

For the very first time, Elsie wore the mink Mr. Bunterbart had given her, not entirely sure it was appropriate—but it was the warmest item she possessed, even with its too-short sleeves. The buttons were tight over her chest, so tight she had to wear her scarf knotted on the outside. Not for the first time, she wondered what she was doing there and if her Alfred could really be found.

A group of men introduced themselves to her now: a motley crew that had worked with Alfred at the River Rouge plant before they'd all been laid off. When they finished expressing their sympathies, she found herself alone again, the boat chugging slowly about fifty yards from the shore. It occurred to her to wonder why Mr. Krim wasn't aboard. After all, he'd been the one to tell her of Alfred's disappearance. She had taken it for granted that he would be there. She supposed he must be careful about maintaining respect as a pharmacist; perhaps his association with her husband wasn't well known. As she scanned the crowd around her, she spotted the grocer with whom she'd had the hasty dalliance. He wore a slightly out-of-date suit and stood beside a woman who must be his wife. Inside her coat, Elsie itched with shame. How pitiful, to be the figure of charity even from those one had wronged!

AN HOUR OUT, everyone was red-nosed. Elsie trembled. It was only one o'clock and Prangley had already preached through his megaphone toward onlookers along the shore about the evils of alcohol. But now they were passing farm country where there were fewer and fewer onlookers to be preached to, and through the hiss of the spray she could hear the reverend starting to lose his voice. The men on board had taken over watching the breaks in the ice, gloves gripping binoculars, studiously squinting at the banks. On the main deck, the women huddled under the roof against the life buoys.

"That's her there," Elsie overheard one of them say, a woman whose hair was coiled like licorice wheels beneath her hat. "That's the Moss widow."

Elsie flinched. It was as if she'd been called a vulgar word. Although Alfred was gone, and she'd been grieving in her own way, she hadn't thought of herself that way: "widow." She turned her back on the group and stared out at the water. It was too late; they swarmed her—in sable and fox and gray marten, in mushroom-colored mohair, in cranberry bucket hats with feathers, in brown angora cloches with bows or brooches, and the older women in poke bonnets with ostrich. Each had something that they wanted to say to her, some sympathy or pleasantry. "You're so brave!" one woman gushed. Another claimed she had to shake her hand, and grabbed at Elsie, giving a forceful pump. One more braised Elsie's cheeks with kisses and warned her not to give up. A fourth touched her elbow and said in an overly sweet manner, "It's not your fault—we understand life has brought you to this level," as though Elsie were but a dog with a certain station.

The horde hauled her in one direction and tugged her in another. She swallowed, and tried not to appear as though she were gasping for breath. They bounced her this way and that between their double-breasted wool and their stoles. Finally, she realized she had to accept their attention as a form of kindness, even when it was the opposite. She smiled weakly and thanked them.

≥ ≤

PRANGLEY WAS STARING out at the water with a concentration he hoped looked natural; inside he was gleeful. The expedition had netted thousands, and all these women wanted for their money was an adventure on the high seas and a paper cup with something hot afterward. For Elsie, there would be hundreds, and for Prangley much more.

Behind him, the ladies had been gossiping freely. The cruise had begun to bore them. Prangley wasn't surprised, though he *was* amazed at how quickly these rich wives forgot their manners and began to treat the tugboat as if it were any bridge party. The missus of a judge was telling another woman about a powerful attorney they knew, how her husband was sure "Old Tom gone bug-eyed" over a girl named Ruby he'd met at a Chocolate Dandies concert at the Graystone.

"Besotten!" she whisper-exclaimed. "Getting his kicks with some flat-chested girl with wide-set eyes and a yellow fringe dress. So he tells me, but that's confidential."

"Oh no, we must tell Tillie," the shocked recipient of the information countered.

"No, no, dear! If it were your husband, would *you* want to know? Especially when she's not even a looker?" The woman finally thought to glance left and right to see if anyone was listening. "It will pass," she said quietly, as if the husband had caught a bad cold.

Behind them, Prangley thoughtfully assessed the globs of ice along the shore and smiled beneath his binoculars. A certain attorney was about to receive an anonymous letter about this "Ruby." It would be easy to look the man up. And after that—well, a bag of money dropped to some hotel bathroom would stop the information from reaching his lovely wife Tillie, would make it all go away. Prangley inhaled the smell of ice and trout. Vern Bunterbart had been right—grabbing cash in this type of situation was so easy, and Prangley had done it well in the past. Hell, their operation had been funded by such tidbits. The dunderheaded attorney would never know one of his colleagues' wives had blabbed. Why oh why were these women such reliable sources of gossip, Prangley wondered. It wasn't as if he wanted to take advantage—it was just that they all made it so damn easy.

⤢ ⤡

BY MID-AFTERNOON, the wind had died down and the sun had begun to play hide-and-seek.

"Oh, look at this *splendid* coat of yours," an older woman in a large bucket hat cooed. She'd introduced herself as Mabel . . . or was it Mildred? Elsie wasn't sure.

"Yes, but you can see it's too small," Elsie admitted, holding her arms out so the woman could mark how the coat constrained her movements, laughing a little in spite of herself.

"Nothing a good tailor can't fix." Mabel dug in her purse and pulled out a Bakelite fountain pen. "Hilda, come," she said to another woman, possibly her daughter, turning her around. She used the young woman's wool back as a board. In a delicate, flowing hand, Mabel wrote the name of her tailor on a thick white card.

The boat was on its return now, chugging through the Red River, emptying into the St. Clair, turning left against the current. It scraped against some ice and let out a blunt shriek.

"Oh, but I can sew," Elsie said. "I just hadn't thought you could let out a fur."

"You can't, dear. But *he* can." Mabel tapped the card. "Trust me, Lucien can do anything."

Elsie thanked her. The quavering feeling in her belly had subsided. She smiled and tucked the card into her pocket—and that was when she heard the yell. All heads turned toward the source.

"There! That's him!" hollered one of the men. He was wearing worn work boots, and Elsie recognized him as one of Alfred's Ford plant friends who had introduced himself to her early in the cruise. He had one leg up on the rail, his hand wrapped around a pole, the other pointing. The binoculars had fallen onto his chest.

The women wouldn't let Elsie through, so all she could see was the man, perched a head above the others on the deck, pointing, and, directly in front of her, hats and feathers bobbing. She heard gasps. Her legs seemed to turn to string.

Prangley waved to the captain. The boat slowed, and as it did, Elsie fought her way through her new friends to the rail. The reverend stood there, eyes narrowed, one gloved hand pressing his lips flat. When she reached him, he grasped her bracingly about the shoulders. "Don't look," he said, turning her toward his chest.

Elsie smelled mint on his breath and, to her surprise, aftershave rolling off his chin. She had forgotten the smell. Then she broke free, saying, "Let me see. I have to see."

"We should pray—" Prangley insisted, a rough edge of disapproval in his voice.

But already she was free of him. "Where?" she demanded.

His gaze fastened over her head, and she quickly located the thing that had drawn the men. It wasn't a body, just a slick of black among the reeds. It looked like black ice—a hard expanse. That was why they hadn't spotted it earlier in the mission: as the day wore on, the sun had faded, and now the glare off the ice was gone. Partly sunk, the hard corners of a car were obvious. Not much showed and it was on its side, Elsie saw, craning her neck. As if the car itself got drunk and tipped over. Reeds poked through it and out the window. Late winter cattails, shedding a cottony substance, bobbed like small flags all around.

Elsie craned her neck again. She leaned over the rail to try to see through the open window frames, but there were more and more people in the way. "Is he in there?" she whispered to Prangley, who did not answer. Then she could no longer peer at the box shape in the marsh because she was vomiting into the water. Everyone sprang back. When she finished, she looked down at her fur, hoping she hadn't ruined it. By the time she looked up again, Reverend Prangley was directing the men, and they were untying a small lifeboat and debating who among them had the training to go. Most had been in the war, and all of them wanted to do it. Elsie found her handkerchief and cleaned herself, then the women surrounded her and urged her to come with them into the deckhouse.

In spite of Prangley's earlier preaching against alcohol, the thin young woman whose back had been written upon by Mabel was beside Elsie with a flask. She said to drink, and before Elsie could protest, a dose of gin had passed her lips.

={ 30 }=

CHARLES PRANGLEY WAS MORE ASTOUNDED than anyone. When he'd hired the boat, he'd told the captain not to expect much, "just a run down the river. A way for a congregation to come together." Couture, as the captain was known, didn't seem concerned—he acted as though he hosted search parties all the time. Like a stray dog, he had a hungry look to him, and Prangley was pretty sure he'd have accepted any offer.

As the winched-up vehicle rose slowly from the water, Prangley watched it, unblinking. Behind him, some of the women gasped, covered their eyes with their fingers. A couple of the more tomboyish ones, in short fox fur jackets and sporty plaid, leaned out in morbid curiosity, as riveted as the men. But there was nothing to see, other than the car. The body wasn't there. The front seat sat empty of all but seaweed. In the back they found a single bottle of Scotch, unbroken, and an old coat, sodden and black. If it was really Alfred's car, it ought to have been loaded tight with cases of whiskey, Prangley knew. Hadn't Bunterbart said they'd found some bottles scattered on the iced river that night?

The volunteers laid the coat out over the hood of the car to dry. Prangley checked the pockets: a red poker chip, a ticket stub for the movie *The Jazz Singer*, and a folded handbill from the Powhatan Club.

The ticket stub broke apart in Prangley's hands. The nightclub flyer had bled its ink in a dark ghost, but it was still readable. Prangley turned the handbill over and peered at the back, where something had once been handwritten.

"What's it say?" one of the men asked.

Prangley peered at the words *Gin Ing* in a flowing hand that couldn't have been Moss's. The card stock was swollen and the ink faint.

"*Ginning*, I think. Is that a phrase, to go 'ginning'? Or maybe it's 'ginling'? But what's a ginling? A cocktail? Like a gimlet?" Prangley shook his head. "Any of you frequent the Powhatan?"

One man shrugged, said maybe he'd been on occasion. The club was deemed aristocratic, and said so in all its advertisements, including the one Prangley cradled in his glove. Prangley had never been to the large dance clubs—too easy to run into someone one shouldn't.

"Any of you know what this means?"

The men shook their heads.

"Puzzler," Prangley said to the man who'd first spotted the car. "We must get Mrs. Moss, ask her the license plate of her husband's car, if she knows it." But when they shouted to the moored tug, they were told that Elsie was recovering. Prangley realized she wouldn't have known this license anyway. Moss would have used this car only for midnight runs. Prangley would need to check his ledger for records, though more likely there weren't any—Bunterbart was the only man who would have known the license.

Prangley laid out the paper scraps on top of the car; if he held them any longer, they would fall apart. He shivered and pressed his lips together. He was sweating from the exertion of clambering around in the marsh, and the wind now chilled the perspiration on his skin. Just like the ones the men used for running, this Model T had its doors stripped off. Charles put one hand on the frame and leaned in—but saw nothing more.

Embarrassed by his own uncertainty, aware of not wanting to reveal his intense interest, Prangley extracted himself and stood tall, his back to the vehicle, shoulders rigid.

"Do you suppose he got out?" he asked the captain, who'd come ashore to stand with his arms folded, smoking a cigar and watching the proceedings. "Why wasn't he wearing his coat?"

"Don't know, but I'll gladly take it," Couture replied, releasing a waft of chocolate-smelling smoke from his mouth. It was a cheap stogie.

Prangley made a sour face. "When it's been down there for months?"

The captain glanced at the coat where it lay over the hood—and could see it was a blue-black nubby wool, now that it had been spread out to dry. "Still good, ain't it?"

THAT NIGHT, PRANGLEY put his feet to soak in a pan of hot water. He sat with a blanket around his hunched shoulders and sucked in the steam coming up from the water. On the dining table beside him lay the handbill from Moss's pocket—assuming it was his. He'd given the wife the poker chip when she'd been able to pull herself together. And he'd found a passage to read from John, chapter 6. Even though it was not quite right, he knew that any words would help the situation. At any rate, they helped put him back into the frame of mind for his performance as a man of God, which he had to maintain until the tug got to shore:

And when even was now come, his disciples went down unto the sea, and entered into a ship, and went over the sea toward Capernaum. And it was now dark, and Jesus was not come to them. And the sea arose by reason of a great wind that blew. So when they had rowed about five and twenty or thirty furlongs they saw Jesus walking on the sea, and drawing nigh unto the ship: and they were afraid. But he saith unto them, "It is I; be not afraid."

His voice had almost given out when he read the words, and the women had to lean closer to hear.

A strange thing had happened when they finally docked back in Detroit. Prangley had found himself reaching into his jacket and handing his secretary a wad of bills for Mrs. Moss. He didn't count it, just shoved it at Faye McCloud and told her to give it to the young widow. It was a good deal more than he would have parted with, he realized, if they hadn't found the car. All those years ago, when his mother said to him, "Lester, my son, you've a good heart," she must have been right.

When the water in the pan around Prangley's feet turned cold, he dried in between each of his toes and pulled on his socks and slippers. He coughed hard into a handkerchief, then went to the phone and dialed the men he'd met at Christmastime.

"I think I would like to meet this King Canada," he said into the receiver. "I deserve to know more about how he operates."

"It is competitive, this business. Maybe he needs some convincing," the voice on the other end argued with him.

"That is not a problem," Prangley said as he went into his coat and drew out the rest of the bills he'd collected. He had plenty, he thought, to make the first payment on the airplane. Enough of this river importing. He hoped never to see another cattail in his life.

={ 31 }=

IT WAS STILL EARLY when Ernest Krim arrived to open Sweets'. He flicked on the lights but locked the front door behind him. He threw his coat on the wall hook, put the float in the cash register, and took stock of the back area, then unlocked the rear door for deliveries. He wouldn't open it until he heard Irving arrive. A few minutes later there was a faint exclamation and the sound of Irving shuffling around outside—yet the assistant didn't come in. Krim's mouth pressed into a straight line as he walked back and opened the door to look out. There Irving stood, three or four feet back, looking down, his face pale as a candle. Just outside, on the square of pavement, a red-brown bundle lay, not more than a pace from where Krim stood.

The boy yelled, "Don't touch it," as Krim knelt and examined the dynamite.

"It's not lit," Krim told him, though as soon as he touched it he could see that it had been. One end of the wick was blackened and it had been allowed to burn partway down before someone's gloved fingers had snuffed it out.

Irving put his hand over his mouth as he spoke, folding at the knees. "I just—I saw it there." The assistant's behind hovered a few inches above the slushy alley as he tried to regulate his breathing.

Krim straightened, the bundle of dynamite still in his hand. He could smell it: a whisper of carbon, his whole life vanishing. He held it gently as he took it inside. Clearly, he couldn't leave it in the alley, where it might be used against him. He looked for someplace on the shelves to stash it. He passed by the jar of nitroglycerine that he dripped onto sugar pills for heart conditions—as far from there as possible, he thought. In the end, he snuggled it into a cardboard box of Kotex napkins.

By the time he came back out, his assistant had recovered. "Who would do this, Mr. Krim?"

Krim took out a cigarette but didn't light it. He turned it over in his hand and said nothing. Instead, he peered through the alley, wondering if the silent threat was all that would come that morning or if there would be more.

"I know," Irving said solidly. "It's that Cleaners and Dyers War I keep reading about. The laundries. Have you been following? These thugs have been bombing businesses that don't unionize. It's been going on forever. They're br-branching out—coming after us now, aren't they?"

"Cleaners and druggists don't have much in common," Krim said, though he realized he ought to be happy for the explanation his assistant had just provided. The boy had reached straight for the Purple Gang without assuming Krim was tangled up with them in any way.

"Go home, Irving. Take the week." Krim put his unlit cigarette away. He rubbed a hand along his torso, realizing suddenly that his chest hurt. He'd been holding his breath from the instant he saw the dynamite.

Irving didn't argue.

Inside, Krim checked his watch and saw that it was time to open the front door. He walked to the windows and looked out. He stared past the green show globe that had hung there since Mr. Sweet had run the pharmacy. Then he unlocked the door and stood outside, looking up and down the street. Was there a man out there, in a car perhaps, watching? No one came in.

He ducked back inside and picked up the phone. He dialed the parsonage, which was the number Prangley had allowed him. "We need to talk about the Purple problem," he said, glancing up as the front door rattled. A blast of cold air came in with an old lady who browsed a rack of hosiery. She was wearing a tall brimmed construction on her head that looked like a birthday cake.

On the other end of the line, Prangley coughed and said gruffly he'd nearly caught his death patrolling the river that weekend. Surely this could wait.

Krim turned his back to his customer and said quickly and quietly into the mouthpiece: "I don't care. My business has been threatened."

KRIM LIT A MATCH off a headstone and touched it to his cigarette, cupping his hands around it. He had been in the graveyard long enough that he'd already had to bend down and roll up his trousers to keep the cuffs from dampening. As evening fell, he felt himself sliding into the shadows, enough that he felt comfortable leaning against a tall gray tombstone, certain he would not be seen. Finally, Prangley appeared, as if from the ground. His tall frame ascended a staircase at the other end of the cemetery—a stone entrance of some sort, probably linked to the church, Krim surmised. Prangley rose, step by step, then strode across the patchy grass.

Grim-faced and reticent, the reverend handed Krim a funeral program for a woman named Anna Hoffman. Hidden inside its fold were two bundles of bills.

"Tell me that's just to start." Krim stashed the money in his over-coat pocket. "I read about your river voyage. There's money in the pot, and we need it. You use my friend's name, you can spare some more."

"Mr. Krim. Fear is a base animal emotion and no good business can come of it." Prangley suggested they walk. "Let's talk about the car we found. I believe Bunterbart said you were east of the bridge construction when Moss's car went under?"

"No, west of it," Krim lied confidently. After standing for an hour in the snow on a day when he'd almost been bombed, he found that the necessary tone came surprisingly easily. "And we have more important things to talk about." He stepped ahead of Prangley, head-ing up one of the walkways.

"I take it they've come around before?"

Krim stared at him. "I told you they had."

Weekly, ever since Bunterbart's fall, two suits from the Purples would lean in the back door of Sweets' and make their presence known. Krim didn't know how they'd found him—when they watched or how they knew about his importing role—but he sup-posed they could hire anyone from boys to bums to follow and trail and ferret out whatever they needed. He had heard they routinely hired hoboes for odd jobs and heavy lifting, then put two bullets in them when they held out their hands for payment. Last week when the Purples had come, they'd mentioned the incident that put Bunterbart in a pine box.

"Thanks to that Kraut cocksucker, I think we'll take fifty percent now," one of the Purples had declared through a square smile that showed every tooth.

Like Bunterbart before him, Krim had made a more robust pay-ment, but still not the expected amount. He believed himself lucky they had simply taken the envelope and not exacted revenge upon his body, or his business, though now, with the dynamite, he fully expected that might come. All day he had broken into a sweat when the bells on the pharmacy door rattled. They had no reason not to bleed him, he realized—and unlike his and Prangley's men, who were fathers and autoworkers, philanderers and failed laborers, men who liked to drink and were fond of the extra money that came from moving liquor at night, the Purples were a real gang. Bleeding was what they did best.

"Fifty percent!" Krim said again. He watched Prangley, who had stooped to brush snow away from a small juniper. "If they know who *I* am," he said to the reverend, "what makes you bet that they don't know you?"

Prangley didn't answer right away; instead, he slowly turned in a circle. On two sides they were fenced into the cemetery, and buildings pressed against the third. The fourth side was open to the street, though a low wall with gates and some beaten shrubs offered a limited sense of security. Krim could see the hats and shoulders of people who walked by, but few glanced in.

Prangley swore. He stood still, looking at the sky, then smiled crookedly. "What if I had it—whatever they wanted? The whole sum. In cash."

"Well?"

Prangley resumed pacing, this time around a stone that said *White* and another engraved *Weaver*. He glanced back over his shoulder at the church.

"Have you ever loved a woman?" Prangley asked Krim in a rhetorical tone, his gloved hands wide apart. Krim nodded. "So you know how it goes," Prangley continued. "She is impressed, flattered, oh there she is swirling her skirt around and blushing—she can only talk of you! Do not look at me like that, because I see it every day. I talk to people, and I see the patterns. What happens next?"

Krim wrapped his hand around the small bundle of money in his pocket that Prangley had already provided. He didn't answer. They stood, Krim on the front side of *Weaver* and Prangley behind it.

"She loses interest," Prangley announced. "The man is stunning to her—at first, then not so much, then maybe not at all. After a time, nothing is good enough. She wants more. He has to do this, he has to do that. He does it all, and it is still not satisfying."

"More," Krim echoed.

Prangley leaned forward, his elbows resting lightly on the headstone. "What would stop *them* from asking for more?"

Krim felt the tightness in his neck as he looked at Prangley's gloves instead of his face. "We must give just enough," Krim said softly.

"I agree." Prangley straightened. "Wait," he commanded, and without another word he walked across the uneven ground of the cemetery and disappeared the way he'd come.

Krim wasn't certain if Prangley meant for him to wait the Purples out or to wait there for his return. As he stood there, Krim saw the secretary go past the graveyard without glancing in. She walked briskly, staring at the sky as if at any moment she would fly up into it.

Krim too looked up, and watched an airplane buzz overhead: its dark silhouette drifted birdlike. The sky was darkening, turning from blue to steel. He could envision the space where the pharmacy was, burned out, bombed. The image of his own door blown out had flickered through him all day. He was beginning to understand Alfred Moss, envy him. That ability to go: to disappear.

Just as he was thinking he'd misunderstood Prangley, the reverend emerged again. This time he hadn't bothered with the formality of cloaking the money in a flyer. When he reached Krim, he grabbed his lapel and stuffed it inside. "Just do not forget whom you owe," Prangley said when they parted, and he didn't mean the Purples. Whether it was enough was the question—but Krim could feel its weight tugging at his chest the whole way home.

When he got in, his mother was asleep, a feathery sound rasping from her wrinkled lips. He counted the money on his bed, as a child might with his empty piggy bank beside him. In total, Prangley had handed him twelve thousand. Krim took two bundles and set them aside. Either ten large would hold the Purples or it wouldn't. If they were going to blow up his store, they'd do it, the extra two grand wouldn't make a difference. He picked up and fanned out the bills in one of the bundles.

"Prangley, why didn't you give it to Bunterbart?" Krim whispered to himself—because clearly, if the reverend had, Bunterbart wouldn't have behaved so crazily. Or would he have? Krim tapped the money against the fingertips of his other hand. "Because you're afraid," he answered himself, though it was almost impossible to believe, especially of a man with so strong a grip.

Krim put the two grand into an envelope in the nightstand. The other ten went beneath the bed, in a safe box where he kept his medical supplies away from his mother. He checked his clock and saw that it was still only eight at night. He would at least be able to leave a message. He picked up the phone and dialed Sanford Hospital. "Please let the doctor know that I have the down payment ready for Gertrude Krim if you still have room for her as a patient."

When he hung up the telephone, Krim lay down on top of the quilt with his shoes still on. Tears ran down his face into the pillow, which surprised him.

={ 32 }=

ERNEST KRIM DROVE along Lafayette Street. Steering under the new crossing, he glanced up at the recently constructed T-bar railing of the bridge. Concrete pillars stood proudly on either side of the road, mirror images of one another. He knew the men would be counting and loading already, and ever since Moss double-crossed him he didn't trust anyone anymore. Gerald Zuckerwitz was a solid guy, sure, and for all his fooling Jake Samuel was reliable, but anyone could miscount while stowing away a couple of extra cases for his own use. And the Kid, Willie Lynch, was learning from them.

"Sleepy Z," Gerald had been called in his boxing days, for his calm, methodical circling followed by his sudden knockout punches. Years before, just after the war, Krim had gone with a group of fellow soldiers to blow off steam. Everyone was drunk and weaving by the time they arrived at the hall—all but Krim. The men stood and shouted, hands on either side of their faces, warping their already-weathering good looks by hollering for blood—as if they hadn't already seen enough of it. The collective roar of pent-up anger. Any excuse to make noise: even Krim, sober and out of place as he was, had raised his voice, and it felt stupendous. He went hoarse quickly.

There was blood on the ring floor, blood on the fighters' bare chests, blood on the front-row audience members. It gushed with each touch. Their heads snapped and sweat flew. Some finely dressed spectators in the front row caught Krim's eye. One in herringbone took out a silk square and, laughing, wiped away a bright dash of blood from his beard. The man's upturned face called out for more. Krim had also watched the boxer—Gerald "Sleepy Z" Zuckerwitz as he was known then, "the iron fist of the shtetl"—shuffling and nodding in the ring for nine rounds before he lifted his fist and hit his opponent with awe-inspiring force. By that point the anger had long drained out of Krim, and a fatigue had set in along the edges of his body, like the pale light of dawn, telling him the darkness was over. He stared as his drunken buddies were reanimated: their hurt suddenly shot through with fierce joy as they leaped in the air and whooped the punch. They shouted, "Lights out!" and whistled on their fingers, almost carnal as they clapped and grabbed at each other's shoulders, slobbering happy obscenities into each other's necks—even his.

Booze had cut Sleepy Z's career short, and Krim didn't see much of his army brothers after that night. The group of them faded back into the gray of daily life as girlfriends became wives and work became routine again. If they woke at night, as Krim did, clutching the bedding in fear, they did not speak of it when they met, only nodded and *Howyabeen*-ed. But sometimes, when Krim looked at Gerald, he saw the slick, shining face of that boy in the ring, the exhaustion of glory, and how Krim had stamped his feet with the crowd, in part to put feeling back into his toes after standing so long and in part to wake himself up from the long, awful dream of the war. For Krim it was just under two years of trenches—and every day he'd known that if he took a drink there, he'd never stop, would numb himself until he was facedown.

Survival. He hadn't said this to Faye McCloud that day in the church—that it was another good reason not to drink. Krim didn't know why he had been listing these things off in his mind for the past month—creating an index for a woman he barely knew.

As he turned the vehicle toward the river, Krim tightened his grip on the wheel. It was now his job to give orders to Gerald "Sleepy Z" and more than a half dozen others—instructing who was picking up and who delivering to whom, where, and when. In the weeks since his one and only visit to Prangley's church, the crew had made several runs, and now, already March, they were close to the thaw and everything would start over as they switched from car to boat.

He'd taken care to partner the men differently than before. Gerald and Jake and Willie were a fine group, because Gerald still had strength and Jake and Willie were both fast. If anyone were to hijack them for the shipment, they stood a chance. Some of the others didn't have enough brawn to them, or enough wits even to watch the shadows. Krim shuffled and redistributed the distributors, or made sure they were sent to areas where they were familiar with the streets and the hangouts, where they'd have friends if trouble came. He felt like the coach of a motley baseball team, aware that he spent far too much time thinking about something that had functioned without a struggle under the imposing gaze of Vern Bunterbart.

Krim cut the lights before parking his vehicle among the long grass and trees. The shipment tonight was from Amherstburg, had been hidden on one of the little deer shit–covered islands along the river. Jake and the Kid were to have brought it over, and Krim could already see the knot that formed the rest—Otto, Herman, Bob, and Tom—at the edge of the ice. Bob had brought in a dark-skinned man from Black Bottom named Wycliff to help out, so he was there too: a big fellow who could carry three cases with ease, exactly what they needed, and bright enough, too. In caps and coats, the group stood so still in the night they could have been pillars on a dock.

Krim began to climb down the bank. Where was Gerald? He glanced about, took in the faint dark shape of the cars speeding across the ice. One weaved gleefully, showing off—that would be Jake. The slower, slightly more cautious car would be Willie. Then Krim spotted the former boxer, standing half under a small pier, a hand visible against the snowy wood planks where he leaned.

A focused exhalation seeped from Krim's mouth. He was glad to have arrived before the cars reached the bank. He needed every bottle counted.

Every day Krim checked the post office, but there was still no money order from Alfred Moss to ensure his silence. He was less desperate for it now, but that didn't cancel out the deal. He still wanted Moss to come through, prove him wrong. The Purples had accepted his payment, grinning, and although his mother hadn't gone without argument to the Sanford—there had been two appointments for talk therapy and she was to move in April—she had been manageable. His stock investments were doing well, too, but there would be ongoing expenses and he certainly didn't trust the Purples to stop pressing him.

But he'd taken the turn in his fortunes as a sign that he could be in control if he chose to be. A strange source of inspiration had come from his assistant, Irving. After the dynamite scare, the shy, bookish fellow had become emboldened. He'd run out and asked a girl to marry him. To Irving's amazement, she'd said yes. It didn't hurt that he'd bought her the biggest, brightest stone in the case, one far beyond his means. Krim had seen them saying their goodbyes one morning. She was a pretty girl with a sleek jet helmet of hair and eyes like stormy skies.

Testing new ground at the pharmacy, Krim had begun to make elaborate displays of underarm deodorants. His female customers parted easily with their dimes. When he saw how well this item sold, he bought a small amount of stock in the brand. Then he'd ordered a kiss-proof rouge—the kind of frivolity old Mr. Sweet had never allowed in his store. Its sales prompted Krim to go one further: he stocked a new soap that promised, with "acts like magic," to wash away double chin, abdomen, ungainly ankles, superfluous fat on the body without diet or exercise. It brought in two extra bucks a box from gullible women. Not much, but enough to keep stocking it.

As Krim stood on the bank watching the men and watching the cars, he lit a cigarette.

The first car arrived with its shipment, its wheels skidding slowly to a stop on the ice. He put out his cigarette between gloved fingers, pinching it carefully so he could save the rest for later. The men hadn't seen him yet, and he was about to step down the bank and onto the river when he heard a hum of vehicles above him. Glancing back over his shoulder, he saw two fedoras bumping along the horizon and bounding through the snowy reeds. The two Purples were familiar to him—but unlike at Sweets' when they came collecting, this time they had their weapons out. Krim halted where he stood, uncertain if he should remain hidden or join his men.

"Good evening and don't fucking move," one of the Purples—a man Krim knew as Abe Kaminski—called out to the figures on the lake, the drum of his tommy plain to see in the moonlight.

The importers slowly raised their hands; Krim knew that, in the cars, Jake and Willie would have theirs raised too.

"Looks like a nice selection," said the second Purple member, Simon. He had a slender, haunted face. Unlike his partner, he carried only a pistol. He walked up to the beat-up Brush motor car with the ragged roof. Krim watched as he reached in and relieved Jake of his revolver. Inside the vehicle, Jake said something uncharacteristically quiet, and the man responded: "No, park it right over there. Then you and your buddies can load it for us. Don't even think about flooring it."

Jake did what the man said, and climbed out carefully, his fingers spread atop his hat. The Purples took a gun from Willie and pointed for him to park his car near where Jake had parked his. Willie emerged, his chin locked in a hard line, eyes shadowed by his cap.

The first gangster, Abe, hadn't had a good-enough time yet. He pointed the submachine gun at each of the men, laughing. "I know whores with bigger balls than you."

"That's just how you like them, too, Abe," Simon shouted.

Wycliff tried not to snicker. Abe saw him, leaned in close to Wycliff's face, and said something that Krim couldn't hear.

Wycliff said nothing.

Abe then patted him down. He found only a knife. He instructed him to empty his wallet, and Wycliff did. Then each of the other men was separated from his weapon and wallet as well. The Purples took it all, though it wasn't much. Abe shoved a pistol into the back of his pants. Simon kept the knives.

Standing silent in the dark above the men, Krim appraised the situation. Although he was a good shot, he had never carried a gun, and he realized now he ought to. If he entered the scene, coming out of the dark bulrush, he feared being shot himself. So he stayed, shoes planted, monitoring the takeover.

Abe pushed the gun against the chest of another man, Bob Murphy. Bob was a big-boned farm boy with a freckled face, not more than twenty, the kind of fool who could list the name of every football player at the University of Michigan even if he couldn't read.

With his hands still in the air, Jake spat in Yiddish at Abe, *"Paskudnik."*

Abe seemed to smile at the insult before pulling the gun away. The bullying theater stopped, and instead came the instruction to load. The men began doing what they always did, only this time they were to move the shipment up the bank inside the iron sight of the Thompson gun. The two Purples stood back, their weapons trained as the men worked.

A cold sweat gathered beneath Krim's coat. What if the Purples' tactic was to do what they did when they used hoboes, retaining the men for their muscle then dispatching them quickly? Krim edged a noiseless step or two closer.

He was still a good distance away when he spotted Gerald below the pier, about twenty feet behind the two gunmen, lurking in the shadows just as he was. Krim watched the short, compact shape, which had begun to silently circle. Krim had seen it before, this roundabout dance—the Sleepy Z trademark. Gerald moved only slightly, but his stance said he was readying himself for the fight. Krim watched as Gerald softly came out from under the dock; Krim opened his mouth to shout, too late.

It was the mean one, Abe Kaminski, who took the blow. Krim watched as Gerald swung: one knock and the man folded into his spats. The Thompson went off. It was pointing down and all the bullets nuzzled into ice, though they cracked violently. The lean man, Simon, spun and fired his pistol. Gerald took the hit in the right knee: a splatter of red flew and his scream soared.

Simon was above Gerald quickly. "You fucking prick," he swore. He pressed the trigger without aiming and shot Gerald square in the groin. The boxer fell over, gasping. But the Purple had one gun and only himself, and he realized he needed to keep it trained on the men. He faced them again. The boxer wept in agony.

Abe was sitting up now, dazed from the blow Gerald had delivered but already reaching for his machine gun.

"Run!" Krim shouted from the shadows, shocked by the force of his own voice and how it carried. "Run!"

Scrambling up the bank, the men passed Krim in the weeds, their faces flickering in the dark like flames.

"The whiskey?" one of them asked.

"Leave it," Krim barked.

"Gerald?" asked Jake, his face white-hot with fear.

Krim peered over the water, waiting for the sickening crack of more bullets. But he and Jake both saw that the Purples were bent with their heads together. Apparently Sleepy Z still had some punch. Abe faltered, and Simon grabbed him to shoulder-and-step-walk back to the bank. His pistol had been tucked away and the Thompson dangled from his hand like an afterthought, flapping with each step as the larger gangster leaned into him.

"I got him," Krim whispered to Jake, and gestured around the curve of the riverbank. Then he was sprinting, under the dock and out, grabbing Gerald under the arms and pulling, his boots slipping as he scuttled backwards toward shelter. Gerald groaned and Krim slapped a hand around his mouth to keep the Purples from turning at the sound. He tugged harder, watching the trail of red they left behind, and the water that was coming up in hungry tongues through the ice.

"I saved us," Gerald said later, between high-pitched gasps, as they bumped along in Krim's truck.

"Nah," Jake said, beside him on the seat, rubbing his shoulder. "Not really. But ya still a champ."

"Where's Willie?" Gerald asked between gritted teeth.

Krim said he'd seen the boy race across the ice, jump the bank, and hop in with Bob Murphy. Fast as a jackrabbit.

Krim glanced at Jake. The Purples would regroup at their car, Abe would shake his noggin and nurse his pain with a swig of something, and then the gangsters would load the liquor themselves, however slowly. All of it was gone, and under the full March moon the two abandoned vehicles still sat on the ice like tombstones.

"It's over," Krim said. Then he repeated himself, realizing that in those two tiny words he felt a magnitude of relief.

={ 33 }=

ALTHOUGH ALFRED MOSS had told himself a hundred times that the boy he called his son was the product of some indiscretion of Elsie's, and he'd just been the soft-hearted clown she'd pinned it on, he often thought of her and the baby. Recently he'd gone on a tear and tried to drown whatever was left of Alfred Moss, family man—but had woken in the night shivering, thinking he heard the child crying, before realizing it was only coyotes far off across the fields, their fluty voices carried on the wind.

When had he last written to Gin? Couldn't say. He pinched cocaine to stay awake for the driving and chewed the last of his Chinatown hop to fall asleep. After a few days of that, he'd collapsed in Oklahoma and hallucinated Prohibition agents, G-men with X-ray eyes, lurking outside his highway hotel. Then blackness.

BANG BANG went the door. Moss started awake. Had the G-men finally broken in? When the voice called out, "Mr. Swanson? Wake up, Mr. Swanson," he knew it was the desk clerk. He'd checked in under the name Algernon Swanson.

Moss asked the clerk what the date was, and discovered he'd been asleep for two days. The clerk was as short and friendly as a calf. He accepted Moss's apologies and three dollars, and said his wife would bring around some stew to make him feel better.

"Yes," Moss answered. "That might help this damn cold I've caught."

"There's no cause for cussing, sir. I know you are married to an actress, but I don't care how they talk out there. This is Oklahoma and Jesus Christ died for a reason."

"Amen. And I apologize."

Moss splashed water on his face from the basin and waited for the stew to arrive. He found a pen in the desk and the hotel stationery headed with the address Lawton Arms Motor Hotel. He wrote to Gin:

My Jade Tiger,

As you know, my business, which must remain secret still, even from you, has taken me far from New York. Should I tell you the mission I have been tasked with, ordered on high from British Parliament itself, the knowledge would only expose you to danger, so I ask for your continued patience. I also ask for a small loan.

My employers originally provided me with a sufficient stipend, but unforeseen circumstances have stalled me in Oklahoma. It is God's country in appearance, but populated by Hell's minions. Should I make it to my rendezvous in the West, I will be paid my final fee and will reimburse your loan. But until you send the money, I am a prisoner of the Lawton Arms Motor Hotel, torn away from your love, your sweet amber persimmons—

There was another knock. Moss opened the door to the clerk's wife holding a cast-iron Dutch oven. She had a grin on her face, as if she were standing in front of the prince of Heaven himself. "Is it true, about Gloria Swanson?" she asked. The wife was a decade younger than her husband, and taller—a cornstalk to his weed—and her hair was gold as silk. "What's your wife like? I mean, in person."

Moss smiled. He took the oven out of her hands and led her in gently. "She's just like you, ma'am. A good woman."

={ 34 }=

THE RING OF THE PHONE startled Elsie because she used the device so seldom. The only person who ever called was her mother—and Elsie tried to extract herself from those calls as quickly as possible. Her mother had come only twice since the baby was born, and both times the old woman had almost dropped Baby John because she was so zozzled. Elsie stared at the unsightly rectangle on the wall for three rings before answering. It was Saturday morning and she wasn't due at the restaurant until evening shift. The phone was an extravagance given how little she used it, but she kept it because a part of her still held out hope—hope that Alfred was out there, no matter how furious at her, hope that his business associates were wrong, hope that he'd call.

It was Constable Van Beken.

"There's no way to sugarcoat it, so I'll just tell you: we got a body here. Recovered along the river. Same height as your husband, but it's a long shot. Might be him, might not."

He asked her to come into the station. He mentioned some of the personal effects they had recovered along with the body. He gave her a brief description—pipe, tobacco, hair pomade tin, ring, and watch chain—did any of these sound familiar? Alfred smoked cigarettes, she said, but she would come as soon as she could. It was the description of the ring and the hair tin that started her quaking. What Constable

Van Beken didn't say, and what she feared to know, was how much of a body would be left after ninety days. She didn't want to think about being shown any corpse—either that of her husband or of some poor random wretch. Both were horrible.

She dialed the neighbor who usually watched Johnny for her, but the woman was out. Elsie phoned her best girlfriend. Judy was the one she'd waitressed alongside when she'd first met Alfred, the one who was now involved with the race man.

Judy answered, but said she wasn't free until at least two that afternoon.

Elsie could feel her own breath blooming inside her chest, and she fought to suppress the sob. "Wh-what if it's him?" she said into the receiver.

"I don't know how to say this, doll, but . . ." Her friend hesitated on the other end. "Maybe it'd be better?"

"Better?" But even as she said it, Elsie could see the faces at the bank, how the will would be executed and accounts would open up to her—how, subject to lender approval, the house would be finally in her name. Alfred had been missing for more than ninety days and had moved into the category of "long-term" missing person, according to the police.

"I mean, so you'd know finally what happened. Look, hon," Judy was saying. "Maybe someone should be with you. What about that man?" she whispered. "You know, the older one that you—"

"Frank Brennan."

Was he still in the picture? Judy asked. Could he offer moral support?

"I sent him away. Haven't seen him in almost a month. I got a letter from him from New York. He's working on the George Washington Bridge there. He lives with his wife there, so I didn't write him back."

Elsie didn't tell her that Frank had tucked a few dollars into the envelope and told her in the P.S. to buy herself a new dress—*pale blue, like your eyes.* She hadn't felt she deserved it. She'd used it instead to pay the phone bill and buy material to make Johnny new onesies, since lately she'd been making them out of Alfred's old shirts. Even those purchases she felt guilty for, dressing her son with another man's money, though truthfully, as the days went by, she was learning that all money was good money. What Alfred had left was mostly inaccessible, and the Cream of Michigan paid her enough to cover only the most modest of their needs.

"I can do this," she said aloud, as much to herself as to Judy. "I have to do this."

"I'll see you after. I'll be at your door at 2 p.m. on the nose, I promise." Judy was known for promises she didn't keep.

Elsie thanked her, and Judy said it was the least she could do, given that Elsie had stood by her after she started dating Oscar—when all their other friends had deserted her. "Yes," Elsie said distractedly. She still hadn't met Oscar and kept forgetting his name, mostly because Judy and Oscar didn't go around together during the day, and nights kept Elsie home with the child.

Elsie hung up and glanced around the house. Knowing how unreliable Judy could be, she was already resigning herself to dealing with the situation alone. She was sweating under her dress, so she went to the bathroom, unzipped the side of the garment, and patted her belly dry with a towel. Unsatisfied, she stripped the sheath off. She had three black dresses, but one was too worn under the arms, another too tight in the bust, and the third a little grease-splattered from work at the restaurant. Elsie had many good clothes that Alfred had bought her in the flurry of the romance, but she had lost weight and neither the pregnancy nor the pre-pregnancy ones fit. She would have to sit down

222

with her sewing machine and make some modifications to her whole wardrobe. She scanned the closet for dark blue. This one would do. She realized it was silly: it was not as if the dead could see her. She zipped herself into it, touched up her hair, then gathered the baby's things and packed them. Soon she had blankets, coat, hat and mittens, bottle, soother, and a soft toy stacked beside the stroller, but the idea of dragging them and the child through a police station unnerved her. Where would she put the baby while she looked at the body?

She felt shaky in a way she hadn't since the early days of motherhood, as though a large wave were pulling darkly over her head, and she squatted down on the floor next to the baby's things and breathed in and out with her head between her knees. Down the street, she heard the scrape of someone pulling in the garbage cans. "Willie Lynch," she whispered.

She stood quickly and looked outside, but it was some other boy. The sky was high and blue and Willie had not been by the house in days. She ran to the telephone and thumbed through her address book. Soon she found the number he had left earlier that winter. A distrustful-sounding woman answered and took several minutes to locate her son. "Tell him it's Mrs. Moss," Elsie said, "and that I have a small job for him if he's available."

Twenty minutes later, the boy pulled into the driveway in his father's car, a fourteen- or fifteen-year-old girl in the passenger seat beside him. "My sister, Annie," he said as introduction. "She has tons of experience with kids, even newborns."

Willie had exchanged his usual cap for a gray fedora, and he had a vest with a watch chain on it. Elsie tried to press a dollar into his palm, but he wouldn't take it. He said he'd take care of Annie, and she'd take care of the baby. If Elsie didn't mind his sister trying on her makeup while she was out, she'd probably do the whole morning for a lipstick. Elsie nodded—she hadn't worn any rouge since Alfred had disappeared, sticking only to a pale powder. She rushed about the house showing Annie where Baby John's things were kept.

"Do they actually think the body is Mr. Moss's?" Willie said as she was leaving, his eyes still big like a child's in spite of his attire. "I was there that night on the ice, you know."

Elsie said yes, she knew, but she didn't know, and he touched her hand in a way that was not childish at all. He had offered to drive her, and Elsie realized she might have accepted the ride if not for that touch.

ON THE WAY over in the cab, Elsie made a list in her mind of the things she could identify about Alfred's body. There was surprisingly little. Long feminine fingers, a few back freckles, and a small, grotesque tattoo of a Kewpie doll on his left shoulder.

Constable Van Beken took her from the station to the coroner's office himself. He was a good-looking brown-haired man who seemed as though he could have been carved from wood, all of his features were so perfectly defined and proportioned. By way of preparation, he said, "I would not put you through this, Mrs. Moss, only you said he had a tattoo he kept hidden."

Elsie blinked rapidly. She did not know how to respond. "And this . . . person?"

Van Beken nodded as they walked briskly along. "There is one. The body is well preserved from the cold water." He consulted the file in his hand. "You say at the time of his disappearance your husband was—"

"Ice-fishing." It was the lie Mr. Bunterbart had given her to use when she first filed the report.

"Of course," the constable replied, as though he didn't believe it but also didn't care to correct her. "Well, we found the body along the riverfront. Not as far as you said the car was, though. Delray. We have the possessions at the station and you can view those too, though frankly, it's better to get it over with."

Elsie nodded again. Van Beken showed her into the building without hesitation. She remembered now that she had met this officer twice before, but even though he could see she was rattled by being in a morgue, he didn't offer comfort or lay his hand upon her back or elbow as they went in. He led the way as they descended the stairs.

"You'll see that part of the head is missing—from a blow, most likely a rock—but the face is intact, more or less, and it should not be hard to make an identification."

Elsie could hear herself breathing hard.

He told her that they were listing the cause of the man's demise as "death by misadventure"—which was to say that it was a death by drowning—and in spite of the damage to the skull, they did not suspect foul play.

Elsie did not gasp when the medical examiner pulled back the sheet. She simply shrunk back. The body was the color of winter sky. One hand went to her throat, the other held tightly to her handkerchief. The skin of this thing, which Elsie could hardly call a man, reminded her of a half-deflated balloon. She didn't even look to see if it was her husband, she simply looked, then closed her eyes, then looked again. The corpse—for it could hardly be called anything else—was indeed the same size as Alfred Moss, and dark hair flopped back from its forehead. A large part of the hairline was gone; the nose remained, but the cheek on the side farthest from Elsie seemed to have melted away into nothing. This man had a similar facial shape to Alfred, at least going by what was left, but the hands were undeniably different—thicker, broad-knuckled working-man fingers with short, square nails, though some of them were missing. Eaten? The middle finger looked like a cigar that had been smoked partway down.

Alfred had the long, slim fingers of a musician, with flat, pink, rectangular nails, even though he'd spent at least some of his days laboring at River Rouge. It was one of the first things Elsie had noticed about him—the noble grace of his hands when he lit her cigarette—that and his smile.

Elsie covered her mouth with the handkerchief, afraid of vomiting. She glanced at grim-faced Constable Van Beken. The medical examiner and the constable both stood off to one side, a respectful distance from her. She watched them, solid in their professions, unflappable; they must do this every week. It was the medical examiner who broke the silence, in a gentle tone, saying, "Take your time."

Her eyes went back to the dead. To the legs, which were still covered by the sheet, even though it had been drawn partway back, baring the chest. There it was on the left shoulder, a tattoo: an anchor—not Alfred's Kewpie doll. Her gaze turned again to the anonymous face of the corpse.

"It's him," she said quietly, so quietly she couldn't believe she had said it, and yet the two men seemed to hear her, because the medical examiner covered the body again and Van Beken for the first time expressed his sympathies. What she heard when the examiner moved the sheet back over the cadaver was not the ripple of linen but the rustle of paper—the will, the mortgage, the insurance policy, the sound of dollar bills. But the tears that fell were real, one for each step she climbed back up, because she knew her husband was still out there somewhere, undiscovered, and that she'd just claimed someone else's. A convenient body, because she badly needed one. She hadn't known she was going to do it, and through her shock she heard her friend Judy on the phone again, saying, *Maybe it'd be better.*

As they walked back to the station, Elsie felt feverish in her winter coat. How bright Van Beken's neck was in the sun beneath his studious face! It didn't seem fair that spring should finally come that day.

At the station, she touched the dead man's things. Each item was catalogued in its own envelope. "Are you sure?" Van Beken asked when she confirmed the hair tin. He consulted the first report she'd made. "It says here Murray's Superior."

"He did buy this kind sometimes."

The ring was a plain gold band, not unlike Alfred's wedding ring, though larger in diameter. As she held it up and looked at the station lights through it, Elsie's unhappiness was genuine. She held the circle between bleach-bitten fingers. Her husband was gone. Whoever the man in the morgue was, one thing was certain: the body was as ugly and startling to her as the fact that she would never see Alfred Moss again.

={ 35 }=

AFTER ELSIE LEFT the station, she walked for about half a mile before she stopped into Old Mariners' Church. She knew burial arrangements would need to be made through her own church, but just then she could not bear to see the face of Reverend Prangley or anyone she knew. She knelt and prayed. Asking forgiveness from God for her lie, she cried into her gloves. Then she went home.

It was almost half past two and, as she'd expected, her friend Judy hadn't shown up. The boy and his small sister looked at her with large eyes.

"Ma'am?" Willie took her by the elbow and helped her up the porch steps.

The baby was sleeping and the sister now wore a bright red mouth, so different from her own.

"Mrs. Moss . . .?" Willie asked again, unable to put words to the question.

Elsie realized she would have to lie again, and that she was going to spend the rest of her life lying.

"Funeral arrangements," she said, sitting on a small wood bench at the door where normally she would perch to remove her boots. But she didn't bend to take them off. "First Lutheran—the number is in my book on the table below the telephone."

Willie didn't move, and neither did the sister. The boy's face had a pinched expression. He dropped down beside her on the bench, nearer than a man should sit to a woman he was not intimate with. "Was it him? Was it Mr. Moss?" He swallowed.

Elsie couldn't stand to look in his eyes, so she focused on Willie's adolescent mustache, the pale hairs on his lip that he must be attempting to grow to look older. They were thin and blond, and above his coral lips they stood out from one another in odd directions, like vines that had not been tended or trained to grow up a trellis.

"I can't—" Elsie's voice choked. "I can't tell you about the body." That at least was the truth.

The boy mistook her emotion, and reached out and clutched both her hands in his own. "Okay, okay, Christ Almighty, here's what we're gonna do. Annie, don't just sit there. Go get on the horn like the lady said. Call the priest!" Willie commanded, and no sooner had the lipsticked fourteen-year-old gone from the living room than Willie pressed Elsie's head against his shoulder. "Mr. Moss was my friend," he told her. "I'll take care of you now."

His breathing was uneven and Elsie could feel moisture from Willie's cheek as his tears slipped against her skin. She straightened uncomfortably, stood up, and patted his head. "Should I call Frank in New York? I should call Frank," she muttered to herself as she left the entrance and paced the living room. The boy didn't ask who Frank was, or even seem to hear her.

"Every cent I ever made I owed to Mr. Moss." Willie looked straight up at her. "My dad brought me into the business, but Moss taught me. When my father was killed—" The boy stopped his speech and coughed several times.

Elsie knew that Seamus Lynch had not died on the river—he'd been cut down at his business, and the murder remained unsolved. In their brief interactions over chores, Willie had told Elsie just enough to make her not ask about his father a second time. It was clear to her now that the boy had a hard time separating the two men in his mind. Elsie moved across the room and rummaged through her purse, looking for the pill container Mr. Krim had filled for her earlier in the year.

"Let's have a drink," Willie suggested. He went out to his family's car, and when he returned, he offered her a bottle of whiskey.

The sister, Annie, came back from the kitchen and sat blinking at the edge of the room. "Reverend Prangley says he can meet with you at four today."

Willie turned from the sideboard sharply, and one of the drinks he'd been pouring sloshed. He pushed the drink at Elsie and downed his own. "I'd like to meet this Mr. Prangley. Make sure he does things proper for you. And for Mr. Moss, of course." The boy stood a little taller, with his legs spread wider, his shiny shoes firm on the Congoleum, his face, Elsie noted with surprise, less shrunken with grief than it had been only a few moments before.

ELSIE ALLOWED WILLIE to drive her to New Lutheran. After he dropped his sister off at home, Elsie stared out the window and noticed again the sunshine, the fact that the air was almost warm. People on the streets were wearing jackets instead of wool. She pulled off her own coat and the baby's hat.

Willie had a cigarette clamped between his boyish lips. "You know, Mrs. Moss, I could teach you how to drive. It would help you, wouldn't it, for running errands with the baby?"

She nodded automatically, not really listening.

"There are a lot of things I can show you. A lot that I can help with."

"Yes, Willie, that's sweet." She shifted the baby around in her lap. The child's eyes were dark and wide. At six months, he was sitting up almost unassisted now, and eager to see the world outside the window. Elsie lifted him up a little so he could watch the signs flash past. For a split second she felt her failures melt away—the child did not judge her. The child did not know her lies, only the fact that it was held.

={ 36 }⊨

PRANGLEY WAS A NAME Willie had heard on some of the men's lips, whispered. Moss's and Bunterbart's. Not Gerald's or Jake's, because if he'd heard the name from them, they'd have been more forthcoming about its owner. Willie removed his fedora as he and Mrs. Moss walked into the church. The first glimpse he had of Prangley sent pins and needles into his knees. The man had hard eyes and knotted hands, even though his voice rushed out soothing as a fountain. Moss had taught Willie plenty, and one thing he'd learned was that there was always someone else to answer to. Willie answered to Moss and Krim and Gerald and Jake and the others. They answered to Bunterbart, and now to Krim. And it stood to reason that Bunterbart had answered to someone too. At one time he'd believed that person was his own father, but after his pop was killed, Willie understood his old man could not have been in charge of the night runs—after all, the business seemed to continue just fine without him.

This was the man in charge, Willie was certain. He extended his palm and watched the reverend's reaction to his name. "Willie Lynch, sir."

Reverend Prangley clasped his hand and pumped it strongly, looking him in the eye. "I knew your father," he said, catching Willie completely off guard. "Seamus Lynch. He sold me a car. About four years ago."

The Kid did a double take. His brow scrunched. Between his hands, he turned his hat around by the brim twice. Had he heard the name Prangley from his own father? A yawning sensation opened in his gut.

"I was sorry to hear he died last year. My condolences," Prangley said to Willie. Then, placing a hand on Elsie's shoulder, "And to you, Mrs. Moss. This is terrible news. Worse," he said, gesturing to chairs, "is that I can't offer funeral services for you. I can help you find a funeral home, and certainly I can guide you through these trying days, but our church simply doesn't conduct them except in very special circumstances."

The boy had planned to interrogate Prangley a little, watch him squirm, but he found himself sitting by dumbly as Elsie and the reverend discussed other locations.

Seamus Lynch had been a hard man to live with, and Willie had seen the wrong side of his belt at least twenty times. Seamus dealt in used cars not far from where the new bridge was being built, and he'd supplied half the importers with the old vehicles that they used to drive across the ice. At fifteen, he'd pressured Willie to drop out of school and assist him—both on the lot and on the river at night. When Willie's mother objected, Seamus had railed that she had the girl she could educate and he'd take Willie and that was that. It only made sense that Prangley knew his pa— especially if they had been involved in the same operation. Yet there was something about the reference that prickled the back of Willie's neck and made his mouth dry. Seamus had been robbed at the lot the night he'd died, shot clean through the heart for four hundred dollars. There was only one car missing from the tiny dealership—a 1921 Roamer town car. Whoever blasted him had done it alone, and had good taste.

"You say they found Mr. Moss east of where we took our boat?"

Prangley inquired. "*East* of the car? Upriver? You're sure?" To Elsie's nod, Prangley said, "Well, perhaps God does work in mysterious ways."

Willie watched as something rippled across the reverend's face. He noticed that Elsie too seemed uncomfortable. In fact, as soon as they'd set foot inside the church, her shoulders had stitched up, and now she perched right on the edge of the chair as if she might bolt at any moment.

Willie broke in to ask what kind of car the reverend was referring to. An old Model T, Prangley said, with the doors stripped off. "No," the boy clarified, leaning forward, an edge to his voice. "What kind did you buy from my father?"

"A 1922 Buick coupe. Still runs fine. Did you want to see it?" Prangley locked eyes with the boy, and Willie noticed a gentle challenge in the uptick of his voice even as he smiled.

"Yeah, I'll take a look," Willie said, words that made Prangley's olive face turn pasty. Of course, the reverend replied smoothly, they'd go out on the grounds as soon as they finished, and he turned his attentions back to Elsie. But Willie wasn't satisfied. "That's all right," he said, and rose abruptly. "Don't trouble yourself." And he let himself out of the office.

THE BUICK WAS AN odd shape—almost like a horseless carriage. It was the smallest coupe Willie had seen, and try though he might, he couldn't remember it from his father's lot. But four years prior, he'd been only twelve—in school and much more obsessed with yo-yos, pogo sticks, and soapbox cars than with real cars. Willie walked around the billiard-green Buick, examining it from all angles. He picked up a stick from the mud and poked the ground with it as he walked, occasionally tossing up dirt that pelted the wheels of the coupe. The idea of the six-foot-three Prangley nimbly climbing through the twelve-inch door was enough to make Willie snicker aloud. The reverend hadn't bought the vehicle for comfort, of that Willie was sure. If anything, it was a joke—and a mean one—definitely his old man's brand of humor. Maybe his pop had given it to Prangley to pay down some debt, but selected the most preposterous car he could find for the gangly priest. It was a nice-looking vehicle, nice enough that Prangley had kept it—but to Willie's eye there was something about it that didn't jibe.

He threw down the stick and glanced over his shoulder at the parsonage. He stalked to the building and tried the door, but it was locked. A window with gauzy curtains allowed him glimpses of a drab sitting and dining room. He went around the other side of the building, but the bedroom shade was down. Still, there was a sliver at either side not covered by the white paper, and plastering one hand against the brick, Willie shoved his face into the window, trying to see past the crack into the room. He tapped his fedora backwards on his noggin to give himself more room to get close. He found himself looking at cedar—some kind of cabinet or dresser stood to the left of the window. Nothing could be seen past it.

He pulled back and glanced around for something to stand on; maybe he could get a better view if he were more level with the top of the cabinet. He spotted a large brick near the gate to the cemetery, ran and pried it from the mud, carried it back, and climbed onto it. Through the opening, he still could view only a sliver of area on the dresser top. There were some papers and a box, nothing out of the ordinary. Even these Willie could see only through the veil of his eyelashes, because he had to squash his face so near the window there was no room to blink.

A cigar box, he thought. He looked longer than necessary at such a mundane thing, then pulled away and climbed down. He stood blinking. Then he said aloud, "A humidor," and got back up on the brick to check. It was true, the box had a nice lacquer instead of the usual cheap paper band. It might actually be a larger humidor under-neath, not a dresser.

Again peering through the crack, he made a slick clucking noise with his tongue. Reverend Prangley was not merely a man who indulged on occasion; he was a man of distinguished tastes. "Fucking *dandy*," the boy said aloud, leaning over to spit.

THE LYNCH BOY had the coloring, the size, and the voice of an angry Chihuahua. Prangley watched the boy sailing down his hallway, the sound of his shoes clattering through the empty church, and felt, for the first time since he'd been a young man himself, helpless. There was no way to control youth—impulsive, never-satisfied, never-expended youth. Who knew what the boy would get into, left to wander beside the parsonage, while here he sat, advising Mrs. Moss on a funeral he wasn't even planning for her.

With the body now recovered, Elsie Moss had summarily dried up what had become in recent weeks an excellent source of revenue. Every second he sat here with her was a drain on time he could be spending elsewhere. Still, Prangley pursed his lips and nodded, because that was what he did best. The widow, meanwhile, smoked more than usual, and the baby played with her cigarette case, turning the shiny surface of it over and over, until it slipped one too many times from his chubby fingers and hit the floor and spilled open and Elsie jammed it into her purse.

She didn't seem particularly upset, Prangley noticed. Sad, apprehensive, yes—but not a bit like that first morning she'd come back to him.

"You know"—Prangley leaned forward—"the church usually does not conduct funerals except for very large supporters and donors. But these society women, I believe they have come to feel a real love for you, for your husband's story. Before I call the funeral director, let me think on this. Perhaps we could find a donor and hold it here after all."

"Oh, I couldn't ask that—" Elsie protested, but Prangley waved his hand.

"I think it is best."

The idea was taking hold of him now: it was a way to find the answers he needed. After hauling that empty car out of the river, Prangley had been questioning everything he thought he knew. And now Alfred Moss's wife walked in here, one of his other rumrunners in tow, and said the body had turned up upstream of the car—a body found a full four weeks later? Where were the Scotch crates and the money? Why hadn't they been in the car? Prangley had to have the body in his possession, whatever the cost. He had to see it with his own eyes.

A furrow appeared in Elsie Moss's forehead. "Will you prepare the body yourself? It's . . . how do I say this, it's not, he's not whole. It must be closed casket."

"Closed casket," Prangley echoed, and nodded. He told her the name of the funeral home and the embalmer who would handle the preparation of Mr. Moss. Then he set his hand on hers ever so lightly. "You know I care more about souls than bodies."

CHARLES PRANGLEY MOVED a tree of roses from one side of the pulpit to the other. A wreath of carnations as wide as a tractor wheel was tied with a white ribbon behind the stand where the casket would sit. Florists had been in and out all the previous evening, and Prangley had barely had time to reflect on practicalities. The body was to be delivered from the mortician's at seven that morning, and Prangley wouldn't have more than an hour before Mrs. Moss and Miss McCloud arrived, and others soon after that.

At the wheeze of truck brakes outside, he turned quickly, and as he did, he caught his thumb and opened it on one of the roses. Without looking to see if it bled, he stuck it in his mouth and jogged down the center aisle. There it was: the body. A man in a cap got out and unbolted the back. Prangley went out to meet him, but the man had already pulled out a contraption that looked like a gurney to wheel the coffin inside.

"Oh good, give me a hand here?"

As they worked, Prangley realized this was not the man he'd spoken to on the phone. He waited until they'd got the box inside and positioned, and the man had presented him with the paperwork. Prangley's request couldn't wait any longer. "The casket—it's unlocked?" he asked. "The wife asked to see him one last time to say her own goodbye."

"I haven't got the key," the man said.

"I understand." Prangley waited a beat. "Mrs. Moss will be disappointed. I hate to ask, but is there any way to go get it?"

The man stalled and Prangley made his case again, saying what a shame it was. Finally the driver went, promising to be back in twenty minutes.

He was gone thirty when the secretary arrived—she was early and, worse, she wasn't alone. Prangley had gone into the office to get a screwdriver, then, standing over the casket, realized he had no way to explain his actions should he wound the wood. With the number of people who were sure to come to the funeral of the Great Missing Alfred Moss, an imperfection would not go unnoticed. That was when he heard the clunk of the door. He just had time to stash the screwdriver inside the podium as Faye McCloud came in. Prangley flushed with anger at the intrusion, the fact that the key to the casket had not yet arrived, and the hand on his watch that ticked forward.

A slim, boyish woman was with his secretary. "This is Kitty," Miss McCloud said, a flame across her cheeks, "my sister." To Prangley's eye, the girl looked cobbled together. She had styled her hair down, but it didn't reach her earlobes and had no curl to it. Her skirt hung awkwardly around her legs, and her shoes were boy brogues. "To play the organ. Because it was so last-minute, we couldn't get Miss Warwick."

"Do you even know how to play this?" he lashed out at this unwelcome stranger, and gestured at the new organ system. It had come to the church by way of honest donations from Mabel Abbot and her daughter Hilda.

He heard his secretary draw in a breath with embarrassment.

The sister, Kitty, straightened her shoulders, walked over, and eyed the instrument. "I can handle her, sir. I've played at the Redford movie theater, and the opening of the Grande Ballroom too."

Prangley assessed this odd creature. "I did not know they would hire a woman." He kept his gaze fixed on her to let the sting of the comment linger. Though he had only been acquainted with her for ten seconds, he enjoyed letting her know he'd seen through her. Kitty bowed her head slightly before folding her body onto the bench. Finally, Prangley turned away, toward the double doors where he heard the *whuff* of the funeral home hearse. "Bear in mind: this is a church, not a nightclub or a picture show."

With that, Prangley headed outside, a line of perspiration on his upper lip. There was no way he could look in the casket with the secretary and her ragtag sister there. Unless he could send them both off on some errand—for what? A special piece of music? But the girl needed to acquaint herself with the instrument, so even if he could concoct something believable, he knew they wouldn't both go. *To spend so much money and fail!* he thought as his shoes scraped across the stones.

The capped man hopped out of the hearse with the key and pressed it into Prangley's palm. "Thank God," Prangley said, and glanced heavenward, meaning it.

Then the driver was off and Prangley was back inside to deal with the McCloud sisters. With relief, he saw that Faye had stationed herself in the kitchen to wait for the caterers. So it was just Kitty he had to contend with. He approached her where she was warming up, running fingers up and down the keys in a succession of major chords that rumbled through the narrow hall.

A pointy grin was pasted across Kitty's face until she glimpsed him. Then she eased off and played more slowly, head gently nodding.

He hovered over her until she stopped and gazed up at him. "It's the ant's pants, all right," she said.

"I'll take that as a compliment."

"You should."

Prangley could see that below the hem of her skirt she was shuffling her shoes around on the pedals. "Apologies about before," he said stiffly. "I am not always good with change."

The young woman nodded, in spite of his wooden apology.

Prangley cleared his throat. "I came to ask: did your sister discuss payment with you? No? Well, we must get that sorted. But I also need ten minutes alone with the body. To . . . say a blessing," he improvised.

"Oh, quiet, I see. I can wait to practice."

Kitty McCloud didn't seem to understand that he was asking for privacy. Prangley was so close to getting what he needed. With one hand he stroked the organ, wiping away imaginary dust. "No, no, it's just that I don't want you to see—they tell me Mr. Moss . . . Well, the face is not all there, you understand?"

"Get out of here!" Kitty belted out, and it was clear she very much wanted to see. But at his disapproving glance, she stood up and made her way back into the kitchen to talk with Faye. He heard her asking how much Miss Warwick usually received for playing the music.

Finally, he was alone. Prangley went directly to the casket and wedged the key into the lock. It seemed to jam at first, then he felt the lock loosen and the poplar lid lift between his fingers. His shoulders went rigid. He stood very still, imagining that if anyone had come into the church just then, they might think they were witnessing a man paying his respects to the dead. But Prangley knew that if they could see his expression, they'd witness him red-faced, paralyzed. After a long moment he dropped the lid shut with a *crack*, strode across the stage, and kicked the rose tree, then, still unrelieved, pushed it off the stage onto the floor below, where the pot shattered and dirt flew like confetti across the floorboards.

He wondered if Elsie knew, or if in her grief she saw her husband in a stranger's face. But this was a fleeting thought. He cared more about the burning sensation that consumed his ears and neck: Moss had robbed him and disappeared.

"Clumsy!" he breathed, looking down at the mess of mud and petals when Faye and Kitty dashed in to see what had happened. His voice ragged, and his neck choked by his own collar.

={ 38 }=

EVERYONE WHO ENTERED the church passed by Gin Ing. She sat in the final row and kept her angular face down, dark blue jacket buttoned up tight—even though spring had finally grabbed the air and shaken it into birdsong. She knew there was no reason to act so diffident; no one here knew her. Still, she was well aware that she stood out in any crowd. People were curious about a young Chinese woman alone, especially here. There were twelve Chinese restaurants downtown, but Gin was certain the men of Detroit saw only the neon flash of *Chop Suey* and did not pay much attention to the people who cooked their food. It was not like New York, where such men would have dined among a room of Asian faces.

What she minded about being treated like an oddity was that she was American—American-born at least—and she spoke and wrote in English better than many of those who spoke to her, slowly, with sideways grins on their faces. When she'd come in, the preacher had spotted her and made exactly the type of stiff conversation she dreaded. Gin had found him so off-putting that she'd quickly accepted his proffered funeral program and seated herself without more than a nod of acknowledgment.

She knew his name: *Prangley*. Like the sound of a toothy zipper doing up. She knew he thought he was very smart, too—*look at his clothes,* she observed, shocked that although he'd been candidly described to her, the description did not do justice to his arrogance. He wore his robes today, and yet beneath them were those cassimere trousers with the dark chevron weave, those embossed calfskin shoes. How obvious that he was not what he appeared to be. Surely, Gin was not the only one to see it. Her slim eyebrows twitched as she watched him seating the many friends and acquaintances of Alfred Moss.

The organist, enthusiastic, fingered notes that reverberated throughout the space, plaintive and loud, and a little faster than the tempo at which dirges would ordinarily be played. Everyone in the church turned to see and admire the organ pipes as they took their places. Gin listened to some women in the row ahead of her gossiping about who had donated the funds for the instrument. One called it "the Abbot Organ." Both were stumped at who had paid for the funeral itself, however.

The casket at the front of First Lutheran was closed, but a large picture of Moss faced the crowd. Gin stared at it. Some of those in attendance leaned forward into the front pew and offered condolences to the wife, who turned her head and nodded. This was what interested Gin, more so than the others assembled, the glimpse of this taut face. The flaxen curls surprised her, the brightness of a woman who'd sounded so dark. The real question wasn't about who she was, but how and when it would be best to approach her.

Just then, a man came in and stood alongside Gin, glancing down her row. There were seats farther up, but she could see he wanted this one. She ought to have moved over into the space and not made him push past her, but Gin kept the aisle. She stood and he brushed by. He sat down but continued searching, scanning the crowd. He was tall and tense, and under his center part a pair of green eyes stared out of a studious face. Gin followed his gaze. Twelve rows ahead, she spied the men who must be the distributors; they were clearly uncomfortable in a house of worship. They took off their hats and dropped them, stooped to pick them up, swatted their knees with them, whispered in one another's ears.

ErnestOttoHermanBobTomGeraldJake—their names wafted over her in a puff: the memory of an exhalation of smoke from between her lover's lips. That was how he'd said them, as if they were one thing. Only five men sat in the pew. Well dressed and sober in polished shoes—she wondered if it was the first time the motley crew had ever sat anywhere in public besides a watering hole. From the back pew, Gin Ing could not hear what they were saying, but she figured the man beside her had a good idea. He had a professional look to him, so he must be Ernest. The Doctor.

She unbuttoned her jacket and feigned interest in the funeral program. She liked the idea that, without knowing one another, she and this other watcher sat together, in some ways providing easy cover for each other. She was pretty sure he was looking at the men Alfred Moss had worked with: farm boys and factory men with a little extra business on the side. Then her pew-mate let his gaze travel again over the crowd, still searching. Again, Gin followed his gaze. His eyes fastened onto a thick-haired woman standing with a fistful of programs—and he immediately stared down at his lap, as if afraid to be caught looking.

Gin observed this woman. She was not slim and not fat, not old and not young. Her skin was a golden pear, and her shape too, though she hid it somewhat in a drop-waist dress. The man took out a pair of spectacles and put them on. He opened up a book from the pew to "Song of Songs" and began—or pretended—to read silently. Gin glanced over at the page.

Let him kiss me with the kisses of his mouth—
for your love is more delightful than wine.

The man shut the book and dropped it into the rack with a soft thump. The group of men was trying to get his attention. A slim, dark-haired fellow raised two fingers in a solemn wave. Now Gin was certain they were all Alfred's associates. The man beside her lifted his hand and nodded, but didn't move from his seat. She knew why he didn't want to sit with them: like her, he had too much knowledge. The church was packed full now, enough of an excuse.

"How did you know Alfred Moss?" the man said, turning to Gin, surprising her. She glanced at him, but was slow enough in answering that he provided one for her: "He knew a lot of people, I suppose."

Gin Ing nodded. Her hand crept up to the beaded choker she wore around her throat. She fingered the necklace's thick pearl strands, a gold lotus pendant hanging from its center. She chose her words carefully. "It's hard to go to a service where the only one you know is the one who's gone."

"Yes." The man removed his glasses and put them back in his suit pocket. "I'm sure it is."

The organist was now sailing joyously through "Abide with Me," and Gin noticed that the man beside her continued to sneak glances at the woman in the drop-waist dress. Then he turned his attention up to the front. But the reverend didn't seem about to start anytime soon; to Gin, he appeared strangely nervous. Finally, after a few more minutes, Reverend Prangley gripped the podium. The organist banged out the last few notes abruptly. The chatter among society ladies and workingmen stopped, and all eyes—including the carefully watchful eyes of Gin Ing and the man beside her—turned to the front.

PRANGLEY WRAPPED HIS hands around the pulpit to keep them from shaking. He looked out and saw the mob of faces, the women who'd thrown money at the disappeared, the pharmacist in the back pew, the distributors grouped together, and around the edges the workingmen Alfred Moss had known. Here in front was the wife, who wore a new black dress and white powder that made her cheeks seem ghostly. And here came her parents, sodden drunks, climbing through the rows late. As far as Prangley could see, no one there had loved the man, and yet he was expected to deliver a proper elegy for a stand-in body, a body that was not the right one. He cleared his throat and spoke, so quietly he wasn't sure his congregation could hear:

"Now I say this, brethren, that flesh and blood cannot inherit the kingdom of God, neither doth corruption inherit corruption. Behold, I show you a mystery: We shall not all sleep, but we shall all be changed—in a moment, in the twinkling of an eye, at the last trumpet. For the trumpet shall sound, and the dead shall be raised incorruptible, and we will be changed."

Prangley looked up again to see Elsie in the front row, held on one side by her friend Judy and on the other by Willie Lynch, the boy who'd asked him too many questions considering his name appeared in Prangley's ledger of men who distributed with Krim. Freckles and moles dotted his face under a spray of tawny hair, making it hard to take him seriously. Nonetheless, the boy had seemed to be sussing Prangley out, and he'd come back into the church with dirt on his shoes that day, as if he'd walked around the entire graveyard or else spent a good deal of time in the lane where Prangley parked the Buick. The fact that he was Seamus Lynch's son didn't help matters. If the Kid knew who Prangley was and what he did, Elsie would soon know too. That much was clear by how the boy practically clung to her. Youths were not known for carrying their secrets in the way that men could. Well, what did it matter? As of that morning, Charles had made as much money as he could from her suffering.

Elsie's face had a pinched look, as though she might sneeze as much as she might cry. He stared directly into her eyes, and said with a voice that held no kindness:

"For the trumpet will sound, the dead will be raised imperishable, and we will be changed."

The widow made a sound in her throat like a scrub jay—a dull yelp. She put her head down, and her friends leaned in and rubbed her shoulders.

Prangley swallowed, but his mouth was dry. It was the first time in years he hadn't been able to maintain his confidence, his calm, or summon any tenderness into his voice. He could feel himself dying before them as he stammered out the rest of the verse. Behind him, in the black-and-white photograph, Alfred kept his thick gray lips pressed tight in a line, as if he would break into laughter. Prangley tried not to glance over at it, even as he gave the worshippers before him a brief biographical sketch of the man. If he looked into those eyes, he feared he might reach out and tear up the picture in front of all of them.

={ 39 }=

THE SCRIPTURE WENT ON, but Ernest Krim wasn't listening. He watched as Prangley's secretary made her way around the back of the church and quietly closed the doors to the hall.

"Excuse me," Krim said, and fumbled past the woman beside him. He had exchanged pleasantries with her mostly to look as though he were engaged—he hadn't wanted the men to motion him to sit with them. He wasn't a good-enough actor to sit through an entire funeral for a man he knew to be alive while his friends grieved him—not at their sides, anyway. Now he turned and slipped out into the passageway where Faye McCloud was setting down the funeral programs.

"Miss McCloud?" he asked, and she smiled. "You remember me?"

"Yes, Mr. Krim."

He moved closer to her. He touched her hand.

"You haven't been drinking again, since that time?"

He shook his head, but his head was very near to hers now, and Faye followed his eyes with hers. She looked out the window at the bright spring sky. She breathed in. He knew he didn't smell of whiskey, but of shaving lather. She seemed willing, if uncertain.

"I could ask you out, but I don't want to risk your saying no, so I'm just going to kiss you now," he informed her. He gripped her harder around the waist than he meant to, and heard her staggered breath.

To compensate, Krim softened the kiss until there was scarcely anything to it. He pulled back slightly, asking for permission.

"We should be in there, for the funeral," Miss McCloud said, but didn't move.

"That's true," Krim said. "Probably we should." He put his arm behind her back and his fingers climbed into her hair as he pressed his mouth against her throat, watching her lips part.

WHEN WOMEN CAME through the doors, crying, Krim was caught off guard. He had not missed the swelling of "Amazing Grace" (which had been played in an almost swinging double time), and yet it seemed that he and Faye had barely stepped away from each other when the double doors opened and crowds surrounded them. Faye left the passageway, no doubt to seek privacy in the ladies' room and fix her hair, and Krim put his hat on and left the church altogether. He found himself outside on the steps, and farther on he could see Mrs. Moss was already there on the walk, smoking a cigarette, Willie the Kid at her side, and the Chinese woman he'd spoken to in the service approaching them. They had been the first four out of the church. Most of the throng would be winding into the hall for olive-stuffed celery and mock-chicken sandwiches.

Behind Krim, some men filed out: Jake and Bob, Otto, Herman, and Tom. Gerald was still convalescing. "Hi, Doctor!" they jeered him, even though their faces reflected the awful finality of burying a man.

"Willie," they called, now having spotted the boy. "Get over here a minute."

The Kid reluctantly left the women and ambled over. Krim waited to join them until they'd all started in on Willie: Didn't he already have a mother and sister to support? What did he want with a second family to bankroll before he'd even hit eighteen? Why did he want to get tangled up so tight with Moss's old lady?

"Oh, dry up. I was raised to be a gentleman is all," Willie protested.

"Nothing gentlemanly about your thoughts," Jake reprimanded him.

"Listen, we been talking," Otto Schultz said to Krim. "The Purples are all getting bogged down in this extortion thing. Whaddya think?"

"Risk it? Get the boats out and do the summer months?" Herman asked Otto.

"You think they're too busy with their Cleaners and Dyers War to care about us?" Krim saw what Otto was thinking. He hadn't considered this, but it was true that no one had come around to the pharmacy since the incident on the river.

"Yeah, that's what I'm thinking," Otto said. He was a stout man with a bald head, which he now scratched.

"You got some stones, buddy," Bob told him. "I'll bet you a C-note they come around with those tommy guns before you even hit shore."

"Yeah, without Sleepy Z they'll put *us* out to dry!" one of the men joked—but his voice held an edge—an attempt to plaster over the too-vivid memory of the machine gun pointed at them.

"I wouldn't import without Gerald," Jake said, shaking his head.

"Without Gerald or Vern."

"Or Moss."

"What about you, Krim? Still in?"

"You're nuts," Krim told them.

"Look, I got gambling debts," Otto muttered. "I either face the bookie's crowbar or face the Purples' guns."

Krim glanced at Willie, then followed his gaze over to Mrs. Moss and the Chinese woman with the choker. He saw his chance to distract the men from the only topic they had in common: liquor. "Hey, Kid," he said. "She'll be okay for ten minutes without you to hold her hand."

The other men sprang on the joke, and in the chaos of their ribs and jabs, Krim was able to fade back. He dodged through the church to get away. He passed through the main hall and out the side door he'd used the one other time he'd been to the church. He glanced down the hall toward Prangley's office, and saw him sitting there with his head on his fist, instead of out among his wealthy women thanking them for coming. But Krim kept moving. The only one who could have stalled him was Faye, and he expected she was trying to keep her whirling thoughts together while making sure the kitchen didn't run out of clean cups.

Along the side of the building, Krim dodged past the organist, who leaned with one brogue crossed over the other, enjoying a triumphant drag on a reefer. When she saw him, she rubbed it out between her finger and thumb and pocketed it. She smiled to herself and tipped her head back, breathing out into the blue sky.

$$\equiv\!\{\ 40\ \}\!\equiv$$

GIN ING APPROACHED Elsie Moss quickly. She didn't need to say anything, it turned out. Mrs. Moss was edgy enough that just coming near made her look up expectantly. She was not crying, had not cried the whole service as far as Gin could see, although she did wear a look of anguish beneath her dark-brimmed hat.

"I know your husband," Gin said.

"You do?" Elsie stared at the woman.

It was only one word, but Gin noticed she used the present tense, not the past.

"Who are you?" Elsie asked, an edge in her voice.

Gin glanced left and right to be sure the boy who'd accompanied Elsie was otherwise engaged. "I first met Al in New York—"

"New York?"

"He wasn't Alfred. He told me his name was Big Al Baxter. He stayed at the Waldorf. He must have told you *that*. Honestly, he never stopped bragging about it."

"Baxter?"

Gin waved her hand. She knew they had only a minute or two before someone would retrieve Mrs. Moss to join the others inside and accept the endless condolences. She'd played the Waldorf card because she knew there was no way he hadn't mentioned it. It was shorthand, telling Elsie Moss that they knew the same man. "Listen,"

Gin hissed, taking Elsie by the arm and pulling her along a stone path toward the parking lot. "I know Alfred is still alive. You know it too."

Elsie stepped away from her, off the path, her buckled pumps sinking in the soft spring mud.

When Elsie didn't say anything, Gin said, "Most women weep. Where are your tears?" She nodded at Elsie's handkerchief, which, although she clutched it in her hand, puffed out, dry and clean and white.

Elsie did begin to cry then. "Who are you? Leave me alone. I don't want to talk with you anymore."

"Yes, I think you do. You see, I know where he is—because he was supposed to take me with him." She put out her hand to stop Elsie from walking away. "Before you hate me too much, you must understand . . . This is the result of loving your husband." Gin reached up and undid the clasp on her choker necklace. The fat pearl strands and the gold lotus flower lowered. Beneath the jewelry, a thin black scar showed, straight across and circling around the sides of her neck, etched into her skin like a tattoo. "We both have had enough of his abuse, haven't we, Mrs. Moss?"

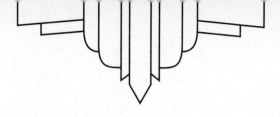

BOOK THREE

AUGUST
1928

PURPLES BRUISED, BUT DETROIT'S LAUNDRY STILL DIRTY

Detroit Free Press, **June 3, 1928**

In a courtroom today Abe Bernstein sat bemused as he listened to opening arguments that detailed a five-year campaign of terror against the city's cleaners. Bernstein, along with eight other members of the Purple Gang, was arrested in April. Prosecuting attorney Richard Tuttle argued that after years of running protection rackets among city bootleggers, Bernstein used those same threats of violence to earn a top position in the cleaners and dyers union with an eye toward also controlling the Michigan Wholesalers Association. Soon after, guns became a common sight at union meetings and those that did not fall in line under Bernstein found their tailor or laundry shops the recipients of fire and other vandalisms.

With the fearsome gang off the streets for what is predicted to be a months-long trial, local leaders believe the tide is turning against the rackets. However, anti-bootlegging campaigner Reverend Charles Prangley of First Lutheran Detroit is less hopeful. "Our efforts to stem the flow of liquor have been effective, but corruption is a hard currency among our leaders. Curing that illness demands vigilance. For every whiskey operation that falls, another arises," the reverend warns.

={ 41 }=

THE TRAIN PULLED into the Chicago junction and Mary Joy Davis climbed aboard—a white silk glove grasping the handrail, her hat making a yellow halo around her face. It was not unusual for a well-dressed black woman to be on the platform in Chicago, yet all the porters knew Mary Joy. The back of her hat was held in place by a large ornamental pin that looked like a relic from another era. Its stick had tarnished, but a mother-of-pearl oval topped it, locking the brim firmly in place in Mary Joy's hair, which was pressed and curled in the manner of Madam C.J. Walker. Wearing a summer traveling suit, she swished up the steps on heels that looked made of lace—Grecian in style, with cutouts across the top of the foot. The conductor—a white man—nodded at her. She nodded back. Behind her, a porter struggled under the weight of two large trunks, tagged with the name *Mr. Sergio Bucci.*

Mr. Bucci traveled often, and all of the Pullman porters knew his name. Mrs. Davis was also known, but was far less famous. She often brought Bucci on board in Chicago, but only ever rode to the next station before departing. She turned now from the step box, and for a moment her age showed in her handsome face. A woman of almost fifty, her skin was a deep brown. She had large dark eyes that were wide-set and heavily lined, both with time and with Maybelline cake. Her dimples conveyed not happiness but worry. She spotted the porter in his dress blue coat, and watched as he wheeled the trunks farther on to a baggage car and hefted them aboard with help from another set of hands at the far end of the platform.

Once on board, she found Hubert Henry. He was head porter and had worked for Pullman since he was twenty-five, like his father before him. He was trim, as Pullman required—not too tall and not too short. He'd grown up in the South and she could still hear the lilt of his accent just like hers, though the railroad had long ago instructed him how to speak in a manner white riders would find acceptable. The porters called him Mr. Davis, but to his wife he was, and always had been, "H.H."

She pulled at his elbow. "It's only two trunks."

"Why's that?" he asked without looking up from a baggage list.

She breathed out heavily. "I suppose I did make someone very important mad."

"Suppose?" Glancing up and down the corridor, H.H. said as quietly as he could: "You stabbed a man's eyeball like a cocktail onion with that damn hat pin."

"You know what he called me."

Mary Joy could feel her jaw tensing, but before she got herself worked up, H.H. cut her off. "Only what every porter working this train is called every day."

"Then you stop bringing them drinks, towels, and bed linens. Leave them for the rest of the ride."

"We had to threaten a strike at rail yards from here to St. Louis to keep you alive. Bit of a difference, I'd say."

Mary Joy watched as the other porters pulled up the stairs and the carriage doors closed. The train whistled and began to hunch forward. "H.H., there is a time to stand up," she said. "The Outfit is charging every Irish saloon keeper half of what we pay. *Half.*"

H.H. put his pencil in his upper coat pocket and stroked a finger across his clean-shaven chin. "It surely doesn't matter what price they ask if they are not supplying us."

Mary Joy felt her shoulders let down with shame. Only H.H. could make her regret her actions. At the time, she always felt so certain of herself. Oftentimes her snap judgments were audacious but led to better deals—but occasionally they had more sobering effects.

Two well-dressed white businessmen came along the narrow corridor, already heading for the dining car. They didn't even seem to notice the head porter or his wife, and neither one of them moved an inch to accommodate Mary Joy's hips.

"These are the last two cases of olive oil from Mr. Bucci," Mary Joy said, stepping closer to her husband to avoid being bumped by the men. Looking H.H. directly in the eyes, she nodded. "After our disagreement, he cannot supply us any longer."

The men passed by.

"*Your* disagreement," H.H. corrected her. "And you better head back and take your seat."

"We don't have to work with folks who don't respect us," Mary Joy said, laying a silk glove on her husband's arm.

"Can't talk now." H.H. found his specs and propped them on his nose.

"Yes, you can. Remember that young man—fellow couldn't stop talking. He parted his hair like Rudolph Valentino. A more delicate face, though, like Buster Keaton. You remember."

H.H. snorted and told her she'd just described every young white man he'd ever met.

Mary Joy sighed. The train rocked side to side and she placed a gloved hand on her chest. She knew the conductor would be through soon—a white pear of a man in his late fifties named Eugene Needle. H.H. had assured her the porters paid him well to look the other way about the alcohol. Mr. Needle knew about other operations too: the waiters who sometimes divided the beef portions by half, especially if they were headed for lady diners, sold them at full price, then, after selling another half at the same rate, pocketed the price of a dinner plate. Needle was getting cut in on everything, but although he looked the other way, everything needed to appear to function at top standard. The porters had a joke about him and *the eye of a Needle*—the man was chubby and didn't fit his name, but he was nonetheless all-seeing.

H.H. put a hand softly on her elbow to steady her, and Mary Joy understood he was also signaling that she needed to take her seat. At the same time, she could see H.H. was curious about the young man she had mentioned. In the South she would not have lingered so long, but this was a Northern line and Pullman followed the customs of the regions it traveled through.

She began to catalog the details slowly on her gloved fingers. "This young fella wore a ring right on this finger." She held up her pinkie. "Said he was in the distribution business in Detroit. Went on and on about big German muscle and a preacher who ran things. Now tell me you don't remember that."

As she spoke, a grin spread across his face. "Alfred," H.H. said. "Alfred Green, I believe. But I don't think he was as important as he thought he was. Least, that's how I saw it."

A porter came by to ask about olive oil.

H.H. put a hand up. "Big tippers only, if you can, and water down what you take out."

"Salad seasoning at market prices today. And Los Angeles?"

"There's just two cases from Chicago." H.H. pointed the white-shirted man toward the baggage car.

Mary Joy had begun to perspire. She pulled out a dainty square of fabric and used it to dab along her brow line. "What *was* that preacher's name, the one Alfred Green talked about?"

H.H. chortled. "A preacher, you say? What are we talking about, a Reverend Bernstein? You know it's the Purples that run Detroit."

"The paths of God are infinite."

"And the road to hell used to pay well."

"That is a blasphemy, H.H." Mary Joy's face flushed with the August heat. She knew that to any onlooker she seemed composed— she had been taught grace and comportment at all costs—but sometimes what she felt inside and what she allowed out were at vast odds. As fall approached especially, when the leaves dried and rattled and skittered through gutters, a deep worry could push through her as though a wind had blown up inside, carrying dirt and grit. They were still more than a month away from the leaves turning, but already she felt her nerves seizing on certain days. She focused on H.H.'s face and the feeling subsided.

The porter who'd asked for the olive oil came back along the corridor, the bottle hidden enough in his arm that it did look like salad dressing—though the amber liquid inside was too dark, and sloshed too much, if anyone had been paying close attention. But all of the porters were in on it anyway. Many of the travelers clearly knew too—at least those who were looking to buy. As the porter reached the passage end, he turned around and hissed to H.H., *"Mr. Davis . . ."* He tapped a finger to his eye for *"eye of the Needle"*— the conductor was approaching.

H.H.'s hand pressed Mary Joy's shoulder as he urged her toward the car where black passengers were permitted. Mary Joy didn't protest.

She had almost reached the end of the corridor when she stopped and came back toward H.H., who had picked up his clipboard and pencil. "Prangley," she said, a smile broad across her cheeks.

=⟨ 42 ⟩=

THE STARS HELD their own in the dark. That's all there seemed
to be: stars, dark, and, below them, the smell of cow pies. Charles
Prangley stood in the field, his white suede spectators sinking in mud
and shit, next to a bedraggled farmer in long-sleeved plaid flannel,
even though it was August. Mosquitoes tittered at his earlobes and
Prangley lifted a hand and slapped. A hum drifted toward them from
a long way off. Prangley pivoted.

"Ya hear that, eh?" the farmer said. "That'll be our gal."

Prangley squinted into the dark and kicked his shoes between
the tomato plants, wishing he'd remembered that, after you hand
over your money to bigwigs, you still have to deal with the grunts.
He'd met with Blaise Diesbourg so briefly he could barely remember
what he looked like. The famous "King Canada" had shaken his hand,
taken his money, then shown him to a car that would drive him out
to the farm. Even so, Prangley believed himself lucky. Everyone in
Detroit, it seemed, wanted to meet with Diesbourg. He was the one
with the planes, the one with the plan. He'd smuggled throughout
the dry years, and now that liquor was legal again in Canada, his business was that much easier. This farmer, Prangley knew, was just one of
the men Diesbourg rented; in fact, King Canada had probably bought
this field as a runway for twenty dollars.

But for Prangley, this new business investment was sizable. He'd cultivated the idea for a long time, and concluded that with Bunterbart gone and the men at odds and ends, it was time. If anything, he was late to the party. So he'd cleared out several stacks of bills, leaving behind a huge black space in the casket, put the money in a suitcase, and ferried it to Canada. He didn't like the way that hole looked. It had been several years since he'd been able to see the wood at the bottom of the coffin.

And now this bearded nobody with his unpainted house and mud under his nails was saying, *Watch those beefsteaks, eh,* as Prangley tramped between garden rows. But the airplane that would land in this field was Prangley's—he'd agreed to buy it outright, sight unseen. He listened to it come, rattling overhead, her belly visible: black with a white stripe, like a killer whale.

"Sweet Jesus!" Prangley cursed, clutching his trilby before it could roll off into the dirt. He crouched as the pilot put her down to the ground scarcely ten yards away. The field unfolded in smoke. When Prangley stood up, coughing, the farmer was laughing, a real belly laugh.

"Dirty business," the man said, clapping Prangley's shoulder as if they were school chums. Prangley saw now that the haze wasn't smoke at all, but clouds of thrown soil. "Just chews up the field," the farmer went on. "Look how many plants he took out. But there's your pretty girl."

The pilot was climbing down from the large biplane, goggles already pushed back on his head. Prangley coughed again, collected himself, went over. He looked up at the magnificent vehicle he'd purchased. The boy in him was silent with awe. When Prangley was growing up, his father hadn't been able to afford a horse and carriage—the family walked everywhere through the streets of Philadelphia, soles thin from wear, dodging steaming piles of dung. Prangley made a show of examining the aircraft carefully, although he knew little about such machines. It was not like buying an automobile, since he could not drive it himself. But it was a fine-looking plane. A bomber from the war, but recently painted and in decent condition.

"Bonjour. Ça va bien? Je suis Michel."

Prangley took the pilot's hand and peered at him. "What's he saying?" he asked the farmer as the pilot chattered amiably in French. He would need to get some schooling from someone, maybe beg a few phrases from Rosine at the Riviera, if he was going to retain this French flyboy he had hooked himself up with.

"Nice flying," he said sarcastically, knowing it wouldn't translate. He asked the farmer to tell the fellow to land a little more lightly next time. The pilot received the message and smiled mischievously, then pointed to the barn. The three men made their way through the field. After the farmer pulled the splintered wood door open, Prangley slowly grinned and nodded. Two old milk trucks held dominion over the space. A couple of sleepy cows blinked at them as they drove across the field, and the farmer and the pilot loaded the whiskey from truck to plane. This definitely beat dealing with a troop of unreliable men and an unpredictable river.

The pilot and the farmer spoke to one another in French as they worked, syllables that drifted thickly past Prangley. When the pilot spoke to him directly, Prangley thought he understood and nodded, but as the minutes wore on, Prangley realized that the words were like a stream, swirling and choking him, and he felt his power fading. He hadn't the slightest idea how to direct this fellow, who nodded and snickered at him in a foreign language. To the farmer, he said, "Tell him—"

The farmer grabbed Prangley's shoulder to reassure him. "Ah, don't worry. He knows. Boss told us where you want this taken."

The plane was meant to land in Ecorse township on a tract owned by Noah Zuckerwitz, the brother of one of Prangley's own men, Gerald. The boxer had been incapacitated for months now, but the brother was a fine connection and Prangley did not mind that this new business would help pay for a wheelchair and nurse for one of his men. It seemed a small penitence after all that had happened that year. Was he getting soft since Vern died, Prangley wondered? Or was it logical to put some money down to rebuild? Or perhaps it was because of the injury itself. The boxer got his balls shot off—one amputated, the other still intact but black as a monkey's paw, or so Gerald said—and there was something more pitiable in that than death.

Prangley stepped forward and shook the aviator's hand soberly before he departed, trying to communicate the solemnity of this first mission. He touched the side of the plane, ran his fingers over the rivets with reverence, then stepped back. He had never been so close to his own operations before—the realization came in a wild rush, and his face reddened with exhilaration and confusion. In his embarrassment, Prangley laughed. A small hiccup of joy.

The pilot laughed too, and climbed up into the plane. *"À demain,"* he called.

The engine ripped to life, sudden and enormous in the quiet of the farmland, the horizon that surrounded them with a thousand blind eyes.

={ 43 }=

ELSIE MOSS LOOKED out the boxcar diner window and could feel hard knots gathering in her shoulders, a flush of embarrassment on her cheeks. As she watched Gin Ing exit a cab, Elsie regretted phoning the woman. She'd tossed and turned half the night, and it showed in her eyes. She had painted her lids with makeup to try to hide the darkness behind a pale, shimmery powder, and now she felt overdone for daytime. She had only an hour before she had to be back to get Baby Johnny.

Gin Ing was the first to speak after the coffee and tea were ordered. Confidently and quietly, she thanked Elsie for meeting with her. Then she said, "He told me he was going to try to get away, but I didn't know what that meant. And I never would have started with him if I'd known he was hitched. He never wore a ring. You must know how clever he can be."

Elsie flushed and snapped her purse open and closed angrily, but said nothing. She watched Gin's hands moving across the table as she spoke. She didn't like to think that these were fingers Alfred had held, that those were arms he'd entwined, and beneath that blue dress was a bosom he'd rested his head upon, any more than, she supposed, Gin wanted to think these things of her. Elsie had known he wasn't altogether hers, but knowing it and having this mistress across from her were altogether different things.

"I hate myself for it," the woman insisted. "I met him because I caught him lying to my father. Don't know why I thought he wouldn't lie to me," Gin continued, as Elsie opened her purse again and this time took out a cigarette case. "He wrote me letters. Recently—that's how I know he's out there."

"Where are they?" Elsie said, her pink lips curling around the cigarette. "Show them to me."

But Gin hadn't brought them. "I could not let you read such intimate things."

Elsie drew back as a waiter arrived. He slid only one cup and saucer onto the table, serving Elsie and leaving Gin without the tea she had ordered. Elsie looked up at him, confused, but Gin didn't seem fazed.

The waiter returned with the pitcher of cream, but again no tea.

Elsie leaned into the table and whispered to Gin, "Without the letters, how can I believe you?"

Alfred had made off with a large sum of money, continued Gin, but she was certain he'd stashed some in a safety box here in Detroit. He'd written her from New York, which was cruel of him, because he knew she'd never go back there. And he'd written her two letters from Oklahoma in close succession—lonely, nonsensical missives begging forgiveness.

If he adored her so, Elsie asked abruptly, why hadn't he taken her along with him? As angry as she was, she still couldn't drink her coffee—it would be rude to do so when the other woman hadn't been served.

Gin gazed out the window. The sun was streaming in and Elsie felt suddenly that it was too bright and hot inside the restaurant. "I know you don't trust me," Gin said. "I wouldn't either. But we are on the same side."

"We aren't at all," Elsie replied quickly, though when she looked at the Chinese woman again, she could see the hardness in the bow of her mouth, the stiffness of her shoulders and neck. Behind Gin's dark eyes was a hollowness that Elsie recognized from her own mirror. She set down the cigarette and picked up the coffee cup at last, managing a mouthful. She swallowed, her gaze on the table. When she looked up again, her eyes went to the other woman's neck, which was covered by a pale silk scarf. "You said he mistreated you?"

Gin put her hand up to touch the knot of fabric, as if checking that it was securely fastened. She deflected, "Was Alfred always kind to you?"

Elsie pondered the question as she took another sip. Then she too deflected: how long had Gin and Alfred been together?

"You don't want that answer," Gin assured her.

"Then tell me more about the letters," Elsie insisted.

Gin took out a piece of paper and unfolded it. "These are the addresses where he stayed. If you want to phone them, they may confirm a man of his description stayed there. I think they have a forwarding address. But I can't say what pseudonyms he used. He didn't tell me."

Elsie took the paper and watched how it twitched between her fingers. Elsie had never placed a long-distance call—that was something she'd seen only in pictures—and now she was supposed to call up strangers on the other side of the country and ask them questions about a man with no name?

The waiter returned with the bill, dropping it on the table. Elsie quickly looked at the total, noting it was for both her coffee and the tea that hadn't arrived. "Excuse me." The waiter stopped. "We never got the tea."

"Owner said dishwashers ain't customers." The waiter offered a defeated shrug before leaving.

Elsie felt her head rear back, dumbfounded at the insult, but Gin didn't flinch or look at the man. She collected her hat and purse from the bench seat beside her and continued their conversation. "What if the money is just sitting here in Detroit while he's who knows where? If there is money, shouldn't one of us have it? You deserve it, and now that he's officially deceased, I'm sure you could get it." She stood up to go.

Elsie grabbed Gin's arm.

"I ... loved him," Gin said, though Elsie noticed the woman's voice quieted as if she wasn't certain she should use the words. "Look, I just want to know where he is. They're more likely to tell his wife than me."

With that, Gin left, hurrying past the window and across the street. Elsie looked down at the paper on the table with the hotel addresses. She could feel the eyes of the other diners on her. She dropped a dime on the table, snatched up the note page, and tucked it into her purse. She left no tip.

={ 44 }=

IN RENO, NEVADA, on the edge of town, the cream-colored Duesenberg sat outside a mechanic's shop, waiting for a buyer, under a hand-painted sign that said, *Cars for Cash*. The admirable vehicle had sputtered to a stop and its owner had been forced to walk twenty miles through the night in his fine shoes. It had been waiting for parts from the Midwest for three months—but even if the parts arrived, no one in Reno seemed to know how to fix the custom automobile.

Alfred Moss himself ducked under the hood and tweaked a few things, but nothing had helped. A mechanic had offered to tow it, along with Moss, to San Francisco, five hours away, but although the coastal city intrigued him, Moss disagreed with the man's price. So now the automobile sat, grass around the wheels getting long. Everything about its slick exterior said that it would be the best ride of your life, and Moss had assured the garage owner of a generous cut if it were to sell. Still, no one got lucky enough to blow that much coin on a beauty that wouldn't test-drive.

Inside the Hotel Golden, Moss went by the name Freddy McGee. Sun-baked a deep tan, he'd left Alphonse Novarro and Alfred Maxwell behind—those names didn't suit him in the new climate. Reno was post–gold rush but still actively mining in places with names like Bald Mountain, Lone Tree, Ruby Hill, Starvation Canyon. Gnarled miners and sad, lovely whores were still everywhere, and as

Freddy, Moss watched the men stream through the town on summer nights, heading for the cathouses. To fit with the rougher working environment, he'd grown a mustache thick as a squirrel. Above it, his black hair swooped back, glossy and immaculate as ever.

"Usual, Mr. McGee?" the bartender called.

Moss nodded and collected his drink the instant it was poured. An unopened package beneath his arm, he steered himself and his whiskey over to a private table by the window looking onto Center Street. This was the street that Betsy Vargas would walk up when she came to meet him.

Fortuitously, he'd hooked up with a vine of a girl whose father ran a sawdust-floor casino that was looking to expand. Moss met her his third week in Reno, and clearly saw that she was the one to seduce—but slowly. He wouldn't get tangled up in promises and babies again.

The only problem with Betsy was that she pursued him like a bloodhound on a scent—if he didn't sleep with her soon, he was sure he was as likely to get thrashed as if he'd done so too quickly. It occurred to him that the girl's determination might be because she was in love for the first time, but what he saw was opportunity. Her father, Mr. Felix Vargas, wore a white straw hat and was never without a silk scarf in his pocket. Like Moss, Vargas had a mustache, though his spiked down into a small pointy black beard. Wherever he walked, he kept his eyes straight ahead, as if he needed no one he passed along the way—and it was that, along with the rumors of the casino's expansion, that told Moss this was a man to get into business with.

Moss sat down and examined the postmark on the package: Oklahoma City. It had been months since he'd phoned the hotel where he'd bunked to see if any mail had come—and through laziness or incompetence, the hotel hadn't bothered to forward it on until now. He couldn't remember if he'd written to Ernest Krim or Gin Ing. He tore through the first envelope, exposing a second one inside. Grubby along the edges, it bore the mark of Detroit. He recognized Gin's stretched-out handwriting.

From the envelope, he freed a newspaper clipping—and stared down at the dark version of himself that had appeared in print. *Obituaries*, it said at the top of the page. He gazed at the photo. In the nine months since he'd left home, he'd forgotten it had ever been taken. A clean-shaven face with mischievous eyes glared back at him. It almost made him nostalgic.

He read the first three paragraphs of Gin's letter, but some instinct, or fear, made him fold the paper up hastily. He scrunched it back inside its envelope.

"Who's that?" Betsy said, joining him at the table. He had missed seeing her pass the window, and now Moss jammed Gin Ing's envelope and letter inside the larger one before the girl could see it.

"Cousin on my mother's side," he lied, turning the news clipping around so she could read it. "Alfred."

Betsy sat down and gazed at the facts of his death. "Long article— he must have been important."

"Sure wasn't," Moss declared, taking a gulp.

She busied herself with reading the clipping and Moss stashed the envelope and letter under the table. Betsy glanced up, her heart-shaped face dark with emotion that, from experience, he knew would hold her in its entirety for a minute or two then flit away. She was a sincere young thing, but her interests waned quickly. In the nine weeks he'd known her, she'd tried horseback riding, embroidery, driving, golf, and dance lessons. Even those activities she excelled at were quickly abandoned. Her favorite drink changed almost daily. The only thing to which she seemed deeply committed was him. It was possible that few had paid her much attention—for although she was not a bad-looking girl, she was a little horsey in the mouth, and she seemed less mature than she claimed to be in years.

Betsy looked up. "What a sad story. The resemblance is striking, though."

"Really, do you think so?" Alfred Moss lifted a finger for the waiter.

"Oh yes, you could be brothers." She raised the page beside him in the air, pursed her lips, and studied the two men.

"Funny, I always thought he was a bit of a nance." Moss grinned at himself in the photo.

"Well, you *are* the more handsome, Freddy," the girl said, leaning forward, fist tucked under her chin, the sympathy she'd felt for the unknown dead man abandoned. Her ups and downs were tough to stay attuned to. He did his best: laughed and ordered a drink for her. He picked one she hadn't had in at least ten days—a Tom Collins.

"So, when are we meeting with Felix?" he asked, but Betsy evaded the question.

"You aren't a bit torn up?"

Moss waved his hand, the emerald ring now absent from his pinkie, only a white circle of skin where it had been: hocked to invest in Betsy's father's joint. "I barely knew him."

The girl wasn't shy; she kicked back half her drink as soon as it was brought over. She swiveled around in her chair and uncrossed and crossed her legs again, one shoe bobbing rhythmically beside him. The shoes had scarlet bows that tied around her ankles. On her head, in a light kasha color, the latest Joan Crawford hat smoothed down her hair, leaving her eyes and the tiniest fringe of bang peeking out. Domed with embroidery floss, the hat had been designed for the movie star out in Hollywood, and now it sold at Sears, Roebuck and Co. for $1.95. Moss knew because he'd ordered it himself for Betsy—it came in a box along with a western shirt he'd picked out for himself. He'd been a bit floored, and disappointed, that they'd arrived faster than the hypoid axle for the Duesenberg. The girl's father was wealthy enough that he could buy her anything, but Betsy remained charmed by the gesture.

"How far apart are New York and Detroit?" Betsy wondered, wiping a fingertip across her glass to move the beads of condensation.

Moss scrutinized her before glancing out the window at the street. "Twice as far as here to San Francisco, I reckon. Maybe more."

She said she guessed that was a long way, and no wonder he and Alfred hadn't been close relatives. She wanted to know more about New York—the girl was always pressing him, asking him about the shops there and the shows. Then Betsy said something that almost made him spit. "How'd you get so hooked up with the tongues there, anyway?"

"Pardon me." Moss set down his drink, picked up his napkin, and dabbed at his mustache. "I don't know what you're talking about."

"Well, isn't that what you called them? The tongues? You know, with the Chinamen."

Moss knew she meant the tong. But he wasn't about to correct her any more than he was about to admit that his name was Alfred and his own photo was the one in the *Detroit Free Press* obituary. She'd forget the tong again when they'd had another drink. Though chances were it was drink that had loosened his restraint in the first place.

Back when Elsie was just one of several girls he met up with in the clubs, he'd made a trip to New York. While stumbling through Chinatown one night, hoping to buy something to smoke, he met Wei Ing, Gin's father, and talked a good game, offering to connect the tong with an opium source in Canada. Fearless in his friend making, he knew his charm and stories could cut across all kinds and creeds, and his vision was acute for spotting the hungry, the comers, and the strivers. Moss probably would have got out of there without more than a kick in the pants if it hadn't been for Gin. She inserted herself into the room and handed Wei Ing a message, calling her father away to the telephone.

As he reflected on this, Betsy pouted, stirring her Tom Collins with the straw. "I'm still jealous you had a girlfriend before me. An Oriental one."

Moss knew that, every time he spoke, Betsy's small world got bigger. He couldn't resist; he dropped his voice and spoke low. "She was a jade tigress. Daughter of a warlord."

Betsy set her glass down hard on the table. "What's that mean?" A hitch in her voice told him she was angry more than hurt—and also that he'd better shut up quick.

"It means she was an unknown land," he said, leaning back in the hard chair, testing her a little. He tapped his pinkie finger on the table between them and smirked.

Betsy picked up her drink and rattled her ice. "I think you're reading too many serials, Freddy."

"You sure got a nice library here in Reno." He smirked.

"I can think of better things to do than go to the library," she said, one finger rubbing his knee beneath the table. He moved slightly and the package with Gin's letter crinkled between his shoe and the wall.

"Not before we meet your father," he said, catching her hand and bringing her fingers above the table. He kissed them, to take the sting from the rejection.

"Oh, what is it with you and my father?" Betsy pouted. "Honestly, sometimes I think you'd rather sleep with Felix than with me."

"Hush, now," Moss told her, moving his thumb up her arm, circling the tender spot on the inside of her elbow. Betsy smiled. Moss fixed his gaze on the window, watching for her father, even as he continued to stroke her bare forearm, making the delicate black hairs rise from her golden skin.

Gin Ing had written to tell him that Prangley was making a fine fortune off his disappearance. And that the only one in the whole charade who'd got nothing was her. She'd stopped the tong from killing Moss (her words), then left her father and her family in New York and followed him to Detroit, and all she'd got for her time and efforts was a broken heart. Moss knew this version of events to be untrue. He didn't know if she was threatening to expose him, but the tone in the letter implied she might—to tell his wife would be bad, but to tell Prangley would be much worse. Still, it would be much *much* worse if she were to return home to New York and tell her father about their continued affair. But Gin wouldn't dare go back, would she? As for him, during the two weeks he'd been in Manhattan that winter, he'd been sure never to travel below Houston. Hell, he didn't even dip below Fourteenth.

Reading Gin's letter, with its surplus of heartbreak and malice, Moss knew that Reno was the best place for him—two thousand miles from all his troubles. Thank the stars he'd not written to Gin since Tulsa. At least, he didn't think he had. Why he'd written to her at all, he couldn't say—he blamed it on some bad marijuana. As his fingertips climbed Betsy's lace sleeve and rubbed the skin there, making her large teeth bite her lip in a smile, he wondered if he ought to bed this girl after all. He imagined himself as a ranch don, riding across wedding-gifted land, a brood of blue-eyed, olive-skinned children following behind him. He also wondered if she had a sister.

"With women it's just like standing on the edge of a perfect deep black lake," Moss found himself saying. "You want to jump in, but you also know that you'll come up wet, or maybe you won't come up again at all." His gaze slipped from the window to Betsy, then back again—he felt her shiver beneath his touch—but it was New York two years ago that he saw in his mind.

GIN ING'S FATHER was not one of the Four Brothers in the Hip Sing guild, but he was nonetheless close friends with, and a hatchet man to, Mock Duck—the portly leader of the powerful tong. There was nothing subtle about Mock Duck. He dressed in butcher's chain mail and carried an ax and a pair of revolvers at all times. Unlike the tong leader, Wei Ing was a slim man who favored bowler hats and hidden blades. At 105 pounds, he was probably slimmer than Gin. Gin once told Moss that by the age of fourteen she'd seen three assassinations right before her eyes, that the blood of men who'd betrayed the Hip Sing had splattered across her lips even as she took cover. Moss supposed he should have interpreted this as a warning. Instead, it had magnetized him. Who was this woman who could see a man chopped up before her eyes and still display so much gentility?

The tong dealt in opium, and also cards, but Gin claimed she didn't smoke and didn't play. She might have avoided Alfred Moss entirely except that, on the evening they met, she was the only person present with impeccable English. Her father's understanding was just good enough that Moss got through the door—spinning a story from half-truths about how the Canadians provided opium to their Chinese railroad workers as relief and reward. Straight from the Silk Road to Royal Navy ships, Moss elaborated. And they still got too much of the stuff. Oodles of opium! Why, living within spitting distance of the border, he knew customs officers ready to go on the take. He'd be happy to share such information with the tong for a finder's fee. Imagine: legal opium, with King George as your importer.

He held up his fingers as if they grasped a golden ring. His tale had fascinated the tong, even if they weren't entirely sold.

There were a thousand Chinese people in that area of New York, coming and going into tearooms and herbalists, laundries and fan-tan parlors, conducting business on the narrow sidewalks, but until Gin stepped into the room with a message for her father, Alfred hadn't realized that every face he'd passed in Chinatown had been male. Where were the wives and the daughters—left behind in China, or cloistered in back rooms? In the hard world of men, Gin had seemed that much more feminine, more intriguing.

She wore a tourmaline dress, a translucent neckline showing her collarbone and the draped skirt making her swish through the place: she nearly shone. Her neck was pale, and perfect as a swan's. She leaned over and said something in Mock Duck's ear, then moved on to speak with Wei Ing, the skinny man with the grin like a knife, who turned out to be her father.

Later that night, Gin had said to Alfred, "You're full of bunk."

He remembered how she leaned down to grab her toes, stretching her legs where she sat on the silk-covered mattress, naked. "I believe you that the Canadians kept their workforce anesthetized during the building of the railroad, but not since. That's a bald-faced lie—and it won't take the Hip Sing long to find you."

"You knew?" Moss turned from where he was urinating in the bath-room. "So you like to make love to liars?" He pulled his pants back up and staggered through the darkened room. "But you won't tell?"

"Tell them what? That the opium connection is baloney, or that your name isn't Al Baxter?"

"But my name is—" He faltered and smiled. He was coming down from a high, and his eyes were still dreamy. Their lovemaking had been lethargic.

"Big Al Baxter," Gin prompted him. "Walked up Baxter Street on the way here, didn't you?"

"Won't confirm or deny." Moss flopped beside her on the mattress on the floor. He studied her face through foggy eyes. "You didn't enjoy yourself enough."

In a noncommittal tone, Gin said that she had. "But that has nothing to do with it. Did you think I was fooled by you?"

"I'd never underestimate you, doll." He kissed her foot on the sole. Gin scrutinized the dome of his hair. Moss kissed the underside of one of her calves.

"Well, then what makes you think I won't tell?" Gin cocked an eyebrow.

Moss climbed up her thighs, leaving wet trails with his tongue.

"Oh," Gin said, lying down, her hands cupping his ears. "I see." Then eventually her hands didn't need to guide him anymore. She raised her arms above her head, tipped her chin back, and grabbed at the air—her inner thighs clamping hard on either side of his face. She had not quite completed her climax when Moss suddenly stopped. Gin looked down. She patted his head. Then she grabbed his hair and pulled his face to one side. It was no use. He was fast asleep with his mouth still firmly planted in her lap.

MOSS STROLLED BACK into Chinatown three days later, not yet aware that Wei Ing had heard that a smooth-talking *gweilo* had kept his daughter out all night, practically within sight of the opium dens and everyone he did business with. As soon as Ing caught sight of Moss, he threw a knife at his head—and missed, he told his target, only because he intended to. To kill him with one jab would be too generous. No *foreign ghost* was going to touch his family, Mr. Ing said—although Moss understood only because the words came out of the mouth of a well-dressed young Chinese translator at Wei Ing's side.

Mr. Ing pressed Moss against a wall with a second blade hovering above his belt. A stream of venomous syllables fell from Mr. Ing's lips as he ushered Moss down an alley, through a door, and downstairs into a basement used as a soy pit. The acrid smell of fermenting soybeans assaulted Moss's nostrils. Then the small assassin punched him in the abdomen with the force of a sledgehammer. It was several minutes before Moss could breathe again, but the translator and Wei Ing waited. As Moss straightened, the knife appeared again at Moss's gut, and Ing was speaking ferociously.

The young translator cleared his throat and said nervously in impeccable English: "He asks you to spread your legs, so he can . . ." The young fellow paused, fidgeting with his suit buttons, as Mr. Ing continued in Cantonese. ". . . cut off your balls more effectively . . . with two smooth strokes," he interpreted.

Moss choked out a protest. He begged the translator to remind Wei Ing of the opium connection he had offered—praying Gin had not already exposed him as a phony. The two Chinese men consulted, then Ing pulled the knife back slightly.

The translator said grimly: "He can let you live, but his only other option is to kill his daughter. This is an act that cannot go unpunished."

"That seems fair," Alfred muttered, mopping his hand across his forehead.

The translator gave Mr. Ing the response.

Wei Ing stepped forward, his face kissing distance from Moss's. "Names," Ing said crisply, glaring. "Names in Canada."

"Rosine Perrault at the Riviera," Alfred said, as confidently as if he were giving directions to a good restaurant. This was the only place he had ever smoked opium—and he'd done it only once. So far as he knew, it wasn't the usual stock-in-trade of the Riviera. Rosine was just a barmaid and a madam who kept a little for herself and indulged on occasion, in a back room.

Wei Ing stepped back, his face unreadable. He spoke to the translator in muted tones. Then came the English: "Next time you come to Chinatown, he says 'your balls will drop to the ground like small oranges from a dying tree.' He only spares you now because you bring business connections, and as a man of business, you may have some value."

Moss boarded a train that day back to Detroit. Upon arrival, he learned one of the young ladies he'd been seeing in the speakeasies in Black Bottom was now in a family way, and claimed he was the father. Elsie was no Gin Ing, but to Moss she was a fine-looking gal. Better than that, she had a sleepy-eyed father who had never thrown anything more than a pint glass and left all knives in the kitchen for his wife to cook with. The decision was easy. Alfred dashed down to Simmons and Clark and nabbed a frosty diamond in a geometric silver setting, all cash, no layaway. He used the five hundred he'd taken off the Hip Sing tong the night he first gave them the opium railroad story.

He had never expected the girl from the tong to follow him back—in part because he was confident her father would murder her as he'd said. But Gin showed up that summer, just as Elsie was beginning to swell in the midsection. Her initial story was that as punishment her father had promised her in a blind marriage; *I am hiding*, she told Alfred. Well then, hide, he said. It has nothing to do with me. But with Elsie blotchy and bloated, and the threat of Chinatown very far away, the tug of Gin Ing was like a moon to the tides.

={ 45 }=

KITTY McCLOUD FLOPPED on the bed, Rosine Perrault behind her. She took a hit from the pipe and lay back. In Rosine's room, everything was a deep blue and Kitty always felt as if she were floating in night sky. Rosine leaned in and kissed her deeply on the mouth. Rosine's bedroom was located behind the office, which was in turn just off the bar, and above them were the rooms of the Riviera hotel. Sometimes, when Kitty stayed over, she heard the girls entertaining Rosine's customers, and sometimes Rosine had to get up and let someone in or out, or broker deals, but Kitty only ever visited the bar and this one room. She had no interest in the business, only its owner. When Rosine would return to her, it was always as a silver streak of flesh in the dark. Tonight, though there were interruptions, the pleasures being had upstairs sounded like the squeaking of mice.

"I can't move," Kitty said into Rosine's mouth. "Touch me." She wasn't aware she'd voiced the desire; it seemed as though Rosine simply knew it and moved to accommodate.

Rosine slid her hands over Kitty's shoulders, unbuttoning her collared shirt. Her mouth eased down Kitty's slim neck. Rosine slung herself over Kitty and left her red lipstick on her breast. Kitty lay back and breathed in deep, closing her eyes, Rosine becoming an ocean that churned up all her emotions, pushed her under and buoyed her up and carried her.

They lay together for a long time, sometimes kissing, sometimes just still, sometimes Rosine fiddling with matches and sucking on the stub of her cigar.

"*Je t'aime,*" Kitty said. The only French Rosine had taught her besides curses. "*Je t'aime, ma garce.*"

WHEN KITTY AWAKENED, Rosine and her cigarillo were both gone—she was somewhere beyond the office, in the front bar, doing business. Kit crossed the bedroom and put on her pants. She went into the office and found a pen. Standing there in pleated trousers and a man's open shirt, she jotted down a series of black notes, large dots with long flags. When there was a whole row of them, she stopped and carefully drew in straight lines behind them, giving the musical notation a staff and bars. Holding the piece of paper, Kitty walked back into the blue bedroom and sat down on the bed, humming what she'd just got down. She dressed herself more properly, eager—in spite of the pull of Rosine—to slip away and find a piano. She threw her fedora onto her head and glanced at herself in the mirror she usually only looked into while she and Rosine made love. Her eyes were still hollow from the opium, but she could think of nothing to correct the problem, so she pulled the brim of her hat lower. She quietly left both bedroom and office, the piece of music clutched in her hand.

A Chinese man was speaking in hushed tones with Rosine at the door, but that was much less unusual to Kit than the man who was slumped on the corner of the bar. Kitty was nearer to him, and maybe that was why he caught her eye. Hunched on a bar stool, he was finely dressed but passed out, a thick strand of drool hanging between his lips and the bar surface. She knew his face, and at first she thought she was hallucinating. She put a hand out and steadied herself against the wall, dropping the music. Then she walked behind the bar and helped herself. Picking up the ice pick, she stabbed and chipped. Rosine noticed her then, and looked at her sharply. Kitty shrugged and continued fixing a Cuba Libre. She downed it, staring at the passed-out preacher, as Rosine closed the door behind the Chinese man.

Rosine came around the bar. Paper crackled beneath her heel, and she bent and picked up Kitty's dropped notes. "What are you doing?" she asked. "You shouldn't be out here."

Kitty took another sip of the rum and cola and nodded at the passed-out man, his hat beside him on the counter. Then she nodded to the office, and both women silently exited, leaving Charles Prangley to his dreams, alone in the empty bar.

"Why are you dressed?" Rosine wanted to know. "Stay with me."

Kit said only, "Who's that man out there?"

Rosine waved her hand, the one with the music in it. "Who cares? A customer. Over-celebrating a purchase he has made."

"Does he come here often?"

Rosine weighed the question. Not often, she said finally. Enough.

"Well, I never seen him dressed like that, but I think he hired me to play the organ once."

"Is that all?"

"No." Kitty watched as Rosine paced around the office, straightening things. "It was at the church where my sister works."

Rosine said there were lots of them who came in one wouldn't expect: priests, doctors, barristers, or accountants. "If it has *les couilles*, it fucks. If it has a mouth, it drinks. It comes here, but you did not see it."

Les couilles. Balls. It was one of Rosine's favorite words, and that was why Kit knew it well. It was the kind of disparagement Rosine tossed out without thinking. It was Kit's suspicion that such moody statements made Rosine feel better about the other part of her business—the young women, much younger than Kit herself, who came there to make money, escaping from fates that Rosine said were worse than anything they would know within her walls.

Rosine spouted off in French before realizing she was talking only to herself. Then she said pointedly: "I don't care about that reverend. What I do not understand is why these Chinese men keep coming in here requesting opium from me. I tell each of them, 'I do not have it,' and each acts as though he does not believe me. This is the third time in four months."

"But you do have hop." Kit jerked her thumb over her shoulder at the bedroom.

"For *us*. This is not some opium den. If they are regulars and want some after they pay for a girl, then maybe, fine, what do you call it, a taste? *Peut-être.*"

Kit still felt languorous from the drug. The gut-punch she'd felt when she saw Charles Prangley in the bar was fading. She sank down on a hard chair and said, "The dreaming I did! Holy hell!" She ran a hand through her short hair.

"You did appear happy," Rosine said more softly, and Kit looked at her, in her thrown-on slip dress, and realized she was barely more present than Kit was. How did the woman conduct business while stoned? At all times, she had a clarity Kitty didn't possess but admired.

"What is this?" Rosine peered at the scrap of paper with musical notation she still held in her hand.

"Oh." Kit smiled sheepishly and put her hand out for it. "I dream music sometimes—but usually by the time I can get to a pen, it's already vanished. It's something I'm always chasing, like a ribbon torn away by the wind. This time, I caught it."

"What do you know about hair ribbons?"

Kit hummed the sketched-out melody. "Oh my. Big Sister dressed me up proper—or tried to—after my father died. Then one day she found me standing in his closet, wearing one of his suits with the pants rolled up, struggling to get a four-in-hand knot into his tie."

A flush came to Rosine's cheeks as she tried to imagine it. "How old were you?"

"Twelve, maybe."

"I think we look alike," Rosine said, taking a compact out of the desk drawer and using it to assess herself. She plucked out a lipstick from among the plain lead pencils and reddened her mouth.

"Who? You and Faye?" Kit asked, only half paying attention.

"Yes, your sister."

"Faye?" Kit asked again. "You can't mean that."

"*Oui.* I thought so that time we ran into her on the street."

"You're crazy," Kit said, slipping a finger under the thin strap of Rosine's dress and pulling her in for a kiss.

A little while later, as Kit walked out of the bar, she passed by the unconscious pastor. She glanced at him, remembering what Rosine had said about not seeing him.

Kitty stumbled through Sandwich town—the Dominion House was already closed for the night, so she couldn't go knocking there—and under the bridge construction, where the tower loomed up, three large black *X*'s like strike marks against the periwinkle sky. Earlier that month, the footbridge cables had been raised and in Detroit the band had played "God Save the King." The bridge workers, small as tin soldiers, had climbed on the tops of the towers. Even here, the last girder for the road deck would soon be positioned. Against the night, long footbridges connected the towers, but they looked as flimsy to Kit as crepe paper birthday streamers. A car was what she needed, she realized, looking at the pale wood planks. If she could afford to buy a car by the time the bridge opened, there would be nothing to stop her from driving across it every day to see Rosine. Kit nodded and kept walking, humming the scrap of melody louder, working out the next bit.

ELSIE MOSS SAT on the bedroom floor, Alfred's shirts strewn about, chests and dresser drawers overturned. Nine-month-old John crawled nimbly across the mess and tried to stand, clutching the wood boards of the dresser where the drawers normally sat. He stood teetering and smiled at his mother with large eyes. "Yes, aren't you good?" she said, but there was no happiness in her tone. "Johnny," she told the baby, "I been looking for this damn security box key all summer. Tell me if you find a key. *Key*. Do you know what a key is?"

The boy promptly fell onto his bottom, spilling a box of cigarettes that had been atop the dresser. They rolled across the floor, and with chubby fingers he reached for one.

"That Chinawoman is a liar, Johnny. There's no security box. There's no stash in our home. There's no—" Elsie lunged forward and snatched the cigarette from the boy, who was picking out strands of the tobacco and lifting them toward his open mouth.

She scolded him, and he cried and reached out for the tobacco he'd lost. She put away the cigarettes, pressing the lid down firmly on the box and setting it again on top of the dresser. As she did, her gaze settled on her hands and she stood looking at the geometric setting of her wedding ring. If what Gin had said was true, her whole marriage was a lie—not just the end of it, when she strayed, but all of it. She took off the ring and handed it to the child to play with. The baby stopped crying and turned it round in his fist, fascinated. Then, bored, he dropped it onto the floorboards.

"I'm going to pawn that thing," Elsie said out loud, although the child had left the room, crawling over shirts into the dining room. She bent and picked it up.

She heard Willie Lynch call her name through the screen door, and told him to come in. She tripped over hangers on the way out of the bedroom. Willie had picked up her son and was bouncing him. He glanced over at her unusually clumsy entrance and saw the ring pinched between her fingers. He paused, assessing. "So . . . you're still looking for that secret security box key that woman from the funeral told you about?"

Elsie didn't say anything.

"She's trying to get something from you, and she was willing to tell you anything. I know a liar when I see one, and I never saw her with Mr. Moss. Sure, Gerald said there might have been a woman, but that's Gerald. Not once did I see your husband with anyone."

"Never?" Elsie asked, because she felt deep down that Gin had been telling her the truth.

"There was a couple times Mr. Moss didn't want me to tag along. A few times he went to the Powhatan."

"Never get married, Willie."

"Okay," Willie said. He was wearing a summer suit, and the baby had become fascinated by the orange flower he'd stuck in his lapel. How many times had she seen Gin? And how many stories had the woman sold her? Willie asked.

"Just two times," Elsie said.

Willie replied, "Two times too many."

"Do you know that the bank had Alfred's accounts locked up until after the funeral—and there was only a hundred dollars in there *in total*?"

"You told me that already."

"Did I?"

"Yeah, like all summer. Forget the hundred bucks. Look," Willie said, smiling and watching the baby grab for the zinnia, unable to pull it out of his lapel, "if you do the run with me in the cab, like we've been talking about, you'll make three thousand dollars in a day."

"I can't do that. I'm terrified of being arrested or, worse, shot at by these Prohibition agents you hear about."

Willie scoffed and insisted, "Think how much you would make." He slid the stalk from his buttonhole and twirled the flower over the baby, just out of reach.

"Where do we get the cab?"

"Two cabs," Willie corrected her. "Ever since them Purples got themselves all locked up on extortion charges, it is a wide-open market." When he saw her anxious expression, he said, "You can do this. I had you out there practicing your driving all summer."

But she had never driven alone, and it was so far, Elsie argued. "Those are roads I don't know."

"You'll follow right behind my taxi the whole way. I'll be waving to you in the rearview. Taxicabs, innocent yellow cabs. No reason to ever pull us over as long as we follow the rules of the road. Suitcases full of hooch loaded tight right there in the back. It's beautiful."

Elsie watched as Willie twirled the flower and let the baby catch it, his fingers pulling at the petals. She protested again, saying she didn't look like a taxi driver—how many lady cabdrivers were there? They'd get her a man's coat and muss her hair and she'd pass for the part, he said. What about the baby, she asked. Willie had an answer for that too: his sister would take him. For three days? Elsie persisted. Well, said Willie, look how strong he was—almost weaned, wasn't he?

"Where will we stay?"

"Wherever we like. At a hotel."

Willie grinned at the baby and the mess he was making of the flower, but Elsie had a feeling it was not the child he was thinking about. She had made certain Willie understood she had a boyfriend in New York—she knew he'd heard her mention the name, Frank Brennan, to her friend Judy.

"I'm sure that, with the amount we'll pull in, we can afford separate rooms," he reassured her now. Baby John had finished mashing the flower, and the petals had fallen all over the dining room.

"I don't want to be a criminal." Elsie turned her wedding ring in her hand.

"Everyone's a criminal," Willie said as Elsie sat, her resistance loosening. "My dad was a good man because he provided, not because he listened to some cockeyed government. You'd be surprised who's on the take. Especially the fucking hypocrites."

Elsie shushed him as if he were a child. "Don't you talk that way in front of Baby John." But she wondered even as she reprimanded Willie if it was because she herself didn't want to hear what he might tell her.

Willie rose as if to go, but instead paced around the room, his smooth face bent in a grimace, the two moles by his eye wrinkling. Finally, he went to the door. "There's one thing about our trip," he said before he left. "You might want a gun—just in case. Do you have one?"

Elsie guessed she must have made a horrified expression, because he backtracked, holding his palm out flat. "No, don't worry. You won't need it, you won't need it, I promise. Never mind."

293

={ 47 }=

THE SECRETARY'S HANDS kept climbing her neck nervously, Mary Joy Davis noticed, to make some adjustment to her hair, though the fingers found little there. She had cut it recently, Mary Joy concluded, and was not yet accustomed to the shorter style.

"What is it like being so close to Canada?" Mary Joy asked. "I've read that Reverend Prangley campaigns very actively for temperance."

Faye McCloud scrutinized her. Cautiously, she admitted, "He preaches against it. But Prohibition has been in effect so long now, I'm not sure how many really listen. It's legal over there." There was a flicker in her face, but Mary Joy couldn't tell what it meant. "Once, he chartered a boat to search for a man who was rumored to have disappeared while rumrunning on the river."

"How terrible!" Mary Joy exclaimed.

"Yes, it was. But it's strange how many new members it wound up bringing to the church. Alfred Moss, the poor fellow, became quite beloved." Faye McCloud nodded at a folded flyer that lay on the sideboard near the church newsletter. "That's his obit there." Then she frowned at the accounts ledger she had been working on. She picked up her eraser again.

Mary Joy stood and went over to pick up the handbill. She gazed at the photograph: the handsome face of the man she and H.H. had met on the train showed a slight twist of a smile. She reached back, took out her hat pin, and reinserted it, straightening the large-brimmed hat on her head. Then she turned as she heard the *whump* of the outer door.

Charles Prangley entered the church quickly, his tall, hard frame propelled forward at a good clip. He stopped abruptly. Mary Joy smiled. The secretary came out from behind her tiny desk to make the introductions. "Nice to meet you, Mrs. Davis," the gangly preacher replied, though his eyes said otherwise. "Who did you say had referred you to our church?"

"I'm here to ask you to keep an open heart. I think we have like-minded attitudes, and there's much our two communities can offer each other." Mary Joy took pains to answer the question without providing a name as referral. But charm and evasion were how initiatives always got going, in religion as in business. H.H. had taught her well—he'd picked up a lot listening to men pitching one another on trains in between reading their newspapers and drinking on the sly.

Reverend Prangley led her into his office and they seated themselves with the door left open.

"The Pentecostal congregations are mixed. Do you mind if I ask if that is why you are here?" He said it with a smile, but the words landed sour with Mary Joy Davis.

"I am pleased that more churches are truly living by the words of Jesus. But it is not at all why I'm here." She set her purse down at her feet. Neither the reverend nor the secretary had offered to take her jacket, and for mid-September it was still warm. She kept the tweed bolero on but removed her silk gloves. "I am a Christian woman, but I also have business, much as you do." She dropped her voice. "You see, I met a fellow from Detroit—told me he had been in the importing business for some time. He mentioned several associates, and you were among them."

Before Prangley could react, Mary Joy went on: "Now, my husband is one of the head porters on the Pullman cars, the Santa Fe line. That's three days from Chicago to Los Angeles—and there are certain products that we need a great quantity of in order to keep travelers comfortable. All that way, you can imagine one goes through a great deal of food and, of course, drink. Though myself, I have never had a drop."

"I am against imbibing as well. I have led many local campaigns—"

"And I'm sure they've been very successful."

"Oh, they have been. We have been using boats and now an airplane to help Prohibition agents apprehend offenders and criminals."

"You have access to an airplane?"

"Yes, yes, I do. Just recently." Prangley grinned proudly and leaned back.

"So you are a man who knows how to look to the future. Businesses have to grow."

"That takes money." Prangley corrected himself, "And faith, of course."

"We have union funds. Can you really not see how we should be working together?"

"Protecting my congregation, Mrs. Davis. That is what I am doing with our new airplane. We in Detroit are surrounded by degenerate Canadians who think nothing of promiscuity or drinking. It appears to be normal to them. I myself suspect their behavior is brought on by the long-lasting defects of venereal disease." Prangley rose and lurched toward the door, which he shut gently. "I wrote a pamphlet on the subject, if you care to read it."

Mary Joy cocked an eyebrow, her dimple deepening. "You appear a learned man, so I will be direct. What I'm offering are customers, served by a unionized, organized group. We are under no jurisdiction.

We are in control of the cars. What I need are the beverages. We can only bring so much on the Canadian line. I can no longer work with these rude Italians in Chicago. Now, to work alongside a man of God—that *would* be a welcome change."

Prangley cleared his throat. "What I can supply you with is some basic advice: do not go calling on someone in business without a referral."

"Mr. Moss, that was his name. Alfred Moss." She slipped on her gloves and stood to leave. Just as she was about to thank him for his time, the reverend cleared his throat.

"Wait." Prangley put out his hand.

Mary Joy stopped but did not take her seat again.

"Tell me about Moss," he said, his voice suddenly gravelly. He stared at Mary Joy, taking in all the details of her manner and attire. "When was the last time you saw him?"

THE NORTHERN DISEASE!

Reverend Charles X. Prangley,
Master of Divinity

14 pages, Temperance Press

5 cents

The beaver is the filthiest of forest creatures and only one step removed from its cousin, the rat! The beaver lives a life of thievery and destruction, in disease and squalor. It is a well-known fact that even the Indian will not eat the pitiable animal. Therefore, it is wholly appropriate that the country of Canada, which profits so handsomely on the gnawing away of the American Christian spirit, should choose the beaver as a national symbol.

With a society built on generations of drink and lawless perversion, is it any wonder they seek to import their ills to America? Sin procreates itself, and as long as alcohol consumption is rife, we must beware of the beaver! If the gentle reader shall turn to page four, a chart will compare the cranium sizes of American criminals with those of Canadian criminals . . .

={ 48 }=

AS SOON AS THE SUNLIGHT from the stained glass ebbed into two tiny rectangles on the hardwood, Faye finished her afternoon tasks. Prangley must have heard her tidying up; he came out of his office to speak to her. She was eager to go—Ernest Krim would be waiting for her around the corner in his truck, but she knew better than to mention this. Krim had warned her several times that he did not want her to say anything to her employer about the two of them seeing each other.

"You will never guess what I found." Prangley clutched an envelope in his hand. He held it out to her.

She took it dumbly and flicked the opening back, exposing the bills. They were all fifties. This in itself was surprising; their funds were never in a single denomination, whether tens, twenties, fifties, or hundreds. They weren't fortunate enough to receive such uniform donations, and Faye took care to deposit everything the week it came in, if not the day. She pulled her hand back and the envelope dropped onto her desk.

"It was in the file cabinet," the reverend explained.

"In your office?"

Prangley nodded and smiled. "It is the donations from Ladies of the Morning. I do not know how we missed them."

The Ladies of the Morning was a meeting of women doing Bible study once a week. Many of them were women of leisure; still, the fact that all the bills featured Ulysses S. Grant gave her pause.

Prangley rapped on her desk. "It should help balance the columns." He appraised her. "My dear, I just realized you have cut your hair."

The reverend had never before called Faye anything so affectionate as "my dear," and with the timing of the money in the envelope, it had the opposite effect to the one he must have intended. She felt her spine stiffen. It was as if a draft had come into the church, in spite of the warm fall day outside. "Time for a change," she said, the words catching in her throat.

"And it does make you look younger, I think." Prangley smiled at her again, his eyes lingering on her face.

Having her new haircut complimented by the reverend before she met Krim made her feel suddenly cheap and ashamed. The hairdresser had styled it in finger curls, to look like Anita Page. She and Krim had just seen *Our Dancing Daughters* in the theater the week before.

Prangley rapped her desk again. "I was so tied up with that Mrs. Davis this morning, I must have looked right through you. My apologies."

Faye reached out and picked up the envelope, crammed it into her purse. "Good night," she said.

⟋⟍

INSIDE THE TRUCK, Ernest Krim was waiting. Faye was taking longer than usual. Earlier that day, in the back room of the pharmacy, he'd had the radio turned on as he worked. He'd heard the new Happiness Boys song "Etiquette Blues." It had put the comedians in his mind, sing-shouting their ridiculous "Mr. Hoover and Mr. Smith," and Krim now beat a rhythm on his dashboard with his hand and murmured the words to himself:

Who is the grandest, greatest man
This country ever knew?
Oh, it's you, Mr. Hoover
No, it's you, Mr. Smith

Excepting Georgie Washington
He was a good man too
He's not running, Mr. Hoover
What a break, Mr. Smith

Are you dry?
I can't remember—but
I'll know, know, know in November
Well anyhow, you'll get one vote
Because I'll vote for you . . .

He wished he had a car radio—the new vehicles rolled off the lot with them installed right there in the instrument panel. At last, Krim spotted Faye McCloud in the rearview mirror. He turned to watch her over his shoulder; he had never seen her run before. She arrived at the truck and pulled open the door and smiled somewhat anxiously, her fingers creeping up her neck. Her face was a flushed peach.

"I'm sorry I'm so late," she panted.

Krim reached out and touched the ends of her hair with one finger. "I always knew what a looker you were. But now the rest of the world will see it too." Krim put an arm around her and slid her over on the seat, burying his mouth against neck and earlobe. After a few minutes Faye tugged her hat back on her head and Krim pulled out into five o'clock traffic. "I think you should meet my mother," he said.

"Now? In my work clothes?"

"Yes," Krim said lightly. "Gertrude won't know work clothes from evening ones since she mostly wears her dressing gown."

He quickly glanced at her; Faye was squinting out the window into the sunlight.

"It's been such a funny day. Why not?" she said. She told him about Mary Joy Davis's meeting with Prangley. "Nicest-dressed woman, and she smelled like roses. Do you like perfume? Well, Charles toured her through the whole church—even that dingy basement! Then later, just as I was going to leave, he dropped by my desk with an envelope thick with cash, all fifty-dollar bills, every one. Did he get it from her, I wonder? But I don't even feel right for thinking that—she was so nice."

Krim put both hands on the wheel and tightened his grip. *I am out of the business*, he told himself firmly.

Faye didn't say anything for a long while. He glanced over at her again, and saw that she was scowling. "My sister told me she saw him at a cathouse."

Krim coughed. He let his cigarette stub fly out the window. Then he pulled the car over to the side of the road. "What did you do with the wad of fifties?"

Faye hesitated, then dug into her purse and extracted the envelope. She passed it to him. He flicked through it.

"I'll go to the bank in the morning," she said. "I would have deposited it, but I didn't want to keep you waiting."

Krim lifted the bills from the envelope and brought them to his nose, sniffing. "Smells like mildew."

"What does that mean?"

"It means they probably didn't come out of the purse of a woman scented with rosewater. I wouldn't worry about Mrs. Davis." He handed the money back to Faye and she put the envelope deep in her purse.

He suspected she wanted, now more than ever, to ask him how he knew Prangley—after all, he'd met her when he'd come into the church looking for the reverend. But she gazed out the window and said nothing.

$$=\!\!\!\{\; 49 \;\}\!\!\!=$$

AT THE SANFORD HOSPITAL, the receptionist greeted Krim and signed him in quickly, saying the doctor wanted to update him. Krim left Faye to wait on a bench in the hall.

It had come to Dr. Marentette's attention that there were other documented cases of "glass delusion," but that all of them had occurred in the fifteenth through the seventeenth centuries, and in Europe. Apparently, King Charles VI of France had been a sufferer and refused to let anyone touch him.

What did this finding mean for his mother, Krim asked.

"Well, it is curious that it only occurs in the wealthy and educated classes."

"It only occurs in them, or is it only documented in them because they're the ones who can afford treatment?"

Dr. Marentette folded her hands on top of the file. "That is an excellent point, Mr. Krim. Either way, we now have a reference point."

Krim asked how the condition had been treated in the past, and Dr. Marentette acknowledged that the most effective treatment had been beating, which proved that a person could feel pain without shattering, that the person's body was indeed made of flesh. This was not the best solution, she said. "We have made some progress with the psychoanalytic sessions."

It had taken Krim a while to get used to receiving reports on his mother from anyone, let alone a female doctor who was a handful of years younger than himself. When he sat in Dr. Marentette's office those first few months, he almost always felt the urge to squirm like a small boy. He'd worked hard to suppress this feeling, until one day Dr. Marentette acknowledged it openly, saying, "I suspect this is hard for you, after being the one to manage her illness for so long, but please try to trust in my opinion and ability."

Now she looked directly at him. "Tell me again, Mr. Krim, when did she first believe her head was made of glass?"

He couldn't say exactly, though the condition had seemed to emerge after he and his brother had both returned from the war. Morty had been shot and did not have much use of his right arm, Krim explained. His brother was told he might never do manual labor again. "My mother spent a good deal of time nursing him, but he was very bitter and angry. Neither of them was very well. Of course, it may have begun before that. She was alone for the first time while we were both away."

"This is helpful. From her account in our last session: 'I was always made of glass, but I especially began to feel an anxiousness about my head when I left my husband.'" Dr. Marentette looked up at Krim from her notes.

"Oh, but that would have been years before," Krim protested, his forehead wrinkling.

The doctor jotted down his objection. "Nonetheless, it's worth knowing why she has focused on that particular time. There's a scientist named Watson who believes in behaviorism, which is to say that fear is learned and not instinctual or inherited. He's been doing good work for the past ten or twelve years now. Have you heard of him? No? Well, if we follow this line of thinking, it's possible there was an event that produced this intense fear in the patient—in your mother. Even if she didn't believe entirely that she'd become made of glass, perhaps that was when she first started to experience attacks of nerves. Is it true that your father beat her? Around the face, perhaps?"

Krim pulled back slightly in his chair, but didn't answer.

"What was happening in your life at that time?"

Krim stared at the diploma on the wall behind the doctor. For a moment he could smell apricot brandy just like the kind he and Moss had been drinking the night of their high school graduation—the night they had wrecked his father's car. He shook his head slightly; that had nothing to do with his mother. He glanced around and saw a paper bag on the file cabinet with the doctor's leftover lunch in it: a peach rested at the bag's edge. That was the apricot scent. He shook his head. "I didn't spend a lot of time at home in high school."

The doctor nodded. "She's responded well to the electric stimulation therapy too. I think we should continue with both, if you agree."

Krim asked if Gertrude was still on the sedatives, and was told it was a light dose.

"Of course, there is another option. Alcohol has anxiolytic effects. Your mother said she gave up drinking a few years before the Eighteenth Amendment. It might not hurt to try it."

"You want to give alcohol to my mother?" Krim dropped his hat on the floor in astonishment, and bent to scoop it up.

"Only with your permission. In the days when she did take a drink, did your mother seem happier or of more sound mind?"

Yes, Krim said. She had seemed so. And he leaned forward and signed the paperwork the doctor spread out in front of him.

AFTER THE TRIP to the Sanford Hospital, Faye moved slowly through her dark house and set her purse on the oak dining table. She heard Krim honk his horn as he pulled away. She reached up and turned on the lamp that hung there. The two sides of the shell handle parted and there in the middle of her bag was the envelope of fifties Prangley had thrust upon her that afternoon. She had forgotten all about it at the sanatorium.

Faye reconsidered the bundle as she took off her jacket and unbuttoned the top of her blouse. She left the room and hung up her clothes. She came back in her dressing gown, and picked the envelope out of her purse. Earlier that evening, when they all sat together, Krim's mother, Gertrude, had mentioned something about taking pictures in her mind. How much did a camera cost? Maybe if Gertrude could take real pictures, it would give her some autonomy over what she thought she saw, what she perceived, Faye reasoned. She pulled two fifties from the white envelope and looked at them. She put one bill back and took the other through the house into the dimly lit bedroom. She climbed into the closet and lifted down a box.

Inside were the letters she'd exchanged with her first sweetheart all those years ago. *Arthur Baldor*: the shape of the handwriting, as much as the name itself, was like an old, sad song. *My dear sweet Faye. My darling. My heart.*

Beneath a bouquet of crumpled flowers was Mrs. Moss's pistol. She'd almost, but not quite, forgotten she had it in her keeping. Faye touched it with one finger, the way a child might pet the nose of a hamster or some other small creature it feared would bite.

Then she put the fifty in on top, and closed the box up.

={ 50 }=

GIN ING SAT on the park bench, watching the children playing. The three boys were rocking in a large cradle-like swing, making it swoop up faster and faster. The little girl, Emily, dressed too fine to play in the dirt, had borrowed one of the boys' abandoned sand buckets. Emily sat alone, her knees spread, the bucket between them and her hands digging into it, scooping up fistfuls and releasing sand into the wind. The particles blew, gliding across the pages of Gin's notebook. When Gin didn't say anything, the girl released another handful, watching the fine veil of it blow and fall. Gin wrote another line, careful with her script. Then she blinked as the wind shifted, dry sand flying into her eyes as Emily, emboldened, stood and swung the tiny shovel, flinging the dirt into the air. Gin rubbed at her eyes, closed them.

The sand turned to snow in her mind's eye—and she saw large ashy flakes falling past the bedroom window of the apartment she shared with her father. She watched the frenetic dance of the snow hitting the glass, the tall frame of it, as she swayed. Her hands clutched at her neck and she kicked out her feet. She bucked and thrashed and kicked backwards, but Mr. Ing avoided her blows, yanking the wire tighter. She couldn't say anything, couldn't beg him not to. No time to get a finger up in between the wire and her neck's pale flesh—it would be over in a minute. Her eyes bugged with tears and the snowflakes outside seemed to melt between her lashes.

Gin knew that her father must be dragging on the wire as force-fully as he would for any man he'd been ordered to assassinate. Then, suddenly, he released. Gin fell to the floor, coughing, the wire beneath her hands. At first she thought someone else must have come into the room and forced him to stop. She realized Wei Ing was sobbing—a sound she had never heard before.

"Forgive me," he said. "I could not do it." He retreated into the dark apartment and she could hear him fumbling in the kitchen, pouring himself a drink.

"You must disappear," he told her in Cantonese, his figure dark-ening the door of the bedroom. "I have killed you."

She lay on the floor for a while, but he did not strike again. Instead, she gradually became aware of his movements—a small light had been turned on and he was moving around her room stuffing things randomly into a bag. Gin stopped sobbing—crying brought too much agony. She looked down at her fingertips, which were bloody from where she had grabbed at her neck. The wound was open, and when she touched it, it felt as distinct as the edge of a page that she could have pulled and turned. She did not let her fin-gers linger.

She pushed herself up and ran into the tiny bathroom and closed the door. She found a silk scarf hanging from one of the hooks where she usually kept her necklaces. She threw water up into the cut, gasp-ing, then wound her neck with the scarf and tied it tightly, wincing. Her whole neck felt as if it were on fire. She had been preparing for bed when her father attacked her, and she was wearing pajamas and a silk dressing gown. Now, instinctively, she grabbed the rest of her jewelry and filled her pockets with it, along with vials of drugs from the medicine cabinet. Afraid though she was, she knew her father was giving her an escape and she had to take it before he changed his mind. He had killed a hundred men, and she had never seen him show mercy. She opened the bathroom door tentatively.

His morose face was blotched. His lean frame sagged. He handed her the bag and her coat. She flung it on over her sleepwear and buttoned it as she ran, still wearing her bedroom slippers, through the snow. She did not say goodbye. Large snowflakes fell into her dark hair. In their haste, neither she nor her father had thought to reach for her hat.

"YOU'RE GETTING ALL THAT SAND in your hair," Gin told the girl. The Eriksson children were often disobedient, but she didn't care. As long as she could brush them off at the end of the day, or get them changed and scrubbed before their mother noticed, she figured it would not kill them. She had taught the children how to lie about where they went and what she'd allowed. But hair . . . hair was noticeable. Gin had lived with the family as a nanny for six months, since just after Alfred left—the four hundred dollars he'd given her had long since run out, and no more had been wired. She'd had two letters from him, one with a fifty shoved inside, the other asking *her* for money. The first had been full of promises sent from New York, where he knew she could not return, and the second had regaled her with tall tales from Oklahoma. Nothing since. Mrs. Moss hadn't phoned her at the Eriksson house, and she couldn't tell if the woman had intended to try to reach him.

Hartwig Eriksson lived on the edge of the city. Hartwig was high up at General Motors, and for him the draw of having a Chinese nanny was that she could tutor him in Cantonese, which he hoped would help in business. Gin taught both handwriting and calligraphy to the kids. Two of the boys were old enough to practice poems for choral speaking. The third boy, at seven, spoke better with his set of pastels. Gin had always been good at pretending, and she had convinced the whole Eriksson family that she was fond of them and was grateful for their employ. Even the children believed she dearly loved them, but she did not. She had stopped feeling, as if something inside her had frozen. She looked them in the eyes and smiled. She always made the face appropriate to the situation. The Erikssons gave her a couple of almost-pretty rooms in a coach house, and although it was too far west to go downtown much, the job kept her busy enough that she could pretend, most of the time, that she had never come there for Alfred Moss. She hadn't at first, not really.

The night of the attack, before leaving New York for good, she had gone to Paul and Joe's on Christopher—far enough from Chinatown that no one would recognize her. At the door, a black man in a beaded dress blocked her entry with a smooth leg extended from a bar stool. "Little late for laundry," he said. Gin flashed a handful of opium bindles and the leg folded like a scissor blade. He reached out an open palm. "One for mama."

In the bathroom, she dug into her bag and pulled out a second scarf because the first already showed spots of blood. At the bar she sold several of the bindles for less than they were worth. The room was solid with sailors and uptown couples laughing through the smoke. Onstage, a man wrapped in tulle was lying on the piano and singing a Marion Harris number. *"I'd love to love you baby. But I'm afraid of you,"* he sang in a high, brittle voice.

Gin remembered how she'd snatched a purse dangling from the back of a chair by its strap, its owner gone for a minute. She had watched herself do these things as if she were an actress in a picture show. It was easier than she could have guessed.

Having gathered what she needed, she had headed south. Her goal was Florida, but she made it only as far as Virginia. At least it wasn't snowing there. She spent two months in Richmond, wrapping her neck with gauze and later concealing the wound with chokers, scarves, tall mandarin collars, makeup. Richmond was a stately, lonely city, full of columns and devoid of conversation. She got a job in a bar, but was regarded largely as a novelty by the rich white men who frequented it. It was after a particularly dehumanizing shift that she decided to try reaching out to the man who'd thrown her into her new life.

Detroit was eighteen hours by train—but what was a day and a half if at the end of it was a foolish, familiar face? There were lots of wealthy, good-looking fools in Virginia, and perhaps she ought to have found one to become a mistress to; but Gin didn't see herself as a mistress.

She found Alfred by asking around the most fashionable speak-easies. Finally, she ran into him at the Powhatan. From across the room she spotted that silly white vest, his thick hair combed to one side like the drift of a river. His plush lips sneered. He didn't seem happy to see her, but part of that might have been the threat of her father that she carried. Nonetheless, Alfred slept with her for three months, and she was committed to him, until she discovered he was married and had a child on the way.

Her father had always maintained that murder could be kind. Gin had never understood what he meant. If he didn't spare some-one, how could it be kind? But on the day she found out Alfred was married, she understood. Pain could be delivered quickly or slowly, and the former was indeed the more agreeable of the two methods. Alfred had chosen the latter for her.

"SHAKE IT LOOSE," Gin told the girl. Emily complied. In fact, the child seemed to take as much glee in whipping her hair around as she had in getting it dirty. Gin sat her down on the park bench beside her and rebraided the thick brown hair. Gin watched her fingers flying through the locks, yanking sections tight; Emily watched the boys still rocking on the swing set. When Gin had finished, she sat staring at the girl's head, not saying anything.

"Are you mad?" the little girl asked her, and Gin shook her head, her eyes not straying from the braid she'd just completed. "You're far away again," Emily told her. "Are you in China?"

Gin smiled and shook her head, tried to make her eyes focus on the four-year-old's face. "I've never been to China."

"That doesn't make any sense," the girl informed her.

"If you expect everything in the world to make sense, you will have a hard life," Gin told her.

The child crinkled her face, a threat of tears. "Why are you being mean?"

"I'm just telling you the truth," Gin said, even though she knew one should never tell one's own truths to a child. She had been raised without blinders, and it had done her no good. She reached out to smooth a hand over the girl's crown in what seemed an affectionate manner.

The girl reached up and touched the black velvet strip of fabric that looped Gin's throat, an emerald medallion in its center. She asked to play with the necklace, and Gin shook her head. When she asked, "Why?" Gin said nothing. The insistent Emily eventually won. No one was near them in the park and the boys were enraptured with their own play. It was better than a fit of tears, and Gin thought the girl would hardly notice the scar. To her own eyes, it seemed to be fading. She rubbed it every morning with aloe, and every night with a liniment from a brown bottle called Dr. Thackery's, which promised to remedy a variety of ailments including rheumatism, neuralgia, burns, scalds, sprains, bruises, insect bites, chapped hands, corns, toothache, stiff joints, or frostbites.

Emily put the necklace around her own neck and Gin fastened it. It sagged down on the girl's chest, but she paraded around the park happily, tossing her new braids and acting coy for no one. When she came back, she pointed to the thin black line above Gin's collar. How did that happen, she demanded. Did it hurt?

Gin grinned. "I fell into a grand piano and somebody slammed the lid. I couldn't get out and I got tangled in the wires."

Emily was aghast. "You did not."

Gin shrugged. "I slid down a rainbow and some of the purple came off on me."

Emily laughed. "You're lying!"

Gin took the necklace back and refastened it, tight enough to hide the scar. "I fell out of a thirty-eighth-floor window in Book Tower. I would have plummeted into the street, but I got caught on a telephone wire and it saved my life. I always have been lucky." She hadn't anticipated how easy it was to lie about the wound, and, strangely, how pleasurable.

"That's the one that really happened," the girl said confidently.

When Alfred discovered the scar, he had been only mildly curious. Even the little girl showed more interest than he had. It was odd, Gin realized now. There was not an inch of her his mouth hadn't touched, except this.

"I don't remember you having a scar when I met you," he'd said, but already he was turning away, toward his pipe, packing it with a fragrant marijuana, holding the match over the bowl. He didn't look at Gin as she refastened the choker that had come loose during lovemaking, nor did he glance at her when she told him her father had tried to strangle her in her own bedroom.

Gin rose and crossed the room suddenly, standing at the window, looking out; she couldn't tell the story to his face. He was the first she'd told. "The snow," she'd said. "All I remember is the snow outside falling as the wire went around me, silently."

She felt a jolt of alarm when tears fell from her chin onto her breasts, and the rush of breath in her throat grew thick. When she turned back to the room, Alfred was lying on the bed, looking bliss-ful, the weed now burned and his eyes foggy. He picked at his tongue with his finger, as if an ember had burned him. He seemed indiffer-ent to her emotions—or was it that she had revealed too much? *The details of our lives are ours and ours alone,* she thought. *Sharing them is like trying to impress upon someone else the beauty of a flower they have never seen, or the horror of a death of someone they've never known. A ridiculous exercise in imagination.* She was stupid, she concluded, to try to share this awful act, or anything besides carnality, with Alfred. Why wouldn't he want the perfect mistress, one who came without any problems of her own?

"That why you came looking for me?" he muttered. "Because your father cast you out?"

Gin dashed the moisture from her face with the back of her hand. "Oh, did you think you were so absolutely irresistible?" Her voice was angry, but she didn't know why.

Alfred nodded that he was pretty sure he was. "Traveled halfway across the country, didn't you?"

Gin laugh-cried as she pounced on him, seized the pillows, and swung them at his head, let him roll and pin her. She kissed him, seeking comfort, to remember she was alive. Although he had kissed back, it was with reluctance. Then he'd rolled off her and returned to the pipe for another hit. Gin stared at his back, his thin, muscled shoulders, the brown freckles and moles she was learning, the small

Kewpie-doll image etched in green-black ink on his skin. She sat up, leaning on one elbow, and wiped at her eyes again. She wished they would stop watering. Trying not to be so serious, she smiled as he looked over. "I'm surprised he didn't try to kill you too," she said.

Alfred shook his head dumbly, leaned down, and kissed her, exhaled marijuana across her tongue.

Had he mistreated her, Elsie had asked her when they'd met in the diner to discuss him.

No, she thought now, watching the Eriksson children play. He had never left a mark on her.

FRANK BRENNAN PACED the hospital corridor, his hands folded behind his back as if he were just there for a stroll. The casualness of his stance betrayed nothing of his emotions. Below his domed forehead, his eyebrow twitched upward as it often did, giving him a haughty look—but that was the only sign of anxiety. He pursed his bow lips, which were pale pink like a doll's.

The Oncology Department behind him, Brennan stood in front of a window gazing down at the green lawn below. The doctors had told him his wife's cancer could be cut out. He imagined it like a faulty structure inside her; the surgeon would go in and excise the defective part. One of the large sycamores outside had already begun to turn and shed its leaves. Brennan peered into the top of the tree, which was like looking down at the part of a woman's hair when it has begun its move from brown to silver.

O silver,
higher than my arms reach
you front us with great mass;

no flower ever opened
so staunch a white leaf,
no flower ever parted silver
from such rare silver . . .

It startled Brennan to find that he still remembered the poem. He'd meant to give the book to Elsie, but never had. Now they were seven hundred miles apart, and he could not fathom when he would be able to return to Detroit. The wires for the bridge had been raised and the catwalk built in August. Ceremonies were set for that weekend—the first walk over the river—but he'd had to send his regrets to the Detroit International Bridge Company. From experience, Brennan knew the construction of footbridges was one of the most dangerous parts of the work on a suspension bridge—the time when accidents happened. The wind shook the walks, and often shrugged workers loose. Catwalks were just that, and one had to be nimble as a cat—they were not pedestrian bridges. Bower, Austin, Henderson, and others were set to walk it, but Brennan would not be there to see it. He would have to wait for photos in the newspaper.

He had not even picked up the phone to call Elsie in two months. He had wired flowers for her birthday in August, and she'd telephoned his office to thank him. It surprised him she'd done so, but he hadn't been in and had only got the message, which was suitably awkward and veiled. There had been another message from her this week, something about coming to New York on business.

To think of another woman now was unfathomable. All his attentions were for his wife, Sarah, with her insides of disease—the kidneys, the filterers. She had grown so gaunt, even their children had come home to be by her side. Their daughter, Maggie, boiled apples into applesauce and fed it to Sarah on a baby's spoon that somehow had remained in their drawers since the children were little. One bite, two. To think of leaving a woman in good health was easy; to watch her die was something else entirely. Brennan drew in a shaky breath. It rendered a person helpless and without any will of one's own. He had forgotten the desire to be anywhere else. He knew that he had to tell Elsie. There were promises he'd made to her—yet he could neither break them nor fulfill them.

Brennan reached up and loosened his tie. His gaze held on the tree, the soft whisper of the leaves that still clung, dry and shimmery, to the gray-green branch. He closed his eyes and tears slipped silently down his face.

≡(52)≡

WILLIE LYNCH REACHED OUT and grabbed at Jake Samuel as the man tried to slide through the crowd. "Hey, pal. Jake! Jake!"

"Kid, what are you doing here?" Jake said, stopping as Willie's fingers brushed his sleeve. Willie saw now that the other distributor was with a woman, but Jake let himself be pulled aside nonetheless. He introduced the blonde, saying, "This young man and I used to work together."

The woman raised an eyebrow but asked no questions, turning instead toward the river, lifting a delicate set of binoculars intended for opera more than bridge openings.

"My mother and sister begged me to drive 'em." Willie shrugged. "I don't get it. Look at this. They got no road, ain't got nothing." He gestured at the structure. The ceremony was for the footbridge, which had been strung across where the real bridge was to be, but was mostly to be used by workers. "Looks like someone just drew that bit in with a pencil."

Jake ignored the boy's complaints—as he always had, thought Willie. "You still clinging to Mrs. Moss's skirts?" Jake ribbed.

Willie grinned. "She just agreed to come to New York with me in October. Stay in a hotel, the whole thing."

"I don't believe it!" Jake said. "What are you cooking up? You think you'll get a wife outta this?"

Willie told the whole story: how he had a connection to some cars, someone he'd known his whole life through his father operating the car lot. "We're set to drive two vehicles, yellow cabs, as if we're taking them to the company. Only we got our own reason for taking them. Liquid money."

Jake shot Willie a look and put his hand out for him to shut up. He leaned over and said to the blonde, "Listen, why don't you run down there by the railing and get us a spot. I'll be along in a jiffy." When she'd gone, he said, "I got lucky—said she likes 'em tall, dark, and handsome. I told her I got one of the three. Made her laugh. We been going steady for twenty-four hours now, but I'm hoping to make it forty-eight. Listen, just yesterday I had word from Gerald—"

"Gerald?!" Willie exclaimed. "How's he doing?"

"Fine, Kid. Probably never screw his wife again, but then he probably wouldn't of anyway." Jake dropped his voice. "But he's working something big—we're meeting at his place next Friday night. It's Prangley. The nut's got a plane. Comes soaring in with product. Drops it down in a field. We repackage it. I'm not sure where it goes from there. I just heard yesterday and haven't even been out to see it yet. Might need hands. You in?"

Willie pulled back, his face hard. "You mean that old priest down at First Lutheran." His instincts had been right, but he was hurt Jake had known about the reverend and never said a word.

Jake rolled his eyes and jabbed his wiry head to one side. "Look, Kid, I just know what I've been told. There's a plane, some fine juice, some fine dough. Everything's set to move fast. I'd think you'd be glad to be working again."

"Well, I got bad business with Prangley." Willie sucked back on the cigarette, then dropped it at his feet and crushed it angrily.

"Seventeen years old, you already got bad business?" Jake shook his head, then twisted to see where his new woman had posted herself. The crowd had grown thicker.

Leaning in, dropping his voice, Willie said, "They never did find the hoods who shot my father—and there's that priest driving around in a funny little car my father sold him. If we always worked for him, then my father worked for him too. Who's to say he didn't just walk in one night and bust him up?"

"For what, though?" Jake shrunk away with alarm. He made a clicking sound with his mouth. "That's a big accusation. Watch yourself, Kid. I mean that. Be careful." And with that, Jake smacked Willie's back and quickly left.

After a few minutes of surveying the crowd, Willie spotted Prangley's secretary among the onlookers by the main tower. He swiveled and headed back to the street, hoping he wouldn't cross paths with the reverend.

⇘ ⇙

CLOSE TO THE MAIN TOWER of the bridge construction, Faye McCloud stood alone. She had asked Krim to come with her, but he had to work. She hoped that was the reason, rather than his being reticent to be seen with her. She watched the businessmen as they got ready to go up. She had read all about them. There was the face of the financier, Joseph Bower. He had removed his woven hat and she recognized him from his newspaper photo: his stiff rounded collar, his large square head and glasses. He was the one who could've had the bridge named for him, Bower Bridge, but chose not to. They ascended and reassembled at the top of the tower. They were just about to make the crossing when Bower himself faded back. Faye couldn't be sure what was happening. Someone seemed to have had second thoughts.

The announcer filled in the space with facts about the bridge construction. It was the first bridge across international borders. Total bridge length was to be 7,500 feet, and the suspended length 1,850 feet. It would rise 152 feet for boat clearance. "Those main pillars are called a cantilever structure. Here's a clever way to remember that: I can't believe her, it's a cantilever!" the voice ad-libbed. Then the presenter gave a quick roll call to the engineers from McClintic-Marshall.

Down below, Faye McCloud saw it was fear that had dropped the man almost to his knees. As Faye raised her binoculars again, all she could see were the backs of the men huddling in consult. It was only a moment or two, and then the crowd gasped and pointed: a young girl and a man with a dog were making the passage. The voice crackled through the speaker, saying this was an unexpected turn. Crossing the footbridge was Helen Austin, the financier's game young daughter, same one who'd driven the first spike a year and a half before. With her, one Mr. Zundt, the paymaster of the construction company, McClintic-Marshall.

They had not gone far when her father began frantically waving for the girl to come back, but she did not turn.

Everyone watched the couple. Heads tipped back, hands clutched hats, hands shielded eyes from the sun. They stepped across the planks easily, as though they were crossing any walking bridge in a park over a pond instead of a temporary structure—shaky as a swing porch— a hundred feet over a knife-blue river. As the structure undulated beneath their shoes, they held each other arm in arm.

People on the opposite shore cheered as they reached the tower on the Canadian side. But they did not descend onto Canadian land—

the announcer said they'd just learned the construction elevator wasn't working. The pair turned, and slowly the two figures and the little dog on the leash made their way back to the United States, he holding on to his hat, she holding his arm.

Faye breathed out, light-headed from watching their brave steps. As they came down amid roars and applause, Faye dropped her gaze and shielded her eyes from the sun. She stared at the ground beneath her shoes. All she had to do was ask Ernest Krim how he knew Prangley—at worst, he would be dishonest—it wasn't as if she had to walk through thin air.

={ 53 }=

TO FAYE, IT SEEMED to come out of the blue when Elsie Moss phoned her and said she wanted to come round to her home, and would Faye mind? Faye wasn't used to company. She cleaned the rest of the day. She had forgotten how much housekeeping and cooking she'd done in the early years, when she was helping her mother raise Kitty and holding things together, all while working. Lately, she kept the place nice in case she did, indeed, want to invite Ernest in—but as she looked around now, she realized how worn and drab her things had become. Working at the church, it was always easier to grab something to eat from the deli than to cook. Kitty had moved out two years ago to a room in a boarding house, where they didn't care if she crept in at 1 a.m. or at 6 a.m., so long as the rent got paid. Usually, in one way or another, Faye paid it, and though it wasn't much, she wasn't sure why she continued to throw away money for her sister to sleep elsewhere, except that Kitty preferred to be away from her judgmental eyes.

When Elsie arrived at seven that evening, childless, Faye was grateful. Dealing with one adult was simpler in so many ways. She saw immediately that Elsie was tense. Through the door, she watched as Elsie stalked up the driveway, her shoulders hunched. When the pleasantries had been made and refreshments offered and accepted, the two women sat in the living room, picking at their desserts and moving spoons around on saucers. Neither knew what to say. Then Faye laughed and said, "I'm not much of a host."

"I'm not much of a guest." Elsie leaned forward and set down her plate on the coffee table, a carved hexagon in need of refinishing. As she looked around and took in the lived-in surroundings, Elsie seemed emboldened. "You know, there's a fabric sale right now. If you put some new draperies up there, this room could be even lovelier. Dusty rose is what you need in here, a little flush of color to temper the brown."

Having lived in this house her whole life, Faye found it hard to envision any change. She turned and looked at the windows. Pink? Yes, Elsie said, it had to be. But a subdued, dignified pink. "I don't know why I'm suggesting it, I've barely decorated my own house since Alfred bought it. What if I pick out fabric for both of us, and whip them up? I'll have time and money after my trip to New York."

Faye protested feebly. "Although," she conceded, "it might be nice to do more around here. There's someone I've been seeing, and it would make it easier to have comp—"

Elsie stood up and strode to the window. "A tape measure?"

Faye ran to get one, though it wasn't long, meant for measuring for a dress, not a window. Elsie slipped off her shoes and climbed on the back of the davenport. She shouted down the numbers and Faye wrote them on a piece of paper. Then Faye took Elsie's hand and helped her down.

"You said you got a new fellow?"

"Yes, sort of. Only . . . he doesn't want anyone to know. Is that how all men are?" Faye wasn't sure why she was telling Elsie Moss about her personal life. She went into the kitchen and came back with her purse. She laid out a few bills for Elsie for the price of the fabric.

Her head tipped back, looking at the woodwork around the three long windows, Elsie said, "Don't ask me about men. Everything I thought I knew about men is backwards."

"Oh, you know him!" Faye clapped a hand over her mouth. "I'd forgot. He must be an acquaintance, because he was at Mr. Moss's funeral."

"Now you have to tell me." Elsie gave her a curious look, arching her eyebrows.

"Ernest Krim."

A cloud passed over Elsie Moss's face. After a pause, she congratulated Faye in a numb tone. Then she stuck her shoes back on and gathered her purse and cigarette case. She tapped the case with her fingernails. "It was him, actually, who came to tell me about Alfred. Middle of the night. I barely knew who he was."

Faye had picked up the teacups to clear, and now she fumbled. One fell to the floorboards and smashed. "Oh, damn." She bent to pick up the violet-patterned shards. With the pieces cradled in her hand, she looked up at Mrs. Moss. "The middle of the night, really? But how would he have known?"

Elsie said nothing, and Faye got up quickly and crossed into the kitchen to throw away the porcelain before it could cut her hand. When she came back, she asked Elsie what it was she had wanted to talk to her about.

"My gun, of course."

Faye blinked. "The one you asked me to keep?"

Elsie nodded. "I'm making a trip to New York. I would feel more comfortable if I had a pistol in my purse. For protection." She touched her bright curls when she said this, combing them forward nervously.

"I'll get it for you." Faye made her way through the house, but hesitated halfway up the stairs. She returned to the living room empty-handed. "Are you sure you want it?" she asked. "I just—" She placed a hand on her chest. "I would feel responsible if anything were to happen."

Faye felt the warmth between them fade.

"I need it back," Elsie Moss insisted. "It's *my* gun."

={ 54 }=

THE BOTTLES THAT SAT in Gerald Zuckerwitz's living room were clear with rounded tops, and the whiskey inside them was bright as sunlight. New labels were applied with an adhesive. Yellow and green, with a bold black type that read: *Mr. Bucci's Olive Oil.*

Prangley knew that the men were desperate to be back in the game, and it didn't hurt that applying labels was something Gerald could do sitting down. He'd been importing longer than the others, though Prangley had never dealt with him so directly before. Now the reverend stalked around Gerald's living room, unsure of himself. It was becoming clear to him that he was good at intimidating men but not at leading them.

"We gotta get a warehouse," Gerald offered. "That's how the Purples always done it."

"The Purples stole their damn warehouses." Jake Samuel took the bottle and sniffed it. "They would walk in with baseball bats. Snap the shinbones of the biggest man. Jab an ice pick into the balls of the owner. 'Here are the keys, sir.' You gonna do that, Sleepy Z?"

Gerald turned to Prangley. "What happens in this racket? The porters collect the bottles, and the label's just in case one gets left behind on the train? We don't gotta mix with those porters, do we?"

"None of that is our business," Prangley reassured him in the tone he used for sermons. "We supply this one source. Our role is clean and simple. There will be no more chasing down Irish mothers and overdue accounts."

"Do we need more men? What about the Doctor?" Gerald asked outright.

"Forget Mr. Krim," Prangley said. He chose his words carefully. "We buried your friend Alfred Moss, but Mr. Krim was the last to see him alive. Do you ever think about that?"

Prangley took the bottle back and poured himself a drink. Since the funeral, he had thought a great deal about where Moss might actually be, and how much Krim had been paid. Krim had also relieved Prangley of a large sum—for the Purples, Krim had said, but there was no way to follow up on the veracity of the claim. It enraged Prangley to think about it.

Jake and Gerald exchanged glances, but neither rushed to Krim's defense—nor, Prangley thought, did they have the brains to pick up on his innuendo. They were excellent at picking up whiskey cases and pasting on labels, and that was that.

$$\Longrightarrow 55 \Longleftarrow$$

WILLIE LYNCH USED his smallness to remain hidden. As soon as
Reverend Prangley pulled out of the churchyard lane in his billiard-
green Buick, Willie rose and slid along the wall where he'd been
crouching beside the garbage cans. Jake had let slip that the reverend was meeting some of the gang that night at Gerald's. Willie
had declined to join them, but he hadn't forgotten. He watched the
humped roof until the vehicle passed out of sight. Then Willie went
to the entrance of the parsonage and knelt down, getting familiar
with the lock. He pulled a couple of picks out of his pants pocket.

He held the lock with a brace and moved the pick in. It was a cheap
three-pin tumbler and the lock turned in seconds. Willie smiled, dipping his head sideways and giving it a shake. He crept in and closed
the door behind him. His father, Seamus, had been hard-fisted, but
he'd taught Willie a few things. One was locks. Cars, doors, or safes
and compartments. Willie had been halfway to lock picking, halfway
to driving for the smugglers, when his father died—and Alfred Moss
had taught him the rest.

Now Willie stood in the darkness, letting his eyes adjust.

The space was much as he'd expected—a bare front room that
matched the personality of a clergyman. There were the calendars, the
Bibles, the table with a dusty cloth, the cups along the sideboard, the
single slouching armchair. An old clock hummed and ticked. Even

though he didn't expect anyone to notice from the church or grave-yard, he didn't light the room. He took out a flashlight, tugged open a couple of drawers half-heartedly, peering into them but not touching the contents. Then he moved quickly to the back of the dwelling.

Entering Charles Prangley's room, the discrepancy between the poor pastor and the wealthy rumrunner was obvious. The man must have counted on never having a pushy guest. All of the furniture was lavish, the bed laid out with silk. Willie touched the linens, then bent down to check for guns that might be stashed under the bed. He found only satin slippers. He went and helped himself to a cigar from the cabinet he'd guessed was a humidor. His instincts were good, and so was the tobacco. He lit up in the dark and paced to the closet, coughing after his first few puffs. He flicked the flashlight around at the extensive wardrobe, pulled out a houndstooth suit, and held it up to himself, looking at his reflection in the mirror across the dark room. Prangley towered three inches above six feet, and Willie had topped out at five-six. He sighed and hung the suit back up, mutter-ing, "When the fuck do you even wear them?" He leafed through some more, then rolled up three silk ties and shoved them into his trouser pockets.

He went to the bureau next and shifted the contents of the draw-ers around lightly. His hands were hunting for keys: the keys to the missing 1921 Roamer town car from his father's lot. He didn't know where he would find them, but his impulse said the back of a drawer, inside a valet, shoved back and hidden—the way one did with dirty pictures or things one used only on occasion. It would not be some-thing the man carried on him, and it would be too risky for him to leave them on some hook or in his desk at the church. Willie puffed the sweet, earthy smoke out of the side of his mouth. He tapped the ash into a silver tray on the dresser.

Walking back through the room, Willie encountered the steamer trunk, which he split open. Slipping out the drawers and shining the flashlight into them, Willie inspected the contents of enough shoe compartments to understand Prangley was a man obsessed. He whistled at the crocs. Then he pulled open another compartment down toward the bottom. Plain rough black slip-ons. He inspected the left one with the flashlight. It was beat-up, practically worn through— unlike anything else in the room. He turned it over, and in the dim light he could see it had been stamped with an emblem of some sort. He angled the flashlight: *Property of Eastern State Penitentiary.*

Willie drew a breath, and the cigar in his mouth wobbled and fell onto his shirt. He jumped at the scorch of it, grabbed it before it could burn, fumbled the flashlight.

Willie's own father had spent time in the clink. He'd almost forgotten. He had been young—four or five—when his father went away for a couple of years. His sister wouldn't even remember. Where was Eastern State? Obviously not Michigan. Had Seamus been as far away as that? If it were a federal crime, Willie supposed so. He'd heard his father talk about his time in the big house; when Seamus got drunk, there were stories. What exactly had his pop gone away for—breaking and entering, rumrunning, reselling stolen cars, or stealing them himself? Willie had never pretended his father was a good man nor tried to take a different path.

"Prangley, you fucking goon." The prison shoes were too large to be anybody else's, and they were exactly the same size as the fancier ones in their compartments.

Willie tapped out the cigar and shoved it in his shirt pocket. Then he went back to the humidor and relieved Charles Prangley of a whole box, tucking it in the back of his pants. He plucked out a pair of diamond cufflinks from the valet on the dresser. He collected three watches. Then he went back to the trunk and grabbed a prison shoe in each hand. He kicked the trunk closed so that nothing would look out of place except the shoes and the few trinkets he'd decided to crib. Without aid from the flashlight, he stalked through the dark little house and knelt down beside the door and placed the shoes neatly on the mat beside the hat rack.

He snickered.

He was about to let himself out when he noticed a bowl on the hutch in the corner just inside the living room. It looked like the kind of place one would throw a set of keys, or stash a letter. Willie dipped his hand into the dish. He touched three stamps and a spool of thread and a button—nothing else. As he stepped away from the hutch, he ran one finger along the tops of the books, tipped one out, and flipped the soft leather cover. His mother would appreciate a new Bible. Willie pulled up his shirt and tucked the good book into the front of his pants.

THE NEXT MORNING, Willie woke late and dressed slowly. He liked to put on a full suit even before he knew what the day held. He knotted one of the new ties, a burgundy stripe, and headed downstairs around eleven. His sister Annie was already at school. He found his mother doing the dishes in her housedress. He had made sure she had a closetful of nice things, but she seldom wore anything except housedresses, saying, "That's all too ritzy."

Now she gave him a flinty glance.

"What?"

She handed him the newspaper, as she'd always done for his father, and brought him coffee.

"Got you a gift, Ma," Willie said. He left the room and returned carrying the Bible. She hesitated to take it, then she touched it gently and sat down with it in her lap. Willie knew she hated the way he dressed, the same way his pop did: the fabric fine and expensive, but the cuts too loud for daytime.

Over cornflakes, Willie questioned his mother. What had Seamus gone away for? Was it rumrunning or stealing?

No, she said, that was all before the Amendment. "He was in for two years, 1915 and part of '16. He said it was just a couple cars, that it only takes one, but he lied like a cat on a windowsill and I knew better. So many tricks, that crooked bastard. He broke the Mankind Act, they said. A federal offense."

"The Mann Act, Ma," Willie said through a mouthful of cereal.

"Well, I cried just the same. I was so angry at him for gettin' caught."

Willie didn't care much about why she'd cried, but he could see he was going to get a story. Once his mother got going, he couldn't cut her off or she would chastise him for his rudeness.

"Your sister was just a tot, and Little Willie, you must've been four, but ya could barely string two words together."

She went on about his great-aunt Margaret and great-uncle Patrick and how they'd leaned on them and borrowed from the Cleary side of the family the whole time Seamus was put away, but cousin Eoin was a pervert, could never bring him to a birthday party, so there was that going on too. Willie stroked the new tie and waited. He knew this story could run on a long time, and most of it wouldn't be of any interest to him—him or anyone.

"Well, you don't got to worry about that anymore. I'll always take care of you," he said finally, when she'd finished her rant and brushed her hair out of her eyes.

"Sure ya will. Till you get yourself a wife. I know how ya look after that Mrs. Moss. Don't think I don't know what you're thinking. Your sister tells me everything."

Willie swore. "I told her I'd bust her in the mouth if she said a word."

"You will not strike your sister, William Lynch." His mother jabbed her finger at him, and Willie held up his hands in surrender.

"And they sent Pop where?" Willie leaned back and felt his jacket pocket, extracting the cigar he'd been smoking the night before.

"Don't light that dreadful thing in here. You're going to turn your beautiful teeth black as walnuts, and you'll stink this place up like a men's room."

"Hardly," he protested. "It's like cedar and blackberry. Couldn't ask for a better tobacco." But Willie did what his mother said and put the cigar back in his pocket. "Pop know a Prangley? When he was in stir, I mean?"

"Oh, Prangley, sure. That's a name I heard a lot. Not when he was in jail, though. Later."

"When?" Willie pressed her.

"Oh, he went to a men's group at the church. I mean, Seamus was Catholic, but over at that Lutheran church they started a group for men to talk about their struggles with the booze."

"Pop probably had a flask in both pockets." Willie laughed, but his mother frowned.

"The man was like a fish in a river," she said. "And he swam along just like we all do—but there were certain things that helped him swim, see?"

Anger was a game Willie and his mother played every day; he imagined it like a ball being bounced back and forth. But today, Willie needed her knowledge. "You know, you're probably right, Ma.

I bet he worked on it even if he didn't stop altogether. I mean, who stops altogether?"

Mrs. Lynch smiled faintly. "Your father was a good man, even if he sometimes had his troubles. And Lord, he had as many troubles as rats in a cellar. Yet I know in his heart he was good."

Never mind that she'd called him a bastard five minutes before, thought Willie. That was his mother's way. He remembered Seamus's temper and the back of his hand as well as he remembered his father's heart, but he didn't argue. When he pictured his pop's doughy face, what he felt half resembled resentment and half resembled love.

"So where was he? Which jail?"

"Eastern State. Pennsylvania."

Willie raised his hand as if he were testifying. "You're dead certain it was Eastern State?"

"I waited for those letters in the mail every day for two years. A wife ain't gonna forget that address."

The last thing Seamus had said to her, she told Willie, her eyes shiny with tears, was, "'No matter what time I come in, be sure and get me up for my meeting in the morning.' But he didn't come home that night at all. I rolled over at six, and the sheets were cold."

CHARLES PRANGLEY ENTERED the parsonage and put his house keys in the dish on the hutch. He paused, glancing around in the dark. He crossed the space with three strides and turned on the light in the dining room. Nothing seemed out of order.

"What's wrong with me?" he breathed. He went into the bedroom, took off his shoes, and put them away in the steamer trunk. Again he paused. Some of the compartments were not pressed in evenly. He pushed his hand against one, making it flat. Another he pulled out and peered into. He closed the steamer trunk and stepped into his slippers. He took off his suit and hung it in the closet, peering into the darkness there. Then he slipped on a gray silk dressing gown and lay down on the bed. He took out a pad of paper from the bedside table and began to write some notes for that week's sermon.

He wrote *Ruth 4:7* and a question mark. He didn't write the quote, though he knew it: "Now this was the manner in former time in Israel concerning redeeming and concerning changing, for to confirm all things; a man plucked off his shoe, and gave it to his neighbor: and this was a testimony in Israel."

Suddenly, Prangley got up and walked once more through the parsonage, turning on every light as he went. He came to the front door and faced the hutch. The books there had slumped slightly to one side. He straightened them and determined that one was missing.

He turned around and there, under the hat rack, were the prison shoes, blunt and black, positioned neatly as though he had put them there himself.

"Fuck," he said as he knelt to examine them. "Fuck," he said again as he snagged them in his fingers and dashed down the hall back to the steamer trunk. He dropped the shoes on the floor and threw open the trunk. His hands ran over the delicate drawers, and when he came to the one he was looking for, he rammed it open. Inside, a pair of camel-colored oxfords were still in place. They shone. He had never worn them. He took out the left and turned it upside down, shaking it. Out fell a car key.

Charles Prangley breathed, gratitude rushing through his tense frame. Then he dropped the oxfords on the floor and went to the closet. He dressed again, and left the parsonage immediately, climbing into the little Buick. The tires threw mud as he turned out of the lane.

To be sure no one was following him, Prangley wound unpredictably through the streets before he headed toward the garage just off Schaefer Road. A cobblestone shop that looked as though it still ought to be serving horses and buggies, the building was long and low, with four roll-up metal doors. The mechanics' shop used two, and two were private parking that "Elmer & Son" rented out. Prangley had keys to only one door; the other spot was occupied, which was just as well since he didn't fancy keeping all his cars in one place. Too easy for someone to get inquisitive. He rented three separate spaces, like this one, with cash, under his old name, Lester Lewis. He didn't visit them often, and he didn't make conversation when he did.

He was still shaking as he got out of the Buick and opened up the metal door. There was the 1921 Roamer. A fine layer of dust had settled over her veneer. He tried to get out to check on the car and start it up once every few weeks, but never took it farther than a few blocks, usually looping up around the Ford plant a couple of times and back. He didn't want to be seen, although he was careful to drive far enough to maintain the car. On these brief sojourns out, he felt a buzz in his testicles, a thrill as if he were flying, even as he motored the car along at exactly the same speed as the other vehicles on the road.

Now he got into the Roamer and let her catch and backed her out into the laneway. He left her running while he got out and back inside the Buick, pulling it into the spot where the Roamer had been. He closed and locked the roll-down gate as the Roamer idled nearby. As he was securing the door, he saw that there was a light on in the first bay, even though it was almost midnight. Elmer or his son must be trying to finish up a repair for the next morning.

As Prangley sunk the hook below the latch, he heard someone say, "Hullo." There was the older mechanic, in a pair of grubby overalls and a flannel shirt, smoking a cigarette against the building. "Think you'll bring her back tonight?"

"Good evening." Prangley straightened and clapped his hands together to get the grit from the door off. "Working late?"

"I only ask 'cause I try to check all the locks before I leave. Every night."

"I appreciate that you keep everything safe. I may not tonight. I have a collector friend who wants to see the car and give her a drive." Prangley nodded, but the explanation felt unnecessary once it hit the air.

"Sounds like a good friend to have. What business are you in, Mr. Lewis?"

"Real estate." Prangley nodded at the mechanic and said good night. He got into the Roamer and the man waved, and Prangley took off into the night a little faster than he normally would.

THE MECHANIC INHALED on his cigarette, cast it away into the dark alley, and went back inside. His son was bent over a Nash Advanced Six with half a dozen tools nearby. "Mr. Lewis just told me he's in real estate."

"He's the crazy preacher gets his picture in the paper all the time. Name ain't Lewis. Probably got himself some whore that lives around here."

"Well, I think you're wrong about that," the father said, making a saliva-slick sound deep in his mouth. "Just doesn't strike me as a liar."

$$\equiv\!\!\!\mid 57 \mid\!\!\!\equiv$$

CHARLES PRANGLEY DROVE, sitting tall, almost breathless. It was painful to know that this was his last ride inside her. It was the first time he'd ever had her out on the highway, and once he was well away from Detroit, he let her rip—the Roamer jumped joyously at a touch of the pedal. He knew that he shouldn't keep souvenirs from a murder, especially not ones that were so large and conspicuous, but it was hard not to. It was the first time he'd done it, for one thing. And for another, the Roamer town car was a handsome slate green with black hubs and detailing. But it was more than that.

He had known Seamus Lynch well—at Eastern State they had been lodged close enough that they could call across the hall to one another. He hadn't meant to meet up with Lynch again in Detroit, but it was inevitable. Lynch kept his secret, until it seemed clear he might not, and then the man had to go. He'd always been steadfast and yet, like Prangley himself, he was hotheaded, a furious fellow, which sometimes impaired his judgment. Prangley knew there had been a detective coming around, and that Lynch wasn't happy with the split of the money they had agreed on, or that Vern Bunterbart was always playing the big man and running the show.

"I did not have a choice," Prangley said to himself as he headed south for Cincinnati. But he had found he couldn't let the man go that easily—and so, the car. There was a practical reason for the theft too, which was that he and Seamus had ridden together to the dealer-ship that night, and if Prangley hadn't swiped something, he'd have been stuck sitting there with a dead man, waiting—for a cab, a bus, the coppers to come pick him up and give him a lift? The Roamer seemed to whisper, *Choose me.* Prangley had reached over the bloody muddle on the floor and hooked a thumb through the key ring on the pegs on the board. Even now, there was blood deeply hardened and etched onto the key fob.

Now, in the near-dark, Prangley glanced down at the fob, dan-gling from the keys in the ignition. He took one hand off the wheel and fingered its edges. He would have to take it off, he realized, before he sold the car. The plan was to leave the Roamer with a small lot in Cincinnati in the morning—Cincinnati seemed far enough away that the vehicle would never come back to Detroit. Whatever lot he could find that looked shady enough to take it for cash, no registration, he'd give them a sweet deal—then he'd ride back to Detroit on the train. He could phone Faye McCloud at the church and simply say he'd got stuck with car trouble while out that morning and that he'd be in late. With luck, he'd be back by lunchtime.

He glanced up at the road again, held her steady between the lines—very little traffic at this time of night.

THE CAR HAD BEGUN TO WEAVE and Prangley jolted upright. Checking his watch, he saw it was quarter past three. Up ahead, the lights of what must have been Dayton, Ohio, sprang up. Prangley rubbed a hand back over this forehead. A twenty-four-hour diner flashed its sign: *Cain's Café.* The wheels of the Roamer eased through the dirt parking lot and stopped.

"A coffee, please," Prangley called to the counter girl as he entered the vacant diner. Thankfully, there was a restroom, which Prangley headed for. He pissed and sighed, washed his hands, and cupped water and splashed it over his face. When he returned, he saw that the girl was pretty, and the cup was there—steaming hot. She had short blond hair and was so small she looked like a doll cut from paper. She wore no rings on her fingers and didn't look any older than twenty. White apron and a paper hat, a name tag that said *Millie*. Right away he was imagining knocking the uniform loose, and her body in twenty different positions across the counter.

"Busy night," she said to him as she wiped down the already-spotless counter.

Prangley laid his car keys next to the coffee and lowered himself onto a stool. He looked at the menu and ordered a hamburger because it was at the top. He wasn't hungry, but he hated to linger without something in front of him.

"Sometimes we get the after-hours folks, but not usually. We're too far out of the city. You got to be downtown where the clubs are for that. Got the train station there." The waitress nodded vaguely in the direction of the window and the street beyond. "But that don't yield many customers at night. Course, it's good for me this way, ain't no one to give me any trouble." Millie talked over her shoulder as she posted the order chit for the cook. "You look tired. Far to go?"

"Cincinnati, maybe. I really do not know. Just as far as I have to so I can sort some things out."

"Business?" Millie guessed.

"Sort of."

She refilled his coffee. He hadn't realized he'd drunk so much of it already.

"Oh, real problems, huh? I got lots of those," Millie said.

A little girl who thought she had problems. Charles Prangley smiled at her, his mouth twitching until the corners split wide and actually showed his teeth. It felt remarkable. He couldn't remember the last time he'd smiled without faking.

"You need more cream there?" She turned around and snagged a tiny pitcher of cream for him. She set it down next to his keys. "Oh, you got engine oil or something on your key ring there. Let me get some soap on my washcloth. I'll rub that right off for you."

Prangley stared at the leather fob on the key ring. To the unknowing onlooker, it was just a couple of black flecks, whatever tar or grime might have been picked up in a pocket or during a driver's travels.

"No, that's all right." Prangley's hand encompassed the key ring. He slid it off the counter and slipped it into his pocket. He couldn't say why he hadn't wiped it clean.

The waitress pursed her coral lips and gave him a funny look.

"I'd just rather leave it on there. It's like . . . a piece of the journey." He made his voice as calm and quiet as he could, reflective.

Millie cocked her head. "I see. Proof you left home?"

"Something like that," Prangley said. He knew he presented well, but just touching and talking about the fob in a public place made him pick up the creamer and dump in more than he meant to, over-flowing the cup into the saucer.

Handing him a napkin, Millie asked where he was from. Prangley lied and said Saginaw. He had to get rid of the car, tonight. Did she know the story of King Solomon and the baby? The car was like that— it had caused too much of an argument, he said. Two of his friends wanted it, and rather than cut it in half, he had to find a way to spare

345

it. Maybe he could find a dealer right there in Dayton. Did she know anyone who opened early?

A bell dinged on the kitchen pass-through window.

Millie shook her head. She fetched his hamburger, then looked out the diner window at the car as he ate. She leaned her chin on her hand and said it looked mighty swell. "I'd like to have me one of those—you know, when I'm rich! I read about this thing, reincarnation, where you get born again, and how you're assigned depends on how good you been. I been real good. I always was a good girl. So who knows, maybe I'll get reincarnated as someone else and be able to afford one of 'em in my next life."

"Sure, the philosophers have their discussions of Indian scripture. But I ask: what is wrong with our concept of God? God is not good enough for you?"

The girl said nothing was wrong with it, she just liked to read, that was all. She certainly hadn't meant to offend him.

"Ah, bookish. Tell me about those real problems of yours," he said, but not derisively. The girl had wide blue eyes and was too innocent to mock.

"Oh, you don't want to hear," she protested, but she went on to tell him that her youngest brother had contracted polio. He was now paralyzed in his legs. She had been supposed to go to a women's college that fall, but they'd spent the money on his treatment, so now she was working nights. Millie said she went home and slept and then got up and helped her middle brother with his homework, and helped her second middle brother get his newspapers folded for his paper route. How many brothers did she have, Prangley asked, finishing off his pickle. Four, she said. She was the only girl. Her older brother was twenty-one and was already out working as a door-to-door salesman, though it was a hard business. Now that she wasn't going to be educated, her mother hoped she'd marry a well-off man, but she had no time for dating and dancing. No offers had been forthcoming yet. Millie laughed. Beneath the french-fry grease, she smelled of oranges. Her eyebrows were fine as feathers.

The cook came out and called Millie aside. Prangley could just hear him telling the girl he was going out the kitchen door to get some air, and that she didn't need to talk so much—a man would either leave her a dime or he wouldn't. The cook handed her a broom.

Millie cleaned for five minutes then came back and refilled Prangley's cup a third time.

"You can help me figure something out," Prangley said. He picked up the salt and pepper shakers. "These friends of mine I have the argument over the car with, this one is a boy, seventeen, son of a friend—but not a good friend, friend I had a falling-out with." He touched the saltshaker to indicate Willie Lynch. "And this one here is a business associate." He touched the pepper for Krim. "He has lied to me before, and not a small lie, either." Prangley looked up into the waitress's alert face. She nodded, got it. "One of them broke into my house, nosed about. The question is, which one?"

"Why, whatever for?"

"The car, maybe. Looking for the keys."

"I can see why you're hot to get rid of it."

"Or maybe not. It does seem like the kind of thing a boy would do—just because boys can be . . . reckless and wild, doing things for kicks that do not mean a thing. You are closer to seventeen than I am. What do you think?"

Millie said she would hate to condemn a young man she didn't know. Was the only reason to blame him because he was young?

Prangley licked his lips and nodded. He put his head down as though thinking it over, but doing so also put him more even with

347

Millie's cleavage, and he snuck glances in the silence. Willie Lynch had prowled around the whole churchyard the week Elsie Moss identified her husband, but he had no real relationship to Prangley and hadn't been back since. The boy was a nuisance, and belligerent—but this girl was right, in many ways, to question whether it was simply his youth that made him suspicious.

"The other one lied to you, you said." The waitress touched the pepper shaker, indicating Krim. "So you're really not copacetic."

Yes, Prangley said, he had lost thousands because of it.

"Thousands?" Millie's hand crept up to touch the back of her hair. "Well, I wouldn't trust him, then. Already he seems guiltier." She tapped a clean, unvarnished fingernail against the napkin dispenser.

Krim didn't know or care about the car, of course, but the car was part of the story Prangley had told the waitress. His motivations were perhaps more hidden, Prangley decided, but the pharmacist did have more forethought than Willie. The boy would be likely to just toss the place and leave it a mess for the hell of it—if he were even able to get into the parsonage without making it look burgled. Prangley didn't think him restrained enough for something as subtle as simply leaving a pair of shoes at the front door.

"You know, it's none of my beeswax, but I have to say it: you just seem on the level, too nice a man for friends like these." Millie took the salt and pepper shakers away and refilled them. The cook came back and handed her the bill, which she brought back down the counter to Prangley.

"Thank you," he said, taking out his wallet.

The door opened and a small group of half-soused men and women came in, dressed sportily and smelling like wood smoke.

"Busy night," Millie said, and hurried away to gather menus for them, the bow of her apron bouncing on her small round buttocks.

He could sleep with her, he thought, imagining that backside naked before him. But he liked her too much. Besides, he knew he'd wind up thinking about the polio brother while he was fucking her, and her whole sad, paralyzed house, and then he'd never be able to achieve his climax.

Prangley took out a dollar and his keys. He wriggled the blood-stained leather fob free, and left the keys behind as a tip. The fob he put back in his pocket; that he could not part with. He left the diner and patted the 1921 Roamer on his way past it. "Attagirl," he said to the vehicle, and kept walking, down the street in the direction Millie had nodded at earlier, toward the train station, a pink dawn swelling.

={ 58 }=

WILLIE HAD DECIDED that a lady cabdriver would wear a man's coat, so Elsie Moss went digging once again through the closets. Alfred's winter coat was missing—he'd probably had it on. But rummaging past his dinner jackets, she came upon the taupe trench. It was perfect for the late fall weather, and she could wrap herself up in it and hide her physique. As she pulled it on, she noticed it smelled slightly musty, like stale cigarettes and earth. She sniffed the collar, unconsciously looking for some whiff of Alfred, but found none. She stood peering at herself in the mirror, tying and retying the generous belt.

Elsie inspected the contents of her suitcase, then pulled some stockings and a pair of panties from her dresser drawer. She held them a moment before she put them back.

She went to the phone and dialed Frank Brennan's office. It was her third-ever long-distance call. The secretary there said to hold on, and in a minute she heard Frank pick up. She spoke in a rush. "It's Elsie. I'm so glad you're there. I've been trying to get through."

She couldn't tell if there was crackling on the line or if it was the sound of Brennan doing something else in the background, folding paper maybe. He sighed. "I've been distracted, Elsie. You're lucky you caught me."

Elsie leaned against the wall. "It's so nice to hear your voice."

"When are you coming?"

She told him they would leave in the next few hours. They hoped to be in New York by nightfall the next day. With whom was she coming, he asked. Was it safe? Yes, of course, she told him more confidently than she felt. She was traveling with a boy, just a kid, a friend of her husband's.

"Oh," Frank said, a low note in his voice.

"Frank, I just want to see you," she insisted. "This kid, his father was a car salesman, and that's how he got us hooked up to drive these taxis there. It pays swell, and I jumped at the chance, hoping you'd save time for me."

She could hear again some commotion in the background. Was it a bad time, she asked.

He didn't answer for a moment, and when he did, it was with a nonanswer. "Be careful, Elsie. The road can be a hard place."

"Will you be happy to see me?" she asked finally, a waver in her voice.

There was a hiccup of silence. "Of course." He gave her the name and address of a restaurant. Did she have a hotel already? She didn't. He would arrange a room for her at the Roosevelt.

After she hung up, Elsie took the delicate undergarments from the drawer again and stashed them in the suitcase beneath her clothes.

She scarcely had time to prepare the baby's food and lay out all his things. She tried to reassure herself that Willie's sister had baby-sat enough times that she would find whatever was needed. The girl was to stay over, and although Johnny seemed unperturbed as Elsie gathered up her bags, she had a pang and went to him, lifting him away from his toys, hugging and kissing him though he thrashed to be put down again.

={ 59 }=

THE MAN WITH THE CABS was Mr. Ciccone. Seamus Lynch had ensured that every car on his lot was checked over at Ciccone's garage, and so Willie had known the mechanic for most of his life. The taxis were parked out of sight. Willie and Mr. Ciccone would pull them around and then they would load Elsie's things in for her.

"Spanking a mare and you ain't even tall enough." Mr. Ciccone whistled as they trudged around back.

"You got it wrong. It's business." Willie said she was a widow, needed to make some money.

Ciccone raised his eyebrows.

"You remember my pop's last day?"

Ciccone said that he wasn't likely to forget anytime soon. He pulled out the keys to both taxis and pitched one set to Willie. They stood inspecting the vehicles.

"Don't happen to recall what he had to do the next day, do you? Ma said he had to get up early in the morning."

Ciccone scratched his head, which was bald on top. He said he didn't rightly recall. "Your pop and I shared plenty of customers. Got his schedule book inside. If it's important to you, I reckon I could go check."

Willie said that would be swell, and the mechanic went in.

"Van Beken," Ciccone said when he returned. "I remember now: guy who wanted a vehicle for his wife."

"Van Beken," Willie repeated. The name meant nothing to him.

={ 60 }=

THE FIRST CROSSING WAS EASY. They took the ferry and drove through Canada. Elsie had nerves about driving but nothing else, since the trunks of the taxis were empty except for their suitcases. They would floor it all the way to Niagara Falls, where they would stop for lunch and load their shipment. Then came the Peace Bridge. It had only opened the year before.

Smoky tendrils of cloud scrawled a pale sky. Elsie followed the bumper of the cab Willie was steering, mindful not to get right up close, nor to lapse behind. She kept her speed steady the way Willie had shown her. It wasn't as hard as she'd anticipated. She glanced over at her purse an arm's length away on the seat. Her cigarette case was there, perched in the top. Elsie took a hand off the wheel and reached over. There was a truck coming in the opposite direction. She jerked back and put both hands on the wheel. When it had passed, she tried again, but just as she reached for it, Willie's cab slowed significantly and she had to jam on the brakes. She succeeded in knocking the purse onto the floor—out spilled the cigarette case, her matches, a compact, and the pistol.

"Damn!"

She glanced down at the contents. There was no way to reach them now. It would have to wait until their first stop. Ahead of her, Willie's cab pulled out and passed a farmer's cart and horse. Elsie hesitated, then followed. When they were in line again, she remembered that Alfred had always kept his cigarettes in his upper coat pocket, probably, she realized now, because they were easy to extract while driving. She could feel a hard, slim object beneath the fabric, and she removed her hand from the wheel again and patted the coat. Dipping her fingers inside, she extracted a box. It wasn't a package of cigarettes, though. Without even opening it, she could see it was a jeweler's box.

"Mother of God."

Using her right hand, Elsie split it open, her left still on the wheel. Inside lay a choker of emerald beads. It hovered there in her sight, then it fell from the box into her lap, and Elsie swerved to the side of the road. She bumped roughly onto the shoulder then brought the car to a stop. She reached down and found the ends of the necklace, held the beads up between her thumbs. Looking in the rearview, she leaned forward and fastened it around her neck.

It wasn't for her. That was what she thought as she leaned into the tiny mirror. Alfred hadn't bought the necklace for her.

She closed her eyes and saw Gin Ing the day of the funeral, lowering her choker, the slim scar there. Elsie stroked the weave of the jewelry, then she tore it from her neck, breaking the clasp. "Alfred, you lying rat." She shoved it back into the box and threw it in the glove compartment. She picked up her things from the floor of the car and lit a cigarette.

Up the road, Willie did a U-turn and returned to find out what had happened to her. Elsie was slumped, smoking and crying in the driver's seat, when he appeared at the car door.

She showed him the choker, and Willie said he was sure Mr. Moss must have meant it for her. He'd disappeared at Christmas, hadn't he?

"Balls!" Elsie spat. "That Gin Ing must have had him wrapped right around her finger. Oh, what does it matter? I hardly knew how to be a wife. After the pregnancy, I went through a terrible bout of the blues." She laughed. "Really, I can hardly blame him. The way I acted, I got what I deserve."

"Well," the boy said, still leaning in the window, "if everything that Chinese lady said was true, then Mr. Moss is alive somewhere—only . . ." Willie took a step back from the car as though she'd punched him. "Only . . . you saw the body."

"He made the choice to leave all of us, not just me, Willie," Elsie said flatly.

IN NIAGARA FALLS, Willie's contact saw that he was young and tried to put one past the boy and unload several cases of wine on him—even though they would take up too much room and the markup wasn't enough. Elsie knew enough that she exchanged nervous looks with Willie. The boy argued as politely as possible, but in the end he compromised and agreed to take two crates of wine along with the whiskey. Elsie suggested they go downtown and buy two more suitcases to pack the extra bottles, but she could see that Willie was still rubbed the wrong way after their conversation on the roadside. It took him longer than necessary to admit that this was a good idea.

Once they were parked, Elsie proposed they go down and view the Falls. They could see the halo of misty blue, the spraying mouth of the massive chasm right there in the middle of the town. She imagined the 165-foot drop off the edge. They still had two blocks to walk there and the murmur of the water was already caught in their ears.

The sky had brightened somewhat, and she opened her coat. Her pants were cinched tight at the waist with a sash that was a scarf on other days. She could sense Willie staring at her, and quickly wrapped Alfred's coat around herself again.

"We should have lunch, but just a quick one," Willie said. "A half hour. And I'm saying that for you. Unless you prefer to drive in the dark. We got to get there tomorrow by four to meet with Poonface for the drop."

"Do you have to call him that?" Elsie was put off by his brashness.

"I do—it's the only name anyone gave me."

As they neared the waterfalls, though, his tough-guy act fell away. He gawked just as Elsie did. The churn of water made her dizzy, and he seized the opportunity to put his arm around her and hold her close as the wind lifted the spray across their faces.

61

MARY JOY DAVIS and Charles Prangley had settled on volume needs and price points and he was damn giddy. Every week, Mary Joy would buy as much as Prangley had previously sold in a month to all his customers combined.

"Reverend Prangley," Mary Joy said. "Don't you think we should pray? After all, our meeting each other seems to be one of His works."

"Of course. Perhaps a silent prayer?"

Mary Joy clasped her hands and closed her eyes. Prangley looked at her across the desk but felt a star's distance away. He had said few prayers to himself since he'd left Philadelphia after Eastern State.

Mary Joy Davis stood to leave, and Prangley finished recording the shipment numbers they'd agreed upon in his ledger book. As she opened the door, light fell in, blocked partly by another woman who stood in the frame, as if she'd been about to knock. Mary Joy politely acknowledged her with "Ma'am." She passed, and Jean Philby came in, her equine face framed by a blue hat with a brim full of pink flowers. Jean did not respond to Mary Joy.

"My Jeannie," Prangley said as he stood. "What a lovely dress. Is it a Chanel?"

The woman glanced down the now-empty hall. "Who is that Negro you were talking with?"

Buying time, Prangley's fingers snapped over the desk, straightening papers. He put the ledger away. When he finally spoke, he smiled and gathered all the enthusiasm he could into his voice. "I was not going to mention this until the next board meeting, but you have just witnessed the beginning of a plan to make Bibles available on trains. Bibles for Berths."

"Berths?"

"A brilliant opportunity. You see, Mrs. Davis is a representative of the Pullman porters' union over in Chicago. A very important contact, you must admit."

"Of course." Jean accepted the cup of tea Faye McCloud brought her and plucked out three sugar cubes with a pair of tongs. Faye skittered off down the hall before Prangley could acknowledge her—his secretary had been making herself scarce lately, barely reminding him of his schedule and skipping their morning meetings.

"But Charles, why change our focus? I have to tell you: when I raise money from the ladies, I've told them it's for temperance. I'm sure the rest of the board will agree with me."

Jean Philby was old money who had married new money out of necessity. She was a Rumsey, from a century-old manufacturer of carriages. However, the family had bet on horses over cars and went bankrupt after the war. Her husband, Joe Philby, had earned the nickname "Crankshaft Joe" because he'd gone from one shop to a five-acre factory in Flint and now produced half the crankshafts used in the country, his lathes turning all day and all night to fulfill the demand. Joe, who had a feminine face with grayish eyelids, loved men—the rough-speaking, broad-shouldered kind laboring in his shops. And everyone knew except his wife, although even she had her suspicions. She'd previously confided problems of marital intimacy to Prangley, who promptly wrote an anonymous blackmail letter to Crankshaft Joe. Prangley received a handsomely thick envelope in return.

Now Prangley placed his palms flat on the desk and leaned forward. "Jean, I think you are forgetting the temptations that people face while traveling. You may think Detroit is a city, but I like to think of Detroit as the biggest small town in America. Out there is a whole world—dangers, enticements, questions, and choices. Why, imagine an important man of business, maybe someone like your Joe—though God forbid a great man like him be led astray. But wouldn't you feel better if there were a Bible nearby that he could reach for? Just at the very moment he catches sight of leering eyes, whispers from deceitful lips, or even the touch of a wandering hand."

Jean Philby looked drained as Prangley continued his sermon about her husband.

"We are human, Jeannie. God has gifted and cursed us with that. We need to turn these berths into hearths. The work I will be doing with Mrs. Davis is also part of the great work of temperance." Prangley smiled, bowled over by his ingenuity.

$$=\!\!\!=\!\{\ 62\ \}\!\!=\!\!\!=$$

"HOW ABOUT THAT? We were through the border faster than you can say 'Jack Robinson'!" Willie said.

Elsie allowed him to squeeze her shoulders. They stood in the parking lot of an inn that looked welcoming enough. He kept touching her, and although she didn't care for it, their jubilance over the victory meant she didn't protest. Besides, she knew he would be the one paying for their two rooms and their meals. He was fronting the whole journey until they made their score in the Big Apple.

"Let's get outta these ugly duds and drink some of that wine and find some spaghetti," he insisted, grabbing her bags from the cab.

But inside, they discovered there was only one room available. Impulsive Willie laughed and said they should do it, but as he opened his wallet, Elsie peeked in and reminded him they also needed gas and food for the next day's journey. They had just enough money to get there, but should resign themselves to the idea of a night bundled up in the car blankets and sleeping in the cabs. Willie confessed he had planned to sell a couple of things along the way, to help with their finances. She asked what he'd been planning to pawn and Willie said, "I got a top-drawer watch."

Elsie arched her eyebrows at that. Was he intending to sell it to cattle? Willie's grin faded quickly and he accepted their fate.

They sat on the bumper, drinking the wine out of a thermos lid and a mug that Willie had pinched from the restaurant. Parked at the back of the lot, no one seemed to care that they were there. They had a view of a wooded field, and beyond it a green hunched shoulder of mountain. They sang "Yes Sir, That's My Baby" and "Button Up Your Overcoat" while Willie refilled their cups.

After a while, Elsie held out her hand to stop Willie from giving her another refill. "I've had better wine at church."

"Church wine is piss water. At least there's some color to this." Willie poured the rest of the bottle into his own cup and glugged it.

"The last time I drank wine was at my wedding."

"Don't go getting all maudlin now," he warned her. "Not when we've had some day. You're not gonna have to work again till 1929. Boy! I wish that dumb priest could see us. If he knew what a score we were going to get outta this, what kind of green glorious he's missing..."

"Why do you hate Reverend Prangley so much?" Elsie asked, and Willie said that explanation called for another bottle. He flipped up the suitcase lid and pulled one out, uncorking it and filling his own glass. He sloshed it in her direction, and to be amicable Elsie agreed to half a cup, which she knew even as she took it she probably couldn't finish. The wine left behind a sour taste like aluminum foil.

He now realized he'd been working for him, this Prangley, three years all told now, Willie said, swinging one leg up on the bumper and leaning in as if he was going to pitch Elsie a fastball. Only he hadn't known it for most of that time, Willie said. He'd worked alongside his father Seamus, Mr. Moss, Mr. Krim, and Mr. Bunterbart—a pack of others, too—and all the while there's this sanctimonious preacher hiding in the shadows, calling all the shots, only Willie'd never met him. "He's the one," Willie breathed, his finger notching a number one in the air. "Thinks he's the duck's quack while we're all running around: we pick up the liquor over here, we drive it over there, we lug it up the stairs. We got coppers on our heels, we got gangs breathing down our necks. I been held up twice, I had the muzzle kissing my cheeks. And what's he got? All the ladies in furs, name in the newspaper, pretending he hates the juice joints. Oh, don't he?"

Elsie's thermos cup tipped sideways in her hand and half her wine had dribbled onto the ground.

"Oh Lord." She placed a hand on her belly, scared she might vomit. "Don't tell me this. Don't tell me—" She thought of Reverend Prangley touching her hand while praying for her husband, her husband who had apparently run liquor for him.

"I'm just sayin'." Willie set his empty cup beside her on the hood of the cab and smacked one hand into the other. "This grafter has got it all figured—he makes the money and we're the ones who pay. What does he do but shake some hands and talk to some Canadian bootleggers, write some numbers down in a book? I went to his parsonage and—"

"When did you visit him?" Elsie asked.

"Well, let's call it a *visit*. That's a polite way to think of it. Pour me another drink and I'll show you something."

Elsie knelt down to pick up the new bottle where it stood in the dirt. She hesitated, reluctant to refill Willie's cup because he was already bobbing and weaving. She watched as he went into his car, and when he came back, he held out two pocket watches and a wristwatch. "Check out these lovelies. Couldn't you just fall in love?"

Elsie looked at the timepieces. She reached out to touch and examine one. Then suddenly she hiccuped and clapped her hand to her mouth, ran behind the car, and heaved. Out came the two cups of wine and most of a spaghetti dinner.

"Guess the bank's closed," Willie said behind her. She lifted her head and saw him kicking at the dirt. He pocketed the watches and poured himself another glug of wine, took it back in a shot. "You okay?" he called to Elsie, but didn't approach.

When she came out from behind the car, she apologized. She climbed inside the cab and took out a new blouse. "Do you mind?" she asked, and Willie turned his back to give her some privacy. When she had changed, she opened the cab door and sat inside, her legs hanging out.

"You know, when Alfred died—or when I thought he had—I went to Reverend Prangley. He's been my family's pastor since I was sixteen. I went to him for comfort and advice about how to manage without any income."

"That weasel. What'd he tell you?"

"A long story."

"Full of static." Willie poured yet another for himself.

Elsie nodded her head slowly. Her insides still felt quivery. "Gave me a watch to pawn to put some change in my pocket. Said it had been donated to the church by a woman who'd also lost her husband. Oh, it was a heartbreaking tale, and I believed him. Most beautiful piece I ever saw—"

"Windbag."

"Prayed with me. Good Lord." Elsie looked up at the sky. "Pretended to care about Alfred going missing." Suddenly she was shaking.

"Oh, he did care," Willie said, taking out a cigar stub and lighting it. Walking around the car, Willie cataloged the number of collections Prangley had been able to make after Mr. Moss died, including the collection when the church chartered the boat. "If I'd known then, I'd have told you."

"I'm a sucker. I'm the girl men take advantage of." Elsie scrubbed a hand hard across her lips. "My mother always told me, you don't trust a man unless you have your hat pin on you. I was twelve years old when she showed me hers, how she wore it partly to keep her hat on and partly so she'd always have a weapon. There it is, four-inch blade always within reach. 'Why?' I asked. Geez, I was naive. 'In case he thinks he can lay his hands on you,' she says. But even when she told me that, no one was wearing hat pins. I just laughed at her for being so passé. I should have listened."

"What are you talking about?" Willie wobbled and hung on to the car door.

"The reverend. He tried to get off with me when I was just a girl. In Palmer Park."

"What'd you do?" Willie's face turned ghostly.

"What do you think?" she said, remembering how she'd cried and begged the reverend to stop. "I wanted to think it was a one-time slip on his part. But I see now—he's a bully. Takes what he can."

"That's putting it kindly." Willie's cigar had gone out and he shoved it back in his pocket. "Move over." He squished into the front seat beside her, shutting the car door. They sat looking out the windshield at a hunter's moon. "I think he snuffed my father."

He told Elsie how Seamus had seemingly been killed for a meager sum in his kiosk, and about the car missing from the lot, and how Prangley had admitted to knowing his father but never to working with him. Then there were the prison shoes Willie had found on one of his "visits" to the parsonage. "If he knew my pop in prison, maybe he didn't care for old Seamus knowing that part of his life. Then there's the question of my pop's morning meeting. My ma says Seamus had to get up the next day to see someone. Mr. Van Beken.

I don't know who he is, could be nothing, but that's the last thing my father never did."

"Van Beken? I know a Van Beken." Elsie hesitated, then said, "The detective who handled Alfred's missing persons case. Of course, there could be others."

"A cop?" The boy spat out the window. "What are the chances?" His head dropped onto her shoulder.

"But didn't they solve your father's death?" Elsie asked. "Weren't there other clues?"

Willie shook his head sadly against her shoulder, looked in her eyes. "Just a missing Roamer town car from the lot—and it's never turned up nowhere. We're living in Murder City, U.S. of A. Five hundred homicides in '26 and Seamus Lynch was just one of 'em. Ain't that the luck?"

She reached over and patted his hair. She felt her throat grow raw as she tried not to cry. "And I can't believe that man took advantage of me—twice. I hate myself. I'm such a fool." Willie told her that wasn't true, but Elsie persisted, jerking away from him. "My husband and my priest both put one over on me. A stupid, empty-headed dunce, that's me."

Willie took her chin in his hand. "You aren't. And any man who would take advantage of you is swine." Then Willie pressed his mouth to hers, and before she could protest, he was bowling her over on the front seat.

"Stop it, Willie." She pushed against his shoulders, panicking as she realized she'd walked right into the situation. Just like that time with Charles Prangley, she was in the middle of nowhere, surrounded by trees, and no one was going to come along and pull her out of trouble. She thought of Willie as a boy, a small man at most, yet his body was stronger and harder than she'd imagined and wriggling beneath him did nothing to help her free herself.

Willie stuck his tongue into her mouth and crushed his groin against her, hoping to persuade her.

She reached for the purse on the floor and brought out the pistol. "Get off me," she said with no warmth in her voice.

Willie stopped. "Jesus, Mary and Joseph! I didn't think you were gonna bring it!" He scrambled off her quickly and out of the cab. "You pulled a gun on me for a kiss? A kiss?!" He tripped over the wine bottle they'd left outside the door and fell in the dirt.

"Well, didn't you just prove me right?" Elsie muttered. "I'm the girl men think they can exploit. Even you." She grabbed her purse, kicked the wine bottle, sending it spinning, and walked away through the trees into the field without another look at him.

AS SHE STRODE AWAY, Elsie shoved the gun into her handbag. She could taste the tears dripping into her mouth. She came to a clearing and stood in a farmer's field that ran all the way up to the side of the black mountain. With her head tipped back, breathing hard, she rummaged around in her purse. The moon was a full bright orange and had risen high enough in the sky to illuminate the farmstead. Her hand wrapped around the pistol and she pulled it out again and put it to her temple. What she'd said to Willie was true: she was a dunce. She hadn't made her life; life had happened to her like a terrible accident.

She dropped her purse onto the ground. She stood staring down the row of the field she'd been walking through. It was eggplant, she saw, mostly harvested, a few bulbous vegetables scattered on the ground or still bumping out from the plants, dark purple. The left-behinds. Aubergine. The plants weren't tall, but tall enough that she wouldn't be found immediately. She didn't like the idea of a hole in her head. She put the revolver to her chest, but the sight of the gun was like a tooth, nipping against her skin. Was she really going to do it in a field of eggplants? There was something sadly comical about the oblong vegetable.

She dropped the arm with the weapon and said Psalm 23 quietly to herself: "Lo, though I walk . . ." She got only as far as "Thou preparest a table before me in the presence of mine enemies" when she stepped to one side and her shoe turned on something, and she stumbled. There was some small object down there that had fallen from her purse. She stooped and, in the dirt between the rows, found her baby's soother. She picked it up and ran her thumb over the nipple, wiping away the dust. For a moment she looked at it, then she dropped it back into her purse and placed the gun on top, and buckled the clasp.

When she returned to the taxis, Willie was passed out in the front seat of hers, one shoe sticking out the rolled-down window. She smacked his foot till it fell inside the door and he grunted and rolled his mouth into the upholstery. She opened the door and rolled up the window, knowing the temperature would drop overnight. She pulled a blanket out of the back and threw it over the top of his bent body. "Lucky kid. If I'd done it, they'd have blamed you and electrocuted you."

She got into the other cab and fell asleep to the sound of a train going by. She heard it rumbling in the distance, and before it had completely passed, she was dreaming.

={ 63 }=

THE HOSPITAL WALLS were the color of old towels, not white and not yellow, and the smell in the room was just as stale. Frank Brennan checked his watch for the sixth time in an hour.

"You've been distracted all day," his wife told him.

"They should offer you a room with a better view."

"It's not a hotel. Is it me?"

"No, it's ... business."

"The bridge?"

Frank's brow furrowed. He rubbed his cheeks, and stood up. "I suppose. The George Washington is almost as far along now as the Ambassador was when I left it."

"Yes, I know how you hate to leave a project in the middle." The door to Sarah's room was open and they sat listening to the clock out in the hallway tick. "You could always go back when the Ambassador opens."

"There's no point!" Brennan burst out, pacing to the window. "This bridge will be twice the length. It's amazing, really—why does it depress me so?"

Sarah's voice was soft when she spoke, but he knew it wasn't out of concern for him, it was the weakening. Talking had become harder and harder for her. Her mouth had dried as though a great wind were blowing through it. Every day her voice became thinner, transparent. Every day she faded. "It's the duty of the future . . . to punish us."

"Well, that's silly," he raged, turning to face her. "I'm not trying to build something that lasts forever. Nothing does."

"No," she said, "not even marriage."

"Don't say that."

She looked at him, and he held her gaze. A woman who had gained weight over the years but worn it well, along with hats and furs from Bergdorf Goodman and Barneys, now she was a sliver of herself, a willow branch lying on the pillows. She wore a thin cotton gown and the skin of her arms was yellowed and dry.

"I don't care who she is. Go—" she forced through parched lips, and Brennan offered her water, which she declined with a facial expression. "—see her."

"There's no one."

She gave him a knowing look.

"All right, there was. But, Sarah, it ended. I came back here, and it's done now."

"I will die."

"Don't say that." Brennan felt a jolt throughout his body. Every day he watched it happening, but they didn't say the words. Their grown children worried the words between themselves, though never to him. He overheard, though he pretended not to.

Sarah wriggled her fingers for him to come closer. Brennan went to her bedside. Up close, he could see how her eyes had jaundiced. Her teeth stood out now like a wolf's, but only because her cheeks had sunken so awfully. It was a terrible injustice, what was happening to her—a woman who had been so good her whole life, never complained, and scarcely uttered a curse. In a city as brusque as New York, that in itself was a feat against nature. If Frank Brennan had been a believer, he'd have turned his back on God for letting it happen. As it was, some Irish schoolboy part of him did anyway, feeling his sense of right and wrong slipping like sand underfoot as it sinks and falls away with each movement.

"I didn't care for it when we were young. But I knew." Sarah paused, and he could see her trying to gather any saliva in her mouth up onto her tongue. "You were away so much. It's natural. I want—"

She closed her eyes. She couldn't talk anymore and Frank could see he had exhausted her. He felt bad, selfish. He took her hand and stroked the skin, her veins large blue pathways running behind the flesh.

"Be happy."

"I want *you*. You are going to beat this," he answered too quickly, dashing away logic.

They were silent for a long while.

After falling asleep for ten minutes, Sarah awakened as though she did not know she had been dozing. She started back into the conversation. "Is she good? Why her?"

Brennan mulled it over. "She's young and a bit impulsive. But strong, like you. She has . . . moxie."

FRANK BRENNAN HAD BEEN GIVEN PERMISSION, and that ought to have made it easy. He'd made the dinner reservation at Delmonico's himself, along with the booking for Elsie's hotel room at the Roosevelt, and he'd had his secretary secure theater tickets on Broadway to see the Ziegfeld Follies. When he left Sarah at the hospital that afternoon, he thought he owed this to her in some way, to go through with it: a romantic night out with Elsie, where he pretended that nothing was wrong.

Now he sat at a table in the restaurant on Beaver Street and, across the dining room, saw Elsie enter—her gleaming hair and intense blue eyes beneath the brim of her black hat, looking startled by the city, its mass and movement. He watched the maître d' show Elsie to his table. He knew immediately that the dress she wore was one she'd chosen specifically for him: it was a corn-blue lace, diamond cutouts down the front and some kind of sheer fabric underneath. The skirt hung like petals around her lily-white legs. Her beauty only made everything harder; this realization brought a white band of pain stretching inside his brow.

"Mr. Brennan," Elsie said, taking his hand, suddenly shy.

"Mrs. Moss," he returned.

When she was settled and the wait staff had retreated, Brennan gazed at her and she gazed back, then she blushed and laughed, a sound like a fork tinkling against a glass at a wedding.

"It's good to see you, Elsie," he said, but his words were stiff.

ELSIE SMILED AND EXAMINED Frank Brennan's face, its smooth plains and deep-creased eyelids. His skin had paled since she'd last seen him. His hair had turned ashier. There was something so noble about his face, but something sad too.

She leaned forward. "Frank, what is it?"

"It's my wife."

"Oh no. I've come at a bad time. Why didn't you tell me on the telephone?"

"I couldn't."

Elsie felt a deep sinking feeling. The restaurant was the most luxurious she'd ever seen, but Frank's demeanor told her this would not be the reunion she'd dreamed of. She'd eaten nothing but a tomato sandwich all day, so she reached out and plucked a bread stick from the bowl. There was no reason now to pretend to be demure.

"I can't be with you. Stay at the hotel, we'll have a nice dinner, but we can't—" He fumbled for the words, glancing at the other tuxedoed diners.

Elsie broke the bread stick in half. She put it in her mouth but then felt a lump rising up as the bread crumbs went down. Her throat and eyes burned with shame.

As she collected herself, she heard Frank say, "This is the finest place in town. It's been here since 1837. Of course, they had to remove the wine cellar, and it isn't really the same Delmonico's it was. New owner—some people complain about that. But I don't, because it's in the same place and I've been coming here for years. It's top-notch."

He made a show of ordering for them. The dinners arrived and Elsie ate without speaking. Frank too was silent. Their knives screeched on the plates and the hushed tones of people speaking around them only seemed to amplify their own silence. The beef was succulent, so delicious that Elsie almost cried. She cut and swallowed, cut and swallowed. This was the last meal she would ever have with Frank, she told herself, and when she looked back, she'd remember the slab of porterhouse more than the slant of his face.

"I rode all the way here in a taxicab stacked with liquor," she told him finally.

"You didn't!" He took a swig of water.

She had felt it necessary to say something—one of them had to speak. And it seemed pointless to try to impress him, so she might as well tell the truth. "We sold it in the Lower East Side. Fellow who bought it was named"—she dropped her voice—"Poonface Jimmy. I'm sorry to say that here, but they called him that at least *ten* times, as if it were his Christian name."

"He was a ladies' man, I take it?"

She shook her head. "The kid I drove down with said it was the way his face looked." Elsie looked down at the table. "Like a ladyhood. On account of too many fights, I suspect."

But Frank didn't snicker. He took what she said very seriously. "Imagine that, a human being going to work and that's his name. Day in day out." Frank laid his silverware down. "The law is wrong anyway. All these politicians supporting the Amendment, half of them were socking away enough gin to make martinis in heaven. My brother in Detroit, Gabriel, I told you about him, he's a Prohibition agent—only Catholic the Bureau took—and even he doesn't understand why he has to round up the bootleggers anymore."

Elsie's eyes widened, and Brennan just smiled. How many times had he and she drunk together? He wasn't going to call his brother and rat her out. His brother likely wouldn't care even if he did.

Then his face shifted back into sadness. He looked down at the dessert menu as if the words were written there, and admitted: "My wife is dying. Cancer."

"I'm sorry, Frank."

"No, I'm sorry. I made certain promises to you."

A waiter came over and Brennan ordered dessert for them. Elsie told him to choose; she had no room left anyway. In spite of her protests, he said she had to try the gelato, and the raspberries with maraschino. He seemed to have a deep desire to feed her, and she wondered if he thought the price of the meal would be enough to earn him forgiveness.

"I thought we'd have a nice night," Frank told her. "I really do want to make it nice for you just the same." He patted her hand. "It's just occurred to me that in all this time, it's the first real meal we've shared together."

Elsie took out a cigarette and Frank lit it for her. She sucked back on it hard, nodding too vigorously. It was hard not to cry, and she knew he must be able to see that in her face. He said he could go for a whiskey and she agreed, even though they weren't in a private dining room, which was the only place whiskey was allowed, and they were still waiting on the dessert.

"So you're really breaking off with me?" she said at last.

Frank nodded. "My wife says I should remarry, but I've made up my mind, Elsie. It's no good. I'm an old sod, and by the time I finish this with her, I'll be a *broken* old sod. Is that what you want?" He didn't give her time to answer. "My children will need me here, and with luck, one of them will have children of their own soon. My daughter Maggie has been married almost two years."

Elsie blinked; she'd never understood that his children were so close to her own age. "Well, I'm not much of a wife," she said slowly. "Not much of a mother either. I missed my son's first steps, apparently. I called the girl from the hotel, and she told me Johnny toddled halfway across the parlor yesterday."

"You're a wonderful mother," Frank said. "You just needed time to grow into it. Every woman does. Oldest struggle there is. You know how many women I saw thrashing their kids, yelling day and night, exhausted and vexed? I grew up with five brothers, over a dozen cousins. And I'm sure you will be a great wife again." He said this in a light tone, but the words sat there.

"Tell you the truth, I don't know if I *could* marry again." Elsie laughed, and this time it came out as an acidic little chirp. "It turns out my husband is still alive."

"What? What are you talking about?"

Elsie took a deep breath, then told him everything.

The dessert plates came and they picked at the sweets as Elsie unwound the story: identifying the body; Gin Ing and the necklace; Prangley and the boy Willie. When she had finished, the plates sat between them, dotted with crumbs and smears of chocolate and maraschino.

"Well, he didn't get away on his own," Frank pointed out.

"What do you mean? You think someone helped Alfred?"

"Yes, clearly," Frank said. But then he turned his attention to the bill, and was calculating the tip. When he looked up, it was as if her story had vanished. He had tickets for a show, he said. Would she come?

"Now? After everything, you still want to go?"

He shook his head and shrugged and said, "Shame if they go to waste."

IN THE THEATER, Elsie felt starstruck. During the cab ride uptown she hadn't gathered her wits enough to ask Frank what he'd meant about Alfred using help to get away, and now, as she waited for the show to start, all she could do was look around. Frank whispered to her that Ruth Etting had been part of the act the previous year, and as she sat beside him, she thought how grand it would all be if only they were holding hands! The lights darkened and there were greetings and announcements, then kicking legs and feathered caps, the ladies all looking the same in their tight costumes, the thick muscles of their legs, the red veneer of their smiles. Frank leaned over and said that none of them had a thing on her. In the end, those were the only words of love he offered her all night.

Eddie Cantor came out and told jokes. He was in blackface, and Elsie peered at him, uncertain why such a refined theater would present an act that had been in low vaudeville shows she'd seen in Detroit in her youth for a nickel. She was flummoxed to find this show much the same as those she remembered, in spite of the finery around her.

When the intermission arrived, Frank said suddenly that he was sorry to leave her, but he had a peculiar feeling and wanted to get back to the hospital.

"Of course." Elsie numbly accepted the bills he pressed into her palm for the taxi that would carry her back to the Roosevelt alone. She didn't have time to refuse them or say she didn't need them.

She watched Frank's hand reach into his jacket pocket and feel for an object, then retreat, empty, as if he'd thought better of something. He kissed her high on the cheek, almost in her ear. "A safe journey." He turned and was gone, through the crowd of beaded dresses and black vests, out the double doors and into the street—his kiss a wet whisper still drying on her skin.

In the lobby, Elsie choked down a drink and tried to avoid eye contact with anyone. Then she was back in her seat and the Follies were twisting and tapping, movements smooth as if they were ice-skating. She watched them whirl into a blur. In the finale, the girls came out with hardly a thing on their breasts, and she knew then why Frank had left at the intermission. Couples leaned closer and the room felt as if it was pulsating with excitement. *Why is saying goodbye the hardest thing for men to do?* she wondered.

Onstage again, Eddie Cantor was in a different suit and without the paint. He sang "Makin' Whoopee" and issued a parting round of jokes. He closed the night by asking for another round of applause for the lovely Follies, then wagged a finger, saying, "Husbands, remember you have wives at home. A wedding is a funeral where you smell your own flowers."

Elsie Moss stood, gasping for air, as the audience broke into laughter and applause. She jostled against the bodies that had risen for a standing ovation. Elsie rushed up the aisle and out the doors into the night. She found a pay phone and dialed the number Willie had given her. He was staying with Jimmy on the Lower East Side.

"It was Mr. Krim," Elsie said without preamble, when Willie came on the line.

"What about him?" Willie sounded as if he'd been drinking.

"He was the one who told me. So Mr. Krim must have helped Alfred leave. He was the last one to see him."

"Sure he was," Willie said after a long pause. "Now that you mention it, I remember he saw the car go under. Said he did, anyway. I remember staring at the hole. Wasn't that big." The line was silent for a moment. Then: "I never thought to question it."

={ 64 }=

GIN ING WAS SITTING with the children in the Erikssons' back-yard when the maid summoned her, saying a man was there to see her. No one had ever come to see Gin there. She fleetingly wondered if it could be Alfred Moss, even though she knew this was unlikely. "What does he look like?" she asked, but the answer was not the one she wanted.

Her father stood in the hall, his back to the stairway wall so that he could look up it, ahead, or out the front door—even though it was unlikely there would be attackers from any direction here. His fingers touched the tops of his suit jacket pockets, a pale blue with pinstripes. Gin had never seen him so attired; he usually wore black. When he removed his bowler, she saw that a gray snake had twisted through the front of his hair; when she had last seen him, his hair had been jet-black. There was a scar on his left ear as though he'd stood on the wrong side of someone else's knife. It was only a year and a half that she'd been gone, but it felt longer.

Gin didn't know if she had any voice to greet him, but nonetheless her hello came out in English as she unconsciously touched her fingers to her throat where a velvet choker lay. The maid retreated to keep an eye on the children and Gin switched quickly to Cantonese: "How did you find me?"

How many young Chinese women did she think there were in Detroit, going out and about alone, Wei Ing asked. He'd assumed she would come here—after *him*. Some inquiries at the restaurants downtown. Everyone needed dumplings once in a while, he said. His voice was even, quiet.

Her legs felt wobbly and her throat burned.

"Don't worry. I will not stay long."

"Good," she said before she could stop herself. "It is not my day off."

"Which day is that?"

Gin paused and an expression crossed her face, partly distrust but also an aching. "Sunday."

Wei Ing said he would return then, and Gin realized she ought to have known he was not to be dissuaded—*assassins have patience.* The maid had not taken his hat, so he still held it in his hands. There was nothing to collect; he turned to leave.

"Wait," Gin whispered. "Tell me why you've come."

He pursed his lips together, judging her. "I have business here and need a translator."

Gin put her hand out and held on to the occasional table for support. To cover her frailty, she pretended, halfheartedly, to flick through some envelopes there. "Is that—is that all?" She could hardly meet his eyes, and her gaze fell again on the stack of bills and a pair of porcelain birds positioned as ornaments.

"Isn't it enough?" Wei said. He looked past her.

Gin turned at the sound of a rustle and saw the girl, Emily, who had snuck in the back door and around through the kitchen to peep. The girl turtled back behind the door, and Gin felt relief. But within a second, the child joined them in the hall, pressing Gin's legs like a cat winding her way. Gin looked down at the little girl watching her father. Although it was the polite thing to do, Gin made no move to introduce them.

Wei Ing made eye contact with the child. He reached into his pocket, leaned down, and silently offered a small orange to the tiny hand that was already reaching for it. Gin opened her mouth to forbid Emily from taking it, but the fruit had already passed from one to the other, the child's exultant, doughy face upturned.

"Thank you," the girl said, smiling, proud of herself for remembering to say it. She glanced up at Gin for approval, but saw none.

Wei Ing nodded to each of them and closed the conversation by saying that Gin was looking well. Then he showed himself the door.

"Who's that?" Emily asked, her fingernails already prying up the bright skin of the mandarin.

Gin crouched at eye level with the girl. "You must *never* take things from strangers."

"But you know him. He was in our home." Emily flicked a section free and popped it into her mouth.

Gin grabbed her by the shoulders and shook her. Peel fragments scattered as the orange fell and rolled down the hall. "Not everyone I know is kind. Not everyone—"

"You're hurting me!" Emily yelped.

Gin pulled her in and held her tight, her nose buried in the girl's hair. "I'm sorry," she whispered. She could feel tears behind the words, and she stood up quickly and turned so the girl wouldn't see them. From outside, Gin could hear the twitters of the other children. She took Emily's hand and rushed to return to them, stooping to pick up the orange peel along their way.

={ 65 }=

ALFRED MOSS FOLLOWED the man in the polka-dot tie through
the private casino. It was located up a stair behind a barbershop, on
a second floor with the windows blacked out. From the street there
were signs declaring vacancy and a false number you could call to see
about renting the joint. When he first arrived in the small city, he
called that false number and a real girl answered and took his name,
saying someone would get back to him soon. But he'd found that
going out with Betsy was a faster means to getting his calls returned.

All around him, blackjack was dealt, cards turned up gracefully.
Nevada's well-heeled ranchers thronged around a table, shooting dice,
whooping, and clambering for a better view. Moss, under the name
of Freddy McGee, was brought over to Felix Vargas, who was locked
up in business negotiations at a back table and looked none too happy
to see the drifter who had recently jilted his daughter.

"Five hundred thousand," Vargas said to a man in a fedora.

The man stood up to leave. "Five hundred, got it."

"Mr. McGee, what can I do for you?" Vargas turned to Moss and
put out a hand in welcome, even as his brow wrinkled.

Vargas retracted his hand from their shake almost before it was
finished, but Moss paid this no mind. He smiled broadly. "Mr. Vargas,
I know we haven't seen each other in several weeks now, but that is
precisely why I've come."

"You want to cash out your investment." Vargas curled his mustache and remained standing, as though the meeting meant nothing and would be over in a moment. Moss was less than average height, but he towered a full head over Felix Vargas. "Jose," Vargas called to a man with legs like pillars. "What did we take from Mr. McGee?"

"Three thousand," came the reply. "Eighty-twenty split in our favor on the profits. We've only brought in eight, so Mr. McGee's cut is sixteen hundred."

"I put in three thousand *plus* a Duesenberg," Moss protested.

"That very pretty garbage can?" Jose remarked. "I've got cattle that run faster." Jose had a stare one shouldn't argue with, but Moss did argue, saying the car was worth at least eight, and that he was certain the agreement had been sixty-forty.

Vargas hooted. "Perhaps if you were family."

"Well, sir, that's exactly what I wanted to talk to you about." Moss boldly dropped down into the chair at the table where Vargas had been conducting his meetings. Surely being seated would assure him more respect.

To Moss's disbelief, Vargas lashed out: "Do you know that she cried for hours? Have you any idea what that is like, to catch the tears of your daughter in your hands?"

"I think you're being melodramatic, sir," Moss responded, wondering how, exactly, one caught tears.

Vargas relented and sat down across from him. He gestured Jose away. After the big man left the room, Vargas looked squarely at Moss. Vargas's eyes watered. "Right now Betsy is praying with the sisters at Saint Mary's. Because of you, she now wants to become a novice and take her vows as a bride of God."

She ain't no novice, Moss almost blurted out. He contemplated the angles left. He could save this. He snapped his fingers. "And that's why I've come! It was just a spat."

"You take a young girl out for some wooing and petting, then you leave her on the side of a highway and drive off—in *her* car. Is that what you call a spat back east?"

Moss cleared his throat. "Yes, well, I did return the car."

"Eventually."

Moss leaned forward eagerly. "It's clear I have her devotion, so really it's you I want to win over. An eighty-twenty split? That's robbery. And I'd be a fool to cash out. I mean, you wouldn't treat your future son-in-law this way, would you, sir?"

A dubious sound, someplace between a hiccup and a sigh, escaped Vargas's lips. "To whom are you proposing, Mr. McGee? To Betsy, or my money?"

Moss smiled at Vargas as charmingly as he could. He willed his eyes to turn liquid and soft, as they did when he looked at a woman.

"Now, Felix," Moss said. "I want to make amends."

A knock came at the door. "Yes!" Vargas shouted.

Jose leaned into the room. "Don Vargas," he said. "It's Betsy. She's here with the sheriff."

66

ROSINE PERRAULT MOVED behind the bar, glancing at the patrons in the room. It was a Sunday, and though there weren't that many customers, those she had were well on the way to being soused: a handful of regulars, and two men upstairs with girls. Kitty was waiting for her to come back to bed. Kit never seemed to care how long she had to wait—and if she wasn't expected to play piano or trumpet somewhere, she was happy to wait all night. Lately, she was at Rosine's so often she had picked up enough French to converse.

Rosine heard an unusual amount of racket from upstairs: a man's voice raised enough to carry down the stairs into the barroom.

"Wake up, whore!"

Rosine ducked into the office and hollered for Kitty to come out and take the bar quick. She had a boy who often bartended, but he'd begged for a night off after working two weeks straight.

"Mon Dieu," Rosine muttered as she dashed up the stairs, but she didn't need to rap on the door of the room because it was already open. The man, a barrister who'd been there only once before, was pulling on his coat and leaving.

"You owe me," he growled into Rosine's face.

"Que s'est-il passé?" she called to the girl, but there was no answer. A glance told Rosine what had happened. The girl had passed out

before the man could finish, or perhaps even start. She was fast asleep. *"Pauvre cone,"* Rosine muttered.

"Just a moment," Rosine told the customer. She had a better girl for him anyway—stunning and happy to please—one she promised would make the disappointment fade. She knocked on a door across the hall and called for Audrey to get ready. *"Vite, vite, s'il vous plaît."*

As he waited, the man insisted he should have a full refund, a discount at the very least. "I thought it was the fantasy of every man to have two women in one night. I should charge you double," Rosine replied, and they were saved from haggling further because Audrey opened the door wearing a fine-woven black negligee and garters with pink ribbons.

"Rosine!" a voice hollered from below.

She turned at the sound of her name and saw her bouncer, a massive-shouldered Italian who went by Primo, standing at the bottom of the stairs. He seldom came inside unless the barroom got rowdy, but there was no sound of a din.

"You got a meeting with the Chinese?" he asked as she rushed down to meet him.

"You did not let them in, I hope."

Primo shrugged. "Hard to turn away a woman. Weren't you looking for an Oriental for upstairs?"

"Moi? Non. This is just something a customer wanted, *un homme pitoyable."* She waved her hand. "One of many ridiculous requests."

The bouncer puffed up his cheeks and blew out. "Well hell. I woulda curbed 'em, but she says they got official business and that you're expecting them."

Rosine turned from the stairwell and peered into the barroom. Her visitors were already seated in the corner.

"I have never seen these ones before," she said. She laid a hand on Primo's beefy elbow. "Go back to the door—but listen for my call in case I need you."

"Figured a woman would be—"

"*Oui. Je comprends.* Probably nothing." Rosine drew herself up, her spine stiff, as she crossed the room.

Kit was at the bar, chipping ice off the block and scooping it into glasses. "Rye and ginger for her, plain soda water for him," she informed Rosine.

Rosine watched the couple carefully. Her eyes flicked across the room. It was emptier than when she'd gone upstairs, and two of her patrons who came together to drink and argue with one another were now getting to their feet. "Don't serve them," she said, placing one hand out as Kitty moved to pour the sodas. "Look, they are making other customers leave. I do not want them here."

"But why?"

"*Parce que . . .*" Rosine launched into a long tirade in French that made Kitty blink in bafflement.

"You might as well serve them now," Kitty pointed out. "There's no one left to protest."

"*C'est parfait,*" Rosine remarked sarcastically as Kit poured the drinks at last. "*Et pour de l'eau de Seltz à cinq cents.*"

※

KIT HANDED THE GLASSES to Rosine and watched her walk across the room, her steps quick and hard, heeled boots echoing in the now-empty bar. The man looked up at Rosine and smiled. The young woman appeared much more anxious, although she accepted the drink with a thank-you. She kept glancing at the man, as if waiting for him to speak. The small man was calm as stone. Rosine's back was to Kitty, and although she couldn't see Rosine's expression, she knew by the shape of her shoulders she was angry, and that her face would show it too.

The man introduced himself in English as Wei Ing from New York, and the woman as his daughter Gin. Then he switched to Cantonese and the girl took over, speaking his words in English. "'Our associates have come here many times, but this will be our last visit.' He says, 'I am the last one to be sent. It is time for you to tell us.'"

"*Je n'en sais rien,*" Rosine protested.

As Kit came out from behind the bar, she wondered if Rosine was telling the truth. Did she know more than she was saying?

"What's this about?" Kit said, stepping in with a bowl of peanuts that no one wanted. Kit could feel the young Chinese woman, Gin, fixing her eyes on her baggy man's suit.

"What is she saying?" Gin asked Kitty.

"It's French. She says she knows nothing."

Gin glanced nervously at her father, who grinned and sipped his soda water. Gin turned to Wei and conveyed Kit's translation for her father.

Suddenly Rosine leaned forward, placing her fists on the table. "*Vous êtes comme tous les autres, oui?*"

"Rosine," Kit said, a warning tone in her voice because she did not want to translate this. She knew she'd already overstepped by coming out onto the floor. She had never interfered before in Rosine's business.

"*Je dis simplement que je sais ce qu'ils veulent.*"

What did Rosine mean when she said she knew what these two wanted? What on earth *did* they want? As Kitty moved back to her place behind the bar, she turned and spoke low to Rosine. "*Qu'est-ce que c'est?*"

"Opium." Rosine's eyes flashed, and she looked right at Mr. Ing as she spoke. "It does not take a genius. Three Chinese have already come asking, and he would not bring his daughter if he were looking for pleasure from the girls upstairs."

Gin did not bother to translate. Wei Ing smiled. He stood and leaned in over the table, nose to nose with Rosine. They were about the same age, each dark-eyed and dark-haired but graying. Each unwilling to back away.

"Show me," Wei Ing said, his breath hitting Rosine's lips.

She was the one to break the stance. She laughed and said *D'accord*, and went through the office into her bedroom, where only half an hour before Kit had been stretched out, reading a novel she'd pinched from her sister, *To the Lighthouse*.

While Rosine was gone, Kit picked up a bottle of rum and poured herself a drink. She sliced a lime. She grasped the pick and chipped out ice. Having a task to complete helped calm her.

Wei Ing came around the side of the table and stood at the bar, watching Kitty. He made a remark to his daughter that sounded lilting and perhaps derisive, and Kit felt her face flush because she was sure she was being made fun of.

"My father says she'd better come back." Gin nodded in the direction of the office, but Kit didn't believe it was the only thing the man had said.

At last Rosine returned. She stood directly in front of Mr. Ing. He turned his back to the dark bar and leaned against it, peering into her hand, which she extended. There was a small wooden heart there. Ing reached for it and removed the lid of the box. *"C'est tout,"* Rosine told him.

No one said anything for a moment. Inside was a small, dry ball of opium. Then Kit felt eyes on her, both Wei Ing's and Gin's, as the man craned his neck to look inquiringly at her.

Kit took a quick sip of her drink, then she translated. "She says, 'That's all.' And that is all. I can vouch for that. We don't smoke anywhere near as often as we'd like."

Gin stood up from the table as she translated, and peeked into the box her father held to see what was there. When he'd heard what the women had to say, he tossed the box and the opium onto the floor and raised his fist to his daughter. Gin yelped and jumped, though to Kit it was clear the gesture was only a threat. Rosine bent to pick up the opium, but Kit stood utterly still, staring at the holster with knives, just there, beneath the man's suit jacket. When he had raised his arm to his daughter, it had split open.

Ing and his daughter began to argue in Cantonese.

"Rosine," Kitty urged her, "call for Primo."

But Rosine's face had turned as fuchsia as her lipstick. She berated the Chinese man in French; Kit did not translate. Rosine clasped the box tightly shut and set it on the bar.

"I am sorry," Gin interrupted Rosine, her face full of fear. "He believes I have made a bad translation. You do not seem to understand what he wants. He says, 'I cannot leave without finding your source for opium.'"

Rosine spoke for herself this time, in English. "That is *all* I have."

"No," Gin said directly to the proprietress. "He wants what you *don't* have. He wants to know where you get it."

⌄ ⌄

IT WAS CLEAR to Gin that the mission was not going to end well. The French woman—the one named Rosine—would not give Wei what he wanted. And now the proprietress tipped her head back, stared hard at Gin, and said flatly: "A customer brings a ball from New York once a month. He trades it for a cunt or two." She lit a cigarillo, as if for emphasis.

Gin turned to her father and spoke—not Rosine's words, but her own. "She cannot give you what she does not have. Mock Duck is an idiot. You are too smart to have believed this lie all this time."

His arm shot out, and this time he did backhand her. Gin dropped against the table, clutching her cheek. When the shock passed and she straightened up, she saw both women were regarding her, along with the bouncer, who had pushed in through the outer door. He stood silently on the threshold, his arms crossed. Gin guessed he would not move unless Rosine gave him the nod.

Gin's father challenged her in Cantonese, asking if she believed she was smarter than he was. His eyes were cold, and his voice colder. "It is a very smart girl who believes a man loves her after one meeting. Surely you have seen enough men to know most are cowards. Your friend was offered a choice, and he chose to live and let you die. You are sure, now, that you know more than I?"

Gin said nothing. She clutched a hand to the burning spot where her father had struck her. The others seemed to be waiting for her to make a translation. They did not understand that what Wei Ing had said was spoken for her alone, and although she believed him, she would never repeat it.

"You are the coward," Gin told him, "if you let another man decide what you would do to your daughter."

Rosine exhaled smoke from her cigarillo. "Tell your father I cannot help him. You must go." She nodded to the bouncer before Gin could even make the translation. But Wei Ing required none. As Gin well knew, her father understood plenty. The atmosphere in the room had turned unfavorable and Gin knew what his fury looked like: he was not about to let the women control the outcome. He was already reaching beneath his coat with one hand, the other finding the nearest piece of skin, which was Rosine's.

Gin watched as her father yanked the proprietress toward him, his knife already at her heart.

Then the ice pick came down through his eye from the top of his skull.

Gin heard herself shrieking and shrieking. A urine stain bloomed on her dress and she fell to her knees. She had seen men killed in front of her in much more violent fashion, but this was her own flesh and blood.

As the younger woman in the suit, the one who had been translating, let go of the ice pick, Wei Ing collapsed on the floor. "I'm sorry," the young woman said, looking down at her hand.

Gin heard Rosine and the other woman speaking fast, words in French and in English, but in that moment she did not understand any language. Her father's remaining eye had turned pale and glassy. Wei had placed his back to the bar because he didn't perceive the women as possible threats—Gin saw that had been his mistake.

The bouncer crossed the room and seized the knife Wei Ing had dropped. Gin watched as he checked her father's pulse and declared him dead.

Gin scrambled to her feet. These white demons had killed her father, and she'd witnessed it. It was only logical that next they would kill her. Her brain didn't tell her this so much as her body. Each muscle begged her to run, and her legs cooperated.

The bouncer dropped Wei Ing and chased after her, but the man from the bar was heavy and Gin was already out the door and around the corner. She ran as fast as she knew how. The dog from the tavern chased after her, barking as if it were a game, but she hurdled a fence into a neighboring backyard and the dog lost track of her. She heard the bouncer yelling, but Gin didn't turn back. Her father had taught her: never stop. She broke her fingernails and tore her dress, but she managed to make it three streets over into a dark, silent neighborhood where the houses hunched together, before she ran straight for as long as she could, no footfalls behind her.

67

"I SAW THE KNIFE EARLIER," Kitty said to Rosine. "When he reached for it, I couldn't let him hurt you."

To Kit's dismay, Rosine said nothing. She simply stared at the back of the dead man's hair, his face now tilted downward against his leg.

"I hit him as hard as I could, didn't really think about it. I didn't mean to kill him. Oh my God. Yes, I did. Just at that moment, I did mean to kill him."

"Mon Dieu, mon Dieu," Rosine said, boring the heels of her hands into her eyes. *"Je ne peux pas regarder."*

Neither woman had moved by the time Primo the bouncer returned and said he hadn't been able to catch the girl. She'd dodged through a backyard and jumped a fence. Unlike some, he said, she didn't rabbit—most would stop and crouch down, find a place to hide. Not her, he said, and so she was gone.

"We gotta get the stiff outta here," Primo said, and he went into the kitchen and came back with a large potato sack. "No officer will believe her so long as we clean up good and deny everything."

"It is you that we have to hide, Kitty," Rosine said, her voice high and tremulous in a way Kitty had never heard.

Primo had already bent to shove the body into the sack. He looked up and said, "Not just her, Rosie."

"What do you mean?" Kit asked.

"'Pending on who his associates are, they'll be looking for you too. The girls upstairs. Everyone."

"But where can we go?" Rosine said.

A shiver coursed through Kitty's body, and she stared at Rosine blankly. She suddenly felt nauseous and cold. She trembled and looked down at her body, but couldn't seem to stop it.

Rosine gripped Kit by the arm and steered her. "Your sister's place," she answered herself, her touch quieting Kit's tremors. "To start, and then far, far away."

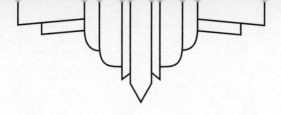

BOOK FOUR

SEPTEMBER
1929

"DRIFTER AND PERVERT" ARRESTED

Reno Evening Gazette, November 1, 1928

Freddy McGee, 28, no known address, was arrested on the eve of October 31st at the Golden Hotel by Reno sheriff Emil Vargas. The charges are illegal gambling, perversion of a minor, attempted oral sodomy, possession of alcohol, and vagrancy. Sheriff Vargas credits his brother, alderman Felix Vargas, with information that led to McGee's arrest. Hotel staff said McGee was a fixture at the shops on Commercial Row over the last two weeks. McGee is set to be arraigned this Monday in the court of Judge Antonio Vargas.

⩵⟨ 68 ⟩⩵

PROHIBITION AGENT GABRIEL BRENNAN sifted through the file that had landed on his desk. It had been almost a year since this Freddy McGee's arrest down in Reno, and now officials from that city's Bureau were telling him the man wanted to make a deal—information about a gang here in Detroit—in return for a reduced sentence. What did Gabriel care about that? He'd never heard of any Freddy McGee in Detroit, even if the man claimed to have ties here.

Gabriel scratched his head and looked at the facts before him. He was being asked to investigate, of all people, the Reverend Charles Prangley.

As Gabriel knew, Prohibition gave many cranks employment— and in his opinion, Prangley was one of them. After the reverend held a benefit or cruised the river shouting his hokum for the newspapers, some ass-ripper from Washington would always phone Gabriel and ask what in holy hell was going on up in Detroit? Gabriel would explain it was a stunt to raise money for the kook's little church. Let the coast guard deal with him, Gabriel had argued. We don't work with water. That was logic enough for Washington. But now, here was Prangley's name again.

Other names from the brief: Ernest Krim, pharmacist of Sweets' drugstore; Gerald Zuckerwitz, former middleweight; Jake Samuel; Vern Bunterbart; William Lynch; Bob Murphy; Tom Fontaine; Otto Schultz.

Several of the names belonged to laid-off Ford line workers. Gabriel flipped through the list. Although he'd have to check, none jumped out at him as having come to the notice of his office. If it were up to him, he'd let the whole thing go—except that a deal had been struck with this fellow McGee.

Gabriel called in the Bureau of Prohibition's best secretary and asked if she could go down to the library and sift through the newspapers for anything that might have appeared on Reverend Charles Prangley.

"Start with March of '28," he told her.

The young woman was whip smart. Every day a different skirt suit. He'd never seen her in a dress, but that was fine by him. He appreciated a tough girl, especially in an office like theirs. She'd been the Bureau secretary for only a month or two. The last one had left after twelve years of service—said she'd seen too many files with photos of men riddled with bullet holes, some of them put there by their own agents. Gabriel had been a Prohibition agent in New York, then Baltimore, before getting moved up North. Although he was not a permanent fixture in the Detroit office, he could see this young girl had missed the worst years of Prohibition.

She was efficient, and came back before lunch.

"Three articles," she said. "One editorial and two items from the social columns."

Gabriel sighed and put down his fountain pen. His eyes were the color of rock underwater and, unlike his bridge-building brother Frank, his face was pale as a baby's, as though he never saw daylight. He was closing in on fifty, but proud of the tuft of reddish curls atop his face. He knew he was thin enough that there was something youthful about him. Someone had told him once that his cheeks looked as though they'd been permanently pinched. His eyebrows were like whispers, and like his older brother he had a strong, straight nose that ran down the center of his face.

"Who protests drinking this many years into Prohibition? Everyone can see it's a fool mistake, and it's brought more damage illegal than legal." He heaved a deep sigh.

The girl looked at him with sympathy. "It is funny when you think of it. I mean, nothing happened after the mayor was arrested," she volunteered.

Mayor Smith made no quibbles with the media that his cellar was never empty, and he had been busted at the Deutsches Haus for drinking.

"Exactly," Gabriel murmured, tapping his pen hard against the file folder. "You know, the only reason the mayor was arrested was because a rookie was on the job that night. Jones. I heard he didn't know who the man was, just brought him in with everyone else." Gabriel felt as though he was chewing on something, or something was chewing on him. "Can you send in Agent Jones to meet with me? Tell him we've got a case all the way from Nevada."

Goering Jones had not been with the Bureau long enough for anyone to really notice his work there. The night he arrested Mayor Smith had been a fluke, and if the other agents remembered who was responsible, it was only long enough for a joke. So far as Gabriel could see, Jones, like all the young agents, had not yet figured out that his task was irrelevant; he showed up early and left late. He was a sandy-haired young fellow with a gap between his teeth that he showed so frequently it was clear he still chose being liked over being regarded seriously. He was good-looking, Gabriel thought, and, more important, he wasn't unbearable. Both attributes made him an attractive partner, and Goering Jones had a dynamism about him, something Gabriel couldn't quite name or glean from a fitness report.

"Let me know if I can do anything else," the secretary said, and hustled out into the larger office.

Jones came in and, without greeting him or looking up, Gabriel read out the names from the file.

"What's that?" Jones asked, sitting down opposite Gabriel. "Roll call at the high school down the street?" He smiled at his own wit, showing the teeth.

"Could be just as easily, couldn't it? Washington says it's an interesting lead. You believe these men have a conspiracy going?"

Jones put his hand out for the papers and looked them over before quoting Bureau scripture: gangs almost always drew along solid ethnic lines and never organized beyond that. "These are just local bohunks putting some extra stout in their cellars."

That was what he had been thinking too, Gabriel said. Except for the fact that Prangley stuck out.

"You want me to come with you and we'll arrest him at the pulpit?" Jones laughed.

Gabriel Brennan shook his head, steadfastly unamused. "This informant, Freddy McGee, if there's anything to it, they'll put him on a train and get him up here to testify at a grand jury first."

"And you want me to help?" Jones seemed dumbfounded.

Agent Jones was in his early thirties and Gabriel could see he was still in denial of the fact that he needed glasses. Jones squinted at the papers in the file. "Vern Bunterbart—I do know that name. He's dead."

"Thank God. One less file."

"He shot up a saloon two years ago. Some agents at the Bureau of Investigation believed it was a political act."

"Well, that would make Hoover dance the Charleston. This Bunterbart. Was he a Red?"

"No. A member of the Teutonia Society. It's a recruitment group for the Nazis."

"The what?"

"Naht. Zee. A political party in Germany."

"Do they drink?"

"We don't know that yet, sir."

"Not our problem, then. But it certainly seems queer," Gabriel mused, suddenly almost interested in his job. "If Bunterbart is connected to the gang, there could be something to all of this." He drew a breath as deep as if it were his last, then made some notes to add to the folder. The amount of work they had ahead of them made him want to take early retirement, but he could see Jones was eager for it.

"Prangley, he's bound to be educated," Jones said, and Gabriel agreed. "We go straightaway and question him, we'll get nothing. He's smart. He'll clean house, won't he?"

"Surveillance," Gabriel confirmed, but he felt an ache of fatigue in his bones just thinking about the long hours in a car. He blew out his breath and closed the file. "I'll consult again when I need you," he said, dismissing the other agent.

={ 69 }=

ALFRED MOSS HAD ALMOST GOT USED to the shackles. He'd almost got used to holding a shovel and working in a chain gang. What he couldn't get used to was defecating in front of other men. If his crimes had been serious, he could have made peace with the whole situation, he thought. But it wasn't as if he'd murdered anyone. He'd been put away on trumped-up charges. Sure, he might have stolen a little here or there, and he'd dallied with the Vargas girl—was it his fault if she went and got her heart busted up over a grope or two with some other woman? He had underestimated her father's power—and his reluctance to pay Moss out. In the end, it was the Vargas family who had turned the tables and taken him for all he was worth.

Now, chained, Moss was prodded in the ribs by a guard, and he climbed into the back of the truck behind the other inmate he was shackled to. All of the inmates stank like they'd been rolling in pig-shit, and they still had a two-hour drive back to the prison. McGee had to piss and there was no way that was happening anytime soon. He thudded down on the floor of the truck, and his ankle jerked as the man behind him climbed up and sat down. The door of the truck slammed shut, and they rode in partial darkness, just a thin line of window allowing a slanting shaft of light. Moss put his head down. He never talked to the others because he found it only led to trouble. All of the other men were at least twice as large as he was and were serving for gruesome acts he sometimes heard them crowing about. He stared at his hands, which were so blistered the blood bubbled up through the dirt.

They bounced forward and side to side, and one of the inmates farted, a toothy zipper tearing through the cramped space. Two of the men guffawed, and two swore when the stench hit them, and then the driver called back for them all to shut up, and after a while the tossing motion of the vehicle put Moss to sleep.

BACK AT THE PRISON, back in his cell, out of his shackles, Moss moved for the toilet, but his cell mate grabbed his shoulder and shoved him back. Moss watched the bigger man lower himself onto the metal seat while Moss sank into the corner holding his stomach and whimpering.

"McGee, tell me again about that sweet Mexican gal," his cell mate said, grunting.

"Now? Jesus." Moss bent in pain. He had to piss, he had to shit, and apparently he had to defend his actions to a voyeur and pervert. "She wasn't no nun when I knew her and I hardly laid a hand on her. Father had half the damn city in his pocket, that's all."

"Didn't like you, huh?" The ogre wiped himself, hitching up his pants. "Boy, you musta given her the business end of everything."

Moss didn't bother protesting. He sprang for the john, shedding his pants and releasing the torrent he'd held in far too long.

"I did lots of no-good in my time—but not to her. If anything, I was halfway decent for once." Moss finished, hitched his pants back up, and lay down on his bunk. "That's the queer thing—you never get caught for what you think you're going to."

His cell mate pressed him for details, but Moss didn't elaborate.

What came to him was the image of the street he'd been driving along with Ernest Krim after high school graduation. A moonlit tower illuminated the area. He and Krim weren't far from downtown, and although he saw no one nearby, he could hear other revelers in the distance. They had been coming from a burlesque house, where a girl with shimmery stockings and breasts that rotated in precise orbits had hooked a leg over Krim's shoulder. Even though Alfred knew Ernest only from sports at school—a tightly wound individual if ever there was one—Moss had stolen a bottle of apricot brandy and managed to talk him into more than a few slugs. They'd hopped, laughing, into Krim's car after the show, Krim insisting Moss drive because he was scared he was going to vomit.

The impact from the pedestrian crossing the street in front of them had knocked Moss's hat and tassel off. Krim had been thrown against the passenger door, conked his head, and passed out, dropping the bottle he'd been sipping, which rolled across the floor and hindered Moss from pressing the brakes as quickly as he might have. The car didn't stop for twenty yards.

When he'd climbed out and seen that the man he'd struck wore police-officer blues, Moss hadn't known what to do. Unnerved, he'd tugged Krim across the seat and slumped him forward over the steering wheel.

Now, Moss closed his eyes. He could see the stranger's face just as clearly as any he'd known: a silver mustache and a white, bald dome of forehead—until it gave way to blood and brain. The cop's eyes had been closed, as if he'd just decided to lie down and go to sleep right there in the street after a night of patrolling. Moss had figured that if anyone heard the noise and came to investigate the crash, it was Krim who could take the rap. He was from a family of means, after all, and Moss was from nothing. But no one came and Krim woke, saw the body, and immediately began to weep. It had only been five minutes since the accident, but it felt like an hour to Moss. "Let's scramble," he told Krim. He knew where they could hide the car.

It was only later that Moss snapped to the fact that he could use the guilt against Krim—and he did. For years, the secret bound them and kept Krim compliant.

Now, from the bunk below, Moss's cell mate whistled and pressed him again. "McGee, if ya don't tell me, I'm gonna believe ya never did anything but drink from the fur cup."

"I pinned a hit-and-run on a buddy."

"Ain't murder if you don't mean it," the voice dismissed.

"It was a cop."

"Well, then that's a service you done."

Moss felt no better for having confessed. He closed his eyes and searched for some comfort behind his eyelids. He found a faraway face looking up at him from deep in his consciousness: it was his wife's. Then his baby's. Both were pale and shining.

MOSS WAS STILL LYING on his bunk waiting for his block to be called to the shower when the guard came to the tiny window of the cell. He tapped hard with his club. "Prisoner McGee! Get up! County attorney here to see you."

They called him by name so seldom that it took Moss a minute to respond. He was taken through the hall and down into the room used to interrogate him a year earlier. He edged inside, sweat riding his skin at the memory of the force they'd used back then. But instead, there was the county attorney he'd asked for months before. He'd written several letters, each revealing more than the last.

"Got your letter, Mr. McGee. Made some inquiries," the man said with a drawl. He didn't bother to shake hands or introduce himself. "The Bureau of Prohibition in Detroit has confirmed the identities of the men you named," he said. "The Bureau is interested." The attorney was maybe fifty, well dressed, and smelled of Barbasol. Moss hadn't seen anyone so clean or decent in a year. The attorney took statements out of a briefcase.

"You'll get me out?" The words jumped from Moss's mouth in a yelp.

"Fed boys can request all they want. But a county judge has to agree to vacate your sentence. Lucky for you, Judge Merkin is fixing for an appointment on the federal circuit court. Wants to make Washington happy, you see? Round the office we say just as soon as Merkin makes the Supreme Court, he'll run for God after that." The lawyer had a dusty laugh. "Now, sign your formal statement, look it over, all the facts you told me are there."

The county attorney stopped talking and pushed the paper toward Moss. Then he sniffed. "Jesus Christ on a steer, McGee, when was the last time they let you shower?"

$$=\!\!\{\ 70\ \}\!\!=$$

CAPTAIN COUTURE LEANED over the rail of the tugboat, sipped from a flask, and shouted at Prangley: "You still have an hour of my boat's time, reverend. I can run you over to Peche Island. Lovely this time of year!" The tugboat captain punctuated his offer with a quiet burp.

Prangley was pacing the dock, Prohibition literature ready in his hand for the fine ladies of Detroit. None had shown up. Jean Philby had promised that she would be there with three friends. Prangley yelled back to the tugboat, "They're probably running late at lunch."

The captain repeated the line. "Running late at lunch?"

Prangley watched him shuffle into the bridge and give the order to stop firing the boiler.

"No use burning half the coal on the lakes waiting for ladies at lunch." Couture laughed and wheezed.

Prangley grimaced. He paid Couture in collection-plate singles, enough to buy two hours on the water. The last fundraising trip on the river had put thousands of dollars into Prangley's tax-free coffers. Those checks signed with the finest names of the city had been meant to buy motorboats, but all of it had been invested in his airplane. Some of the sharper women had asked after the boats, and when they would be put on the river to patrol against the evils of Canada, but Prangley would always charm them toward other topics and bits of gossip. In the last few months he suspected news of his business had entered the chatter circuit and wise husbands had begun to forbid check signing and hobnobbing with the handsome pastor.

Prangley looked at the last trickle of ash floating out of the boat's smokestacks then dropped the pamphlets into the oil-slick water around the dock. He rubbed his face. He realized he hadn't shaved that day, or the day before.

CHARLES PRANGLEY WAS ALREADY BLEARY-EYED as he drove out to Grosse Pointe, drinking from a full bottle of Scotch. No one would notice, and if they did, the alcohol would only give him more appeal, he told himself. The party was in full swing when he arrived. He was glad he'd dressed for it. The mansion was an English manor with three peaks, an atrium, a garden and swimming pool to the side. A valet took the car before Prangley could park it in the already-filled circle. Even from outside, he could hear a live band. A butler took his hat and coat in the reception room, and Prangley was thankful he'd thought to stash the bottle, already bearing a Mr. Bucci's label, inside his suit jacket.

Prangley steered himself across the reception room where men in tuxedos milled, smoking under the carved oak ceiling. Mabel Abbot and her daughter Hilda stopped him at the door of the ballroom. Inside, young debutantes whirled and zigzagged across the floor in dresses like meringue—lovely sixteen- and seventeen-year-olds with their pale skin and their plump cheeks, their exposed shoulder blades straight and thin as crucifixes. Mrs. Abbot glanced nervously across the room even as she placed a hand on the tall pastor's arm and smiled, waylaying him, parking her girth against the door frame so he could go no farther.

"Reverend! We didn't know you were coming," she said loudly, though there was no point—certainly no one would hear her over the music and the din of voices.

"Mrs. Laprise didn't say you were!" Hilda yelled. A painted-on mouth smiled, though her tone cracked a little.

The Abbots had donated the organ at the First Lutheran, but it had been months since Prangley had seen any of the wealthy wives who'd eagerly clambered aboard his chartered boat or packed the funeral of Alfred Moss. Sermons Prangley could deliver, and adages aplenty, but other sorts of social excitement were harder for him to navigate without betraying his own habits. For a time, the ladies of the parish would invite him along to socials, and more than one of the widows would lean against him provocatively—as if such a thing were possible, thought Prangley with a shudder. Always the attention came from the fleshy-armed and hairy-lipped, or the gaunt ones who followed eating programs and dressed in low-cut gowns and wore too much gold. He looked past them all to their daughters. Was it his lack of interest in the matrons, or the absence of exhilarating new experiences he could offer, that had allowed him to slip off their guest lists?

It probably didn't help that at one point in the last deb season he had cornered young Hilda near the ladies' room and fingered the lace shoulder of her dress a little too long. He hadn't gone further than flirting with the twenty-year-old, and she hadn't seemed to mind terribly, but now, when she smiled, he noted some nervousness in it. Her mother continued to look tense. Prangley leaned forward and planted a chaste kiss on the old woman's cheek, telling her she was a vision. Perhaps he could win them over after all. Mabel Abbot smiled—but there was still worry in it.

All he needed was a sliver of space. There—he was in the ballroom.

"You will behave, won't you?" Mrs. Abbot whispered to him, more as if reassuring herself than as a warning.

"Of course, my dear Mrs. Abbot. I'm seeing someone now, actually."

"Oh?"

"A charming woman named Myrna. Delightful young lady. Coincidence gave us our acquaintance, almost as if there were some wondrous hand pushing it into existence."

Mrs. Abbot was more curious than charmed by the story—Prangley could already see the gossip wheels turning in her head as she mentally scrutinized the name against a list of socialites and their daughters and came up short. He was careful not to say more. Though there was indeed a Myrna, he would never bring her anyplace like this. Like all his women, he met her when he purchased her services, at a squalid loft called the Sugar Box, and he still hadn't decided why he'd been beguiled by one so crude. He felt dizzy and leaned back against the door frame he'd only just made it through.

"Marriage-worthy?"

"Early days, but a lovely girl," he replied, staring around the room at the swirl of dresses, the glint of tear-shaped gems, the long draperies and white table linens, the brilliant chandeliers overhead.

The hosts, Mr. and Mrs. Laprise, were nearby but occupied. The husband was bragging half-drunkenly to someone about a yacht, and the wife seemed intent on flirting with one of his associates. Prangley watched her push her generous sequined bust into the man's shoulder as she said something in his ear. It wasn't until Mrs. Abbot intervened that the Laprise couple received Prangley. They were people with faces solemn enough to be printed on money, and Prangley wished they could know how much he belonged with them, how prosperous he really was. The mister grabbed at Prangley's hand and gave it a single obligatory pump and the missus leaned in for a quick kiss that wouldn't have connected if Prangley hadn't leaned in also and smeared his lips across her earlobe. He'd met them only twice before, but they were the parents of a marvelous girl named Piper who was making her entrance to the debutante world that evening.

"Reverend, we didn't get your RSVP," Mrs. Laprise began. "But you got an invitation?" The question pitched her voice up higher than usual, and she rubbed at her ear where he'd left perhaps too much saliva.

"Of course. Stunning. Nice to receive something engraved," Prangley guessed; he had not seen the card. The whiskey he'd snuck in the car made him a little uncertain on his feet, and he held Mrs. Laprise's hand longer than he ought to have, mostly to hold himself up. "That Piper." He lifted a finger as if to scold the girl, though she was on the other side of the room and hadn't yet spotted him. Truth be told, he didn't know if the sweet sixteen-year-old even knew who he was. She'd been dragged along to church events, though, and when Prangley had spotted the notice of her coming out in the newspaper, he'd decided spontaneously to attend the ball.

"Well, more the merrier," Mr. Laprise said. Looking Prangley up and down, he added, "Nice duds. There is a bit of champagne going around, so if it's not entirely a dry event, I'll take the blame. Leave the ladies out of that."

"Everything in moderation," Prangley said.

A woman nearby broke in to grasp Mrs. Laprise by the arm. It was Jean Philby. "Bertie Parker is visiting from England," Jean exclaimed without glancing at him. "She was telling me about terrific fighting at the Temple Mount in Jerusalem. Can you imagine? Men, women, children. Terrible! She's collecting money for the charities. I already gave."

"What kind of charities?" Mrs. Laprise asked as she turned away from Prangley.

"Christian ones, of course." Then Jean seemed to notice him. Her lips stretched in a straight line, a smile that left her teeth concealed. She touched his shoulder. "But please don't worry, Charles. You're still our favorite charity."

It was something he had learned studying this type of woman. Though easily given over to nattering, gossip, and vain obsessions, they possessed a near-animal sense of hierarchy. They could look at Prangley and know the name "Lester Lewis" even if they didn't.

Jean noticed Prangley's long face then. "Charles. Did I miss your river cruise last week? I am so embarrassed. You must tell me when the next one is."

He saw for the first time that her face was sharp as a hatchet. No wonder her husband, Joe, didn't find her attractive.

"If there is one." She laughed and said, "I heard Prohibition is going the way of the cloche . . ."

"Are we really done with the cloche?" Mrs. Laprise asked, rattled.

Abruptly, Prangley left the adults, beelining for a table of young debs in white, most with dates who looked as though they hadn't begun shaving yet. For courage, he tucked one hand into his pocket and rubbed his thumb along the seam of the old leather key fob, the one he'd taken from Seamus Lynch. The parsonage had been broken into enough times he didn't dare leave it behind: the blood-flecked fob went everywhere with him now. Sometimes Prangley thought of it as a good luck charm. Other times he touched it and revulsion overtook him. In his wilder fantasies, he wondered if it was the missing Alfred Moss breaking in.

Behind him, he heard Mr. and Mrs. Laprise trading opinions.

"Was he drunk?"

"Believe so."

"Did you invite him?"

But as he expected they would, they let him stay. The Laprises had their own merriment to make and turned back to guests who were more familiar.

Taking stock of the young people at the round table, Prangley congratulated the girls on their coming out. He bowed down and took the hand of one, asking her name. The fellows, he thought, looked ridiculous in their clothes: boys playing at being men. One reminded him of Seamus Lynch's son, Willie, though he knew that insidious boy was far too low and poor ever to win his way into an affair like this one. "Is this your date?" Prangley asked the prettiest girl, jerking his head toward the young man.

She giggled, and the young man said indignantly that of course he was. "He's on the wrestling team," the girl boasted.

Prangley peered at him. "Have you ever hurt someone? I mean, really hurt them?"

The young man said that wasn't what the sport was about. He extended his hand in a firm shake, pronouncing his aristocratic name as he'd been taught, with all three designations, the middle one a family name that told of the wealth on his mother's side.

"Do you know who I am?" Prangley asked the boy, who shook his head. "Well, I am God's own lawman in Detroit. Been in the paper several times." He secured a seat and regaled the boys with the story of pulling a car that belonged to a dead man out of the river. The girls were aghast, and pleaded with their dates: couldn't they dance now? But when none of the girls wished to dance with him, Prangley produced a full bottle of whiskey and snuck it beneath the table. All of the young people passed their glasses below the white cloth, their manners momentarily forgotten. There were other cocktails going

round the room, but none of the kids had figured out how to get one
without the disapproval of parents and chaperones.

An hour passed, and the band played "I Wanna Be Loved By You,"
"Tip-Toe Thru' the Tulips with Me," and "Happy Days Are Here Again."

"Did you ever hear of the Pullman porter train cars?" Prangley
inquired, now that half the girls were swaying in their seats, heavy-
lidded with the whiskey that topped their sodas. He didn't stop to
question why he had an urge to impress these rich children. Their
poise lasted even through the haze of the booze. The girls tittered
to each other but kept their hands folded. The boys sat as straight as
they could in their crisp clothes, giving full attention with their stupid innocent eyes. Pride coursed through Prangley's veins and lit his
cheeks pink as theirs. He could feel his heart pounding. He glanced
around the room, but if any of the adults noticed him sitting with
the youths, they thought nothing of it. Most were involved in their
own half-ripped pantomimes anyway. "Look at this label. Why, I put
these bottles on every—"

But Prangley didn't finish his sentence. Piper Laprise floated into
his peripheral vision. The young debutante came over because she had
spotted the bottle and what they were doing.

Prangley took his moment, standing and kissing the girl's cheek,
though he could see no recognition in her face. She was wearing a
band of flowers in her hair, and as he brushed her cheek, he breathed
in. "What an honor. Look at you, dear!"

Above the table this time, he poured himself a full glass of whiskey, and one for Piper Laprise. He passed it to her silently, and she
took it with a hand that shook. She glanced about anxiously. Her
dress left her shoulders and clavicle exposed, and dipped a white web
of fabric down into a V of modest cleavage.

"My mother says you're a reverend?" the girl asked, and turned her back to the room so her parents wouldn't see.

"A man can be many things." Prangley smiled.

Piper took a brave gulp. Her mouth split with disgust and she dashed a napkin off the table and dabbed at her lips. She handed the glass to one of the boys. "I can't drink it," she protested.

Prangley pulled her close and commanded her to dance with him. It was her party and he knew she would be the girl who was too polite to say no. She smelled like lilies. They'd only made one turn on the floor before Prangley felt his ankle twist clumsily and he fell. As he stumbled, he clutched the girl. Laughing, forgetting they weren't alone and that she didn't know him at all, he pulled her down on top of him.

Mr. Laprise and several other penguin suits quickly disentangled the odd couple and were none too gentle as they marched Prangley out through the reception room. He muttered apologies, but the men were fiery with drink themselves and didn't care to listen to the party-crashing reverend.

"It was a misunderstanding," Prangley assured them. "Really, now, there is no need for this. I always did have a weak ankle—injured it in the war. Piper is all right, is she not? I did not mean any harm, really. I never do, I never have, and I n-never—"

"He's torn Piper's dress and got half of them drunk!" Mr. Laprise declared to his wife when she tried to intervene.

"Blotto," one of the other men put in. "The girls, too. Hilda Abbot just ran up and told my wife that two of 'em are drink-sick in the ladies' room."

"A dazzling party!" an onlooker interjected. "Finally, I'm entertained."

"You hypocritical poltroon. You yourself said there was alcohol here, Mr. Laprise," Prangley argued. Laprise stared at him but said nothing. Prangley could feel his skin burning, could imagine the screwed-up expression on his face. As he looked at the circle of men, he recognized several he'd fingered as philanderers, buggerers, and frauds. He'd made blackmail money from them. There was Old Thomas Arsenault, the attorney who paid handsomely for his affair with a flapper, which Prangley had heard about from the society ladies on the boat searching for Alfred Moss's remains. Arsenault mailed bundles of dollars to a post office box that Prangley kept under another name.

Crankshaft Joe Philby, another of Prangley's blackmail victims, came forward. "You dare speak to Mr. Laprise that way at his own party? You're not a man!"

"Maybe not, but your lovers are!" Prangley retorted.

Crankshaft Joe laughed at first, as though the comment couldn't touch him. But glancing at Mr. Laprise and the disturbed faces of the other men, he became solemn. Then Joe wound up and slugged Prangley with unexpected force. Prangley heard the crack, and felt the rug beneath his hands as he toppled. It took him a moment to grasp what had happened. He shook his head slowly, and tried to stand for the next bit of the fight. But he couldn't gain his feet and no one remained to argue with him anymore. Tuxedos and gowns were fading as they retreated, beads and purses, tails and cufflinks, leaving Prangley where he was—he realized —sitting on the Oriental carpet in the reception room.

Two servants came over and helped Prangley up, one of them saying, "Please, sir, let's not make any more of a scene."

"Oh, fuck off," Prangley said, but only after he'd let them help him stand.

AS THE CHILD SANK onto the soft linens, Faye gazed down at her. The baby's smooth, tiny face never ceased to amaze her. That there were two babies, almost exactly alike, was stunning. Alistair was already sleeping in a crib placed perpendicular to Catherine's. Faye hadn't expected two, and Ernest had to run out and purchase a second crib, but the room accommodated them. A little larger, Alistair was usually the first to cry, the first to wake, and then again, the first to fall asleep. When the girl had been born, her whole head was only the size of Faye's fist, and even now, two months on, she was delicate, though she was plumping in the cheeks—and those wrists, creamy like ripe bananas. Faye reached down and pulled a flannel over the girl to the shoulder.

The rooms in the McCloud house had changed: repapered, with fresh curtains sewn and hung at every window. Kitty's childhood room was now the nursery, decorated in yellow and brown, although most nights at least one of the infants still slept in with Ernest and Faye. On the dresser were photos of the babies in Faye's arms the first week home from the hospital—and a wedding portrait of the new Mr. and Mrs. Krim. Since Kitty had been unable to attend, they'd kept the wedding simple and small. Faye had worn a white dress purchased off the rack.

As she turned to leave the nursery, Faye almost stumbled over Chaplin the dog. The spaniel skittered out of the way. She had adopted the dog when Kitty had shown up in the middle of the night the previous year, her girlfriend Rosine a pale ghost beside her, the dog in her arms, an enormous suitcase balanced between the two women. Faye hardly believed her sister capable of what they told her. She tried to convince Kitty to turn herself in to the police, but, failing at that, she had phoned Krim, who'd purchased the train tickets: Detroit to New York, and from there to Florida. Rosine said they could get a boat and go where no one would find them.

The dog had become very protective of Faye, as if it knew she had saved it from a street life. Rosine had called the dog Charles or Charlie Chaplin, but Faye didn't care for the name, which was too close to Charles Prangley's. Now the spaniel was just Chaplin. The dog at her heels, Faye descended to the kitchen, where she found her tea gone cold. Beside it was a letter from Kitty, who was camped out in a village called Le Morne-Rouge in Martinique, though the envelope was marked Fort-de-France, the nearest postal station.

Ma chère Faye,

That is how we say it here, as you know, though it does me good to write in English. My French has come a long way in the past year. When I hear it now, it has stopped sounding like absolute jibber-jabber, but I still miss being able to really talk to someone and feel confident and like myself—the way I always did with you. How come I didn't know I had such a swell big sister? When I think of you now, I think that we were always close. I remember how when I was young we used to call between our rooms at night. I miss you terribly.

Although it's always hot as hell here, it's been a sweltering summer, full of hurricanes. For all the beauty of Martinique, it is still a jungle. When the trees toss I sometimes feel as though the whole world could blow into the ocean. I am a long way from Detroit, that is for sure!

When Rosine was just a girl, she visited Martinique, and it was very cosmopolitan. She tells me they called the closest city to us, Saint-Pierre, the "Paris of the Caribbean"—but that was in 1900, before the volcanic eruption, and I'm sure she can barely remember it, let alone remember it right. Perhaps where we are was always a village, though. There are few amusements, and if I spend too long contemplating all the things that brought me here, I really do feel as though I am being punished.

Rosine's distant cousin, Marcel, the one I told you about last time I wrote, has demanded we pay all his expenses now. That is fair since the house is so small that we really have taken over. We leap over each other like mice in the night. None of it is how Rosine said it would be. She had hoped we'd be here only a few months and now here we are, almost a year has passed, and we still haven't saved the money to get to France. They are planting bananas here now, and it is a promising thing for the island, but all that work goes to the men. Making any money at all is . . . challenging. Rosine has found some ways to do so, but I can't. In good news, I've almost given up drinking . . . because I don't want to waste even a dime!

Send me some more books if you can. I devour them. There is nothing else to do here. I have so much time to practice now that I could become the best female jazz musician out there, but Rosine says she can't stand my vamping. *"Ça suffit!"* she yells, and a bunch of other phrases it still sometimes takes me a while to figure out because they're less common. One recently was "you sound like you're poking a pregnant cat." It turns out she is not as big a fan of jazz as you might expect. Marcel threw my trumpet out the window one night. It landed in the stinking passionflower—and I'm not saying that like a curse, that's what it's called. The instrument wasn't dinged, but I am more careful now.

Did you have the baby? A boy or girl? You are fine? I'd send you a gift but the only place to shop is Fort-de-France, about an hour down the road, and I have to get a ride with Marcel, whom you know I am so fond of! But I am sure you are good at mothering. And I'm happy to know you quit working for that old letch Prangley straightaway. When you said that you left him entirely in the lurch without any notice the minute you got engaged, I threw my arms in the air and cheered. Oh dear God, I've just realized it's been months since then. Time is forever here and nothing all the same. Please write.

De tout mon coeur,
Kitty.

=={ 72 }==

KITTY AWOKE to a low moan in the adjacent room. She turned onto her back and lay, unmoving, in the heat. She was wearing only men's boxers and a white undershirt, but still she could feel the damp of sweat between her and the sheets. She closed her eyes again, but the bedsprings were singing next door. She opened her eyes and stared at the foliage that peeked above the window. It was light out, but a thin, milky light, by her estimation 6 or maybe 7 a.m., and already Rosine had a client.

She hadn't felt Rosine leave the bed. She propped herself up on her elbow and reached to the bedside table for a cigarette. Finding an empty box, she plucked the nub of Rosine's cigar from the ashtray and lit it. She took a puff and coughed. *Who wants to screw at daybreak?* she asked herself, but she knew. There were only a handful of clients, and the ones with wives tended to come either right before work or right after. Kitty had a hunch which man it was just by listening. *Ma mignonne, mon ange*, he panted.

Kitty got up and crawled out from under the mosquito netting that cloaked her bed. She dressed and let herself out. She found coffee and cigarettes at a tiny café where the owner and his wife never ceased their conversation to look at or speak to her, then she sat outside, staring at the sky and the volcano in the distance. In 1902, Montagne Pelée had wiped out the neighboring city of Saint-Pierre, killing thirty thousand. A green mountain, its lip puckering up into the sky, she hoped it never blew its kiss at them. She hummed a tune that had been sticking around her head—it helped to distract her from the memory of the sound of Rosine making love with someone else. It was a misty day and in the distance the mountain reminded her of a sleeping animal. She dragged on the cigarette and blew it out, clouding her view of the volcano that much more.

Kitty knew that the sounds Rosine made were fake, they were the overstated kind purchased by a dollar, but at the same time she and Rosine had barely been together lately, Rosine always swatting Kitty's hand away or kissing her chastely. Living with Marcel, Rosine's second cousin, didn't help matters. He was in and out at odd hours—sometimes he worked in Fort-de-France and would be gone for a week or more, then he'd return and go on a drinking or drug jag. There were only two bedrooms in the tiny villa they shared and both were small. Marcel kept his things in the one Rosine used with clients, but said he preferred to sleep in the living room just as he had before Kit and Rosine arrived. He didn't seem to care what Rosine did in there, as long as there was money and the house was clean. Kitty had learned to cook because it was the only thing that kept them talking to each other.

Sometimes Kitty thought they didn't truly live at Marcel's but were only parked here like a car left by its owner next to the curb beyond the usual allotment of time.

Now she sipped her coffee and stared into the sky. She hoped that Faye would send money, though she hadn't been so bold as to ask. The shirt she wore was an old one of Marcel's, but it was two sizes too big for her and she'd had to leave the last buttons undone and use the tails to knot it at the waist. She took a notebook from her pants pocket and scratched a staff onto the page and a few quarter notes. The song was quiet, and a bit like the volcano there in the distance, waiting.

A tuft of green, but with a flashing orange heart deep inside. Then she turned the page and, before she could stop herself, wrote: *Galveston?* She scratched it out. Below she wrote: *New Orleans.* She drew an arrow beside the city name, and wrote *Kansas City.*

She'd written to her sister that she was saving every dime for the journey to France, but it wasn't entirely true—her French was still not as good as she wanted it to be, and it was not France she was thinking of, but getting back to America, with or without Rosine.

The sun was up now in the sky, and Kitty headed back to the villa. She found herself alone with Rosine, who had just washed up and was eating a banana while wearing a towel. Her hair lay slick against her face, but stray stands were already lifting away from the rest in the heat. Kitty knew that by noon, as the day's humidity peaked, it would be a tangle of curls. She leaned in to kiss Rosine's cheek, then pulled away as quickly. In spite of the washing, Rosine smelled of the man.

"Où étais-tu?" Where were you, Rosine asked. She seldom spoke in English anymore. She said she'd been hungry and there was no breakfast.

"Speak English with me," Kitty begged, even though the conversation was simple enough. She moved beside Rosine at the counter and took out a frying pan. "There are eggs, or I can make fritters," she said. But Rosine shook her head. "Coffee?" Kit offered, and Rosine nodded.

They stood in silence at the counter listening while the water in the coffeemaker fizzed and hissed as it warmed. Kitty poured, and Rosine drank the coffee black, burned her tongue, and pulled the cup away, opening her mouth and putting her finger to the scald.

"I hate that one," Rosine said. "He thinks he loves me."

"They all think that," Kit answered.

"Non."

Kitty offered milk to cool the coffee and Rosine accepted.

"Sometimes they curse at me and call me a whore," Rosine said, smirking. "A cunt, a bitch, a dirty girl. Not worthy of them. Then they come back the next week, needy as beggars, and say all the same things again."

Kit took a spoon and swirled it around until she caught a coffee ground and extracted it from her cup. "You don't have to sleep with all of them. We have enough money saved that we could go to Fort-de-France, at least get our own place, be in a larger city."

Rosine walked away from the suggestion and sat down on the sofa. She picked up a shirt of her cousin's and tossed it from one end of the sofa to the other. "*Et après?* I would rather sleep with the locals than the sailors," Rosine said. "Have you ever slept with a sailor? *Non?* Well, they are drunken brutes. And diseased. Then I will get syphilis and lose my face—my *face*. This is what you want? At least here in Le Morne-Rouge, it is quiet. We have family. The city is not that far if you want to go more often."

"You think that you like it here, but look at how much weight you've lost," Kitty implored, this time in French.

"Yet I haven't lost weight. My face is so puffy." Rosine put her hand to her cheek.

"You don't eat. You drink too much, and you do too much of Marcel's cocaine."

Rosine waved her hand as if there were a bad smell in the air. She protested that she hardly ever did cocaine. "Only when I am tired of screwing."

Kitty raised an eyebrow.

"I am always tired of screwing, that is true," Rosine acknowledged. "But so what? So what?"

This was an argument that had arisen many times in the past few months. Kit took out her notebook and flipped through it, humming the tune she'd been haunted by. She was so absorbed by it she didn't notice when Rosine left the room. She wrote down the words *Volcano Blows*. It would need lyrics, she realized, a singer. She remembered Faye saying that the Song of Songs was the only part of the Bible she'd read. Kitty found Marcel's copy—one of the few books in the house that was in English—and there she found the lyrics she was looking for.

> *Until the day break, and the shadows flee away, I will get me to the mountain of myrrh, and to the hill of frankincense.*

Kitty found Rosine half an hour later in the bedroom, lying down and still wrapped in the towel, maybe asleep—it was hard to tell. Kitty leaned in the doorway. "We're never going to Paris, are we? We can't even make it down the road forty minutes from here."

Rosine turned over and looked for her cigarillo on the bedside table, but didn't find it. In irritation, she sat up straight and said, "I never told you to kill that Mongolian."

"He would have killed you," Kit whispered. "Would you have preferred that?"

"Peut-être."

"You're just tired," Kitty said, and extended the pack of cigarettes she'd bought that morning.

"Je pense à cela tous les jours," Rosine said. Then, in English, as though Kit hadn't understood: "I think about this thing every day."

"Me too."

Rosine bent her head, her hair falling forward as she lit the cigarette. She drew on it, then leaned forward and tossed the lighter back to Kitty, more forcefully than needed. "That is why you are miserable, and I am happy with whatever I have."

The towel Rosine had been wearing was still tucked beneath her arms but had fallen open, exposing her belly, her legs, and her bush. There it was: trim, dark, and pink like a cat's mouth. Kit looked longer than she should have, then turned and left the room.

ROSINE HAD ANOTHER CLIENT later that night, which was how Kitty wound up alone at the movie house in Le Morne-Rouge—an old schoolhouse with chairs set up in rows.

"What show is it?" she asked the man at the door.

"It's Joan," he told her, nodding and smiling.

Kitty threw fifty centimes into the bucket at the door and joined a handful of viewers—a mother and her children, an old man already nodding off in the corner. Four French films had been donated to the theater by the French Ministry of Culture, and Kitty had seen each a dozen times already. There was Abel Gance's *Napoléon*, but she found it nearly unintelligible even after eight viewings because the film was meant to be four reels and the government had sent only one. There was *The Passion of Joan of Arc* directed by Carl Theodor Dreyer, *La fille de l'eau* directed by Jean Renoir, and a Dadaist ballet with music by Erik Satie called *Relâche,* directed by Francis Picabia. Strange though it was, *Relâche* was Kitty's favorite, partly because the camera spent a fair amount of time on the floor looking straight up the dancer's skirt at her drawers and garters, and partly because Kit liked to close her eyes and just listen to the music. The school cinema owned an old Edison and usually accompanied the film with the music of French composers, also donated by the Ministry. They had Satie, Ravel, Saint-Saëns, Fauré, and Chopin.

The usual choice to go with Joan of Arc was Debussy's "Clair de lune" suite. But this evening, when the film started, a jaunty tune poured out of the speakers. Kitty got up and went to find the old doorman, who was now running the projector. Although they didn't know each other's names, he knew her well from the number of evenings she had spent there. What could he help her with?

"The music," she told him. "What happened to the Debussy?"

"Eh?" He leaned in as if he hadn't heard her. She repeated herself, with better enunciation this time. In the glow of the projector, she watched his lower lip pull up over his top one in a kind of shrug. "It was stolen," he told her.

"What about the Ravel, or the Satie?"

"Also stolen. We are lucky to have the record player and projector still. Don't worry. Good music is good music." He pointed to a box at his feet full of records he had possibly brought from his own home.

Kitty took her seat and watched as Renée Jeanne Falconetti was put on trial. The projectionist juggled reels and records, changing the music several times. Kit wiped the sweat from her brow with a dingy handkerchief. By the time Joan of Arc signed the confession and was dragged to the pyre to be burned, the calypso song "Sally You Not Ashamed?" was bumping through a wood box amplifier. Kit watched sober-looking women in cloaks and head wraps gather around the fire, silently call out names, their eyes blinking in the pillars of smoke, and Falconetti as Joan burning, her shaven head lolling backwards but her eyes still fixed on the sky above as if on God. The birds flew overhead. The screen turned gray with smoke. All the while, a trombone and a saxophone seemed to play tag with one another in a carefree number, while a steel pan slid and bamboo sticks pitter-pattered underneath.

$$\equiv\!\!\{\ 73\ \}\!\!\equiv$$

"HE'S NOT A PRIEST," Prangley overheard Krim correcting his assistant, but it brought him a deep pleasure when he saw Krim's hand shake as he set down the pill bottle he'd been filling. Krim handed it to the assistant to take to the front register.

Prangley put on a slight smile as Krim came toward him. "Mr. Krim. I had a thank-you note from your wife the other week."

"Did you?" Krim was courteous but stiff, and Prangley could see that he was meant to understand he was not a welcome patron in the pharmacy. "Isn't the church keeping you busy enough? You need a special cure for one of your patrons?"

"Counseling for a death this morning. A wedding this afternoon. It is a Friday. Always a busy day." Prangley didn't tell Krim that Fridays were busy for other reasons too—there was the load for Mary Joy Davis, who always took twenty cases. These days Prangley always had a date on Friday and Saturday nights with Myrna. But he tried not to think about that, and played the role expected of him while the assistant pharmacist was still nearby. "One life ends as others begin, it is always this cycle. Love and death, like twins." He crossed his long fingers over one another. Then he drew himself up to his full height and glared at Krim.

As the assistant moved to the front of the store, Reverend Prangley dropped the niceties. He leaned over the prescription counter. "I have something to ask you."

Krim nodded his consent, but Prangley knew he had afforded him no opportunity to argue.

"Did you come by my parsonage the other day?" He kept his tone conversational, but even he could hear the note of worry underneath, like the ice that hides under a fresh snow.

Krim shook his head.

"It is a curious thing. Someone has stolen one of my suits." Prangley pursed his lips and gave Krim a long look. He tapped a finger softly on the counter. "Would you know anything about that?"

No, said Krim, he didn't.

"Look, I ask because with your height you would fit, and I would hardly blame you if you had decided to borrow it. 'God will not let you be tempted beyond what you can bear,'" Prangley explained, grinning, as if entering the parsonage with the intent to steal something were a common failure. He was hoping to trap Krim into an admission.

The pharmacist's face betrayed nothing. "How did the intruder get in?"

"I changed the locks three times this past year," Prangley said, his tone even, as though they were speaking of the weather, "but somehow things still go missing. Some watches, a pair of cufflinks, and most recently the suit." Prangley paused to recall the details, then continued chronicling, his voice wavering as the items gained importance to him. "Silk handkerchiefs, ties, cigars, a letter opener, a compass and a stopwatch, even a photograph of my mother. Once, a dog's bone appeared in my icebox where I'd had a steak." Prangley's cool faded and he put his hands on the counter between himself and Krim and leaned in again, hissing, "Someone certainly thinks himself very clever."

Krim shrank back slightly. In that moment he struck Prangley as being too meek for such a crime—breaking and entering required some backbone.

"As you know, I don't have time for any business outside here. I'm a husband now, and a father. That is my focus," Krim informed Prangley. He held the reverend's gaze.

Prangley grinned and cocked his head sideways. "Well, that is just it, is it not? You stole my secretary. Suppose you also took my suit?"

Prangley saw a flash of fear on Krim's face, and pressed harder. "Tell me about those sweet babies of yours. What are their names again? Catherine and Alistair? Do they sleep well at night? Do you? All tucked up in that house on Bagley, that little dog running around the yard. What a picture."

Krim stepped back. His face had gone ashy. He dropped his voice and whispered, "I'm out, Prangley. You know I'm out. I've gone straight."

The reverend nodded. "'There are two ways to be fooled. One is to believe what isn't true; the other is to refuse to believe what is true.'" He smiled, as if he had bested Krim in some way. He tapped his finger on the counter.

"You stay away from us," said Krim. "If I see you on our street, I'll—"

But Krim didn't finish the threat, because Prangley turned at the sound of the assistant approaching. He smiled at the young fellow.

Krim turned back to Prangley, reached beneath his lab coat, and pulled a ring of keys from his pants pocket. There were two house keys, the store key, and his truck key—a total of four. "The only locks I know are the ones that go with these right here."

"Of course, Mr. Krim," Prangley said, and put his hand down, skittering the keys back across the counter. "This is not an inspection. I really came by to say hello, and to give my best to your wife." He nodded and turned to go, holding the door open for an elderly woman on his way out.

$$\Longequal\!\!\{\ 74\ \}\!\!\Longequal$$

AFTER THE DOOR had closed and the woman had been helped and rung up, Irving, the assistant pharmacist, said to Krim, "I was trying not to overhear, but that seemed like an odd conversation. Could you smell the whiskey on him?"

"I could smell the crazy on him," Krim said. "If he ever comes in when I'm not here, you phone immediately—me or the cops."

Irving gave Krim a questioning look, but didn't linger; the telephone on the shop wall had begun ringing. Krim gestured for the young man to pick it up. "Sweets' Pharmacy. Yes, Mr. Krim's right here." He cupped the mouthpiece with his hand and said, "Your realtor."

Krim took the phone and *uh-huh*'ed into it. There was good news: the realtor had closed the sale on his mother's house. When he hung up, Krim paced around distractedly, retrieving a briefcase from the back room and shoving papers inside it. "Can you handle everything here? I have to find my brother Morty. They need his signature before the house can be sold, but otherwise it's good."

"Is Mort around?" asked Irving, and Krim nodded, his mood lightening for a moment.

"Found himself a program. Showed me the booklet. He's been sober almost thirty days now." Then the smile faded, and he said, "I'm not kidding about that phone call—if the reverend comes back, don't hesitate."

IT WAS A GOOD THING Mort stood up and waved with his whole arm, because Krim might have missed him otherwise. Mort was clean-shaven and his hair had been shorn off and combed. He was wearing old clothes, but they were neat and included a tie. A half-consumed coffee sat in front of him at the table inside Jacoby's.

Krim stuck out his hand to shake, but his brother clasped him in an embrace. "I can't believe it. You look like a changed man," Krim said.

"I *am* a changed man," Morty said. They ordered lunch and Krim tried to get right down to the house sale business, but his brother wasn't ready. He had some amends he wanted to make. Krim waved his hand, but Mort wouldn't be silenced. He went on about how Krim had been carrying the load for him all these years. "I know was my debts forced ya to run all that liquor. The bad I done led to the bad you done."

"Not true." Krim swallowed a gulp of coffee and looked at the table between them. "Every man makes his own mistakes."

"They told me it's real important to apologize. Let me." Mort leaned forward. His eyes were sincere though his fingers twitched.

"I accept your apology," Krim said. "Hell, I haven't seen you in a tie since you graduated high school!" He pushed his plate aside and pulled out the paperwork for the house.

As Krim expected, Morty grumbled over it, asking where Gertrude would live if ever they let her out of the Sanford Hospital.

"With Faye and me."

Morty said he hated to see the old house go, but in the end Krim prevailed and Morty leaned forward and put his signature on the document. It was a scratchy loop of letters that looked as if it'd been made by an eight-year-old. "This sobriety stuff gotta get easier," Mort said. Then, "One day."

Krim watched in wonder as Mort dug in his pocket and pulled out a dollar. He declared he was paying for them, to make up at least a little of what he owed. Krim told him to stick it back in his pocket. As Morty folded the dollar back into his coat, he said, "The only money ya count on is what's in your pocket. Rest is rainbows."

Ernest put down a good tip for the girl who'd brought their schnitzel, then extended a twenty across the table.

FAYE HAD JUST BEGUN to write a response to her sister when she heard Krim pull in outside. The truck sounded different. She stood and parted the salmon curtains in the living room—curtains that Elsie Moss had sent them. Mrs. Moss had promised to do them up quickly, but in the end it had taken her half a year and she hadn't brought them round herself. She'd sent a young girl to deliver them, while Willie Lynch waited in the car's driver seat. Now, Faye watched as Krim stepped out of a Chrysler, not his usual truck with the Sweets' logo on the side. Through the open window, Faye called, "What is that?"

Krim patted the car door. "It's ours. I thought with the children we could use something more reliable. Come out and see."

Faye hesitated, glancing up the stairs toward the nursery. Then she did peek out the front door. It flustered her a little that he was so independent, so private. Shouldn't a wife be consulted on such a large purchase? But there were many things she'd had to make peace with about her husband, and his past. At least he'd been forthcoming when she had finally asked him—in some ways, it reassured her she could trust him. His admissions about smuggling and his role in the disappearance of Alfred Moss had brought them closer together, to be so let in by someone. Maybe what bothered her was not that he made the purchase without her but that he possessed the same self-determining qualities she did.

"We closed the sale on Mother's house today. Came out ahead," Krim said.

"The truck was fine," Faye contended, although she saw it was a handsome sedan.

He nodded. "You wish I'd saved the money for Kitty to pay her way to Paris?"

"No, of course not," Faye said a little too quickly.

"We can't ride all of us in the front of a truck like that, and certainly not when they get older." Krim was carrying a large paper bag from the pharmacy. Faye could tell he didn't want to leave the vehicle but also didn't want to pull her outside, away from the babies. As they stood there, an apprehensive look came across his face and she watched him glance up and down the street.

"We could have invested it, that's what I was thinking." Faye's hand crept up to her hair. The words rang false even to her own ear. She was still thinking of Kitty.

"We have enough investments—too many, actually. I heard that the market's turning."

"People are always speculating on these things, making their tips, aren't they?" she asked. She said she hoped he wasn't going to pull their money out and put it in some other fellow's pocket for whatever he was selling.

"No one's trying to sell me anything," Krim said, but Faye noticed again that he seemed distracted.

"I'll bet," she said, and kissed him as he came close and handed her the bag. "What's this?" Take a look, he said, and when Faye peeked inside, she was confronted with a stack of bills. "You're not still mixed up in something, are you?"

Krim shook his head and followed Faye inside. He explained he'd seen Morty that day to sign the paperwork. "He was the one really got me thinking, almost more than any news reports. As he took back his dollar bill, he said, 'The only money ya count on is what's in your pocket. Rest is rainbows.' So I took the money for the house in cash, paid for the truck, and brought the rest here."

"Rainbows?" Faye arched an eyebrow. "Sure you only bought him lunch?"

Krim nodded.

She told him to go look in on the twins, and put the bag in the upstairs closet, or wherever he thought was safest. She spooned out their supper, but Ernest was a long time returning.

KRIM LOOKED DOWN at the babies with pride. Sometimes they reminded him of puppies—the way their eyes slit closed but not all the way—and he could only guess at what evanescent thoughts tumbled behind their brows. Especially after this morning's conversation with Prangley, he felt himself wanting to linger. He went to the window and made sure it was locked. Then he passed down the hall and into his and Faye's bedroom. Since he'd moved in, they'd painted it a deep olive and she'd replaced her floral bedspread with a handsome country plaid. She'd said she wanted him to feel welcome there. Faye went about the business of a household with the same efficiency she'd brought to her work—at least, that was how Krim saw it. Now that her focus was here at home, she treated its care and maintenance as a regular nine-to-five.

Krim went and checked the lock on the master bedroom window. Then he opened the closet and looked for the best place to stash the money. He rummaged around, past Faye's dresses and hats. Perhaps under the bed would be better . . . though if he were a burglar, that would be the first place he'd look. Back in the closet, he pushed aside his old pharmaceutical bag and two fedoras on the top shelf. Behind them was a large plain box. He took it down and opened it and socked the money in on top of the other junk without looking. Then the scent of roses lifted into his nostrils. He reopened the box and pushed the bag of money aside and looked at what was underneath. In cursive, Faye's maiden name: *Faye McCloud*. He didn't recognize the hand-writing. He slipped one of the letters from its envelope and glanced at it, not really meaning to read. *All my love, Arthur*, it said at the bottom. Krim slid the paper back in and examined the envelope again.

AS THEY SAT down to dinner, Faye said: "I need you to burn the letter. I can't do it."

"Pardon?" Krim stopped with his spoon raised halfway to his lips.

"From Kitty." Faye nodded at the correspondence on the table with the stamp from Martinique.

"Oh, that."

"You know I can't do it. I don't want any evidence, but at the same time I worry these letters are all I have left of her. Do you think it will ever be safe to see her again?"

Krim picked up the letter from Kitty and took it to the stove. He lit the gas.

"No, Ernest, wait, please! I have to read it one more time."

He brought the letter back and resumed eating. He listened as Faye read Kitty's words aloud to him. Then he said: "I don't think anyone will ever find her. Even if she had stayed in Detroit, who's to say she was at the Riviera that night?"

He didn't tell Faye, but he was thinking of Alfred Moss—the joker had the whole city searching, and no one had thought to look farther than Hamtramck or Royal Oak.

"It's silly, isn't it, that I burn them? I still feel like I have to protect her."

Krim chewed through a stringy onion. "Did you tell her about the twins?"

Faye nodded and said she'd just started her reply when he'd pulled up. "I was going to tell her how their dog pulled a full chicken carcass from the trash and lived to tell the tale. Happiest dog I ever saw! Oh, and I was going to write how Reverend Prangley sent that fancy bassinet as a gift—how mad you got and how you threw it out on the curb."

"I don't like the idea of one of our children dreaming in some bed that came from that man. He came to see me today at the pharmacy—half-corked and nonsensical. I think him sending us that bassinet was a threat."

Faye set down her spoon. Her expression was pinched and he could see she wasn't going to eat anymore. He wished he hadn't said anything. Silently, he finished his bowl and bread, lit a cigarette.

Finally, she said, "I thought you told me everything about the rumrunning. Is he more dangerous than you said?"

"Yes. Well, I don't know, really."

They both turned at the sound of baby cries upstairs. Krim jumped up and dashed up the stairs before Faye could move. He returned with a wriggling Alistair and a sleepy Catherine in his arms. "They're fine," he told her, handing off the girl. Faye eased down onto the sofa. Krim kept the boy, bouncing him slowly, one hand behind his neck to hold up his head.

"We could go for a ride before dark," Krim said a while later. "I've heard the motion of the car can calm them down and put them to sleep." He didn't mention that it might calm him too.

"How would that work?" Faye asked.

Krim explained: she'd hold Catherine, and Alistair could ride in the back in his bassinet.

"You're eager to show me the car, aren't you?"

"It has a radio."

The baby girl began making a soft coo almost like a bird, which her brother then echoed. Their small hands butterflied toward one another and caught.

= 76 =

THE BOY SAT on the living room floor playing with a belt of his father's.

"Where did you get that?" Elsie asked Baby John, who was no longer a baby so much as a toddler.

There was a beep-beep and she looked out the window. A cab had pulled into the drive. Willie Lynch got out of it, wearing mechanic's coveralls. He came up to the door, the keys held up. His hands were stained gray. "Here ya go," he said through the screen. He meant to just pass the keys in to her, but she told him to come inside.

"You're working for that Mr. Ciccone now?" Elsie asked, noting his coveralls.

"Yeah, didn't guess I'd like learning about cars so much as I do. It's in my blood, I suppose. And it's steady. I'll let you take all the risk, long as I get my cut." He nodded out the door at the taxi, which she was now driving regularly to New York. She had assured him he'd always get his cut with her. He'd done her a good turn, bringing her along and getting her hooked up that first time. They'd done two more runs together, then he'd said he didn't have the taste for it anymore. So she'd done four more runs without him. And she never worried about the mortgage payments anymore.

"What's all this?" Willie toed the boxes and bags she'd pushed into the entrance.

"Old stuff of Alfred's. I was hoping you could help me carry it out. I'm going to donate it."

"Thought you woulda been rid of his stuff a long time ago."

Most of it was gone, she said. But Alfred had more suits than she had dresses. She'd put out half of his stuff last year for the block sale when she'd sold the old furniture and got new.

"You'd think he'd have planned to take at least something with him." Willie dug through a bag and extracted a jacket. He held it up to himself and looked in the mirror in the hall. He said he might relieve her of a few items if she'd wait.

"Sure," Elsie said. "But don't you have enough of your own?" He always seemed well turned out.

"Can't hurt to save a few bucks. My sister Annie's having a kid."

"No!"

"Well, she's sixteen now. I worried I'd have to beat the guy into the church, really put the fists to him, but he stepped up."

Elsie listened as Willie explained the situation. He thought his sister would still graduate. The girl was smart enough, and as long as she made it through till January or February, the school would pass her.

He yanked a few more items from the boxes and didn't notice that Elsie was looking at him. He asked to try on some pants and went into the bathroom. He came back in only his undershirt and the pants. He'd changed, she realized, in the time she'd known him—his face, and his attitude. Elsie felt a ripple of something, and even she couldn't say if it was the glimmer of a crush or motherly surprise at the fact that he had grown up. Wordlessly, she handed him a button-up shirt and tried not to let her gaze linger over the new muscle he'd earned in the mechanic shop. He slipped it on, did up the buttons, and stooped to grab the belt off the floor, gently prying it from the child. When the outfit was complete, he eyeballed himself in the mirror. Some of the tough she was familiar with came back as he spun around and cocked a pistol with his fingers.

"You know what I need with this? A peacock-blue tie. And you know who's got one in just that shade?"

Breaking into Prangley's place was too petty a thing for him to do anymore, Elsie said, her eyes narrowing. Too boyish. Willie was eighteen now. Also: Prangley deserved worse.

Maybe, said Willie, but he wasn't going to be the one to dish it out to the reverend. He had his mother and his sister, and soon his niece or nephew, to think about. "Oh, and did I tell you I got a girl now?" An unfamiliar note of pride crept into his voice—or was he trying to make her jealous, Elsie wondered. He put his hands in the pockets of the pants and leaned against the wall. "Sweet thing. She's an O'Neill, so my mom's stopped praying the rosary for me. What's this?" A perplexed expression rippled his face and rearranged his moles.

He withdrew his hand from one of the pockets and showed Elsie what was there. It was a small key.

$$=\!\!\!\Big(\ 77\ \Big)\!\!\!=$$

KITTY KEPT THE SECRET for several days—until she was sure of herself.

The cash had been folded in with the pair of small men's pants and the shirt that Faye had mailed her. There were two packages of Juicy Fruit, a copy of a novel by Thomas Wolfe, and a new one by Virginia Woolf, *A Room of One's Own*. The only thing Faye hadn't put in was a cheeseburger and fries from the corner lunch counter. Kit had reached inside and pulled out the items one by one, smelling each as if it contained some whiff of Detroit—of home. Then her hand found the bills through the fabric of the pants as she unfolded them.

Her sister knew her well, could read the embellishments and see the truths even across an ocean. Kitty looked up at the sky, and what might have sounded like a prayer of thanks in anyone else's mind was in Kit's a single high note.

SHE DIDN'T WANT to leave Rosine without her knowing. She and Rosine made love one last time that morning, though it was strained, and afterwards Rosine cried, something Kit had never seen her do, and she felt awful for going. The plan was to enter at Galveston, with Kansas City to follow—due north by twelve hours. She knew that neither city held any allure for Rosine.

"I like it here," Rosine said in English, rubbing her palm over her nose and cheeks and shaking the thick loops of her hair away from her face.

"*Je comprends,*" Kit said in French, smiling sadly.

"Tell me you still love me," Rosine said, taking Kit's hand.

"*Je t'aime encore.*" Kitty had touched Rosine's lips. Then she'd pulled away and picked up her things. "Follow me if life lets you."

She knew Rosine wouldn't, and Rosine knew it too.

Marcel drove Kitty into the city without a word, angrier about it than Rosine had been. Out the window, in the car's side mirror, Kitty watched Le Morne-Rouge become tinier. When Marcel dropped her off, he asked her for ten dollars for the suitcase she had borrowed. She gave it to him. Then she picked up the portmanteau and her trumpet case, and turned away. As she walked through Fort-de-France toward the harbor, she breathed in the fragrant air—she would miss the island, their garden, the smells and the food, the kiwis and smoked fish, and the mountain, even the mountain. But she knew she would not regret it.

Kitty watched the boats pulling into the harbor. It was a clear day and the ship that came for her was large and white—no way to miss it, long as a city block. People lined up and called to one another in French, checked their belongings and their tickets, made last-minute juggles, and said farewells. Kit was alone, and the seagulls were the only ones that called to her. Behind her, the windows of St. Louis Cathedral and the yellow- and pink-painted houses that climbed the hill were the only eyes that watched her go.

⫘ 78 ⫘

MARY JOY DAVIS dreamed of the girl. She was in between the gawky and cute phases of childhood, but her smile was unguarded and true. It was just her face, close up, a slight smudge of perspiration on her upper lip as though she'd been running. The eyes were too big for the face, as were the teeth. Her skin was a lovely gold-brown. Then the girl turned and walked away, and Mary Joy watched her going, down the sidewalk—stepping off the curb into the street. It was Gratiot Avenue in Detroit. There was no sound then, only a great rush of darkness like a wave crashing through the wide avenue, folding it up into a gray-black blur.

Mary Joy followed, or thought she did, charging into the dark. When she looked down, she saw her hand wrapped around a topsy-turvy doll. It was the kind she remembered from her own childhood in the South. A small white face and arms extended from a hand-sewn floral dress, but beneath its skirt, secreted away, was another doll with a small black face and arms—one to be cared for when white folks weren't near. As Mary Joy stroked the doll's cheek, its porcelain crumbled beneath her thumb.

"Esther! Esther!" Mary Joy shouted until she awakened. Then she whispered the name into her sweaty pillow. She sat up and looked around her: her rooms were the same as always. As far as rooming houses went, it was a nice one, but it was not the private apartment she would have preferred. She shared a wall with a young woman who came in late at night and left early every morning. Nonetheless, it took Mary Joy a moment to remember she wasn't in Chicago. Sometimes she dreamed the girl in Chicago, on Twenty-Second or on State Street, and sometimes on the tenant farm in Georgia where Mary Joy had grown up. This was the first time she'd dreamed her into Detroit.

Mary Joy pushed herself up and walked across the room to her desk, where she had a calendar. She wanted to go to the hall phone and call H.H., but when she checked the calendar, she saw his days off marked clearly—he would not be back in Chicago for another ten days. Mary Joy went down to the bathroom and wet a washcloth, and mopped it around her face and neckline. She didn't cry, because she was certain other lodgers were waking up or coming in. Back in her room, she sat down beside the window. It was almost dawn, and there was no point in sleeping anymore that night.

She made a list of things to do that day but wound up scratching most of them off. *Bible sample*, and *Negotiate terms / Reverend* were the only two she left on. Mary Joy put the pen down and turned off the light, but still she sat—rigid and anxious in the window. The downtown smelled of diesel and maple, and she could hear a street-car rattling in the distance.

Mary Joy was not afraid to live alone, nor was she afraid of her line of work—she had God to protect her, and if there were ever a moment He failed her, she knew she could always protect herself. She had done it before. But she was afraid of the girl, afraid of the image of her face and what it did to her. It left her shaking just to see it. For days after one of the dreams, Mary Joy trembled at the shifting of shadows. The girl reminded her that no one is ever prepared.

After the dream, Mary Joy would keep her head up and her eyes straight ahead and walk one foot in front of the other, but her fists were clenched with effort, her stomach would knot, and she would cease to eat. She would lose those ten extra pounds she struggled the rest of the time to keep off her hips—but she would take no pleasure in it. Even now, touching a hand to her lips, she could feel her face twitching and she fought to find a calm inside herself that she could assemble over the top of it.

={ 79 }=

IT WAS AFTERNOON when Charles Prangley packed his coats and suits, laying them flat inside the trunk. Some of the shirts and trousers had never been worn, yet Prangley was attached to them, enough that he didn't like the idea of some cat burglar thumbing their hemlines. His shoes were already packed and ready to go. He piled four shirts one on top of the other, and ran his hand over the final one, delicately. He would wait until it was dark to move the two trunks outside. He would call one of his crew to come—the Buick was much too small. He hadn't decided yet which of the men to summon.

He had already formed his plan when the young girl who was the new secretary came around the alley, knocking on the door and urging him back to the church. It was only four o'clock and she hoped he wouldn't mind her fetching him back again. She said this as if it was a question, though really there was no question to it. Mrs. Davis was there to see him, she said. The trunks were standing inside the door, but if the secretary saw them, she gave no indication. As they left the parsonage, Prangley turned and locked both the door and a brand-new padlock bolt in place, shutting it across and latching it through the frame. Again, the secretary said nothing.

The new girl was nearly a simpleton and Prangley almost missed Faye McCloud. He followed her. Six months out of stenographer's school, her legs were like chalk in her stockings. She lit strange desires in him—fury and excitement, but mostly exasperation. The church committee had not been impressed when he hired her. At the same time, the church had been desperate for help after Faye's quick departure and he knew this girl would never suspect anything. She hadn't enough experience to discern anything out of place in his practice or demeanor. He could train her the way he wanted.

As they entered the church, Mary Joy Davis stood, wearing shoes that were a little too tall, though Prangley noticed she never wobbled. He wondered if she'd chosen them specifically to gain height on the day she was to meet with such a tall man. They greeted one another formally—not as though they had never met, but as though they had not met in a long time.

"I am glad to see you are well," he said to her.

Mary Joy's face twitched slightly. "God has watched over me, and for that I am grateful."

He showed her into his office and she sat before he could offer a chair. "These shoes sure are pretty, but they are not kind," she remarked, staring down at the indentations the buckles had made on her ankles. "I was on my feet all morning."

"You should view yourself as fortunate to be able to wear them in public. All my best things are saved for private showings to no one." He heard the bitter note that had crept into his voice.

"And that's exactly why we should spend some of our money in a manner that will bring everyone more pleasure. You, me, and the travelers who are lost." Mary Joy's tone of voice was sincere, but her enthusiasm grated on Prangley.

She opened her large purse and extracted several small Bibles. They looked almost as if they had been made for children, though they bore no pictures, only pages and pages of ink so small that Prangley did not think he could make out the words, even up close with his bifocals. The covers were royal purple.

"These are the Bibles for Berths that we've been talking about for so long. I suppose we don't have to go with this particular Bible. There are others we could choose—here's a red six-by-nine sample, you see— only I did think that the violet color was attractive and that the size lent itself to putting into one's pocket."

"You have surprised me, Mrs. Davis. I thought we might be talking about splits or an increase of orders," Prangley said. He avoided thumbing through any of the Bibles Mary Joy had extracted from her carpetbag.

"Oh, of course." Mary Joy smiled widely through her painted coral lips. If she was not happy with his lack of interest in the good book, she did not immediately show it. "Reverend Prangley, it has been a fine thing to work with you for this year, and you are right that, as we come up on the anniversary of our association, we should reexplore and renegotiate."

Prangley removed a cigar from his desk drawer and lit it without asking her permission. Mary Joy tried not to cough, though she did eventually, enough that Prangley was moved to call for the secretary to fetch a pitcher of water.

After the girl had left them, and Mary Joy regained her breath, she asked, "What happened to the woman who worked for you before?"

Prangley took out a small bottle and poured himself a drink. He offered one to Mary Joy and she declined, her face pinched into a smile that clearly did not want to be.

"Miss McCloud became Mrs. Krim, and so she is gone. That is how it goes. You have good help and then they run off, chasing after the devil."

"The devil is not the marrying kind. I truly hope this secretary is serving the church as well, but tell me: is it wise to smoke luxury cigars in front of your staff? Do understand, I ask this as a friend."

Prangley took the cigar from his mouth and looked at it for a moment. "I completely forgot that I was smoking it when she came in," he said, perplexed he'd made such an error. He stabbed it out and dropped it back in the desk drawer. Then he mashed his lips together. He didn't care to be corrected by anyone, but especially Mary Joy Davis. "First scent I ever knew was tobacco. My father was a cigar roller," he said. Yet he was angry with himself for admitting it to anyone, least of all her.

"It is not where we come from but who we become," Mary Joy said.

This gave Prangley pause. He set one finger down on the desk almost as if bookmarking the adage, pinning it there to use himself to someone else at a later date.

"I would like to raise the purchase price," he said suddenly, steepling his fingers. "My airplane has taken some wear and tear."

"I am more than willing to discuss an increase." Mary Joy tilted her face slightly as she peered at him. "But not without a higher-quality product. I believe we agreed that to stretch supply could be advantageous to us both, but I have to tell you, the amount of watering down has become absurd. We must be more *honest* with our customers."

Prangley downed his drink. "But you do not drink, do you? How can you say if the alcohol is pure or not?"

"You are correct. I do not drink. But neither am I color-blind," Mary Joy continued. "I know that amber is the color of whiskey and blood-red is the color of wine. Gin is the color of glass, but unlike water, it should shine and the elderberry scent should lift and make up completely for the lack of hue. Furthermore, I know that when a two-hundred-pound man does not get soused on a twenty-ounce tumbler of Scotch, he is unlikely to buy it again on his next business trip. Should we invite competition? What if travelers begin to bring on their own?"

Prangley pursed his lips together. Raising the price meant nothing if they discontinued their plan to dilute; at the same time, the woman was right. If they lost their business entirely, it would be much worse.

Mary Joy, Prangley noted, was less compromising this afternoon than she had been when they first began working together. She pressed him: "Tell me it is the greed, and not carelessness. If you have negligence, it could harm both of us. But a desire for more—that is a thing I understand. Oh my stars, do I!"

Reluctantly, Prangley agreed to see if he could do anything about "portioning." Mary Joy Davis gathered up the Bible samples and tucked them back in her bag. "I believe you are a good man," she said. Prangley was so taken aback, it must have shown on his face. He had never heard praise like this from a business partner. She amended: "We are on the same side, and I wish you peace and God's love."

={ 80 }=

IN THE CAR out in the street, the two Prohibition agents marked the progress of a woman in a garden hat as she exited Reverend Prangley's church.

Goering Jones leaned forward. "A colored woman should have her own church. What's she come here for?"

Gabriel Brennan sighed and watched the woman walk in her rubber-tipped heels. She carried a small book—a Bible?—in her hand and a carpetbag in the other. "I didn't see any women on our list. No point putting more hours on this than we have to."

After a few moments, the agents watched the reverend lumber across the church grounds. His face had a warped look to it and in the breeze his dark hair rippled over his distinctive hairline. It had gone wilder and grayer than the careful coif in his news photos, sweeping over the dome of his head the way water rushes toward the edge of a long fall. Gabriel asked Jones how tall he thought the man was. Jones squinted and said six-three, six-four.

"Goes in late, ducks out early. *Twice.*" Gabriel tossed his cigarette stub out the window. "Whatever he is, he's not much for tending his flock."

Jones said, "He's hinky, that's for sure."

HOURS LATER, the agents were still waiting, this time with the car positioned so they could peer through the church fence and across the graveyard. Gabriel's legs had locked up and he tried not to groan in front of his partner as he stretched. For some reason he didn't want the boy to realize he had twenty years on him.

"You smell like cigarettes," Jones said, rolling down his window.

"You smell like chewing gum."

The two men locked eyes in a minor showdown. The younger agent's bottom lip tucked in beneath the upper one for a minute, then he swallowed.

A truck pulled into the church grounds and both men turned their attention to the parsonage laneway.

"Jake Samuel." Gabriel identified the skinny man who opened the Ford truck door and jumped out. Jones leaned out the car window and positioned his camera to capture a shot of the reverend carrying his possessions out of the parsonage. The camera was a Memo. New and small, it could take fifty photos without reload. Still, Gabriel thought Jones was taking too many tonight, and told him so. "One roll per day, Agent Jones."

"Think that's booze in that trunk?" Jones asked, blue eyes lit with excitement.

In spite of himself, Gabriel smiled at Jones's enthusiasm. "Oh, probably."

A few seconds later, the truck turned out of the lane between the church and the parsonage and motored right past them. Gabriel waited before pulling out and trailing—it was dusk, still bright enough that he wanted to make sure he wasn't too close.

"Where are we?" Jones asked as they pulled up to a shop on Cass. Ahead and down the block, they watched the two men move the trunks onto the sidewalk, then through the doorway. They went one after the other, each taking a load.

"Five dollars says there's no alcohol," Gabriel said, never taking his eyes off the men.

"Sure. How do you figure?"

"Each took a trunk. Looked heavy, but if there were bottles in there, they'd have to move the trunks together."

"What is that place? A furrier?"

"Cold storage. Keeps furs safe from moths and damage."

"You know much about fur?" Jones asked, and Gabriel noticed his smirk.

He must have been wondering what Gabriel would look like swaggering around in a long fox fur. No, said Gabriel. He doubted he'd ever be part of the dandy trend in men's fashion. He had enough red hair of his own. As he said it, Gabriel saw the other agent measuring him, but his own gaze never left the storefront.

"Well," said Jones. "Cold storage is a great place for booze. I'll take that bet."

={ 81 }=

GABRIEL BRENNAN STEPPED out of the car and walked toward the cold storage shop. Jones was quick to follow. Inside they pulled out their badges, and told the startled owner to bring back the trunks so they could be examined. Gabriel peppered the fellow with questions: Did he know the men who'd dropped them off? Had he stored anything else for Prangley in the past? Yes, the owner said, a raccoon coat and a fox fur.

"Let's see what we got," Gabriel said. He took a small hatchet out of his trench coat, and watched Jones do a double-take. Jones was young enough that he'd missed the days of ax-splintered kegs and Gabriel Brennan could see he hadn't imagined his boss would walk around with that kind of weaponry right next to his chest. As Gabriel unfastened the leather holster on the ax, the owner stopped him. One of the trunks was a Louis Vuitton, he said. It was probably worth as much as whatever was inside.

Gabriel considered it. Then he moved to the other trunk, which was generic, and broke it open with a heavy stroke. He threw the lid back and was greeted with fabric. Black shirts and navy, white, wine, and goldenrod. He exchanged a baffled glance with Jones, stuck his hand in and dug through the orderly piles. As he came to the bottom he breathed out. He'd won the bet, but he was disappointed. He'd hoped their case would end right there. To make up for his displeasure, he muttered orders at Jones: they would phone the bureau for a van to transport the trunks; the other would be seen by a locksmith, but he was fairly certain its contents would be as mundane.

"He's getting ready to go on the lam. Now we really do need to clock in on this one." Gabriel let the broken lid fall with a sigh and a thud that were of almost equal weight.

={ 82 }=

CHARLES PRANGLEY CLIMBED the stairs, slowly. At the top of three flights sat Mryna's apartment. He'd first met her at a cathouse downtown in Detroit—the Riviera had been shuttered and Rosine was nowhere to be found. There were rumors about what had happened, but Prangley couldn't make any sense of them. Although it made him apprehensive to be seen creeping around Detroit, Prangley had been forced to look for his pleasures a little closer to home. That was how he'd found the Sugar Box. The downstairs window displayed candy boxes, but there was no shop, only a set of old stairs, and one only had to climb them to understand that no chocolate was sold there. It didn't have the same privacy or the same attempt at glamour as Rosine's place had, but he concluded this was perhaps not the worst thing.

He'd only bought Myrna's company for a couple nights at the Sugar Box when he decided he enjoyed her. The first night she'd lain beneath him trembling and crying and begging him, "stop," and "don't stop," interchangeably. That was the first time he'd thought to consider what these girls wanted. The second time she'd said she was glad he'd come back—the other men there were so cruel he wouldn't believe; none were like him. But the third time he called at the brothel she was gone. The tight-faced madam told him nothing. Money and physical pressure got him bounced. But he had been bounced from there before. He found himself bounced from more places lately. Still, Myrna's address wound up finding its way to him from one of the other working girls. Myrna had acted surprised when he came calling at her apartment, but now he sought her every Friday, and sometimes Saturday or Sunday nights too.

Prangley wasn't winded when he reached the final step. Excitement outweighed the physical exertion. Myrna opened the door before he could knock and he took in her wild head of wheat hair and impish grin. Then he gazed down and saw that she was not wearing a thing besides her feathered bedroom slippers.

"I couldn't sleep last night, 'cause I kept thinking about you. And I been thinkin' of you all day."

"What did you think?" He pushed her inside, closing the door behind him. He threw his coat off.

"I thought of your eyes," she said, standing on her tiptoes, reaching up to place a hand on his face, though it was almost out of reach for her.

"What else?" He unbuttoned his shirt, leaning down so she could kiss him.

Myrna moved her hand to his mane of dirty gray-black. "Your hair."

"Tell me what you thought exactly. Were they bad, bad thoughts?"

"No!" she protested, looping her arms around his neck.

He kissed her and yanked at his belt at the same time. He was already losing his pants, charging against her, knocking her onto the bed, which was the only piece of furniture in the apartment besides some ladies magazines and odds and ends.

They lay together, her gold hair a tangle above her head, her eyes jet black and almost fearsome with their intensity. She had large rosy cheeks just like that rich Ohio girl he'd known long ago in his youth. Myrna was tiny, no more than five feet, and thin as fishing line. She crossed her legs around him as he pushed inside her.

"Tell me you love me," he demanded.

"I love you, Charles," Myrna breathed into his ear, wrapping her arms around his back. "I love you."

"Now tell me you love my cock," he said, pulling out then thrusting forward powerfully before she could confirm or deny.

"Stop! Stop!" she pretend-pleaded. "I don't. I can't say it."

"Say it," he demanded, stopping for real this time.

"You know I won't, Charles," Myrna said.

"You'll regret it," he said, rising up off of her and putting his clothes back on slowly. They weren't his best, since he'd stashed most of his things in the cold storage.

She lit a cigarette, and shrugged. She went and sat on the window ledge stark naked, her tiny breasts bobbing. Prangley watched her. She had told him she was fifteen, and that he was the first man she'd slept with in the business, or at all, yet somehow she had the instincts for controlling the game. He didn't know how she was able to thrill him so much.

Prangley forced his pants back up his thighs, dragged suspenders back into place. His expression was someplace between furious and excited. "You know you're supposed to repeat after me. Why did you make us stop?"

Myrna dropped her cigarette out the window and smiled. "So we can start again, silly."

={ 83 }=

EVERY TIME THE gangly preacher visited Myrna, she told him she loved him. The games between them were so dirty, she wondered if he even noticed that part of it. She had grown up in the industry and had observed that when trading sex for money that there were certain things a woman never did. Her mother had warned her about using the word "love," but Myrna was intent on doing things her way. From her perspective, the preacher seemed obsessed with innocence and owning it. What could be more innocent than love? The phrase *I love you* was bigger than any set of knockers, bigger than any hard-on. After she'd moved out of the Sugar Box and rented an apartment, Prangley followed, and her mother had conceded that perhaps the girl had been right. Together they refined Myrna's story: they told Prangley that tricking at the Sugar Box hadn't been for Myrna, and that she was intent on getting out of the business.

When Myrna had finished her Friday night date with Prangley, and he'd gone, she phoned the brothel downtown and asked to speak to the madam.

"Who's callin'?"

Myrna identified herself and the woman on the other end said, "Oh, why didn't you say? I'll get your ma for you."

"How'd that new stop-and-start game go?" her mother asked.

Myrna heard the snap of a match as her mother lit a cigarette. Instruction for the evening's activities had come from her mother, based on what Myrna had relayed of Prangley's previous desires.

"I'd say very well. He liked that little break in the middle. Was quite affectionate afterwards. Asked me if I was curious to know more about him. I said I would love to go out for dinner or see him at his place sometime. He didn't exactly want to be seen on the town with me though." The girl, who was really a woman of twenty, laughed. At fourteen, people had thought she was still ten, and at eighteen, fourteen. Part of it was her tininess, and part of it her pale complexion and snub nose. "Maybe a date at his place."

"You don't say." Her mother exhaled, but Myrna knew she was practically salivating. "That necklace he gave you last time. You know how much it was worth?"

Myrna took a guess, but her mother corrected her, saying it was two thousand, and there was more where it came from. She said she knew first time she laid eyes on Prangley's crocodile shoes he had more clams than he knew what to do with. She instructed Myrna to play it cool when she got to the man's place—don't stuff her pockets right away, just take it in, and they'd figure out the best way to bleed him later.

"I almost feel sorry for him." Myrna pouted into the receiver.

"Don't! Don't you remember, when he first came to the Sugar Box I told him you were just an adolescent and it was your first night working here. 'Go easy on her, she never lain with a man before.' That fucker slapped and choked one of my other girls the first time he came in here, and he knocked up another because he wouldn't put on a rubber. Always the young girls too. Don't forget what a snake he is just because you've had some laughs."

Myrna lit her own cigarette and said she supposed that was true. "Please, Ma," she added, "don't spend all the money before I can come back and enjoy it."

"Just be careful," the madam advised.

═{ 84 }═

"GOD, HEAR ME," Mary Joy Davis began, so quietly she scarcely spoke.

Mary Joy had adopted the Second Baptist as her church away from home for many reasons—one was that it had been founded by former slaves and had served as a station in the Underground Railroad. As well, she heard from some of the congregation that they were open to the idea of charisma, an idea that she found so moving in her own Pentecostal church back in Chicago.

"As you know, Lord, it is hard for me to be away from H.H.," she prayed, "and hard to be here, so far away from my community and our house."

She ruminated on what else needed to be said. She believed that what she spoke aloud had more import than the thoughts all jumbled inside her.

"I am in great need of Your guidance. You sent me a man to work with—and I trust in You and the ways You deliver. It has worked going on a year now. H.H. and I have received blessings of money. For this, God, I do thank You. But now I must ask: is this man really of good heart? I have pressed him repeatedly for the Bibles he promised to donate with me. He ignores me and I get no answers. At the same time, the spirits have become"—Mary Joy paused, pushed her tongue into the side of her reddened lips—"weakened. I have spoken to his men about this, and I have spoken to him too. The fact that he is a man of God, that You have given me someone to work with who feels your spirit, Lord, at first this seemed like a dream. But lately he appears—"

She looked for the words, and as she did, she reached a thumb inside her neckline and hitched up the slipping strap of her brassiere.

Every Friday, Mary Joy took two men she'd recruited from the Second Baptist to help load her twenty crates. They picked them up from three of Prangley's underlings, one of whom held himself up pitifully on a crutch. Mary Joy and her men—Marvin and Edgar—would transport it to the train station, where her porters took over. Sometimes the reverend oversaw his business, there just long enough to empty her carpetbag of its bills, but more often he didn't. Even as he pressed her for better prices, he seemed distracted and unmotivated.

"—heretical. He is unpredictable, and I doubt somewhat that he is as pure of heart as I had thought. I had believed we both sought to help our communities as well as ourselves. And his crew—well, they have their own difficulties to overcome, I am sure, especially the lame one, but nevertheless, they disrespect me in small ways and I am sure they call me names when they think I am out of earshot. Names I will not utter here. I am grateful for the riches that have come from this union, the blessings You have given me, but please, dear Lord, tell me what to do. Send me a sign."

Mary Joy heard others coming into the church and taking their places. Soon, Sunday worship would begin. Her back ached, but she knew there was one more thing she had to say.

"This is the hardest time of year for me. Lord, it was when You gave her to me and when You took her. My girl, Esther. She would turn fifteen next month. I thought that grieving would become easier with time, but it has not. You took three babies from me before they could become babies, and I made peace with that. I accepted it. So why can't I make my peace with this? Every day I'm grateful for the time I had with Esther. You saw fit to lend her to me for at least a few years. Still—"

Mary Joy drew a shaking breath that seemed to set all of her quivering.

"This sadness remains with me, every day, like a chancre inside my lips. My tongue touches it while I am speaking of other things. It is still so raw. I feel my body taut as a skipping rope turned by the hands of others, snapping against the pavement. Give me strength, Lord. Help me through these next few weeks. Please, take the dreams away at least. We both know I have my sins, but please do not punish me with my own daughter."

={ 85 }=

AGENT BRENNAN and Agent Jones trailed the Chrysler from Sweets' Pharmacy to Bagley, where the old McCloud house sat back from the road between two hedges and behind an elm. The mostly Irish neighborhood was familiar to Gabriel. Although Ernest Krim was German in name, the wife had clearly come from a long line of Scots, so Gabriel guessed this must be her family home. He watched as Faye waved from the porch and Krim pulled into the drive. She had one of the babies in her arms, the other in a carrier at her feet. The dog was there too.

"What about investigating her?" Goering Jones asked. "She worked for our man Prangley over a year."

"If she's not on our list, she's not on our list."

"Women talk," Jones said as Gabriel slipped the car over to the curb half a block away. They both turned and looked over their shoulders. Mr. and Mrs. Krim kissed and he took the child from her, jostling it back and forth in some kind of game.

"What do you know about the ways of women? You even married?" Gabriel asked, his face brightening as he ribbed the junior agent.

"I know the skirts talk and talk," Jones said.

"A real guy's guy, aren't ya?"

The young agent raised one eyebrow. Gabriel held his breath as long as the agent held the look.

"That's what I thought. Married to the Bureau."

The two men watched as the Krims went inside. The agents remained in their spot, then, when it was apparent no one was coming back out, they reparked in a better position where they could see through the front windows—though there was little to see. A husband and wife eating dinner and talking, then sitting in their parlor, occasionally pacing around, and maybe arguing a little, all framed by a pair of pink curtains.

Gabriel sniffed. "You wearing perfume, Jones?"

"Just Florida water." Jones ducked his head. "They don't look bent," he observed, his gaze on the Krim house.

Gabriel lit a cigarette but, remembering it disturbed his partner, butted it out after two drags. "The crookedest men are always the ones who go the straightest path. Watch. We won't find anything here, but if we dig up dirt on Prangley, he'll be the one to bury Krim. And if not the reverend, then someone else will."

KRIM WATCHED as Faye got up and went to the kitchen to fetch iced tea. The dog padded out after her, then back again in her wake. It was a warm night and they had the windows open. The children had gone to sleep easily, and now Krim got up and put the radio on low. An old waltz poured out of it.

"I have something I need to tell you," Faye said as she came back. It wasn't the kind of tone he'd been hoping for. With the children dozing, Krim had been thinking they could rekindle the part of their relationship that had fallen off under the burden of feedings and late midnights.

Krim accepted the glass. He lifted his eyebrows in a manner that said, *Go on, then*. But Faye hesitated, and he felt a sinking inside. What if what she wanted to say was truly awful? A part of him still waited for her to vanish—she'd come into his life so quickly and changed it, yet she also felt like a dream from which he might one day wake. It was the skeptic in him, and he knew it.

"It's the money," Faye said finally. This was not at all what he'd expected. "The money you put in the closet."

"What did you do?" He braced himself, but already he knew. She began to cry. He hadn't seen her cry since the time in his truck when he'd told her about the rumrunning, his association with Prangley, and the lie he had told on behalf of Alfred Moss. She might have cried a little when the twins were born—that first emotional week. Krim sat straight, not touching her. When it became clear she wasn't going to tell him, he said plainly, "How much?"

"I sent three hundred to Martinique. I couldn't stand it, knowing Kitty was miserable, or that she might be doing terrible things to make money." Faye pulled up the apron she was still wearing from dinner and wiped her nose on its edge. "I used to give her all the money I wanted, because it was mine. I'm not used to being dependent. When it was just me, it was my finances. Now they're ours, but really they're yours."

He asked, was she lashing out at him—for making money, of all things? And she said no, of course not. She was just explaining where she was coming from. Krim lit a cigarette and got up and walked around the room. He passed the radio but was too distracted to snap the sound off. The waltz finished and Louis Armstrong's "Ain't Misbehavin'" replaced it.

"So now there's twenty-two hundred." Krim pulled at his ear. "I suppose I spent ten times that on my brother over the years. What I intended with the money was that it would be . . . insurance."

Faye looked up and retorted that you don't keep insurance in a box in the closet.

"About that. I saw the letters from Arthur Baldor."

Faye's face flushed and she looked stunned, as if he'd slapped her. Krim immediately regretted his words.

"I was in the war with a Baldor," he said, quieter now.

"I was . . ." she began, but couldn't find the words. ". . . very young when I started seeing him. Sixteen. How well did you know him?"

"Not at all," Krim said. He had just known of him, that he was there and was from Detroit too. Stocky kid, blond, wasn't he?

"I'm sorry you weren't the first," Faye said finally. "Honestly, it all happened so quick I barely knew whether I said yes or not."

Krim stood at the window. His gaze rested briefly on a black sedan parked out on the street. The radio in the background switched over from music to a news hour. The French foreign minister Briand had put forth his proposal for a new economic union of Europe. In Germany, Hitler was heading demonstrations against war reparations. And in Boston, a play by Eugene O'Neill that had great success in New York had been closed down for its controversial themes. The dog, Chaplin, sensed the tension in the room and Krim watched as the animal scuttled over to where Faye sat, nuzzling her hand and looking for affection.

Krim stared across the room at his wife. Her eyelids were puffy and half-closed—not enough sleep lately between feedings, though she seldom complained. Her hand absently went to the dog's ears, curling them with her finger. He had seen only one photograph of her from that time in her life. Even at sixteen, standing beside her sister and mother, she'd looked as serious as a building's cornerstone.

He glanced outside again and once more noticed the car parked across the street in the shadow of the elm tree.

"What does Prangley drive?" he asked.

"I don't know—why?" She turned and followed his gaze. "That's not it. It's a funny little car he has."

Krim reached up and tugged the drapes closed.

=(86)=

THERE WAS A PART of Elsie Moss that didn't want to know anything more about her missing husband, and for that reason she had put off trying to find the security box the key belonged to—the same way she'd put off calling the hotels in Oklahoma whose names had been given to her by Gin Ing. It was the end of the first week of October when she finally gave in to curiosity. Willie insisted on coming with her. They tried four banks, and the last was his suggestion. He asked where Mr. Moss had lived before they bought the house, and deduced the closest bank to that. It was near Western High School, where Moss grew up.

The bank clerk said yes, there was a box assigned to Alfred Moss, but that he couldn't take them back without proper documentation. Elsie produced the marriage certificate and the death certificate, the stout clerk apologized, and the odd couple was shown through to the vault.

"You're so quiet, you're making me nervous," Elsie told Willie.

"Well, hell, it could be anything, couldn't it?"

It was a small box, only five or six inches wide, and it bore the number *302*. Elsie turned the key and felt it give. She dragged the box out. They stared into it at a thick envelope that was jammed against the edges and barely fit the box.

"Jesus," Willie breathed.

"Do you think—?" But Elsie Moss didn't finish her question. Her hands fumbled at the paper and she tore it open and dumped the contents onto the table.

She was glad then that the bank clerk had given them privacy, because out spilled at least a hundred photos of nude women. There were dancing girls in skimpy outfits. There were smoking girls leaning against cars. There were girls in the woods and girls on beaches. Girls who pulled their blouses up and their brassieres down, girls bent over with their faces peering through their legs upside down and backwards, showing lacy drawers or showing bush. Women who hiked up skirts, and women who wore nothing at all. Women laughing, and women who were stony-eyed. Two women who were clearly sisters stared at the camera defiantly, their nipples like dimes on their gray chests. There were close-ups of breasts and close-ups of bums with garter straps running down them. Pear-shaped bottoms, and apple-shaped bottoms. Lacy knickers and no knickers at all. Pictures of men and women together, grinning, kissing, nipple-pinching—but none of the men in the photos was Alfred.

Neither Elsie nor Willie spoke. She fanned a few out and he picked up one or two and held them, looking. Elsie could tell that he felt as she did: hot and terrible.

Then he said, "I'm sorry. I really thought it was going to be a score."

"I can't look anymore," Elsie said, and turned her back to the table as Willie stacked them and sifted them back into the envelope.

"It's quite a collection," he muttered. She imagined that if he had been with one of his pals he might have taken some delight in it, but no doubt he could see how pained the images made her. "He didn't shoot them, you know. They're different cameras, different frames along the edges. Buy, sell, trade, that's what you do with dirty pictures. How you build this big of a stash."

Elsie turned around, her face flaming. "You? What do you mean 'you'?"

"Men," Willie said, scraping up a few more photos and shoving them in the envelope. "I mean men do."

"Do you have a collection like this?"

At first, Willie said he wasn't going to answer that. Then, when he saw she wasn't going to back down, he muttered, "Not like this. Traded a handful, starting when I was maybe fourteen. I seen this many all together maybe once before."

Elsie spotted something on the table and covered her eyes. She said she couldn't look, but was that *him*?

Between her fingers, she watched as Willie leaned down and examined the photo she meant. Even at a distance, Elsie could see it was of Alfred and a Chinese woman in a gauzy dress. The woman was wearing a black cameo around her neck. It looked as though they might be at the outdoor ballroom on Boblo Island, the floating carnival in the middle of the Detroit River.

"It's Mr. Moss," Willie confirmed.

"Is anyone naked in it?"

"No," he said, and she extended her hand for it.

"Why aren't I angrier?" she said to the picture of her husband with his arm wrapped around Gin Ing.

The boy put the rest of the photos in the envelope and dropped it back in the safety deposit box.

There was no point in continuing to pay for the box, Elsie said. If Willie wanted the photos or could fetch anything for them, he should keep them. He'd be doing her a favor.

"I'll feel like a creep carrying this around," Willie said, taking them back out.

Underneath the envelope was a white piece of paper. They'd been so excited about the envelope when they first pulled it out that neither had noticed. Now Willie pried the document from the box. He unfolded the giant parchment paper and peered at it.

"What is it?"

He shook his head. "I can't read it."

Elsie stood close behind him and looked over his shoulder. "It's a birth certificate, I think. That date, that's Alfred's birthday." Her gaze went to the top line, where a winding black pen had handwritten *Alfredo Moschiano*. "Jesus Christ," she whispered. She reached over and took the document and folded it up and put it in her purse with shaking hands. "This man couldn't tell me the truth about anything."

The envelope was too thick to fit in his jacket, so Willie carried it in his hand. They left the vault and the bank clerk locked it up tight.

When they got outside the bank, a brisk breeze came along and blew dirt in their faces, and Elsie blinked until she thought she might cry. But she didn't, and it was Willie who voiced what she'd been thinking: "I really thought I knew Mr. Moss, and here he told so many damn lies. I never knew you could live like that, with the lies accumulating fast as leaves in the gutters."

Elsie lit a cigarette. "He was a *rake* after all," she said, and blew the smoke out at the sky. Then they both laughed, though to Elsie's ears it sounded hollow. She knew that Willie would go home and think about the girls in the photos, and the men who took them, and that she would too, try as she might not to. *That's how images work*, she thought. *You don't have to see one long to remember it forever.* She supposed that was why her husband kept them even though they were locked up, far from his home, where he couldn't even get at them. And now, much farther away still.

AS GIN ING MOVED through New York's Chinatown, no one
spoke to her. Men hustled to get out of her way, glancing nervously
at her or taking her in only through their peripheral vision. She knew
what they called her behind her back: sometimes Witch, but mostly
Nou gwei. They said Gin Ing had come back from the dead seeking
vengeance and killed her father. She lived in his apartment now and
used his things and his money. Although many had believed her dead,
none could dispute her claim on her father's possessions once she had
returned. Sometimes she encouraged their chatter by attiring herself
in a blood-red dress like the spirit they'd named her for.

Gin turned onto Doyers and followed the curve past the Nam
Wah Tea Parlor. When she came to the theater, she saw a small throng
of actors waiting outside for her to open the place. Since the actors
were never early, she knew that she was late.

The actors were her people now, and the theater was hers too. The
old theater had been there when she was a girl, but she'd nearly forgotten about it. So many times her father had told her not to play on the
"bloody angle," which was a notorious bend in the street. The Chinese
gangs had fought there because they could shoot at one another while
remaining shielded on either side of the turn.

Not long after her return, walking past the theater one day to a
laundry, it occurred to her that someone with money and too much

time on their hands could easily get it up and running again. Gin handled the paperwork, the opening and closing of the space, maintenance and upkeep, and all the outreach and publicity needed for productions to find an audience and get notices in the papers. And the actors came; the sight of the doors open was all it took to draw them. There, they staged traditional Chinese theater and also more modern radical spoken theater. All of the actors were more versed than Gin was in the new culture coming from China, and she enjoyed listening in. Although she'd always been good at making the face expected in a given situation, Gin herself didn't act. She managed, and once in a while she assisted with directing. After everything that had happened, what she loved most was to watch: to disappear into a story, mime, or dance.

Gin let the actors inside and they chattered about the best scene to practice and quickly took their places on the tiny stage. Gin adjusted the lighting rig, then sat on one of the long benches, watching.

It was here, in the early days of the theater, that the famous comedian Ah Hoon had imitated Mock Duck—the way Mock Duck waddled across a room, the way he handled chopsticks. The way his fat wife browbeat him into nothingness. Gin remembered it well. Although she'd been only a girl then, she knew the tong leader almost as well as an uncle, and to see his gestures expertly mimicked had amused her. The actor drew such ire from Mock Duck for the performance that assassins were sent, and the theater had to secure police protection from the NYPD—yet the show went on. It might have been that rebellious performance that inspired her to reopen the old place.

Now, Gin watched as another actor—a young man with thick, dark eyebrows that seemed to behave like parentheses around every facial expression he made—took the hand of their best singer and led her center stage. Gin was very fond of the young man, though she pretended not to be. In her first year back, she had been enjoying her minor celebrity as a vengeful spirit too much to return to the world of the living—although, if such a reappearance were to happen, she realized, it would likely happen here, in this space, which needed sweeping from the feet, both white and Chinese, that shuffled through it for openings.

The director came over and asked Gin Ing what she thought, were they ready, and without looking away from the actor onstage, she replied, "Yes, I think so."

The director praised her for the bursary she'd managed to secure for them, and they spoke about costumes and which seamstress was best. He asked her if she'd signed the new lease for the theater.

It ought to be in the mail, she said. She'd go check.

As she collected the business envelopes from their box, she found a personal letter from her old employers, the Erikssons, in Detroit. She tore it open in the foyer so that the sound wouldn't disturb anyone. The little girl had turned five and begun school. She'd included a drawing and a few words her brothers or new nanny had no doubt helped her spell. Gin smiled—a genuine one. She missed the children far more than she had imagined she would. She'd left Detroit quickly, taking shelter at the Erikssons' home for only one night following her father's death. She remembered how the girl, Emily, cried the whole time Gin packed her bags and readied her things for the train back to New York. Gin cried too, but didn't tell them it was because of how violently Wei Ing had died.

Mrs. Eriksson wrote all the family news, including that they were all learning Spanish now. Although they couldn't imagine when they might make it to New York, they'd enjoyed looking at the pictures in the theater program Gin had sent them from her last opening.

Mrs. Eriksson said she was enclosing a business card her husband had asked her to put in. Mr. Eriksson had taken Gin's theater program to his office and shown it around, and he thought Gin should get in touch with a Mr. Zhang in New York, who was involved with the Chinese Consolidated Benevolent Association. Women like Gin, Mr. Zhang had said, were important in establishing new businesses for Chinatown, and if she got in touch, the Association would help support her in numerous ways.

There was just one more thing, Mrs. Eriksson wrote. A woman had phoned and then come around for Gin. *She said she found something for you in a safety deposit box—a photograph, which I am enclosing.*

From inside the theater, Gin heard the sustained final note of the actress's song, and the hum of voices as the director gave the players praise and notes for their next run-through. She fumbled through the letter and the child's homemade card one more time, but there was nothing. She found the photo still tucked inside the envelope, and extracted it. A moment later, the actor she'd been admiring was leaning over her shoulder.

"Is that really you?" he asked, peering down at the image of Gin, a full two years before, beside a smiling Alfred Moss.

Gin didn't answer for a moment. It was the only proof she had of him, his swirl of dark hair and flinty eyes. She handed the photo to the actor and said, "That is not me. That is a dead girl. Keep it."

He smiled uncertainly. "But you're with someone else."

"Surely you have heard the rumors?" she asked. The actor was standing close enough she could smell the musk of his sweat. It was not an unpleasant scent.

He hesitated before saying, "Everyone has heard them."

"Well, there you are. That is the man who killed me."

"But I thought—" he started to ask, but Gin was already gone, moving in her ruby dress toward the double doors of the darkened theater. She looked back just long enough to see the actor gaze down again at the youthful girl in the photo, then slip the picture into his wallet to keep it from wrinkling. A perplexed smile hooked his lips.

$=\!\!\{\ 88\ \}\!\!=$

OUTSIDE SWEETS' FRONT WINDOW, Elsie Moss tried to peer between the green and amber apothecary jars. She couldn't discern whether the white coat inside belonged to Ernest Krim or his assistant. She took a deep breath and pushed the door open before she could change her mind.

As Krim looked up over his glasses, Elsie saw his face change—and she recognized the expression. His lips pressed together, and the lines appeared in his forehead. In the past, she'd thought the sad-eyed look he gave her was pity. Now she saw clearly: it was guilt.

She stepped up to the counter and held out the piece of paper silently. He took it, expecting a prescription. When he opened it, his firm face became softer around the eyes, and harder at the mouth as he grimaced in confusion. He tilted his head to the side as he looked at the writing. Then he looked over the paper at her.

"Those are the addresses where Alfred stayed after he left here."

He said he didn't understand, but he lied badly. She realized now that if she had known him at all, she might have seen through the story he'd told her the night Alfred disappeared.

"I've thought about this a long time, Mr. Krim. Believe me, I've thought about it." Elsie shifted her weight from one foot to the other. She might have lost her nerve but for one detail: she noticed perspiration had formed along the pharmacist's hairline in a shiny wet line.

"I hate what you did to me, but I know Alfred lied so much he probably pulled some bunkum on you too."

Krim folded the paper and tried to pass it back to her. "I don't want this," he said.

"Neither do I, Mr. Krim, so do me a great favor and take it from me."

={ 89 }=

MARY JOY DAVIS raised her hand and closed her eyes. She felt the swell and sway of the members of the congregation around her, but did not notice the other people so much as accept His presence. At that moment, all that existed was a buzz, a call to God that she had to answer.

"Jesus," she whispered, but then the whisper turned into a yelp and a fast stuttering of syllables as a glossolalia broke through her and out of her. The language of the angels. The syllables were irrelevant, it was the presence of which they spoke that mattered—an electricity that was absolutely clear in its meaning. As if she had bitten a lamp cord, there was nothing at that moment between Mary Joy Davis and God.

After worship, Mary Joy turned to shake hands with those around her, and encountered a boy staring at her in terror. She locked eyes and smiled at him.

"What's your name?" she asked.

The boy didn't answer at first, then, when she asked again, his voice squeaked, barely audible over the din of others talking. He was a skinny kid. His face said he was seven, yet he was tall enough to be nine or ten.

Did he have something he wanted to ask her, she prompted him, and he shook his head. She said, "Be honest. God knows when you lie."

The boy's mother was turned away, chatting with someone on the other side of the pew.

The boy opened his mouth to speak. Mary Joy had to lean in to hear him.

"When you yelled like that, did you ask God to come to you, or did He just barge in?"

Mary Joy thought about it. "Now that you mention it, I did ask God to come. But I asked Him last week. You think I should be angry that He showed up late?"

The boy didn't know how to take the joke and shrank behind his mother, who continued to ignore him. It was clear he wished the lady who spoke in tongues would go talk to someone else.

"I had a problem with someone at my work, and I said to Him, last week, I said, 'Could you give me a sign if I should go on with this bond?' But now, I know He heard me. It doesn't matter what He said, it's that He *heard*."

MARY JOY NEVER SENT the men to pick up the shipment alone. She always accompanied them and rode between them in the front seat. Reverend Prangley's crew wasn't always ready, though, and worse, Prangley wasn't always with them. As she and her men pulled into the farmer's laneway, she could see from far back, even in the falling dusk, that there were only three silhouettes.

"This damn man is like a tick under a stocking."

She saw her two men glancing at each other.

Edgar, the driver, nodded his head.

"He's slipping," Mary Joy said. "Lord, this is not how to run a business—especially not one of this size."

The men neither agreed nor disagreed with her. The driver brought the car to a stop and they all got out. The man in the passenger seat, Marvin, extended his hand to help her, and Mary Joy took it, dropping down into the dirt as delicately as she could in her heels. "Will you do me just a little favor, Marvin?"

"Of course."

"You drink on occasion?"

He nodded and said only sometimes.

"That liquor over there, y'all are going to taste it. I'll propose a toast and I'll look at you, Marvin. If it's too watery, don't say a thing. But if it's all right, you praise it."

Marvin nodded again.

The driver shot Marvin a look, which didn't go unnoticed by Mary Joy. It was clear he didn't want to get involved with anything more than carrying, and didn't want Marvin to, either. Mary Joy had helped Marvin out of a usurious mortgage—a setup where he never really owned his home, for although he'd put down a substantial down payment, the monthly rates had been jacked and if he faltered on just one month's payment, he'd lose the place and everything he'd put into it and have to start all over again. The deed holder was not a bank but an individual who preyed on men like Marvin—black men who couldn't get loans and couldn't buy elsewhere. Mary Joy had seen his kind before. The louse had sold the same house six times in eight years after numerous families defaulted. After Marvin shared his troubles with her down at the Second Baptist, Mary Joy showed up with a lawyer, who hammered the deed holder into selling the property to Marvin outright. She said he was willing to pay the full amount of the total owing on the house *that day*.

Marvin was now in debt to Mary Joy Davis, and although she was much more forgiving than either the bank or the deed owner, Marvin was not in a position where he could ever say no to her or her activities. It was a simple thing she was asking of him, and she knew he'd oblige.

Now Mary Joy walked ahead of Edgar and Marvin and greeted the white men with dimples and pleasantries. "I am pleased to see you have all my cases!" She whisked a finger through the air, counting silently. "Tell me, where's Reverend this fine evening?"

"Saving souls, but it's all here. Big order this time." The one named Jake did the talking, and the one named Gerald hung back, leaning on his cane. Gerald's brother, Noah, was against the wall of the barn. Sometimes he gave her the stink-eye, and she knew he didn't like working with her even if he appreciated the take.

Jake went to get a dolly and Noah came over to help him load it. Leaning on that cane, Gerald seldom moved more than a case of liquor. Mary Joy's two men started toward the crates too. But Mary Joy held up her hand and said, one moment, if they didn't mind.

"Would you gentlemen join us in a toast?"

Marvin dipped his hand into one of the crates and pulled out a bottle. He passed it to Mary Joy Davis.

Jake told Noah to run and get the lady some glasses. What was the occasion?

"Though I don't drink myself, it would give me great pleasure to see a toast raised to my daughter, Esther. October 25: today is her birthday." Mary Joy filled the men's cups.

"She back in Chicago?" Jake was the only one of the men who tried to be amiable.

"I'm not a mother anymore, but thank you for asking. She'd have been fifteen today." All the men looked somber to be drinking to a dead girl.

Mary Joy watched Marvin's Adam's apple bob with the swallow. She kept her eyes on his face. He finished the drink and said nothing.

Mary Joy thanked the men, then held up the bottle that was still in her hand. "This here looks like toilet water. It should be a bright gold and it's only yellowish. Did Reverend Prangley tell you I wanted the product pure from here on in?"

"Yes, ma'am," Jake answered quickly—a bit too quick.

Mary Joy tipped the bottle this way and that, watching the contents ripple. "No, I am sorry, but I cannot pay you the previous rate. If you like, I can wait until you fetch him, or I can just leave you what I think is fair and I'll discuss it with him myself later."

Jake blanched and Gerald choked on the final swig of his drink.

"He's unreachable," Jake explained. "And I can't take less than he expects."

Mary Joy's face was calm, but she could feel her blood pumping. "We will all thank Reverend Prangley for creating this predicament. If he were here tonight, as he damn well should be, we wouldn't all be standing around watching the sunset, quibbling about prices. Marvin, get my bag from the truck. Take out ten bundles and leave those on the seat. You, go on and load this liquor," she instructed the driver.

Her men jumped at her force.

Gerald came forward on his cane. "This is damn uppity behavior. We've been good to you."

Jake put a hand on Gerald's arm, but Gerald shook him off.

"I'm just telling her. Prangley don't act human when he thinks he's disrespected."

The driver was already loading the crates and Mary Joy took the bag of money from Marvin. She flung it at Jake's feet where it landed with a thud. "You want to talk to me about disrespect?" Her voice rose a notch, then she swept out one of her heels and kicked the cane from under Gerald's hand. He nearly toppled, but his boxer's sense of balance kept him upright. Still, he looked stunned, and he put a hand down to touch his weak knee.

Mary Joy smiled. "You speak to me that way one more time and I'll see that you never walk again."

She turned and trotted back to the truck, where Marvin waited with a hand to help her in. The truck door slammed.

The truck started out of the dusty lane, then Mary Joy told Edgar to pull round again, and he did a sharp U. The men froze as the vehicle whipped back around. Mary Joy could see that Gerald's face was fixed with fear. Through the open window, she called, "Listen here, I'll tell Prangley myself tonight. Unlike you, I know how to find a man when it matters."

={ 90 }=

UNDER A COBALT SKY, Myrna saw the parsonage for the first time as Charles Prangley led her there. It sat in the shadow of the church, across from the graveyard. Headstones dotted the grass, brown as mushrooms, and turning leaves shook overhead, rasping. Myrna shivered and grasped his arm tighter as they moved across the yard. He had told her he was a reverend, but she hadn't really believed it on account of his clothes. He'd told her, too, that he was a businessman.

"How'd you get into the God line of work?" she asked as he leaned down to touch the key to the padlock.

"I saw no other options," he told her. "I would have liked to become a doctor or lawyer, only we had no money for such fancy education— and I sure did not want to roll tobacco like my father. His fingernails were stained brown and he made pennies."

"I'm sure you were plenty smart enough," Myrna said, smiling up at him.

"I am so happy you have come here with me. I never have had anyone to my home, and lately, I must admit, I have felt the loneliness. Especially these past couple years."

She clutched his hand tighter.

"Do you like silk sheets?" Prangley asked her as he led the way inside. He didn't turn on the lights, and she wondered why.

As they entered the front room, she knew her face showed unease. The little house was as shabby inside as outside.

"It is true I have to keep it humble," he told her. "It would not look right for a reverend to put his possessions on display in his front room, you know."

She nodded, and he turned and bent to kiss her. Myrna pressed herself against the front door, realizing too late that he saw this as an invitation to pin her there with his body.

"Stop!" Myrna gasped. Again, Prangley thought this was part of the game and rubbed her flat chest through her clothing, gripping her nipples and twisting them. "Stop!" she said, and broke free.

"Myrna, what is it?"

"I thought—" she said, but didn't finish. "Let's just go to your bedroom. I don't feel very comfortable here."

"Of course." Myrna heard the stitch in his breath, as though she had hurt his feelings. She knew this was when she ought to love him most: he was bringing her where, he said, no one had ever come. She forced herself to take his hand. He led her down the corridor and opened up the room. It was much prettier than the rest, and it pleased her. The bed was dressed in pale blue silk, as he'd promised.

But as she began to take in her surroundings, she saw there was little else in the room. Where were his personal effects? All his fine clothes and shoes? The cufflinks and ties she'd admired? Myrna walked across the bedroom and stood in the center turning in circles. She spied the humidor and went to it, saying wonderful, let's both have a smoke, throwing open its drawers. She found them almost empty.

"I told you I had to move most of my things into storage, on account of the break-ins," he informed her. "But take the last cigar there and let's have a drink."

She watched as Prangley moved to a crystal decanter on the dresser and filled a small blue goblet for her. As he passed it to her, her hands quivered. She hoped he didn't notice. She was worried that he was the one who'd duped her. She watched as he tossed back his own drink in a single gulp.

"Why were there break-ins? What was there to steal?" she probed.

"Oh, many things. Clothes mostly, designer furniture. Watches and jewelry. I love to collect, as you know. I have a keen eye."

"Yes, of course." Her hand went to her neck, which, she suddenly realized, was bare.

As Prangley itemized the things that had been stolen from him, Myrna kept her hand over her clavicle. A real girlfriend would have fastened the necklace he'd given her and worn it constantly. But her mother had sold it and was holding the money for her at the Sugar Box.

She'd had a couple of moments of feeling something for him. Probably not love—love was for nitwits—so what the emotion was exactly was hard to pin down. Now that she saw Prangley's empty house, she realized she'd been fooling herself as much as him. Her mother had warned her that she wasn't ready for the con. Myrna took her hand away from her throat and set it on his arm, gazing up at him, trying to conjure the starlight into her eyes that normally came easily.

"I kind of hoped you might have another gift for me," she coaxed him.

"I do, actually." Prangley went to the closet and opened it, revealing empty shelves and hangers. There were only two hats and two suits in the whole space. Looking past him, Myrna saw a great emptiness.

He went to one of the suits and fished through its pockets until his hand closed over something. He brought it back to her and told her to close her eyes. She felt the cold weight of it as he fastened it over her chest. When she opened her eyes and looked down, she saw a silver locket: an old piece, and not very flashy. He'd polished it, but the edges were tarnished anyway. She didn't think she could trade it for more than thirty dollars. "It was my mother's," Prangley said, pride rounding his voice and smoothing the lines in his face.

Myrna touched the locket reticently. She was silent too long. Her eyes were flat and emotionless. She couldn't act her way through this moment, and when Prangley saw her expression, his own changed radically.

His thin lips snarled and his eyes bulged. "You played me."

⟍ ⟋

HE'D BACKHANDED HER before she could say a word. Prangley almost couldn't believe he'd done it, but there she was, stooped over and breathing heavily. The rage had overcome him so quickly.

Myrna touched her face where he'd struck her, then turned and ran through the parsonage, the heavy locket bouncing on her chest. She was scarcely across the stoop when Prangley grabbed her and spun her around, as angry that she would run from him as he was about her lies. She hadn't said a word, but she didn't need to.

"Get back inside, you filthy little gold digger," he whispered into her face. "I will fuck you until you break."

"No," she said. Tears streamed down her face. "No, I'm sorry. Forgive me."

He sneered, pressing her against the porch wall. "I do not think you know what you have done. I have never brought anyone so close." He reached out and stroked her hair with one hand, even as he trapped her with his body. He could feel how volatile his emotions were, and struggled to gain control.

"Please don't hurt me," the girl whispered. "I did like you, I promise I did."

"But you want money. You want to be paid. For your kisses." Prangley's gaze burned into hers, and he trailed a finger over her mouth. He took in the pale freckles on Myrna's nose. He let the finger fall to her chest and farther down. "For your icy tits and your cage of a pussy. Here, I have money. Do you not see, you foolish child? I have more money than you can imagine. And if you had stayed with me, you could have had it all."

The enormity of the betrayal was sinking in now. She had to have been lying to him for weeks—that was what hurt the most. He would show her how stupid she was, what she was missing. He snapped shut the padlock on his house, then grabbed her and dragged her by the hand into and through the church, all the way down into the basement.

The girl pleaded with him, insisting she just wanted to go, please let her go.

"Not until you see," Prangley said as he thrust her through the corridor and opened up the room with the casket.

Myrna screamed when she saw it, and tried to run, but he pushed her in. He could see in her eyes that she didn't know what he would do to her there. He told her to shut up while he found the key to the coffin, then he threw the old wood open recklessly. Dust puffed up. Still she refused to look, as if afraid there would be a body inside.

"Money," he said. "There it is. That's what you want, isn't it?"

There was more than even he remembered. She had her hands over her eyes and was sobbing. So he took out two bundles and threw them at her. They fell at her feet and she gasped, and finally made her way to the casket, where she saw endless bundles of hundreds.

"Go on, take it, as much as you can carry. It will never be what I could have given you."

Myrna slowly reached out and put her shaking hand into the coffin. It wrapped around four bundles.

"Go on," Prangley told her, his voice strangely soft and paternal, even to his own ear. He almost meant its tone. He lowered the coffin lid and pointed at the dirt floor where the other packets of cash had fallen. "Don't forget those other ones."

As she leaned over to grab them, he pulled his leg back and kicked her as hard as he could, his blunt-toed shoe hitting pelvic bone. Myrna fell and did not move for a moment. Then he was beside her, grabbing her hair, shoving the money down the front of her dress. "Get out of here," he growled, "and never let me see you again, or I promise I will hurt you in inhuman ways. That is only fair, given how you have hurt me."

He released her and the girl needed no second prompting.

={ 91 }=

MARY JOY DAVIS took the booze to the train station directly. For once, she didn't board with Mr. Bucci. Instead, she asked Marvin and Edgar to loop back and drop her at Prangley's church. She told them to leave her there, but they insisted they would wait in the alley for her in case there was any trouble.

As it turned out, their wait was over in minutes. Mary Joy saw just enough at the church that she came back to the truck almost immediately, and told the men to go on. She was fine, she said, and had business to attend to. She didn't smile as she waved them on, though, and again she caught Marvin and the driver exchanging looks. Perhaps they had seen that her hands were shaking and she was perspiring heavily, despite the October night turning brisk. Then the driver simply nodded his head and did what she'd asked, pulling away.

What Mary Joy Davis had seen was the reverend chasing a young girl from his parsonage: one he pinned against the doorway, cajoling her and trapping her, touching her hair and running his hands down her tiny body. Mary Joy was too far away to hear what they said, but what she saw was the reverend violating a child.

It was only a moment, then he'd pulled the girl away by the hand. Mary Joy had begun to shake, and as she watched them go into the church, she spoke softly under her breath: "The nakedness of thy son's daughter, or of thy daughter's daughter, even their nakedness thou shalt not uncover."

That was when she went back to the truck and told the men to go.

Now Mary Joy strode around the corner and up the street to where she knew there was a gas station, and bought a can. The white attendant there smiled and greeted her, and told her cheerfully: "We don't see many niggers in this neighborhood."

He was missing a tooth on the top-right side of his mouth, and as Mary Joy fumbled with the bills in her purse, she thought about knocking out several more. Instead, she said nothing. The man had no sense in his head. Long ago she had come to believe no whites did. When she got outside, she gazed up and breathed out.

She walked back to the church in time to see the girl's small shape as she ran, limping, from the church and flagged a taxi. Mary Joy closed her eyes and muttered, "Lord, I know You let me see this bestial act for a reason, and I will purify this ground for You. No one should have to worship in a place such sins are committed. Give me strength to do this for You."

Gazing up at the sky, she decided to wait until it was darker. She stashed the gas can behind a yew shrub, and went and bought a coffee at a diner.

={ 92 }=

GABRIEL BRENNAN and Goering Jones drove in silence, following behind Willie Lynch's car.

"You see that?" Gabriel pointed to the Ambassador Bridge, which stretched above them, nearly finished, the roadway complete and the final cables being secured in their places—a long structure stretching grand above the river. "My brother Frank made that."

Jones craned his neck against the car window to look, then turned back and gave Gabriel that gap-toothed smile. "Must be fearless, like you."

Gabriel lit a cigarette and rolled down his window to discard the match. "Nah, he's an engineer. In New York now, says he'll be back for the opening. Though if I know him, he'll end up missing it. He's doesn't like parties."

He and Jones had watched as Willie finished a day of work at the mechanic's then went home long enough to shower and change. When he'd ducked out again, Gabriel was ready at the wheel, Jones beside him with the Memo camera. They followed as Willie wove around the streets as if he hadn't made up his mind yet, almost spooking them into thinking they'd been spotted. Eventually, Willie's car began to drift in the direction of the First Lutheran.

"Oh looky, looky," Gabriel said around the cigarette clamped in his teeth. He smiled, but it wasn't joyful so much as seen-it-all. "Our boy here is heading to where it all began."

"This should be good," Jones said, leaning forward excitedly.

"Don't get a hard-on just yet," Gabriel cautioned, tossing his cigarette to the curb as he eased the car over.

Jones grabbed his crotch. "This never lies."

"Don't it."

They watched Willie park his vehicle around the corner then hop the fence and walk through the graveyard toward the parsonage. The lights inside had been dimmed and the padlock was fastened. The kid bent down and, as fast as a dancer kicking, the lock was open and in his hand. Beside Gabriel, Jones pulled in a breath. As Willie Lynch sauntered in and closed the door behind him, Jones caught a picture of it.

After a few minutes, Gabriel said, "Hello." The imposing reverend was exiting the side entrance of the church and striding across the space between the two buildings. "Here's Mr. Prangley."

Jones turned to see. "Look at his face," he remarked. "Something's got him pissed."

"I don't want to think about what he's going to do to that kid," Gabriel said suddenly, just as Prangley reached the door and found it unfastened. "We need to haul these idiots in. We can toss the church later." As he spoke, he opened the car door.

"We have enough for a case?" Jones squeaked.

But Gabriel was already out of the car in pursuit of the reverend and didn't bother answering. Behind him, Jones hesitated, then got out too. Gabriel drew his gun. "Lose your hard-on somewhere back there?"

They went in together after the reverend. Gabriel faltered in the dark, then followed the sounds of struggle into the bedroom. He found Charles Prangley pinning Willie Lynch against the back of the closet wall. Lynch was suspended about a foot off the floor and Prangley's hands were digging into his throat. The boy's eyes rolled white.

"Drop him!" Gabriel commanded. "Hands up."

"Bureau of Prohibition," Jones barked.

But Charles Prangley didn't let go.

Gabriel stepped forward and swung his gun fast against the side of Prangley's head. He didn't care for men who didn't listen. The handle connected with a crack, and both men fell instantly to the floor, their limbs entwined.

MARY JOY RETURNED to the church calmer than she ought to have been. There was no one around—and the night had turned black and windy. She began at the door, because that was where the reverend and the girl had entered. It was also wood, and seemed the logical place to start. She dripped gasoline over it, lifting up the heavy can. She poured more along the perimeter. It didn't take her long to realize she'd need to get inside. Too much damn brick. She went into the graveyard, found a loose brick from the fence, and returned to pitch it through the window, saying, "Forgive me, Lord. It is for the greater good."

If Mary Joy Davis felt guilt, it was only a quiet shaking inside her. She saw her hands were quivering, but she thought again of the tiny figure of the girl, so like her own daughter in stature.

Mary Joy fetched a loose branch and broke the jagged shards. Still, she cut her belly as she climbed inside, and the blood, when she touched it, only invigorated her and reminded her of her purpose. A verse from Hebrews came to her: "And almost all things are by the law purged with blood; and without shedding of blood is no remission."

Also, Leviticus 17:11: "For the life of the flesh is in the blood: and I have given it to you upon the altar to make an atonement for your souls: for it is the blood that maketh an atonement for the soul."

Mary Joy walked down the rows of beautiful wooden pews, splashing them with the gasoline, saying both verses. She opened Prangley's office and spent most of her fuel there, opening any unlocked drawers and ladling gas into them. She splashed it over the ledgers and the fountain pens. The smell was dizzying, and she put her hand against the walls as she walked. She found the door to the basement and soaked it. She was nearly out of fluid, yet she knew she had to go to the bottom of the church if it was truly going to burn. She drizzled a small amount on the stairs, and saved the rest for the tunnels. She cast liquid over the doors downstairs, and one room still ajar that held a casket. She dared not lift the lid but soaked it well, spending the last of her fluid. Back upstairs, she went into the kitchen, where she washed her hands, fixed herself a sandwich, and sat and ate the whole thing beside the icebox. Then she thanked God for the nourishment and fortitude.

She walked back through the church, and as she walked, she lit matches and threw them down. She felt placid, never more beautiful, more righteous. Half the church was aflame when she realized she would need to go back down into the basement to ignite the gas she'd drizzled there. She did, though by this point she felt her lungs tightening with smoke. She lit and tossed matches, and hurried. Mary Joy had not run in many years, and not in heels. But now she ran, and then she came to the main doors of the church, which were already ablaze.

She fell to her knees, for she had no idea how she would escape. It had not occurred to her that she would need to get out. "Lord," she called. "Lord, please help me. Come to me, Lord. I need You now, more than I ever have before."

Then she felt God come through her as if she'd touched lightning. She spewed syllables that comforted her heart. She lifted both her hands to heaven.

Mary Joy stood, opened her eyes, put both her hands out, and charged through the flaming doors, ramming them open. Her palms burned, and fiery bits of wood rained down on her shoulders, but she scarcely noticed and she ran out, through the night, down the street. When she turned back, she saw the smoke drifting upward like its own language, the flames like serpents of orange and red. She hurried down to the riverside, and her heels slipped in the dirt and the gravel, then she plunged her hands into the river, where it was so cool. So beautiful and blue. Her head lolled and she opened her eyes, sighing. The bridge arched in the distance, its perfect lines black against the indigo night.

She removed her hands from the water, squinted down at her palms, and the sight brought her to tears. They were white and puckered, and she could see they would scar. "Thank you," she cried. She knew she would carry the mark of the Lord forever, how He had chosen her for this task.

She turned her head and saw the gleam in the distance: yellow arched windows, the pure, magnificent light hammering through the church.

={ 94 }=

GABRIEL BRENNAN and Goering Jones put the Lynch boy in a separate cell from the reverend. The kid had come to in the back of the car, but his voice was so weak Gabriel could barely hear him. Prangley hadn't revived yet, but they didn't want him anywhere near Lynch when he woke. Gabriel hoped Willie would be in good-enough shape that he and Jones could question him soon. But as he planned their line of questioning with Jones, the other officers who had been sent out to the crime scene called.

"What the fuck are you fucking telling me?" Gabriel shouted into the mouthpiece. His swearing caused Jones to get up from his chair and walk over to listen in. When Gabe first joined the Bureau, he'd heard the rumor that agents would lose a day of pay for every swearword, but he'd been around long enough now that he knew better. "Fuck Jesus, fuck Mary, and fuck Joseph too."

He dropped the phone back on the hook and Jones stared at him, the question unspoken.

"We gotta get everything we can out of them. They're all that's left."

"What do you mean?" Jones asked.

"Prangley. Already he got somebody to burn it down. Torch job. Whole church." Gabriel looked at his fingers and snapped them, a *poof* sound escaping his lips. "Fire department has drained half the river trying to put it out, which tells me that we ain't about to pull any evidence out of the place. Not much, anyhow. The snitch in Reno—Freddy Whatshisname—he was telling the truth."

Jones leaned over the desk on his knuckles so that he and Gabriel were almost nose to nose. "It was the Krims who did the torch job." Jones sounded confident. His blue eyes were unblinking.

Gabriel regarded the younger agent. He scratched his red hair and drew a hand down his cheek. "Or God. Him, or the Krims—bring either down here now!"

⋙ ⋘

ERNEST KRIM STUMBLED through the station toward the interview room, Agent Jones barking orders at him, telling him where to turn. Faye followed behind, one baby in her arms and the other in the carrier. As they passed by an office, Krim spotted another agent, who came out into the hall and followed, a man with ruddy hair and Irish features. "What'd you do, Jones?" the older agent said. "Arrest the babies too?"

Faye turned around nervously at that. "Are we being arrested?"

Krim didn't like the note of anxiety in her voice. She sounded guilty already. He raised his eyebrows at her and pressed his lips firmly together, but he couldn't tell if she understood or even saw him. He needed her to keep quiet.

The group walked past a row of four or five cells, and inside one Krim recognized the shape of Willie Lynch, even though the boy lay on his side, breathing heavily, an arm over his face. What had happened to him? Several cells along, he saw Prangley. Prone on the bench, the reverend's hair stuck right out through the cell bars, a knot of red scabbed onto his scalp. It glinted like a smashed candy apple.

He wondered if the agents had beaten them. He glanced quickly over his shoulder at his wife and children.

At the far end of the hall, Agent Jones opened a door and told Krim to go in, then turned to listen to something the other agent said to him. The two had a discussion in the hall, but Krim couldn't hear it because one of the babies, Catherine maybe, began to wail. The door closed, and the crying retreated. The agents were taking Faye and the children somewhere else, he realized. The only rooms they'd passed had been cells, and although the hall bent and ran on, he couldn't fathom what they would want from her. Krim folded onto the nearest chair and waited. They kept him for what felt like an extraordinarily long time, though his watch said it was only an hour: what *were* the agents doing with Faye and the babies?

A drinking fountain on the wall told Krim the room probably doubled as a lunch area for the agents. Eventually, he got up and paced around. He checked the door, which was windowless, and found it locked. After a while he heard a baby crying, then, as it came closer, he heard his wife also crying. Footsteps passed and went farther down the hall.

At last the older, red-haired agent came in. He gave Krim such a glare that he immediately took his seat. He introduced himself as Agent Brennan. The agent didn't sit down at first. Instead, he stood behind Krim and said, "Tell me everything about Charles Prangley."

Krim craned his neck to look at the agent, and Agent Brennan came around the table and sat down in front of him.

"My wife used to work for him."

"Yes, your wife has already told us . . ."

Krim sized up Agent Brennan. He had at least a day's worth of reddish stubble on his chin and upper lip, and eyes like gray marbles. There was a sullen demeanor to him, but it seemed painted on. The two men faced each other, unmoving, for a full minute. Each stared at the other. If his wife had told him anything, Krim realized, the agent would prompt him with it, or use it to tease more information out. But now nearly two minutes had passed. Krim felt his toes unclench inside his shoes.

"I didn't like my wife working for him, and she quit just before we married," he said. He breathed out through his nose.

"What was your objection?" As the agent leaped on the information, a dimple appeared at his cheek.

"She was a bookkeeper. He was stealing," Krim said in an even tone. In the hour they'd given him, which he expected was meant to spook him, he'd had time to organize his thoughts somewhat. "We both thought eventually it would come back on her, and now here we are. It's why you pulled her in, isn't it?"

The dimple disappeared from the agent's face. It was not what he wanted, and Krim could see it. All he had to do was keep calm.

"Also, and I feel terrible to say this about her, but I should be completely honest with you, shouldn't I?" Krim paused and the agent nodded. "Well, seeing as he was stealing, she also stole, but only once—fifty dollars to buy a camera for my mother."

The agent had a notebook in his hand but didn't write in it. His body had grown tense. "Why do you think Mr. Prangley was stealing?"

"I really don't know him well enough to say," Krim said, allowing his shoulders to rise in a slight shrug.

Krim knew the reverend might sling mud at him when he woke, but it was one man's word against another. The Kid might panic, but he had no beef with anyone so far as Krim knew, and he was just the type to hang himself before anyone else. Krim's only goal was to make it out of the room and back home with Faye, to feel her in his arms and kiss the children.

KRIM HELD HER HAND in the taxi and Faye leaned her head on his shoulder. She still couldn't believe she had done it: she had cried for an entire hour and in the end the agents had stopped trying to question her and started trying to comfort her. "I just kept thinking of them locking you up in that cell next to Charles Prangley's. I couldn't stand the thought."

Krim tightened his grip on her hand, and with the other he reached down and stroked Alistair's cheek where he rode in the carrier. Catherine was not asleep, but she was quiet.

"I figured out you didn't talk, but I can't say I wasn't nervous. I brought all this on us."

Faye put her finger on his mouth and said, "They smelled my hands. They were looking for a propellant. What's a propellant?"

They climbed out of the taxi and took the children inside and up to the nursery. Alistair dozed off, but Catherine wouldn't sleep and they brought her in with them. After a while she closed her eyes, and Faye got up and moved her back into her crib. She came back, but Krim hadn't put out the light yet. She pointed at it, but he said no. "I want to see you. All I could think about in there was how I wanted to see you again."

She undressed slowly in front of him, dropping the garments at her feet then stepping over them toward the bed. He buried his face in her breasts and she let him kiss her belly, her sides, her ribs, her nipples, her shoulders, her neck, her chin, her mouth.

SHE WOKE PARTWAY THROUGH the night because Krim was shuddering beside her. He grunted and cried out in his sleep. Faye watched him for a moment in the darkness, then put her hand on his shoulder and woke him, telling him, "You're dreaming."

Krim sat up, bewildered. His face was childlike and confused, and she was unaccustomed to seeing it that way.

"What's wrong?"

"I dreamed I was in a prison cell. Only it was years ago. I was just a kid, still wearing my army uniform." Krim reached over and put on the lamp. Faye watched quietly as he lit a cigarette. He sucked in and out. Then he mashed out the cigarette, got up out of bed, and found his boxer shorts and her bathrobe. "We all went in kids, pictures of sweethearts hidden in our caps, secretly afraid and shaking in our boots. Or there were those who didn't even have that—just pictures of our mothers. We aren't there but a few months and suddenly we're leaden-faced men, even if we still smelled of Necco Wafers. Some tried to distinguish themselves from the others in bold ways, but more just crumbled, became numb or cruel. You live in a trench and shave with a rusty razor, and over time you don't have steady-enough hands even for that. We had one tub of water to bathe the lot of us."

Faye sat down on the bed and drew her bare feet up.

Krim sank down beside her. He looked ill. "I went into the war because I wanted to get away, not because I was particularly patriotic. I did things, Faye. Not just the smuggling." Then he said, "The lie I told Elsie Moss. I can settle with myself why I did it—I *needed* the money—but the truth is, Alfred talked me into it. He could convince me of whatever nutsy thing because I felt bound to do anything for him."

Faye knew there had been an accident the night of Krim's high school graduation—that someone had been badly hurt and Moss had helped him out of the jam. She gazed at her husband. His face looked as if all the color had been pulled out of it. His hands hung limply between his knees.

"In the dream, I was in that cell. Your old boyfriend passed by as a guard. I don't even know how I knew it was him." Krim cocked his head slightly as if trying to remember. His green eyes were foggy. "It was stitched on his uniform maybe, or somehow I just knew. And he said, 'That's exactly where you deserve to be.' I'm the guy who thinks he has to save everybody, but I'm bad, Faye."

She said he wasn't, and held him and kissed his hair, which smelled of tonic and sweat. "They let us go tonight. You're not going to prison, Ernest. If anything, I worried it was my fault we were there—because of what Kitty did. I kept thinking they'd ask about that! I was so glad we burned her letters."

Krim seemed to lighten then, saying it wouldn't be the Bureau of Prohibition on her heels.

Later, when Krim was asleep again, Faye lay thinking about Arthur Baldor. It seemed unfair that her husband should dream of him when she hadn't in years. She tried to remember his boyish face, but couldn't recall anything more than the curve of his mouth. She got up and went to the closet. She took down the box on the top shelf. In it, she found the bag of money, which she hid back up in the closet. Then she took the box with the rose petals and the letters in it, and carried it down to the kitchen. She opened the trash can and stared at the contents in the bin, which included an apple core and coffee grounds, some potato peelings, an empty biscuit box, and some old rags she'd used to wipe up baby vomit. She picked up the letters and touched them, one by one, before letting them go.

$$\equiv\!\{\ 96\ \}\!\equiv$$

BURST GLASS BOTTLES. That was all the evidence that had been gathered in the church before the firefighters forced the agents out for their own safety. Everything else, including the hymnals, was charred black, the other agents reported to Gabriel Brennan. Didn't the glass indicate possession of alcohol, Jones had wanted to know. Yes, Gabriel confirmed, it might indicate the presence of wine, but since wine was often part of religious ceremony, churches were clear to possess it.

"Hell, I been sipping Communion wine since I was five," Gabriel said with a smile, but after a second he hauled back and punched the telephone on his desk. It fell to the floor with a clatter and ding. Jones jumped back.

Neither of the men in custody had said more than two sentences, no matter how he and Jones goaded them. The Lynch kid had talked about a man named Moss, but neither Gabriel nor Goering knew who that was. When they searched, they found an obituary page from the previous spring. Prangley had conducted Moss's funeral. When Gabriel mentioned the name "McGee" to both Charles Prangley and Willie Lynch, he got only blank looks. McGee was the Bureau's source, though the agents had never met him, but when Gabriel telephoned out to Nevada early on Saturday morning, he was told McGee had been released early for his cooperation. The court clerk there said

McGee was now their problem. Gabriel hung up. Now he had to break it to Jones.

The young agent drew himself up to his full height. He was slim but muscular, and Gabriel let his gaze linger. The evidence of an athletic youth was still present.

"How long can we keep them? Can we beat a confession out of one of them?" Jones wasn't ready to give up.

"I like your spirit," Gabriel said, but he was already putting on his coat. "If they won't talk, and the evidence is gone, it's time to go home."

"We're done?" Jones's face carried more hurt than disappointment, as if a deep wound had been inflicted.

"Shit, let's get a drink," Gabriel said as they left the Bureau offices.

"A drink?"

They got into the car they'd shared for the past few weeks and Gabriel sped through the streets. They stopped in front of a house on Brooklyn Street, only a few blocks down from Bagley, where the Krims lived. Gabriel got out and slammed the door, and Jones trailed him up the walk.

"What is this place?" Jones asked as Gabriel climbed the stoop stairs.

"It's my place. I thought you understood." Gabriel turned to face him, his eyes assessing. Jones swallowed. He nodded.

They went inside and Gabriel wasted no time. He thumbed on a small lamp in the living room and poured them two whiskeys. Jones was still wearing his coat when Gabriel passed him the drink and told him to take it back in one shot.

Jones did, his gaze on Gabriel as he lowered the glass. "Tell me you at least liked the way I brought in both the Krims by myself?"

"I did. Just wish we'd been able to get more out of 'em."

Bolstered by the drink, Agent Jones took off his coat and laid it over the chair. He flashed the gap-toothed smile. "You might be able to get something out of me, if you try."

"Always hoped I might," Gabriel said, but he'd only been waiting for invitation and his mouth was already closing on Jones's. The young man's jaw was firm beneath his hands and his tongue was a river of intoxication, leaving a bitter honey taste on Gabriel Brennan's lips.

$$\equiv\{\ 97\ \}\equiv$$

THREE OF THE WALLS of the church still stood, but the fourth was gone and all of the roof, leaving the structure empty as a doll-house. All the stained glass windows had shattered in the heat. Bricks lay in huge piles where the walls once were, and smoking beams poked up from the rubble. The structure was stained deep black in huge patches, as if someone had painted it. At the top of the front of the facade, the cross remained, but stood crooked and bent.

Charles Prangley dropped to his knees in the street and a car swerved around him. He barely noticed. "God, help me," he called. "How could You take everything?"

He didn't kneel there long, though. The next vehicle, operated by a less observant driver, almost struck him. Prangley scrambled and fell back onto the sidewalk. He lay on his elbows, which burned with the impact of the fall. He was still weak from being hit alongside the skull the day before by Agent Brennan, then from sleeping on a metal cot and being yanked in and out of the interview room several times throughout the night while begging for a piece of toast and water, all the while trying not to give anything up.

When Prangley finally gathered himself, he walked closer to the church, though with every step his throat burned more. By the time he reached the few firefighters who were left to watch the smoldering rubble and make sure it did not reignite, Prangley sobbed. One of the firefighters expressed his sorrow to see such a handsome building destroyed, and clapped Prangley on the shoulder. But no, he said to Prangley's inquiry, the reverend couldn't go in to recover anything yet. The firefighters had been through the rubble as much as they could and so had some agents, but they didn't want anyone else tramping around in there. They weren't sure if the floor would hold or collapse into the cellar. If they found anything of value as they finished putting the embers out, they'd salvage it. He jerked a thumb over one shoulder to a pile of darkened items beside the graveyard. The parsonage and the car had also gone up in flames. Prangley nodded. He patted his pockets and, still crying, pulled out half a cigar.

The firefighter looked at him with pity and shook his head. "We don't want even a match near this."

Prangley put away the cigar and took stock of what he had with him: a pocket watch worth about fifty dollars, a pair of gold cufflinks that weren't valued at much more, one ring. There was a thin four hundred in his wallet. He knew he couldn't go to Myrna, because she wouldn't take him back if she knew he was broke now, and she might not anyway after what he'd done to her. He had a feeling that if he went back to her apartment, he wouldn't find her there anyway, and the Sugar Box had bouncers who wouldn't look kindly upon him.

Prangley went over to the pile of items. He encountered the secretary's typewriter, a couple of smoke-damaged portraits of previous reverends of the church, the collections plate, some candle stands and an incense burner, and a four-foot-tall stainless steel statue of Mary that had always been part of their Nativity. She seemed to hold out her hands to him. Though her dress usually shone silver, it was now blackened with soot. The expression on her face was placid and sad.

There was nothing from his office there, and nothing from the basement. He turned and scrutinized the parsonage, which was indeed as ravaged as the church.

Prangley staggered across the graveyard and, checking over his shoulder to see that no one was paying attention, headed down the steps that led to the passage where Bunterbart had always made his drops. The keys rattled in Prangley's hand as he unlocked the first gate. He stepped down and crossed to the second gate. He could see the basement tunnel beyond, its walls stained black. Whoever had set the blaze had done it right, making sure it would burn from cellar to steeple. Prangley knew the agents believed he had paid someone for a torch job—that he'd had a fail-safe plan in case he was ever arrested. Without evidence, they'd had to let him go. But Prangley couldn't think of who would commit such an act. He hadn't called Jake or Gerald yet—he'd come directly home because he had to see the destruction for himself.

As he ventured in, the debris-covered ground gasped a tiny ghost of smoke up around him. In the dim afternoon light that bled in from the stairs and from the places where the floor had been eaten away, he saw shattered glass dotting the hall. Large rounded fragments stretched along the edges of the corridor, and small dime-sized pieces shone like gems among the soot. That was the reserve, he realized. All the whiskey had gone off like grenades in the conflagration.

The door to the room where he kept his money was a pile of ash. Inside was nothing but charcoal crumbs. All that remained of the casket was a collapsing frame—a few metal bars that had braced the lid and reinforced the corners.

If the firefighters outside heard the reverend's yowl from deep within the church, they wouldn't have been able to approximate from where it came. When he exited, Prangley saw that one of them had come around the back to locate him, but he was already stumbling through the graveyard and onto the sidewalk. His coat flapped out behind him as he ran a zigzagging path, across the street and back again, with no idea where he was going. There was a dreadful fire in his throat and his eyes streamed until he was blind.

={ 98 }=

ON BOARD THE TRAIN, Alfred Moss rattled his way up the California coast. Moss wore the three-piece suit he'd had on the day they'd hauled him in back in Reno. He'd acquainted his face with a razor, but skipped the pomade in his hair. The train was bound for Chicago then on to Detroit. He'd been turned out, given gate money, and paid for his information, so he was certain this meant the deal had worked out well for everyone. Anybody he'd worked with in Detroit who would recognize him would be behind bars. His plan was to find Elsie and slip back into a life with her. If not her, then Gin. One of them, at least, would be happy to see his mug. Even on the train he debated with himself about which woman would be better—it was Elsie's face that had come to him in the prison, floating in front of him, reassuring him. Maybe she'd be so relieved to see him he could convince her to start over somewhere else.

He had a thousand dollars in a security box he'd thought to take out in New York, another few hundred stashed in Santa Fe, though who knew when he'd be able to get back there. He had left some money for Elsie in the account—he couldn't remember how much, but he was sure he had. Just as he'd sent money to Gin and to Krim. He had, hadn't he? He closed his eyes and tried to remember the time he'd spent snaking his way across the country, but it was a blur of

Manhattans and marijuana and, in a couple of places he didn't want to admit to, moonshine and heroin.

As one of the Pullman porters passed by him, Moss reached out and whispered, "Hey, boy."

The man bent and waited for his request.

"You know where I can get a little tipple on this train?"

"No, sir, can't say that I do."

"Come on, George, you must! I can smell it on the other men. There's gotta be something going around?" He knew some travelers called the porters George after the train cars' owner, George Pullman.

"Nope, sorry." The porter showed him no sympathy; in fact, he seemed frostier than ever.

"Well, can I snag that from you at least?" Moss gestured to a crumpled newspaper in the porter's hand that he'd been clearing and taking to the trash. The man gave it to him and moved on. Moss unfolded it and smoothed it out. It was the *Santa Ana Daily Register*. The front page declared: BILLIONS LOST AS STOCKS CRASH, MAINSTAYS OF MARKET IN PLUNGE.

A little farther along in the journey, Moss grabbed another porter and asked the same question about getting a pick-me-up. This time, though, he smiled and remembered to employ the charm that had always got him the things he wanted. The porter said he'd make some inquiries, but the inquiries didn't take longer than a minute and then he was back with a bottle labeled *Mr. Bucci's Olive Oil*. Moss haggled with him on the price—he hated to spend so much when he had so little. Couldn't the fellow come down just a bit for a man who'd spent a year in the slammer and hadn't had anything to wet his whistle in so long? This porter said he had to give kickbacks to the conductor besides. Finally, Moss thrust the bill into the man's hand and the porter smiled and thanked him.

Moss unscrewed the cap and drank. It was not the most robust liquor he'd ever had, but after so long away from drink, it gave the slow burn he sought. Alfred leaned back against the seat cushions and grinned.

⟨ 99 ⟩

ERNEST KRIM WENT into the closet, but the box wasn't there. He tried not to panic, but a surge of anger overtook him and he strode into the nursery where Faye was feeding one of the children.

"Where is it?" he said, curtly enough that the other twin woke at his voice and crowed for someone to come over.

"Thanks," Faye answered sarcastically. "Where is what?"

"The money. The market just had a heart attack."

"What does that mean?"

"Where is the cash?!" Krim raised his voice louder than he meant to, and Faye broke off the feeding and put one baby down and picked up the other. Bouncing the second twin in her arms, Faye led him out of the nursery and back to the closet.

"Up there," she said, nodding.

"Where? The box is gone."

"Yes, I threw it out."

He stared at her, not comprehending.

She looked down for a moment, her brown hair shadowing her face. She sucked in her bottom lip—almost as if she regretted her action, thought Krim—but when she looked back up again, her gaze stayed steady on his. "I was done with it. Who needs the past? I have you and the children."

Krim swallowed. What a heel he was. He took Baby Catherine from her arms and Faye stood on tiptoe and pushed over two hat-boxes, and there was the white paper bag he sought.

"What's happened? Are we in trouble?" she asked.

"The papers are calling it a disaster. We've lost all of our investments."

"But it was our money. How could it be lost?"

He opened his mouth to speak, to try to explain, but no sound came out.

Faye took Catherine from him, went over to the bed, and lay down on her side. He watched as she fished her breast out and fed the baby. The dog, Chaplin, jumped up and stretched at her back even though he'd been told a million times to stay down. It was hard to panic while watching someone nourish a small child. Krim told himself, *Don't think*. Instead, he watched his wife and the padding of his daughter's hand as she pressed the breast for more. Behind them, the dog's sides heaved in and out in sleep.

While Faye finished nursing, Krim took down the bag from the top of the closet and stared into it, assessing.

"We'll have to move Gertrude in with us."

"We've talked about doing that anyway."

"Yes, but now we'll have to. It's not a choice. This is all we have."

Faye said she'd be happy to draw an income again, and Krim said sure, if there was work to even be had. They collected the children and went downstairs and put the radio on so they could hear more of the reports. Faye put on a soup—though Krim told her to save some ingredients for tomorrow, they should cut back on luxuries.

Since Agent Jones had rounded up the family and taken them in for questioning on Friday, Krim had not felt much like talking, but now he was truly in shock.

Over the past few years, men had put dynamite at his shop door and Prangley had threatened him; there had been guns and gangs, and now police, but even so, Krim had never balked. Now he reached for Faye's hand and said, almost under his breath: "I'm scared."

Faye held his hand and didn't say anything for a moment. The children were both lying on the floor on a blanket, old enough to raise their large heads and push themselves up on their arms but not strong enough to turn themselves over yet.

"When I tallied numbers all day for a man and it didn't make sense, I started to think that money is not a quantity," Faye told Ernest. "It's a dream. You can pull it into whatever shape you want," she continued. "You can walk in circles for it and come to dead stops, and even if you make it to the place you're looking for, maybe there's nothing there."

={100}=

ELSIE ANSWERED THE DOOR thinking that the person thumping out "shave-and-a-haircut, two-bits" might be some neighbor, or maybe Willie with a set of car keys for her next drive. She did not expect to stare into that handsome face, somewhat weathered now: its dark eyes still full of merriment, a smile that still haunted her.

"Kewpie doll, what a sight you are!" Alfred Moss leaned in and kissed Elsie on the cheek before she could shut the door. "I bet this is a bit of a surprise, ain't it, but let me come in 'cause I got lots to tell you. How I missed you! Where is that boy o' mine?" He handed her a sparse bouquet.

It was early evening and she had been making mashed potatoes for her son. The pot bubbled on the stove. Baby John stood in the dining room, wearing a bib over his shirt and overalls and carrying a wooden toy car. Alfred was already halfway into the house when Elsie got her bearings.

"This is not your house anymore. You can't barge in here." She turned and watched him try to sweep the boy up into his arms, but Johnny resisted him, saying *no-no-no*. The toddler pushed hard, crying and scuttling backwards on the new parquet she'd had installed earlier that year.

"Sure does look spiffy in here." Alfred looked down at the floor, then up at the painted walls and the new furniture. "What the hell's wrong with this one?" He gestured at the toddler, who was crying and clutching his toy car tightly against his chest.

Elsie felt her heart accelerating in her chest. "He doesn't know you. He can't remember his first twelve weeks. Anyway, I don't want you talking to him. You're scaring him. You just push your way in and grab him?"

She dropped the flowers on the table and went to the boy, bending down to his level, stroking his hair, and talking to him in a low voice. She put a hand on his back and guided him into his bedroom, closed the door behind him. Her son had almost but not quite learned to turn the handle himself, and she could hear him fiddling with it, though the door remained closed.

Alfred asked what she was doing, wasn't she happy to see him? Didn't she want the boy to see his pop?

"You're not his father." Elsie fixed him with an icy stare. "His father's dead. There were people searching for his father for months. His picture was in the paper in an obituary and everything. I don't know who *you* are."

"Kewpie doll, we were good. So good." Moss laughed. "You're joking me, right. Don't you remember? I thought of you so much. If you knew!"

Something roiled inside Elsie and she fought to keep control of her state. She didn't know what emotion showed on her face, but it was obvious Alfred mistook it for passion—weakness, a giving in—because he stepped forward and grabbed her, his hands rubbing over her buttocks, his mouth seeking hers. She let his breath play over her lips, then sucked in air and looked him in the eyes. He tasted like stale gin and pipe tobacco. He tasted like someone she didn't know anymore, and maybe had never known that well. She pulled away and said so: they were never that good—the first four months maybe, then he was off with some other woman. He drew back, shocked at what she knew.

"Well, sweetheart, you were steppin' out on me too. Don't say you weren't." He gave a twitchy grin that showed only two teeth and was someplace between forgiving and accusing. It stunned her to realize how smug he was. How hadn't she seen it?

"Because I felt so alone. I thought I'd die! For a long time I fought that. And I thought I'd lose the house. But I didn't." She jammed a finger down on the table. "This is my house now, and everything inside. All your things went out in the trash. My name is the one on the mortgage. So why don't you just go?"

"Sugar?"

"Get out. I want you out, and I don't ever want to see you here again." Her voice was rising as the little boy got the doorknob turned and peeked out from his room. She saw him and went to the doorway to close it tight again, handing him a new toy to occupy him. When she turned back around, Alfred Moss was looking into their shared bedroom. Then he was inside, shifting through their closet.

"Your clothes aren't there. Your key isn't there, *Alfredo*. I found it and I found the bank and the security box. Your birth certificate is here in the china cabinet drawer," she said. Going into the dining room, she yanked the drawer halfway out. "And you should take it, because you sure as hell can't be Alfred Moss anymore. If you want your French pictures, you can go see Willie Lynch and ask if he still has them."

Elsie heard hissing in the kitchen—the water bubbling over. The potatoes would be mush. He was still standing there staring into the empty spaces where his clothes had been when she went and turned off the pot on the stove.

When Alfred followed her into the kitchen, his face was flushed and his eyes had narrowed. "I love you, you bitch! Can't you see that? Why do you have to throw everything in my face? I know I fucked up. Just give me ten fucking minutes."

She turned and stared at him. But she didn't want to listen, didn't want to look at him. Her face was hot, as if all the blood in her body was surging upward. She glanced at her son's door and was relieved to see it was still closed. "I told you three times to leave, Alfred."

When Elsie saw that Alfred didn't appear to be moving, she seized the handle of the pot with its potatoes and hot water and threw it across the kitchen. The pot missed him, but the water splashed everywhere. Alfred jumped back, singing obscenities. His clothing protected him, but scalding drops dotted his face and neck, and he clutched at the burns before sprinting from the property. She had never seen him look so graceful, and remembered he'd once bragged about being a track star. She supposed at least that one detail was true.

={ 101 }=

AT HIS MOTHER'S CALL, Willie Lynch came downstairs. In the kitchen, she snagged him by the arm. Mrs. Lynch craned her neck as if she could see into the living room, though she couldn't from there. "I can't help thinkin' it's that fella that died in the river. Willie boy, ain't he the one come round and taught you how to drive two years ago?"

"Holy mother of God," Willie breathed. He shook off his mother's hand and strode into the room.

He took Moss in: sitting there with his leg up, making a triangle shape against the other one, a decent suit but looking the worse for wear in the face. His high cheekbones were emphasized by hollowness. He'd lost weight and his eyes had sunk in slightly. There were tiny raised bumps across one of his cheeks, which he kept touching. Moss had always impressed Willie with his polish, his manly elegance, and his whip-fast talking. But whatever Willie had admired seemed faded, like the shine in an old gem.

"What are you doing here, Mr. Moss?" There was a high note in Willie's voice, try though he might to keep it out. He wondered if Moss had come to him specifically, if he might be the first to see him after all this time. He felt a flicker of happiness at the thought. But Moss squashed the thought before it could flourish into a hope.

"My wife said you have something of mine?"

"Your wife?" Willie put one hand on his side. "A man don't treat his wife like that."

Moss stood up. "Let me show you how to greet an old pal, Kid." He grabbed the boy and hugged him, slapping his shoulder heartily. "You see? That's how it's done. But you didn't do that, so I gotta ask you: what do you care about how I treat my wife? And how intimate are you that she'd give you a collection—a mighty large, mighty fine collection, I might add—of blue photographs?"

Willie heard his mother, who was watching and listening in from the kitchen, swear heartily. The men heard her footsteps as she hurried away upstairs.

Willie's voice showed his exasperation. "Is that all you want? Some old smutty pictures?"

Moss touched one of the burn marks on his cheek. "No, it isn't. I want to reconcile, but everyone's acting like some horrible crime has taken place. I mean, you and I"—Moss waved his hand forward and back in the space between them—"we shouldn't have a beef with each other. Unless you screwed her. You screw her?"

Willie stared down his nose at Moss, then he shook his head. He never did get closer to Elsie than one drunken adolescent kiss, and after that he didn't try his luck again. The pistol she'd pulled was a firm deterrent, and although he enjoyed mentioning the girls he went dancing with just to see her flush, he honestly liked the woman too much to really risk angering her. He was wearing Moss's pants, the pair Elsie had given him, but Alfred didn't notice. "I'll go get your nudie shots."

Moss's expression flattened and smoothed. "All right, then. Thanks, Kid."

Upstairs, Willie yanked a shoe box out from under his bed and took out the envelope of photographs. Beneath it was his father's old

Luger, which he'd carried when he was smuggling but seldom brought out anymore. He was lucky to still have it. The Purples had relieved him of a different one of his father's pistols. Willie's brow furrowed as he held the envelope of photographs. His mouth twitched. He replaced the lid on the box and slipped it back under. When he came back down, he asked Moss a second time what he was doing in town, what were his plans exactly.

"Head down to Hertz and pick a car, get myself a big hotel room, and then we'll just see. I got so many ideas I been working on, Kid." Moss was all smiles now, more the way Willie remembered him. "I rode the train clear across the country. That's some scenery. You know you can buy liquor on the Pullman cars? Comes in bottles marked like salad dressing. Clever trick, I thought."

Willie said he'd heard something about that but didn't know all the details. "Gerald and Jake are in on it. They're the only two still working with Prangley."

"How 'bout that?" Moss snatched back the envelope before Willie could hand it to him. He peeked inside and slid a few photos out, flipping through them. He made an appreciative noise with his lips. "Not you, though? You into clean living now?"

"I hate that slippery fucker. Just last weekend—" But Willie stopped himself. Because here was Moss, and somehow they'd all been pulled in by the Bureau just before his arrival.

"Oh, so you know, then." Moss made a clucking sound in his throat, still regarding the girls in his hands. Willie saw flashes of legs and smiles as Moss thumbed through them.

"Know what?" Willie said through gritted teeth. His stance had stiffened, but Moss wasn't looking.

When Moss finally glanced up, he quickly pushed the girlie pictures back in the envelope and said soberly, "About your pa. Bunterbart told me, but I suppose it was bound to get around. Terrible. For Prangley to put him out that way, over what? Some money. Some cop sniffing around. The usual shit. Well, obviously you know how Bunterbart can talk when he gets drinking..."

"Sure I do," Willie lied, his chin tilting upward slightly. He felt curious and cold, as though the blood in his veins had turned to quicksilver. "What else did he say?"

"All I know is what that big German muttered through his cups, but he said Prangley kept that Rambler in a private garage, barely drove it." Moss shook his head. "Warped man. That's why I never cared about buggering off on the operation with all that Scotch and dough."

"Bunterbart is dead," Willie said, his face frosty. "He got himself shot up just after you left."

"Dumb son of a bitch."

"You gotta go, Mr. Moss," Willie said. "I got some business to take care of."

Moss looked flabbergasted. Didn't he at least have time for a drink?

Willie hollered for his mother and quickly she came out of the kitchen, as if she'd crept back in there to listen. Her face was pale and waxen, which told Willie she had. He asked if they had any whiskey and she dug through a cupboard and produced a full bottle. Willie took it from her, his hand closing over hers for a second as it transferred between them. Then he handed the whole thing to Moss.

"You go ahead, Mr. Moss. I got things to attend to."

Moss accepted the gift eagerly and showed himself to the door. The cap was already off the bottle.

After Alfred Moss left the house, Willie looked at his mother. "Listen, you're gonna take a cab to Elsie Moss's house. You're gonna take care of her boy."

It was unheard of for his mother to stop talking. But for once she said nothing, just gave him a sorrowful, questioning look.

"Because I'll need Elsie to help me, and the last thing I want is her dragging that baby along," Willie explained.

His mother shook her head. How, she asked, did Willie think he'd find Reverend Prangley? He stopped for a moment, as if he hadn't figured that part out, though as soon as he spoke, the answer was ready on his tongue: "I'll find out where he drinks. Jake will know. Jake will tell me."

≡{102}≡

CHARLES PRANGLEY DIDN'T LIFT his head for five days unless it was to take a mouthful of whiskey. The bartender refilled until Prangley passed out, then charged him for a bed in the back. When Prangley woke, he walked to the bar and said, "Hit me," and the bartender fished out a new glass and unscrewed the cap on the bottle. He told Prangley he had no problem with how much any man wanted as long as he paid—but he did have a problem once Prangley called him a yellow-bellied cocksucker. What prompted him to utter it, Prangley couldn't remember. It could have been that the bartender called in a bouncer to remove a different patron. Then suddenly Prangley himself felt the man's fist against the side of his face, though he didn't feel it so much as begin to understand it had happened, especially when he saw the sky for the first time in more than half a week.

He shook himself off and walked a few paces down the sidewalk, then checked his wallet. He saw he had a hundred left. As he wandered down to the riverfront, it occurred to him that even though he had no car, he might be able to walk to Canada. Staying drunk was his main priority. The lights twinkled in the distance, and the new bridge was right there arching black above the gray water—as good as finished, even if they hadn't declared it open. Rosine's was long gone, but he doubted he'd have any problem finding another bar to serve him. The Dominion House was a pub along the same stretch, and closer to the bridge even than the Riviera had been.

He walked past his church and tried not to look, but he couldn't help it, and the sight of the burned bricks only gave him more purpose and more desire to cross the bridge. He approached the structure with squinty eyes. The wind was in them, but he was also still half-blind from the alcohol. The customs house was there, beside the entrance to the bridge, but only one kiosk was lit. Sawhorses blocked the roadway, and fencing was stacked nearby but had not yet been assembled: there for crowd control for the grand opening. He spotted some bales of barbed wire, not yet put up. As Charles passed a line of huts, an officer stepped out of the open kiosk. "Stop!" the fellow said to Prangley. "No travelers on the bridge yet."

"Going to Canada to get a drink." Prangley pushed the man aside, intent on climbing the slope of the road.

The man yelled, "Turn it around, rummy."

Prangley did. He took one step back toward the officer, then reached into his coat, yanked out a Smith & Wesson revolver, and shot. He was close enough that, even with drunken aim, the bullet connected and the officer dropped back into the shadow of the building, a web of blood across his face. Prangley put the gun away and stumbled up the long slope of the bridge.

PRANGLEY WALKED a long way up, feeling close to the stars in the sky.

He was sure he'd been that high in buildings, or on balconies, but this was different. The wind rushed through his hair and pushed it over his eyes and around his mouth. He combed it off with his hand. All around him, the night shone deep blue. There was a long curve leading up the bridge and it took him longer to walk than expected. Then the long straight bridge was before him. He'd almost reached the halfway point when he turned and looked back down at the way he'd come.

No one ran after him—the darkness was still.

"'I will go up against the land of unwalled villages . . .'" Prangley said. "'I will go to them that are at rest, that dwell safely . . .'" Then he stopped because he realized he could still see the burned-out church, and from the air it was small and hollow, and almost beautiful, filled with the night, like the set of a play, though Prangley couldn't remember ever having been to the theater.

Thinking this, he felt an ache begin in his chest and wondered why he had never gone. The affluent women who'd buzzed around the church had invited him, for a brief time, to parties and fundraisers, had held his arm and flirted and posed for pictures, but they'd tired of him quickly and stopped inviting him out on the town—partly because they couldn't take tipples freely in front of him, and partly because his charm wore thin after a while, and his bitterness came out, and he knew it. Certainly he could have afforded to go to the theater—or could have once. He owned an airplane and had never been up in it, and now he didn't even have a car to take him to where the plane was, and didn't have the money to pay the pilot.

As he stared at the darkened ruins, he decided God had taken the church from him, that it was an unexplainable turn, like an act of nature. The agents had cursed him when they told him about the fire—a plan, they accused, hatched with one of his men. But Prangley couldn't think of anyone who would do this. The Lynch kid had been locked up with him, and so had Krim—so it wasn't them who had set it.

Prangley turned toward Canada, the wind cutting his eyes. He put his hand up to shield them. Off to the west, he expected to see the

537

Riviera from there, but it was just a bump of bricks among the others. He could see front yards and back yards and the McClintic-Marshall Company's final building supplies stacked around both sides of the pilings. West down the river, factories streamed smoke into the sky, churning its way into the clouds. And just slightly east, there was the steeple of the university church across the water and its windows, unlike his own, still lit.

Charles had never experienced anything so beautiful in his life, and it shocked and frightened him. He couldn't believe how cold it was up there, how cold and splendid. The wind moved and the clouds moved, and the water below him moved, and in their movement he felt his hate carried away. He had no hatred for anyone except himself. He had killed the guard in a moment, and he hadn't felt any alarm in doing it. It was just a matter of efficiency. He looked backwards, but the arc of the road hid the customs houses from view. There were other people too, gone forever, and some he wished he could get back. Still more that he'd hurt, even if here and there he'd helped a few along the way while lying to them. All of it was a glorious game, but what did it come down to? The images crashed through his mind, then stopped in a wave of sadness that dribbled from his mouth in strings of saliva as he cried. He had done nothing with his money when he'd had it, and now he would never recoup it.

"God, forgive me," he said. Prangley stepped to the railing and looked down. The water bounced below, whitecaps that bobbed and disappeared again. Little spots and splashes that flickered. The wind sent his coat flapping as he leaned over slightly. It was far enough down it would kill him. Of that he was certain.

He closed his eyes for a second, and in that instant he heard a voice say, "Don't do it, my son."

He opened his eyes. He saw nothing but the night. He gazed down at the water again, and this time he heard a deeper voice inside him say, "My son."

"You cannot forgive me," he said aloud.

"Even you," the voice told him. "Even a son of a bitch like you I can forgive."

Charles put his hands up and held them aloft. He wasn't sure if what he was hearing was God's voice or his own. The wind rushed between his fingers forcefully.

He turned around to step away from the railing, onto the small sidewalk that ran the entire length of the bridge. Not ten feet away stood a young man. Prangley squinted at him, before recognizing the shape as Willie Lynch.

"I have just spoken with God. He forgives me," Prangley said to the boy. His voice rose in a strange cadence of jubilance.

The Kid pulled his father's Luger from his jacket. "Then I guess heaven is for shit heels."

Prangley saw the gun, but didn't move for his own. The bullet bit through his chest a moment later. He didn't fall right away, but Willie didn't shoot again. The boy came closer to Prangley, who looked down, watching his jacket bloom with blood. "I accept this. This is Your will," Prangley said. His eyes were unfocused. He smiled, and then he fell to the sidewalk like a mountain crumbling. His teeth chattered for a moment as if with cold, then abruptly they stopped.

={ 103 }=

THE BOY CALLED from a pay phone saying they were headed for the bridge, and Elsie sped through the city as if there were no other cars on the road. Willie had insisted he didn't want her to see— didn't want her to be part of it—only wanted a ride home when it was done. She knew she was too early, because as she drove toward the bridge, she looked up. There was the reverend's shape and his gait as he climbed the arch to the middle. He was close to the railing, walking more slowly than he normally did. She decelerated, peering up through the dark, then she spotted Willie much farther back, as though trying to keep his distance. She sucked in a breath, and then her car was too far under the bridge and she was coming up around and back, past the customs houses, though she saw no one there, and no one came out to stop her.

They had changed the roadway since the last time she'd driven it, and now there were sawhorses everywhere in preparation for the upcoming opening, and wire and fencing still to be erected. She parked right up against a sawhorse barrier. She sat in the car for as long as she could, but then she couldn't take it anymore.

Suppose Willie follows too closely? Suppose he doesn't come back down? She contemplated this for about twenty seconds, then she reached over to her glove compartment and took out her revolver. She got out of the car. Her breath tore through her lungs, and although she rushed, she was also aware that if she truly ran, her footsteps would echo. It was eleven at night and she could hear the sound carry over the expanse. She softened her step until she crested the bend of the on-ramp. Although there were no cars on the bridge, and would be none for days, she used the sidewalk.

She glimpsed them in the distance, the gangly reverend facing away from the boy, contemplating the water, then turning back around quickly. She couldn't hear what they were saying over the wind and the sound of the water. But she heard the shot. At first neither figure reacted, and she stopped. She held her breath so long, waiting for one of them to stagger or fall, she wondered if the bullet had missed entirely. Her stare stayed on Willie, willing him to remain upright. Then she did begin to run, and as she closed the space, the reverend toppled, landing sideways on the pavement.

When she arrived at the center of the bridge, Willie still hadn't moved, and she saw that the reverend was dead. The tall man lay as still as stone. She shoved her own pistol in her trench coat pocket and grabbed Willie and searched his body with her hands. "Are you all right? Did he wound you?"

"No," Willie said. "No." He tore his gaze away from Prangley's body and looked at Elsie. He put his hand on her cheek.

She reached down and took the pistol from him, because it was still in the exact same position as when he'd shot it. At the touch of her hand, he let go, looking down. Elsie Moss held the pistol for a second, then walked to the railing and lobbed it into the river below. She thought to glance up and down the river for boats. There was one, coming from the west, but it was a slow, dark shape on the horizon.

"Willie!" she urged him. She went to one end of the body and picked up Prangley's ankles.

Willie stared at her, then came over, muttering, "Jesus. I can't bear to touch him."

"We can't leave him here, Willie. Not if we're going to keep you out of prison. Now help me. On the count of three—one, two, three." She heard herself say the words, astounded at the calm tone, at the fact that her body moved to complete the logical actions required of the situation.

Willie lifted, and Elsie lifted. The body stretched between them, sagging in the middle. Then Willie grunted and found his strength and lifted higher, and all Elsie had to do was help the feet over the rails. They let go, and the body rolled horizontally in the air, then twisted and fell downward headfirst. It seemed to take much longer to land than either anticipated and the whole time Willie was saying, "Oh God, God, God . . ." his bottom lip trembling.

The body went in straight, a dark splash, and didn't bob back up again. Elsie said, "We have to go, Willie. Now."

She took his hand and led him at a fast trot off the bridge, though they slowed at the other end and made sure there was no one near before she opened the door for Willie and helped him into her car. She had never seen the boy so fragile—the gold freckles and brown moles on his face stood out in the ghostly light of the streetlamps as they pulled away and rocketed homeward, a strange maternal feeling keeping Elsie's panic to a minimum.

=(104)=

ALFRED MOSS PICKED out his rental car, a 1929 burgundy Essex sedan with red rims on the tires. He got a hotel room, but there was no one to share it with, so he went out to look at his city. It had been so long since he'd seen it. All the same things in the same places, and then just the one or two new signs or storefronts jarring him or throwing him for a loop. There were new skyscrapers that had been built downtown, new theaters, and other construction still in progress.

He cruised down Griswold Street, where a glorious Art Deco building with an antenna spire on top was all lit up, even at ten at night. It was called the Penobscot Building, and he remembered construction on it had only just begun when he left. Detroit was becoming new. He reached down and pulled up the bottle of whiskey that Willie had given him. He took a nip. "That is fine," he said, of both the building and the blend. He nodded his head. He drove along Fort Street for a while, and then he found himself going by the First Lutheran church. He swiveled in his seat and marveled at how consumed it had been by fire.

"Golly!" It stunned him, the shell of it, and intrigued him, too, that Willie hadn't mentioned it when they'd spoken of Prangley. But the boy had seemed distracted, perhaps by the fact that he, Alfred Moss, was back. Now Alfred shrugged and could only assume the fire must have occurred some time ago. Perhaps it was no longer news.

"Same church where they sang my praises and buried me—ain't that a kick?"

Moss took a long swallow from the bottle and guffawed. He pulled the wheel to take him down to Jefferson, where he could drive along the water and maybe see the new bridge better. He lit a cigarette, took another drink, and held the wheel with two fingers. Out of the corner of his eye, he thought he saw something large and dark plunge out of the sky and break the water, and he grabbed the wheel quickly.

What the hell was that, Moss asked himself, and gazed out the driver's side window, peering at the water then up at the bridge. "Falling apart already?"

He stared out the window so long he convinced himself he had seen nothing unusual. Then he laughed, and said, "Probably some cheap Canadian's fault," and he turned his attention to the road again—only to find that it was the road, and not some phantom falling object, that wasn't there. Where he remembered a street, there was none: only dirt and the bridge foundations. He yanked the wheel hard to the left so as not to drive straight into concrete, and the car skidded and rolled. The whiskey bottle flew up and struck him in the chin, and then his head crashed against the window and the car plunged into the water. It went down slowly, but Moss didn't jump clear. He was unconscious.

Alfred Moss saw and heard nothing. The water didn't fill up the Essex sedan until it was all the way submerged. No one had seen it go off the road. In a few minutes his wife and Willie Lynch would run from the bridge and jump into her car, only a hundred feet from where he languished—but already he was sinking farther in. The water combed out his hair and licked his eyes and his nostrils without him knowing it. He didn't hear it pounding like footsteps. It simply took his breath, and washed him into a forever sleep.

FOR MAYOR, BRIDGE OPENING IS JUST WHAT COUNTRY NEEDS

Editorial, *Detroit Free Press*, November 10, 1929

Even as the belly of the New York market is still roiling, heaving, after the orgy of speculation that has blighted our economy this decade, Mayor John Lodge is smoothing his beaver top hat for tomorrow's gala opening of the Ambassador Bridge.

At noon tomorrow, the good Mayor, along with Governor Fred Green, will walk the 7,500-foot length of the bridge. Following behind them will be a Navy band playing "My Country, 'Tis of Thee." On the other side of the bridge Mayor Cecil Jackson of Windsor will also march. Behind him a band will perform "God Save the King." Music-minded readers will note the songs share the same melody. Of course, even at this moment of marriage by metal and cable, our countries do not share the same problems.

"There are those that would stoke fear in Americans," the Mayor said in the face of calls to cancel tomorrow's gaieties. "But I'm a believer in the future, which is the direction this great project points towards." Let us correct the Mayor; a bridge, by its very nature, points in two directions.

For all the economic miracles promised by the bridge's construction, the failing of our banks has put our future in doubt. Also lingering is the peculiar notion of Prohibition, an increasingly tenuous belief given how connected the two great, and mistempered, nations of North America now are. The Canadian delegation is planning to bring good French champagne to the bridge. Should the leaders of Michigan step but one more foot beyond 3,750 feet, they will also be free to imbibe, and perhaps forget about our economic troubles for a moment, even if the citizens they represent may not.

={105}=

THE TWO BRENNAN brothers sat across from each other in the chop suey house. Frank lifted a teapot and poured into his cup, but not a drop came out. There was no whiskey left. "That's that," he said.

"Well, it was a good time while it lasted," said Gabriel.

They stepped outside and clapped each other on the back. Even though they were nothing alike, they looked and moved the same, and strangers would have had no problem telling they were kin. Before they parted ways, Gabriel turned toward the river and said, "She's a real lady, that bridge."

Frank gazed at him affectionately. He could see that the attention made Gabriel so nervous he fished in his pocket for a cigarette and stuck it in the side of his mouth. Frank asked if he was sure he couldn't come to the opening the next day, and Gabriel opened his jacket to show his brother his badge and said duty calls—partly with resignation and partly as a joke.

"Well, then, until next time."

The brothers walked in separate directions to their cars, but Frank felt the wind at his back and the slowness of his steps, and wondered how many times he had left with Gabriel. The overcast afternoon smelled like wood smoke and, as he passed a bakery, the pasty yeast of fresh bread. He breathed it in deeply, as if he could memorize every moment. It was something he'd noticed about himself in the year since his wife's passing—the minutes took on more significance than the hours.

Frank found himself driving up Woodward Avenue toward Elsie Moss's neighborhood, though he hadn't intentionally pointed the sleek blue Packard in that direction. He circled her block twice. There was a new car in her drive and he took this as a sign she was doing well financially. On his third loop back around, he guided the Packard over to the curb. He got out and walked slowly up her drive. He could feel his breath snaking through his nostrils, and watched his finger rise to push the bell.

He hesitated, and then he saw the boy at the window—her child had grown enough that he was darting around the living room and climbing on the furniture. Frank could see, too, the suited elbow of someone sitting on a sofa. A man's hand held a glass, and when he leaned back, Frank could see his hair, though not his face. It was a sandy blond. A young man, like Elsie was a young woman.

Frank stepped to the side of the porch where he wouldn't be seen. He stood there, uncertain. Then he felt in his pockets for a pen and paper, and found the small volume of poetry by H.D. He had read it two years before, thinking it was by a man, and only recently learned that the author was female. He thumbed the book open and saw that he had written in it before the last time he'd seen Elsie, though he'd chickened out on giving it to her. *To Elsie, a remarkable woman. Yours in friendship, Frank.* He had no pencil with him to modify the message, and it was as true and good as any he could have come up with, he decided. Quietly, he crept closer to the door, and put the book inside the mailbox. He felt the lid close and he breathed out, and turned and shuttled back down along the far edge of her drive to the Packard.

Before he drove away, he glanced at the window once more, and saw Elsie stand and turn the light on, bathing them now in yellow.

The man had stood too, and Frank could see he was a short young man with fashionable hair and freckles. The two of them were drawn around Johnny in some kind of game, but the child was too small for Frank to see. Elsie was looking down, laughing, maybe singing, and even from that distance Frank had never seen her look so beautiful.

FRANK BRENNAN AIMED the car downtown and along the river. He noticed the veins in his hands, and how they sprang from beneath his skin, bushy and blue, silver hairs over the top of them. He drove along the stretch of road that led up to the bridge, paying close attention. It was six thirty and turning dark when he finally pulled the Packard over and got out and walked around the site. There was fencing with barbed wire assembled everywhere, and several human shapes were already gathering, intending to wait the long night to be the first to cross the bridge, bent on owning plaques, prizes, and bragging rights. The area had been readied for festivities, for crowds and bands, and press photographs—even Brennan would be included in at least a couple before he got back into his car and headed home to New York. But these ceremonies mattered much less to him than the structures.

He stood below, beholding the black arch of steel, the 1,850-foot suspended span, and the long lead-up too, which now connected two nations—one that was heading into a tailspin, and the other, foreign and stable, at least for the time being. Brennan had been working since he was a very young man, and had never stopped. He'd grown up with little, and all there was to do was build, and build, and build—to build the wealth, and build the nation. He wondered if what he'd told his brother was true, if this would be the last of the great bridges, the last thing he accomplished. He imagined the empty decade that he was certain would stretch ahead. He had to admit, he liked the stripe this bridge made on the amethyst sky.

Brennan inclined his head and listened to the way the wind passed over and through his bridge. Across the water, he observed lights winking on inside houses as night fell. But even in the dusk, the black towers and the web of cables were distinct. People would walk and drive through the air for decades here, and he could have no idea who they would be, their lives, passions, beliefs, or destinations, but when this crumbled, they would make another. Progress had no keepers; it went on into the horizon beyond where anyone could see. Some of the travelers would be tortured and despairing, and others peering ahead, energetic and eager; few of them would ever think of those who had conceived of the structure below, the documents or policies that went into it, the number of minds developing it, or the number of hands that had touched those rivets or selected that band of cable. Time would pass, Brennan thought, and so would he, but the future would always need building.

He blinked as the bridge lights twinkled on to show all boats on the river its outline. Then he shivered. It was time to get back into his car and drive on, but he hesitated. Beside him, the water whispered and sang.

═{ AUTHOR'S NOTE }═

SOME OF THE characters and events in this novel are based on historical facts, both big and small. The Purple Gang and the Bernstein Brothers were real, as was the Milaflores Massacre and the Cleaners and Dyers War. Mock Duck and King Canada are also real historial figures. The financier of the Ambassador Bridge did suffer a panic attack when attempting to walk across it. All quoted newspaper articles are fictional.

The writing of this novel began with two images from a family story: a great uncle named Alfred going through the ice on the Detroit river with a shipment of whiskey; a pearl-handled revolver, found in my grandfather's drawer by my own father when he was a child. The images are true, but I have exaggerated the words greatly, as happens to all family histories.

=⟨ ACKNOWLEDGEMENTS ⟩=

I WOULD LIKE to thank my publisher and editor Lynn Henry, whose insights were 151 proof. My agent Shaun Bradley has been a part of this book during the entire eight years of its writing. My husband, Brian J. Davis, was my researcher and master of newsreel voice.

Gary Barwin, Kevin Chong, James King, and Eric Fontaine read, and bettered, the instances of Yiddish, Cantonese, French and German in this novel. Curator Kristen Gallerneaux allowed me into the archives of the Henry Ford Museum and offered valuable knowledge. Thank you to Kristin Cochrane, Sharon Klein, CS Richardson, and everyone at Knopf Canada. Thanks to my friends and supporters at *Joyland Magazine*. Thanks to my dear friends, some of whom contributed their names to my characters. I am deeply grateful to the Canada Council and the Ontario Arts Council, who provided funding during the writing of this novel. Thanks to my family: Mike and Vicky and all the Davises, Erik and Brenda Schultz, Ross Schultz, Dave Schultz, and especially my mother, who helped me immensely. Thanks to my father who, though gone now, helped with research during the early drafts, and also instilled in me a lifelong love of film noir and old music.

© Sara Maria Salamone

EMILY SCHULTZ's previous works include *Black Coffee Night* and *Joyland*, which received rave reviews and award nominations, and an acclaimed book of poetry, *Songs for the Dancing Chicken*. Both her novels *Heaven is Small* and *The Blondes* were finalists for the Trillium Award, and *The Blondes* has been optioned for film. Schultz is the co-founder, with husband Brian Joseph Davis, of the influential online literary magazine *Joyland*. She currently divides her time between her native southwestern Ontario and New York City.